Arabian Jazz

Diana Abu-Jaber...

Arabian Jazz

HARCOURT BRACE & COMPANY

NEW YORK   SAN DIEGO   LONDON

Requests for permission to make copies
of any part of the work should be mailed to:
Permissions Department,
Harcourt Brace & Company, 8th Floor,
Orlando, Florida 32887.

Portions of this book previously appeared
in *The Sun,* September 1990.

Library of Congress Cataloging-in-Publication Data
Abu-Jaber, Diana.
Arabian jazz/Diana Abu-Jaber.—1st ed.
p.   cm.
ISBN 0-15-107862-9
I. Title.
PS3551.B895A89   1992
813'.54—dc20   92-41532

Designed by Trina Stahl
Printed in the United States of America
First edition
A B C D E

To my cousins Pam, Marc, Tariq, and Suzy; my parents, Pat and Gus; my sisters, Suzy and Monica; my grandmother Grace; and most especially to my beloved husband, Michael.

ACKNOWLEDGMENTS

Heartfelt and abundant praise, admiration, and thanks to my wise editors, readers, and friends: Larry Woiwode, Jane Smiley, Kevin Oderman, Alane Salierno Mason, Richard Olmstead, and Eric Ashworth.

Thanks and love for their enduring support and friendship to Janice, Amil, Janet, Dick, Bob, Deborah, Claudia, Amy, Mary, Julee, George, Molly, Tim, Gretchen, and Garrett.

And thanks to the Ucross Foundation Residency Program for artistic and environmental support.

Arabian Jazz

Chapter 1

WHEN MATUSSEM RAMOUD opened his eyes each morning, his wife would still not be there. He was amazed by this. By six o'clock, the floors of his house vibrated with drumming and music. "Naima."

He had become increasingly bemused over the years, wandering into abstraction, traveling in and out of conversations like a visitor to foreign places. Only at his drums did he seem to focus, concentrate with the purpose of remembering, steering rhythms into line, coaxing a steady—in his word, *peripatetic*—pulse out of air.

His wife's face was imprinted on his consciousness. He thought of her as he drove to work in the mornings through ice and rain. His sense of loss was sometimes so potent that he became disoriented. His need to drum grew sharp as a knife cut; he tapped and shuffled behind his desk. He made his secretaries nervous, and visitors to his office would stay for only the briefest sessions until his tapping became too much. Matussem's daughters,

1

Jemorah and Melvina, could tell when he was really napping—not just feigning sleep to eavesdrop—because his feet would start jerking rhythmically, tapping out time to Charlie Parker. After their mother's death, they heard him both mornings and evenings, alone or with his band, tapping in the basement, drums humming, tripping and rushing, giddy, loud-voiced. This sound had followed the girls through the years, from their father's first riffs on a child's kit he'd found in the basement to the Snazzy Sound of Mat Ramoud and the Ramoudettes.

None of the relatives in Jordan understood Matussem's life in America; but even those who never left the Old Country except for summer vacation knew that after work at the hospital maintenance office, Matussem made money as a drummer. When he played jazz they heard noise, and when he played Arabic music, they could dance; this was good enough for them. So when his sister Fatima, who lived in Syracuse, heard that the Syrian Orthodox Church was throwing a welcoming party for an archbishop from Jordan, she got on the phone and called her brother.

"We need loud, we need big name, we need free," she said, stabbing at the keys of her terminal. "You fit to all three, perfect!"

"Who's saying?" Matussem said. "You never even *heard* us and you saying loud. You think because it is your family name it makes a big name? And we get four hundreds for three one-hour sets. Sometimes. One time we did."

There was the kind of silence over the phone that made Matussem's skin crawl. Silence was the opposite of his sister, a by-product that resulted whenever she was concentrating her powers. He'd always thought she worked at the library because it gave her a place to charge up. She'd immigrated to America from Jordan in 1960, a year after he did, in order to keep an eye on him. He squeezed the phone receiver, trapped between her silence and whatever was coming next. Finally she said, "Matussem, Matussem, *Ya Matussem*, remember when you are five and I am six and I give you all my *grabia* cookie to eat? Do you?"

Matussem had no such memory. He put his hand over the receiver and sighed as deeply as he could. Then he said, "Yes?"

"And you remember when you are six and I am seven and I make this boys stop pick on you and call you shorty?"

"Fatima, please, take pity—"

"What *I* am saying exactly! I am taking pity on you all your life and *these* how you repay me. *These* how you treat she who give the breads from her mouth, her flesh and blood—"

"Fatima, Fatima"— he switched the receiver from his right to left ear. "We play free for your party. Okey-dokey."

"*Inshallah!*" she cried. "I should be so lucky!"

"What *Inshallah*, what, Fatima?" he asked in the tone of someone crossing the desert.

"*Inshallah* I live till these Sunday! Maybe I drop dead tonight and you dance on my grave. Maybe you and Allah will that I should make carpet for your feet!"

"What time on Sunday, O sister of mine?"

"Seven o'clock," she said, aching to fly full throttle into recrimination. She resorted to punching at the terminal keys again. "On a dot. Look respectable for once. Tell Jemorah and Melvina to wear dresses—there good families there to look them over."

Rather than remind his sister of what she already well knew—that one might as easily put a jinni into a bottle as put Melvina into something she didn't want to wear, he said, "Your wish, my command. Good-bye, O great big sister of mine."

THE AEROGRAMS FROM Uncle Fouad or Auntie Rima always began arriving in winter, mentioning the possibility of a visit. By June, the relatives started to descend and Family Function Season officially began, thick with upstate humidity and sweating relatives who thought somehow that this was preferable to the desert.

It was mid-May, the first real thaw in a season that had been thick with snow; Jemorah was at her desk in inpatient billing. Like Matussem, she and her younger sister, Melvina, worked at Johnson-Crowes Hospital: Jem out of necessity, Melvie—as she put it—out of "destiny." Jem's job was simple, if meaningless; she totaled the previous day's billing on an adding machine and stuffed the itemized invoices—one semiprivate, two catheters, three hypodermics, and so on—into the patient's folder. She filed, sorted, distributed, and stapled. Mostly stapled. She also answered the phone: "Good morning, inpatient billing, may I help you?"

She heard the songs of furies, of the lost and broken and wayward. People with mothers dying or children dead.

"My son's been in the hospital since birth and now

he's going to die if he doesn't get heart surgery. What am I supposed to do with these bills? Seven hundred dollars consulting! And I don't have any insurance. My God! What is this one?—two hundred fifty-eight dollars for an anesthesia tray?"

"You need to speak to one of our patient reps—"

If the caller hung on, if the funnel of tears, illness, and terror had not sucked this caller down into its eddies, then Jem had to take a message and deliver it to a representative. When the patient reps saw Jem coming, bearing a white phone-message slip, they groaned. "God, get away from me." "Please not another one." "Jesus, you're a curse."

Jem had just finished a foot-wide stack of filing; there were a variety of ink blotches on her hands, one heart-shaped dot near her nose; her wild hair was gnarled into a bun and speared by a pencil, and her lower lip was caught in her teeth, her expression something close to perpetual surprise. In contrast, Melvie—skin, hair, uniform, even her mind—seemed sleek as stainless steel.

Melvie called that Monday from her office in critical care upstairs, her voice cool as chrome. "Warning, warning," she said. "It's Family Function Season again."

"What? That doesn't start until June."

"It's May thirteenth and I'm sure you realize Aunt Fatima doesn't take chances on a late start. She had one of my women summon me from a code blue to tell me the Archbishop's welcoming party is Sunday night."

"No," Jem said, shaking her head. "I can't do it; I'm not ready. It's too early in the season, isn't it? No, I just can't do this one."

"What do you mean, you *can't?* Be more specific, Jemorah. Do you mean you're incapacitated, or that you just won't cooperate?"

"You know what I mean," Jem said, voice shrinking. "I never have any fun at these things. *Why* should I go? What's the point of it?"

She heard a background sucking, gurgling noise in the pause before Melvie's answer. She imagined her sister holding the receiver with one hand and vacuuming out a patient's lungs with the other. The sound had an exquisite crispness to it, eloquent disapproval. Jem knew that one reason Melvie made such an excellent nurse was not because of any kindly nature, but because she was annoyed by illness and held patients personally responsible for their own diseases. *A weakness of will,* she'd heard Melvie say more than once.

Jem recognized that Joan of Arc tone in Melvie's voice now, as she was saying, "*Fun* doesn't even enter into this picture, Jemorah. Don't you know that by now? There is no Fun—there is no Why. We're talking about Family."

Jem held her breath a moment, listening to the electric silence that vibrated along the telephone lines.

"Spare me the passive-aggressive tactics, Jemorah," Melvie said. "You're wasting your silence. Guilt runs off my back, as you are well aware."

"I know, I know."

"Just stick with me," Melvie said. "And remember the bedouin saying: 'In the book of life, every page has two sides.'"

Chapter 2

*A*T FIVE EVERY workday, Jem left the business office, stabbed her card into the time clock, and dashed to join the nurses at the Orange, Sutter's Mill, or the Won Ton à Go-Go, bars edging the strip between the hospital and Syracuse University, all rotted by weather, perfumed by beer. The city, slanted into its hard sky, could almost have been by the ocean. But there was no ocean by Syracuse, just the finger of Onondaga Lake, gray as bone. Farther north was Lake Ontario, which, though hidden, made itself felt in the rain and snow that wound sheets around the city, the wind driving people's faces down into their chests like the heads of sleeping birds. Sometimes in the winter Jem couldn't get warm, no matter how many layers she wore, and it was only in the tunnels of the city bars, protected by tavern walls, in nests of peanut shells and sawdust, that she would find some distance from the cold.

. . .

THE WON TON à Go-Go was one block from the hospital, and Merv the assistant manager kept it open twenty-four hours for the nurses. The nurses called it the Emergency Room. Merv liked nurses because they started screaming and laughing after a few drinks, and screaming made him feel like business was good. He especially liked Melvina because even though she never screamed, she looked like she could kill with her bare hands. Eyes dark as Taiwanese girls', too. Merv was from Taipei and he had learned about America from John Wayne and Bruce Lee movies.

Jem and the nurses were sitting in the back, drinking sake, which Merv kept for hospital staff who stopped by after their odd-houred shifts.

"Hey, you pilgrims," Merv said, stopping at their table once Melvie returned. "More karate-sake? How 'bout it, Mervina? 'nother Taiwan-on-Zombie?"

"No, thanks, Merv." Melvie stabbed at the remains of her drink with the straw. "I'm driving."

"Yes, Mervina in driver's seat," Merv said, bowed, then left.

"He talks like a fortune cookie," Hazel said. "You ever notice that?"

A fierce May wind sang in the windows, rattling them and dashing rain like gravel. The nurses all got quiet, looking at each other, then burst into laughter. "Doesn't it sound like the bar is haunted?" Jem said.

They hooted and rolled their eyes. They thought Jem was funny, especially after they'd had a few sakes. They'd drain a couple of bottles with ease before the night was half over. Melvina smiled grimly; she made special exceptions for her older sister, who required extra care and attention. "Validation therapy," she called it. Her goal, she said, was to make her sister aware of reality. As Jem joked with the nurses, Melvina lined her fingertips up. "You realize," she said suddenly, "what Fatima's little party really *is,* Jemorah."

A gust of rain shook the windows and Jem had an instant prescience of fear. "What?" she said.

"You're twenty-nine years old now," Melvie said. "Twenty-nine. Thirty this September. That gives the aunts a little less than four months to deploy forces. This is marriage-emergency in their book. If you turn thirty without a contracted male, you'll be diagnosed as a terminal spinster. Fatima's going to be bringing out the big guns now, all kinds of groom-specimens. It's no more Mr. Nice Aunt."

"So I won't go!"

Melvina put her hand over the top of a glass that Merv was trying to fill. "I'm telling you for your own good. Prevention is the best medicine. You have to go and look the devil in the eye." Melvina sat back, eyes glittering. Jem felt depressed.

I T S E E M E D T O Jem that virtually from the hour of her mother's passing, her aunts had converged around her with warnings about men. They told her: stay with your father, he needs you now; ignore boys, they're stupid and conceited; avoid men, they're stupid and dangerous; you don't know what they can do to you, what they want to do. Each summer, visiting Auntie Nabila or Lutfea or Nejla would take Jem's face between her hands and examine Jem's lips to see if she'd been kissed.

"Not yet," they'd whisper, crossing themselves. "*Al-humd'illah*, thanks be to God. She's a good girl!"

When Jem turned nineteen, the earth made a quarter turn. The aunts got back on the phone and declared that Jem was ready for the altar. College had been innocent play for a semester or two, they said, but enough was enough, she'd have to shape up now, get serious about marriage and babies while there was time. And her father would have to help out, since the "poor orphan" lacked a mother's care.

While no visiting aunts were scheduled that summer, Fatima more than made up for them. "Is your duty, is sacred obligation, to get that baby-girl married," Aunt Fatima said.

"Yes, yes, O great big sister," Matussem said, making a face and avoiding Melvina's look.

While Fatima herself was childless, each of her sisters had several sons. "Ripe for pickings," Fatima said. But not a sister would donate. After all, they pointed out, Jemorah was a wild-American-girl, painted and cunning, not appropriate for any of their sons, not even, Fatima said, poor little one-eyed Nassir. What strange, devil-faced children could come from such a match? A few years later, when several sons immigrated to America to go to school, all they wanted was wild-American-girls, not boring-Arab-cousins. Fatima told Matussem that this was her curse, retribution for her unspecified "sins." Still, it remained imperative to her that Jemorah marry *someone's* son and preserve the family's name and honor.

At Jem's twentieth birthday party, Aunt Fatima and her friends from the Ladies' Pontifical Committee sat together and sang dirges in Arabic about loneliness and aching hearts. Matussem brought home friends from work, anyone from the head of oncology to the guy who managed the used-car lot down the street. All Arabs, all fifty years old at least, and all looked to Jem to be at death's door.

She tolerated these visits for her aunts' sake, making the men pots of thick Turkish coffee with cardamom seeds and little saccharin pills while Melvina muttered over the dishes about chattel slavery and concubines. All of the prospective suitors seemed to find Jem desirable, tolerable at least; all of them she politely declined; none pressed his suit. After a year or so of this, Matussem had run out of friends and neighbors and told the aunts that Jem had decided to become an old maid and stay with her father.

Fatima shoved at her Greek Luxury beehive hairdo, snorted, and said, "Yes, we see about that!"

Jem waited, year after year, but the desire to marry, to love a man passionately—"lassoing hearts together," her friend Gil Sesame once called it—didn't come. She was tucked deep into herself, into the life she led with her family. How strange it was—unimaginable, really—to realize that she'd already lived longer than her mother, that in 1968, when her mother was two years younger than Jem was now, she had already married and given birth to two girls.

Sometimes, though, the thought of having children did come to Jem, like the lambent shadow of a jinni in a bottle. She knew that this idea emerged from another, deeper desire: a dream of rebirth, the longing to move more fully into her own life.

Seemingly without effort, Melvina had made it to age twenty-two unengaged. Jem believed that Fatima and the other aunties had given up on Melvie around the time she turned twelve and had, briefly, taken to smoking Dutch Master cigars. (Her "rebellious period," Melvie called it.) With her wide, charcoal eyes and curling lips, she had an almost Aztec beauty. But her expression was so penetrating that Fatima was once moved to say that Melvie had "never looked like a girl."

Now Melvie was charged with such responsibility and had seen so much that soon she would become like the other nurses, with a laugh of granite, a chest braced like an iron crossbar. Melvina had been making herself into that woman for as long as Jem could remember. Every morning since Melvie was old enough to dress herself, she had dragged a great weapon of a brush through her curling blue-black hair, forcing the hair down with Vaseline and bobby pins till it shone like lacquer. Her pale olive face was always scrubbed, and her eyes were wet stones.

THOUGH THE RAIN had died down, there was a faint moaning in the windows; wind came in at the crevices and swirled peanut shells and ashes across the floor.

"It sounds like Mrs. Niedemeyer is out there," Jocelyn muttered into her beer. Jocelyn was a big woman who sat with crossed arms, biceps tucked up under her breasts. Her uniform was unzipped in front to reveal monumental cleavage that made Jem think of the parting of the Red Sea. None of them ever bothered to change after work; they stuffed their caps into their pockets, walked straight from bedside to bar, then sailed drunkenly through dinnertime toward nighttime points unknown.

"Yeah, Nancy 'Prune-Lips' Niedemeyer," Harriet said. "Remember her? Nobody—I don't care what you say—nobody should live that long. She kept saying I was trying to off her."

"She claimed you slipped monkey blood into her IV," Melvina said quietly, twirling the little parasol from her glass.

Harriet nodded. "First she used to tell me she wasn't gonna die. I mean never. Ever. Then when that didn't look so sure, she told me she was gonna haunt me for all the goddamn rest of my life, walk on my carpet after I shampooed it, turn off my hot-water heater, stuff like that! Christ, eighteen months out of my life, every day having to look at that poison-powder face and stick needles in that dried-out prune rump."

Melvina looked at her nails. She didn't like the nurses to speak disrespectfully of their patients, but she knew it was as much a part of the job as feeding and bathing them. The hospital had made Melvie a team leader after only a year on the job, and head nurse the year after that. Her supervisors told her they'd quickly seen that she was "all nurse."

"We found Sadie Bosquick today," Melvina said abruptly. The women quieted. Jem recognized the name, an older woman Melvie had told her about: post-op, disoriented, a heart patient who'd disappeared from her bed the day before, even though until then she'd needed help to move and trailed tubes and IVs like streamers. She had shared a semiprivate room with a patient named Lucy who'd been experimenting with psychoactive drugs just prior to her admission. Lucy said she'd seen Sadie sprout wings and fly out the window, but there was no trace of Sadie on or around the hospital grounds. The admissions folder was blank under next of kin. Sadie had been admitted through emergency and had received immediate bypass surgery. Three days later, she had vanished.

"Where was she?" Jem finally asked; silence had settled around Melvina, the kind that women working with her dreaded to break.

Melvie took another sip of her pink lady. "On the commode . . ."

The women were looking at her, waiting.

"Making a bowel movement. Her last act in this life and it was incomplete."

"She didn't like using the bedpan," Hazel, another of the nurses, murmured. She was almost as young as Melvie. "I guess she wanted her privacy."

Jem could tell Melvie was rolling the tip of her tongue around the inside of her cheek, a gesture of extreme irritation. "Of course, we all know she was *supposed* to have been closely monitored. She was supposed to have been escorted to and assisted in the bathroom," she said. "She sat dead in that bathroom for six hours, left with her last human function. . . ." Melvie stopped; she looked around the bar, not seeing any of the few other drinkers, silent, stirring their cocktails. Then she looked at Jem. "We let her go."

Nobody spoke. Jem imagined the corpse, small, white, curled up on the john, the terrible isolation. She turned then and saw something fleeting pale as ghost-skin over Melvie's features. "Another death," Melvie said.

Chapter 3

MATUSSEM HAD STARTED out that Monday evening before the party, trying to arrange the kind of drum solos an archbishop might like; but he ended up thinking of his wife. He believed that any music was prayer, sending a message out to the sky. Nora was always his audience; she was *over there* listening. He knew that drumming—its sound and intensity—had the power to penetrate the heavens and earth.

Coltrane's music seemed to have been written for her, especially "Naima," a song so slow and sweetly agonizing that it didn't sound like there were drums in it at all, but on closer listening they were there, on the edges, moving it along so the song didn't just stop and close on itself like a wound. You needed drums, Matussem knew, like bodies needed hearts, the muscle to keep things going. He sat under the flashing mirrored ball, drumming, praying, alone in the back of the Key West. He was asking for help with all this "husband business." His wife had always said that American women didn't

16

need husbands, even though, at age nineteen, she had married him.

"My sister Fatima going to put me in the crazy house with her fifty thousand worries about husbands," he told his friend Larry Fasco earlier that day.

Hilma Otts was sitting at the opposite end of the bar, drinking a Black Label, still dressed in a down parka and moon boots, even though the spring thaw was well under way. "What? She need a husband?" she asked. "She's welcome to mine if she can dig up the son a bitch."

"No, it not for her. I mean, not officially," Matussem said. "It for my daughters. Someone show Fatima something says women don't get husbands after thirty. These country so much the same as Old Country. Only there they says eighteen."

"You want, I'll take that little fireball off your hands," Larry said, wiping out a glass. "She's spicier than Chinese food, ha-cha! I do like that."

"You mean Melvina?" Matussem looked closely at his friend. Larry was radiant in the bar light, his hand inside the glass looking like a prism of blue veins and translucent skin. The thought of having this man as a part of the family struck Matussem as novel and appealing. He compared their hands on the bar, admiring his earth-dark color next to Larry Fasco's crystalline skin. Then he said, "My friend, if you caring to tangle, then *vaya con dios,* but if she ask, *I* knows nothing!"

TWENTY YEARS AGO, Matussem had moved to Euclid and memorized its empty landscape, bare trees like pencil scratches and a few halfhearted houses that stood against the sky. There was also one cement building, a windowless cube alone on a dirt-beaten lot, that Matussem glanced at without seeing on his daily commute to work.

Over the years that big cube had borne the names Joy Unlimited, Bongiorno & Sons, Ellie Mae's Fish Shack, Kiddie Korner, Dino's Studio Twelve, the Zal Gaz Club, and Grange #323. For a few years it simply stood empty, a place for the local teens to get high in, sheltered from the elements and truancy officers. The weeds grew twining around it and the snow eroded its layers of paint.

Then one mid-March, when winter's steel had melted from the air and the snowdrifts had shrunk to clods of ice and car oil, the weeds around the cube were suddenly cut, and its walls whitewashed. The walls were also stenciled with a male silhouette swinging a decidedly feminine silhouette into the air. Driving by on the way home from work, Matussem felt that he had to go inside.

Maybe it was the cavorting couples on the outer walls or the rec room paneling and basement smell of the interior. Matussem could never decide what it was about the place that won his heart. Probably it was Larry Fasco, the owner, in a pair of brown double-knit slacks, polyester shirt, and cowboy boots, sitting absolutely alone at the bar of his two-week-old tavern, pouring himself a drink with a shaky hand. When Matussem opened the door, light shot in and struck Larry, turning his face and clothes white and bleaching the color of his eyes.

"Shut it, will ya?" Larry asked, holding one hand up to shield his eyes. "It's like a fucking laser beam."

Matussem debated if he was meant to shut it while standing inside or out. He let the door close behind him as he stepped in. Once inside, Matussem had been able to see—even by the strings of Christmas lights (until they got the disco wiring worked out)—that Larry Fasco glowed like a painting of a medieval saint. Only his fingernails, eyelids, and the translucent cap of his hair had the slightest tint, and these shone as if heated from within. Larry raised his glass to his visitor, and Matussem watched the tip of Larry's tongue poke out lizard-quick, lick his white lips, then flick back in.

"Well, I please to meet you!" Matussem had said, extending his hand. "I am Matussem Ramoud, many year in U.S. of A. You, by Allah, the most interesting person I seen in America." He had added "in America" at the last minute. Back in the Old Country he'd seen a few doozies.

"Well, Matussem Ramoud, I sure am glad to meet you. Larry Fasco's the name, and I may be the most interesting person you've met so far, but you're the third mortal being to set foot in my bar, after me and my ex-wife, the Psychokiller. So step on up and buy us a drink."

Without any windows or the sort of customers who came and went at regular intervals—for Larry's gradually building clientele rested their elbows on the bar all day and all night—time at the Key West stood still. The only evidence of its passing was the accumulation of dust upon the liqueur bottles and of grime under the patrons' nails. Larry Fasco liked to say of the Key West that it was "The Room of the Absolute Present Tense." He even considered changing the bar's name to The Room of the Absolute Present Tense for a while, but he couldn't fit it all on one wall.

M E L V I N A G L O W E R E D, E Y E S blackening, waiting in the doorway for her father late Monday evening. "Tell me why," she said as he entered the house. "Why must you go to that snake pit at all hours of the night? What attracts you?"

"Snake pit? What snakes? Where? Show to me."

Melvie crossed her arms. "You know who I'm talking about—Joe Brummett, Ricky Ellis, Sam Otts; it's chock-full of shady characters and troublemakers. Don't play dumb A-rab with me, Mr. Ramoud."

"It's probably a breeding ground for bacteria, too," Jem said from the living room.

Melvina waved her hand at this. "Look, Mr. Ramoud," she went on. "Give me one reason why you *must* place your body in such close proximity to that Fasco person's, please?"

At the time Matussem had no satisfactory answer, but he decided to think about it.

By the following day, a new marquee had appeared beside the Key West.

M E L V I N A A N D J E M were driving home from work and the Won Ton à Go-Go on Tuesday and Melvina spotted it immediately. "Oh no. No, no," she said.

Then Jem was able to make it out too. It was a new sign that read: The Big Band Sound of Mat Ramoud and the Ramoudettes, Every Wednesday Evening Till the COWS Come Home.

Melvie didn't even see the marquee board, only the black letters that seemed to hang suspended in the air by themselves. "No! No! No!" she cried, punching at the car horn. She twisted the steering wheel, driving off the road and up onto the dirt lot of the Key West, missing the marquee by inches. They lurched to a stop and Melvie rested her forehead on the back of her hands. "I cannot go on," she said.

Larry Fasco rushed out shouting, wanting to know what the hell they thought they were doing to his lawn.

Melvie waited, watching him gesticulate through the rolled-up car window. Then she rolled down the window and said, "No, Mr. Fasco-*person*. I think you have the wrong question! I think the right question, Mr. Fasco-*person*, is what are you doing to our father in this snake pit of yours?"

Larry Fasco quieted and studied Melvina for a few moments. Then he said, "Well, my my my my my my my! Ain't she a fierce thing! Ain't she fierce?" he asked, peering in at Jem. "I love 'em fierce. Always have. I suppose you know I call my ex-wife the Psychokiller. There's nothing more beautiful, I always say, than a woman who knows how to be really angry."

To Jem's surprise, Melvina had no response. They sat there a moment longer, then Melvie rolled up her window and they drove off without another word.

Chapter 4

WEDNESDAY AFTER FATIMA'S summons to the party, Jem picked up the phone in the kitchen.

"Jem? Is that you? It's me! The Studs Terkel of algebra."

She twisted the phone into the curve of her neck. "I'm sorry?"

There was a pause, then, "You know, that's what I always loved about you, Jem. You appreciated my wit. Okay, it's Gil. Must I give my family name? How many Gils do you know? All right, Gilbert Sesame. You want a photo ID?"

"Oh no, not really?"

"And you're always so glad to hear from me."

"Oh, Gil! I don't believe it!" Jem was flustered, sure he knew she was blushing. "I don't believe it!"

"Darlin', if you don't hurry up and say something more *positive*, I'm gonna have to call the next gal on my list."

◀ ▲ ▶

GILBERT SESAME. FIVE foot three to Jem's five ten. Thirty-four to Jem's twenty-two—eight years ago when they first met. They were in the same journalism class and took an instant dislike to each other. Jem found him obnoxious and Gil thought she was dreamy. Gil would sit alone in a corner of the classroom, rifling off commentary on the classwork, observations that were usually preceded by "no offense, but. . . ." Such as, "No offense, but I've seen cow pies more informative than this article." The rudeness was exacerbated by a down-home drawl, a weird, undefinable accent. No one knew where he was from, but he wore a wide-brimmed straw hat like a riverboat gambler's.

Then Gil submitted a feature story about a spider to read to the class. It was insightful and elegant and moved through a range of emotion that Jem never would have believed Gil possessed. As he read, though, it sounded more and more familiar to her, until finally, at the story's close, she raised her hand and said, "I'm sorry, but I'd swear I read that piece in *Reader's Digest* or somewhere."

Gil flamed; his skin normally had a cherubic cast and emotion turned it fiery as a baby rash. He jumped to his feet and, pointing at Jem, shouted, "You! You are trying to *skewer* me! I will not, I repeat, I refuse to be a shish kebab for you or any other female!" Then he marched from the room, his short legs switching past their table.

That night he called her up and asked if she'd go out with him for coffee. Jem was too astonished to decline. They sat in the student union and he told her she was the first beautiful girl he'd ever met who had a sense of humor.

"*Woman,*" she said. "I'm a woman."

"No, ma'am. You're intellectually mature, but emotionally you ain't. I can see that close up and I can see that across that damn seminar room. You got a skittishness in you like a horse around cows. What you need is an experienced cowboy."

Then he told her she was right; the story was by Loren Eiseley, copied from an essay anthology. "I figured he wouldn't mind," Gil said. "Seeing's how we're both rural types."

It turned out he wasn't a writer at all, but a graduate student in the math department. He was friends with the journalism teacher, Bill Hermans. Bill usually taught proofreading and editing, but the department had asked him to sub in the Beginning Journalism workshop. He'd been so terrified by the prospect, especially by the need to be brusque, bold, and drunken in his commentary—as he saw the offices of a reporter—that he hired Gil on the sly to ride shotgun, a kind of creative outlaw. It was a role that Gil felt—as a mathematician—suited to.

"It's a fine job," he told Jem, "being an undercover character, if only there was a living in it."

Gil was married, but he spoke of his marriage in the way people speak of distantly recalled events, old acquaintances, and faraway cities. He would take Jem out for coffee, sometimes dinner, after their class, and he would reach out and twirl a ring of her hair as they talked. He spoke of places like Laredo, Albuquerque, Laramie. He drew maps in the air with his fingers and told Jem he wanted to show her the Tetons, raft her down the chill waters of the Grand Canyon.

When he wasn't playing at writing student or totaling equations, he was a pool hustler. "This is the one truly good thing my daddy taught me," he said, as he demonstrated his technique at the table for her. It was late, the bar smelled of stale beer, and dust moved in a column through the triangle of light over the pool table. Jem was delighted by the transformation of the man as he lifted the stick, wielding it like a wand, thick fingers curling against green felt, his neck, eye, back all fluid in one swan's arch toward the ball. He made every shot that he called; the few patrons in the bar seemed to know about him. No one would play. Gil was poised and suave, his stocky body transfigured. He twisted chalk onto the stick with a raised little finger and a flourish.

One evening, toward the end of Jem's college term, Gil took her to a new rec room. It was hidden above a hardware store and had a small, makeshift bar and rows of pool tables and pinball machines. Gil walked up to a pinball game called Zontar, Amazon Queen of Steel Balls, dropped a quarter in, and Jem watched the illustration over the pinball table start up. Zontar's anatomy flashed lights and a little number-counter panel in her forehead toted points as Gil worked the machine. He squared his haunches against the table rim, fingers feathering the levers; he became elegant, poised to sail into the arms of Queen Zontar. He racked up points, getting one extra ball after another, the machine encouraging him with clicks, whirs, shrieks, and whistles. A group of teenage boys began to cluster around him, imploring, "Oooh, ooh, get 'er!"

For twenty minutes Gil played past more whistles and bells, vortexes of clangs and fire alarms, and then, somewhere near one billion points, he dropped the levers and let the ball roll down the chute.

Some boys clapped, but others were outraged and watched him as he walked away, saying, "Whadja do that for, huh? What you let it go for?"

Gil turned and faced them, the boys already lining up at the table for their own shot at Zontar. "You know who gets really good at pinball?" he said. "Losers like you who haven't got any friends."

Gil and Jem hurried out of there to the street and down the sidewalk.

"I thought you were going to show me how you hustled," Jem said once they'd slowed to a walk.

"I'm sorry, honey-darlin', but we-all had to get out of there while the gettin' was good. Besides which, I changed my mind about it."

"But why?"

"I didn't want to let you see what happens," he said. "It gets ugly. That pinball was just a taste."

"What do you mean?" Jem said, glancing nervously back. "What happens?

"Well, y'know, it's a perverse kind of thing," Gil said, taking her hand, warming up to an answer. "Just a bunch of wood and felt, like that machine, plastic and lights. But those toys mean something to a person; they can become a foe, an adversary. A pool table can be a wife, or a boss, something feared or respected or loathed. And the hustler is like the poor sucker's psychiatrist, trying to get into that sucker's head, and it's just so easy to pry the damn lid off; nothing to it, really, it's pitiful. There you are, making like their mother or their shrink, stroking their withering egos, showing them the table, first this way, then that, first telling them, sure you can be master, sure you can; you stroke them and stroke them till they're almost believing it themselves, they are believin' it, sure. Then it's not so sure. Up and down it goes. It gets tricky. A minute ago, two minutes ago they were positive. The felt table curled up in their arms like a babe and went to sleep. Now something's waking up. Something's waking up in their brains, too, and it's their boss or their wife or their mother, for crying out loud; something isn't taking no for an answer, something wants a fight, and that's what the mark wants, a fight. Even if he'll have to lay down and die for it, that's what he wants; he wants it so bad he can taste it in his mouth and in the back of his throat.

"And he fights, he does. It's a fine, noble, sad, disgusting thing I'm talking about. Because I'm talking about taking a man down by inches, giving him back some, taking him down a couple more, a couple more, a couple more. You have to be able to stand to do it. Don't tell me it ain't a gentleman's calling; it's got its own code of etiquette. Sometimes I bleed 'em slow and clean; sometimes I do it fast and easy. I calculate what every man can stand and ration it out accordingly.

"I'm just there on the sidelines, helping it along, keeping the movie running. I'm just the messenger, bringing him bad news and more bad news, until at the end of the night, the bad news is that he's cleaned out and more and the game's over and there ain't gonna be no more games, no more messages, not from this messenger, not ever."

Jem stared at Gil, at the way his rings flashed on his fingers as he wiped his forehead, at the way his voice trembled, reminding her of the way opera singers sang, as if delivering up demons. She took a step away from him.

J E M H A D L A S T seen Gil at her graduation ceremony. Backstage before the march, he'd given her a ring with a stone that looked as if it were on fire, so big that when she adjusted her gown it tore a gash in its front.

"My leaving town has been unexpectedly necessitated by circumstances beyond my control and not to my liking," he whispered, clutching his straw hat to his heart. "But do not lose heart, darlin'. I'll be back for you soon and then it's off to the Casbah!"

She hadn't heard from or thought much about him since that day. But here it was, his voice again, after all those years, bursting into the present. She rubbed her temples, dazed and a little dismayed, and tried to make herself sound hearty. "So, Gil! Where are you?"

"The land of legends, over the rainbow, *Salt Lake City*. Mecca for artists and intellectuals of every stripe. And what's more, it's my pleasure to report the time is at hand. Your dreamboat to the West and all the world that waits there has just docked."

"Dreamboat? Gil, weren't you, um, married?"

"Married and then some, darlin', once, twice, and thrice again. But never mind, those spills are all wiped up."

"Oh, really."

"The plan is this: we honeymoon a spell in the New

York environs, maybe visit Niagara Falls, then light out for the open spaces. Escape!"

"Oh, now, Gil."

"Just give me a chance, darlin'. Let down your bayou-black hair. Now that I've found you again."

After she'd finally hung up, Jem shut her eyes and listened to a sound like feathers whisking air, a measure of time, the passage of seven broad, empty years. Everything in her past seemed doused in gloomy work and dark winters, and suddenly the idea of Utah opened in her mind like a sunlit plain. She imagined herself riding bareback, lariat held high, catching the sweet golden air of the desert.

Chapter 5

$\mathcal{B}$Y SATURDAY OF Party Week, Jem had been inundated with daily letters and telegrams from Gilbert, all saying, "Come away with me."

Melvie had been alarmed by the first telegram, associating it, from nursing lore, with announcements of disaster. She watched Jem accept the message at their door and open it.

"'Darling, don't deny your fate, this was meant to be,'" Melvina read out loud over Jem's shoulder as Jem looked back, hoping their father couldn't hear from his recliner. "Oh, my God, what is this?" Melvie ripped the letter out of Jem's hands. "'What we have is Kismet, a concept from the Muslims, your own heritage, come to claim you. Don't deny it, come to me, you wouldn't even have to take off your clothes. Love'—Oh, my God—'Gil'? Not that creep Gilbert Sesame?" Melvie glared at Jem, and Jem raised her hands shrugging.

• • •

GIL AND MELVINA had met only once, very briefly, when after driving Jem home for spring break, Gil had stepped in the house to use the bathroom. Jem didn't want to invite him in, but she didn't know how to refuse his request after he'd taken her forty minutes from the university to Euclid. She knew he was just trying to wheedle his way in, pry open a door to her private life. He lingered in the lower entryway and then tried to go to the bathroom upstairs instead of the one Jem pointed to, just off the foyer. Melvina appeared at the stairs then, arms akimbo, blocking his way. She was fifteen, in both high school and her first full-time year of nursing school. Even though it was a day off she was wearing spotless white slacks and white blouse, more or less identical to those she wore to work.

"And who, exactly, are you, and where do you think you're going?"

Jem sighed. "Gilbert Sesame, my sister, Melvina."

Gil blinked. He looked back and forth from Jem to Melvie. "Your sister? Your *sister?*"

At first Jem thought he didn't believe her, even though, despite differences of style, they looked so alike, their skin the same pale shimmer of olive, the same glints of blue in their black hair. But there was a different, strident tone to Melvie's eyes—she always held them high and regal, as if she were forever impatiently looking over a crowd. Jem's gaze went inward, and if a person looked closely at her they might feel themselves being drawn in.

Gil seemed to be astonished by the mere fact of Melvina. He kept saying, "Your *sister?*" After a moment he recovered and wiped his hand on the seat of his jeans before extending it—an action that Melvina noted. "I'm ever so pleased. A sister of Jem's !"

Melvina barely glanced at the hand. "What is it that Mr. Sesame requires?" she asked Jem.

Jem rolled her eyes. "He wants to use the bathroom, okay?"

"Well then," Melvie said, taking another step down toward Gil and pointing with the kind of gesture that tells a dog to heel, "the bathroom is right there. It's off the *foyer*."

To Jem's dismay, Melvina stood outside the bathroom, arms folded, while Gil was inside. When he stepped out, she said to him, "I didn't hear the faucet run, Mr. Sesame."

"Meaning what, Ms. Ramoud?"

"Meaning that you didn't wash your hands after urinating, Mr. Sesame—if that is your real name."

Gil waited a moment, then he said, "Well, I don't know about yours, but my daddy taught me to piss in the bowl and not on my hands."

Now Melvina was snapping Gil's telegram in Jem's face, saying, enraged, "How could you do this to me?"

"To *you*? What about *me*?" Jem said and tried to snatch the note, but Melvie stuffed it down the front of her dress and locked an iron fist over it. "Yes, indeed!" Melvie said. "The question is: are you going to continue consorting with this criminal?"

◆ ◆ ◆

MELVIE WAS APT to call anyone who was not at least a second cousin twice-removed a criminal, vagrant, or "shady character." After the Family, there was little room over for anyone else. The house was always filled with the thunder of Matussem's drumming, jazz music, and the heated Arabic of visiting relatives and Old Country friends. Jem, in turn, grew up loving serenity and quiet. She was a sweet child but had only a few good friends.

Her one male friend—Bobby Watkins, from tenth-grade Chess Club—was such an invisible, brooding person, she'd forgotten his gender and brought him home one night for dinner and a game. Her father had hovered over them, segueing in and out of Arabic throughout the visit, offering helpful opinions.

"Well, he looks like a withered pea pod, if you ask me. Greenish in the face," he said to Jem in Arabic, smiling and nodding across the dinner table at Bobby. "No meat on his arms. Eyebrows like a dung beetle. Can't you do better than that?"

"Well!" Melvina said, throwing down her napkin, much to the surprise of Bobby. "If that's the way you're going to talk, I'll go eat in the kitchen."

THERE WAS ANOTHER boy who'd caught Jem's attention that year. He was a neighbor from one of the "bad" families that Fatima talked about, an extensive, interwoven system of Ellises, Otts, Beevles and others. Jem had seen him one day sitting in front of the local candy store.

The store looked like a house that someone decided to nail a sign to one day, a big, dirty sign, with the letters O–G hand painted in red. The O–G was a place for cigarettes, chocolates, and newspapers. Jem was afraid of it. Melvina called it a "snake pit" and a "breeding ground for bacteria." Matussem said it was just a "pad" full of a "mixed-up bunch of crazy lunatic dudes." A group of tough-looking boys had made its front steps their hangout.

As a schoolgirl, Jem had passed the O–G every day, her head tilted against the bus window; the school bus wound along the country roads that went deep with fog on spring mornings. Sometimes it would pass the same group of boys on the way home from school as on the way in, and the boys looked as if they hadn't moved all day. Ricky Ellis, Teeny Beevle, Hank Otts, and Darren Bennett. Jem knew their names from the kids on the bus who pulled down the windows, flipped off the kids on the steps, and yelled, "Go to school, scumbags!"

Jem couldn't figure out what those boys did on the steps all day. They appeared sometime in mid-April and lasted through the spring. They didn't talk to each other; they didn't seem to know that the others were there. They stared like foxes Jem had seen in the fields, their minds folded up into themselves, still, waiting.

Even though they were about Jem's age, fourteen or fifteen, they looked much older. Slack and rail thin, they grew their hair over their eyes and past their shoulders. One kid, Ricky Ellis, held a monkey wrench that he constantly turned between his fingers. Peachy Otts from across the street told her that the boys wanted to be mechanics, but the local garages said they were all thieves or crazy. This was especially true of Ricky since his father had blown himself up three years before, trying to supercharge their car using various potions in the gas tank.

Mornings when the sun parted the fog it would catch the bus at a certain angle and all the windows would flare white; then Jem saw angels, white footed and sylph eyed, floating over the children. The windows glowed, and Jem opened her eyes like a person wanting to blind herself.

One school day, Buddy Otts pulled down the window and shouted at them, "Get a job, fucking slimeballs!" As usual, none of the boys even bothered to look at the bus. Jem was staring at Ricky; the bus took the gravel road at such a crawl it wasn't hard to spend some time looking. He was hunched up, black hair stiff with grease falling over his face. Then, for the first time ever, she saw his face turn, parting the curtain of his hair, and recognition shook her. She'd expected eyes that had seen violence and death, seen the pieces of Mr. Ellis's knuckle and kneecap that Peachy claimed to keep in a shoe box under her bed. But his eyes were steady, drawing her into their gaze.

Jem had been studying ancient mythology in tenth-grade English that year, and they'd just had a lesson on demigods and fabulous beasts. Jem's favorite creature was lovely, its upper parts those of a boy, the lower those of a goat. It played pipes, haunting the forest with music that was a thing of the heart or the body rather than the ears. Or so said their English teacher. Miss Potamkin wore gray dresses around a bologna-shaped body. Jem remembered her deep voice as it fluted and followed the dance of her hands, trying to capture this marvelous creature for the class.

"A faun is far more special than either a satyr or a nymph," she had said. "A graceful, shining boy on lightning hooves."

"Wick-ed," Joe Frankfort said.

"It sounds either super-creepy or super-stupid," Pamela Milford said, sucking on her hair.

Jem had thought it was hard to take in. A beautiful monster. Silent music. Later, she understood this was Ricky's kind of loveliness. He looked at her and things went backward. As she sat there on the bus, she felt the quiet fill her head, her breath scarcely moving. His eyes had thick, animal lashes, irises clear as air. When Jem tried to tell Melvina about this discovery, her eight-year-old sister said to her, "Ricky Ellis is a juvenile delinquent; you stay away from him. Have you seen his fingernails? I'm sure he carries diseases. I'd report him and all his delinquent friends if the truancy officer weren't such a shady character, too."

At the time of Jem's preoccupation with Ricky Ellis, Melvie had been auditing basic nursing courses for a year. The community college used the Clay Elementary classrooms—where Melvina attended—after school was out. Melvie was too young to enroll, so she'd sit in the back of the room and pass herself off as somebody's daughter. Between *Cavalcades of Reading* and *Math Fun,* she lugged a tome entitled *Fundamentals of Critical-Care Nursing.*

When Melvie knew a thing there was no sliding around it, and she knew that Ricky Ellis was *no good.* So Jem consigned Ricky to the moments when he lifted the embers of his eyes to her as the bus flashed by, or the moments in dreams when Jem floated over the dividing line between boy and myth. She dreamed of him stretching his long, rangy legs, fine as hooved limbs. The image troubled her in a way that no real boy ever had, and Jem lived with it over the weeks until at last she went to Miss Potamkin and told her she'd seen a faun.

Miss Potamkin listened closely, then caught Jem's hands between her own, and said with round eyes, "My dear, I'm so happy for you, so very, very happy!"

With autumn came the New York freeze; the boys found new shelter and left the steps of the O–G. Then there was nothing for Jem to see but the concrete steps littered with candy and cigarette wrappers, and the screen door with a broken latch, banging above them.

In college, Jem made halfhearted attempts at dating. Young men were drawn to her olive colors, inkwell eyes; they stood close to look at her hair, anoint themselves in her presence. But always she would feel herself stiffening under their gaze, trapped like an animal in headlights, her pulse slowing, her aunts' voices running through her like a river. After college, she decided she no longer had the energy for men. At work or out socializing, she ignored their glances, their tentative observations and questions. Only Gil Sesame had approached her as if from the side, lowering his voice, murmuring to her like a sly cowboy gentling a pony.

THAT EVENING, AFTER Melvie—still clutching Gil Sesame's telegram—drove off to her kung fu class,

Jem walked downstairs. Matussem was in the basement, playing along to Charlie Parker and Sonny Stitt, counterpointing Max Roach and Art Blakey.

"He wails," Matussem said after Jem turned down the volume. "That Bird, he is wailer."

Jem looked at her father's clear eyes and thought of the sky over Jordan. It was a sky that could turn from powder to steel without a wisp on its surface.

She told him about Gil's courtship. "I just don't understand why now, after all these years, all this sudden passion," she said.

Matussem put aside brush and stick and took her hands. He said, "With love, there no reason. Tell me about these Gilbo Sesamoon, he good boy?"

Jem sighed. "Oh, Gil."

"Jemmie, wait," he said, squeezing her hands. "I'm afraid you are waiting for some signs from me, for me to say that you are suffered enough. Well you are, all right? You are suffered enough."

"I don't know what you mean," she said, staring at her father.

"Is like you staying at these crummy job to prove something that don't needs proving. He wants to take you to Utah, right? There desert out there and big skies. And Tim Mox."

"Tom Mix."

"Mox, Tox. In Jordan the same idea. In Jordan we watched his movie. Him and Flush Groodin—"

"Flash Gordon."

"—seventy, eighty, hundred times! We *loved* these. We kids go running all over these movies place, like Beit al Zoon, the bear-man. They don't get the movies like that in these country. What was we talking about?"

"Utah."

"Utah or Jordan. Take pick. Nine of one, half-dozen of other. Why not try it? What's the hurt? Believe me, sometimes I don't know why I move to these balls-freezer place. Only your mother can get me to stay in these refrigerator. So why stick here? These way you will get warmed up and get a man all in one time, and Aunt Fatima will get off my neck, too. Don't think she isn't going to drag some ghoul out the family closet right now for you to marry."

"Dad."

"Maybe I want some place for vacation, too. There some Mormons, sure, but they don't bother you if you are speaking their language. They are clean like you wouldn't believe. And look over there," he said, pointing to his shelves. "*Seven* Books of Mormon! Seven!"

While she was contemplating the spines of the books, her father pulled a telegram from his back pocket.

"Oh yeah. These come for you when Melvina was fussing. I signed for it. I didn't tear it open, but if you hold it to light you can read pretty much it all." Matussem shrugged, sticking his hands in his pockets. "I like his style. I like the way he say you don't have to take clothes off."

Jem opened it, anticipating the message she nearly knew by heart. The words changed, but the substance remained: *run away*. This time, though, the words grew softer and wound tendrils around her fingers. She imagined a white lake, Western wind toppling a thousand white flowers. The paper said, "If love came in glass bottles, I would send you a hundred bottles to line up under your window. They would be full of devotion and if you uncorked one then it would pour out like a genie and say, Come with me to the Casbah of Utah. Come escape. Remember, you don't have to take off your clothes. Love, Gil."

Chapter 6

ON THE DAY of the archbishop's party, Fatima took extra time on her index fingers. They were the most important, and as the fingertips of American secretaries, cashiers, and dental hygienists proved to Fatima, nail polishing was a lost art in this country, sacrificed to the high tech of press-on latex and metal. Fatima was true to the ways of her mother and mothers before her: layers of Dragon Lady Red, tough as concrete and hard enough to tear out eyeballs.

After the fingernails came the eyebrows, tweezed to exclamation points. It helped distract her if, while plucking, she thought of her brother's daughter, Miss Queen-of-the-World Melvina, who'd probably grow her eyebrows in a line straight across her face if she could, simply to aggravate Fatima. It made her angry just to think about it: Melvina and her first-generation attitude, and the sin of the way Matussem was raising her and Jemorah: no tradition, no respect for the elders, *ya'Allah*, if Fatima's parents were still alive!

"But, thanks to God, they not," Fatima muttered, painting on new bayonet-brows. "Baba, it would killed him all over again. Mama, I swear to God, have a thousand heart attacks and rise from dead. Not to mention what she do if she saw what they buried her in." She was thinking about the caftan that had gone to her mother's final resting place, a beige, church-lady affair. Matussem had already made up his mind to investigate America. "He stand around, all hands-in-the-pockets," Fatima muttered, "watched the six miserable sisters grab Mama's clothes." By the time Fatima had returned from school, they'd taken all the good things and left only the church dresses for her and dead Mama. "Look what they left us!" she remembered shouting at her mother's body, just one afternoon stiff and waiting to be bathed. "For you I can see maybe, after all, where are you going? But what about me? They treat me like I am a corpse, too!"

Thinking about this was making her angry all over again, and she pressed the lipstick so hard against her mouth that the tip broke off. "*Ya ba yea! Ya kelbe!*" she shouted, throwing down the tube. Then she remembered she was trying to swear only in English, so she shouted, "Shit, damn, curses! Shit, damn, curses!"—the three swear words that her almost-American nephew Nabil had taught her were the worst and most awful, more powerful than "May your favorite son's camel get fleas," or "May you obtain a great house that fills with leprosy and disfigures you slowly, limb by limb."

The three little words didn't help much, so she ran out of the room in her underwear screaming, "They treat me like a corpse! Like a shit, damn, curses corpse!"

Zaeed was used to his wife's grudges, some decades old and more. ("She laughed at me when I was five and she'll be laughing at me tonight at the bowling alley," Fatima once said of a 102-year-old aunt.) Fatima was Zaeed's first cousin and had lived in the same house in Beit'oon on the edge of the Dead Sea with him and sixteen other relatives since she was three, and, so far as he could tell, she didn't behave much differently from any other Arab woman that he knew, except perhaps a little more so. It was American women he couldn't get used to, nearly as calm and modulated as American men. They'd take a step back for every step he took toward them. They were all so pale and hairless, but at least they were better than the English—he shuddered to think of his short stint as a dishwasher in London—who were pink.

"Pink eyes," he whispered to himself, watching his wife dash from room to room in a bra and slip.

"You know this functions make me so much *stress,*" Fatima said, wrestling with her bra and shoving around the cups that reminded Zaeed of radar cones. "This Old Country types, why don't they leaves us alone? Always reaching, reaching out, like hands from the grave. Nag, nag, nag! Then when they got what they want, they spit in your face, *so superior Arabs.*"

Zaeed knew this was one of a hundred different versions Fatima had of the Old Country. The children born in America would hear how they were descended from saints and how neglectful young people were of the Old Ways. When cousin Samir married an American, Fatima attended the wedding dressed in black and gave them a card written in Arabic, "Samir, this would kill your sainted mother, bless her sacred name, if she were still alive."

Zaeed followed Fatima back into the bedroom. "Of course we don't have to go," he said.

Fatima turned to stare at him. "You are a too amazing man, Zaeed Mawadi. Only you could think that I, Fatima, youngest of seven sisters in the Old Country, would be snubbing the archbishop of our grandparents."

"But they never even met him. He is not from the same districts even."

Fatima raised one eyebrow in the mirror as she threaded the wire of a gold hoop through her ear. "Do you know how that sounds like to me? That sounds like the kind of thing an *American* would say."

Zaeed sighed and laid back on the bed.

"Besides," Fatima went on, shoving a load of gold bangles up her forearm, "what does it matters? Nothing. Old Farouq Mawadi had the right ideas. Pack it up and move to Miami. The only weather a person can take in this God-hater place, anyway."

"Or move to Utah, like Matussem talks about," Zaeed said, then repented. He closed his eyes against his wife towering over him with those eyebrows.

"*Inshallah,* Zaeed!" Fatima shouted. "By God's holy will and in the name of the prophet, I swear to you I go, I throw myself down in the middle of Route 81, if it would make you so much happy! I promise you, if you want to tear my heart out while it beating there better ways than saying evil-evil about my only brother." She caught her breath and went to the closet and began slashing through a thick store of dresses.

"Besides," she said, yanking one dress off its hanger, "Matussem couldn't last two minutes without me. Ask him these yourself. Has he come with one reasonable husband for even his eldest—who going to be now *thirty years of age!* He's helpless, such a mama's boy, an infant."

"He's ten months younger than you," Zaeed said, still with eyes closed.

"So? So what?" Fatima said, viciously pulling the dress over her head. "Ten months, ten years, ten centuries! He's my baby brother and not you or all your fifty thousand important words can change that," she said, zipping with a flourish.

MATUSSEM SMILED AT himself in his bedroom mirror, first directly, then in profile. "Well, well, well, who we has here?" he said, sweeping one hand over hair so thick with tonic that it gleamed like chrome. "Omar Sharif? Or it is Valentino?" He pulled on his western shirt and his arrowhead bolo tie. "'Into your tent I will creep!'" he sang. His belt buckle was five inches of silver, embossed with a bucking bronco and "North Dakota Centennial." "I am the Sheikh of Syracuse! The lovely ladies will be all passing out when they are seeing me."

In the next room, there was a pile of clothes on the floor. Melvie had tried on all four of her mix-and-match outfits and found them wanting. Now she was rummaging through Jem's closet. "Clothes, what do I want with clothes? I'm a *nurse,* for God's sake," she said, tossing another of Jem's blouses on the pile, "not a wax dummy! I don't need a husband and I don't need clothes. If you ask me, we'd all be better off going naked. Skin is water-proof, permanent press, and, furthermore, doesn't stain like cotton."

"Then we'd all have to look at Auntie Fatima naked," Jem said, propped on the bed.

Melvie stopped; Jem could see her stiffening. "The human body is beautiful, young lady," Melvie said. "I look at bodies from sunup to sundown, all kinds of bodies, and I do all kinds of things to them! I have a patient now who has had every one of her limbs amputated as well as both breasts—"

"Really? Have I seen—"

"And I have to disinfect those stumps every day. I also have a patient who was born without eyes or a nose. He told me that he wears a cloth sack over his head to go grocery shopping. His attendant says grown men have stopped in the streets and wept at the sight of him. But you know what?" She turned her clear, hard gaze away from Jem.

"What?"

"He's actually beautiful. His skin is a diaphanous blue, and his tiny mouth looks just like a rose. I've often thought people in general are like trees and flowers. They require light, air, water, nutrition, stability, and warmth. I've also observed that human faces are nearly identical in function to buds; they open up and they attract pollination. People habitually look toward light, and they often turn toward the windows in their sleep. Bodies are little more than stalks when you come right down to it. Would you put a shirt and tie on a stalk?"

Jem lay back on the bed and faced the ceiling. She

tried to imagine herself as a plant. She propped herself up. "Yeah, but I wasn't talking about a brand-new plant, I was talking about one that's getting a little droopy and keeps wearing those down-to-there blouses. You know which ones."

"Some plants are even more beautiful when they age," Melvie said, indignant. "Just like some people. Obviously, you still need to learn how to examine things, to look at the world through a nurse's eyes. Haven't you ever seen anyone with advanced tuberculosis? Their skin becomes amazing, brilliant, even as they're dying." Melvie was standing in just a white slip, her dark hair down and heavy as thunder on her shoulders. Beyond the window, the day was failing, turning toward the hour of parties and celebration. A shadow lengthened over the room, over Melvina's temples. Melvie smiled and said, "Like babies' skin—the promise of blossoming. The reason there's all this wedding pressure on you."

"Babies."

"And, of course, in the aunts' collective mind, your time for sowing and reaping is disappearing before their very eyes. Not much medical basis for that belief anymore, however."

"But what would I do with children? I hardly have a job."

"Obviously, you're going to have to be strong. Resist." Melvie pulled her original outfit—a white, uniform-type dress—back over her head. "Give no quarter and take no enemies. Take liberty or death and nothing in between!"

"Melvie."

"I'm only concerned about you, Jemorah. You've got so much potential."

"I know, I know—and my life's meaning depends upon a professional degree."

"Excuse me, when did I *ever* say that?"

"Well—"

"I simply believe your destiny lies in graduate school."

Jem pulled a pillow over her head. "Melvie. I threw away the application. You made me apply to psychology at *Stanford*. Sure, I'd love to go there, but it's one of the hardest universities to get into. Not to mention the priciest. I don't even have the money for Onondaga Community College."

"The hard battle is the only one worth winning. I fished the application out of the garbage. Organize your priorities, Miss. Fight or flight?"

Jem pulled the pillow off and gazed at the ceiling. "Fight. I guess." She sighed.

THEY DROVE TO the church through the city neighborhoods of Jem's childhood, and she began to think about her mother and the few times they had gone to church together. She remembered there was a church in New Hampshire; they had visited her mother's parents, Nana and Pawpaw. It was before Melvie was born. Her father didn't go. Jem's mother carried a purse of black patent leather, mirror smooth, and wore a coat of black, flocked material, soft as cream. When Jem pushed it in one direction it darkened; in the other it smoothed and lightened. The church had polished pews. Jem fidgeted, snuggling into the coat, looking at her face in the purse. She had forgotten to wear her hat with ribbons down the back so her mother bobby-pinned a tissue to her head to cover it. Every time she twisted around to look, a forest of adult faces bore down upon her. Above the faces, hidden in a secret place, under the colored window, there were angels singing and the breath of God in the organ. Her mother wore gloves that smelled like mothballs. When Jem took communion the host was papery. It stuck to the roof of her mouth as she pressed her palms together, her bare knees on the kneeler.

Once Jem had asked her mother, "Why do we only go to church when we're with Nana?"

It was a Sunday evening and the two of them were driving back to Syracuse. Her mother unplugged the lighter and touched the glowing ring to her cigarette. She put the filter to her lips then blew out through her nostrils, sighing. "Because I don't believe in it. Because I don't believe in any god. I'm an atheist."

Jem kicked her feet up and down; they didn't reach the floor. The shiny patent leather flashed blue lights. Outside rain foamed in the air and rushed up the hood of the car. The evening was dull, lowering around the road.

"Mom, look! Lookit what I can do!" Jem had yanked on the car handle and the door swung open, the street rushing under them.

"Jem!" Her mother reached over and caught the handle. She slammed it shut. "Not while we're driving, okay?"

Jem crossed her legs and watched one foot bob next to the other for a while. Then she said, "So then why do we go to church?"

"To make your grandparents happy." Jem's mother held the cigarette in one side of her mouth and puffed out the other while she played with the radio dial. "And because Auntie Fatty doesn't approve."

"Why?"

She shrugged. "Wrong religion, I guess. Not dressy enough."

"What's an atheist?"

"Someone who thinks what they choose to think." The smoke from her cigarette rose and turned arabesques through the air.

Chapter 7

ORE THAN ONCE Jem had heard Melvie refer to the functions thrown by the Ladies' Pontifical Committee at St. Yusef in Syracuse as "human sacrifices."

"And that's putting it nicely," Melvie said. "What they're doing is feeding their virgins to their raging gods of macho domination and chronic dissipation. And that means *us*."

Matussem referred to them simply as "Arab hoedowns." "Jordan, Syracuse," he said, "it all the same wherever."

If the Ladies' Pontifical Committee had heard Melvie, they would have slapped her name on their Suspicious Laity List. This list, which grew longer each year, noted the latest social indiscretions of longtime offenders and the recent blasphemies of new parishioners. Several Pontificals harbored hopes of one day turning the list over to the police to aid in resolving a murder or drug bust. Many local Arabic matrons aspired to belong to the

Ladies' Pontificals—an elite whose members' reputations were as spotless as their bed sheets. When asked to describe themselves, Pontificals liked to use phrases like: "A Welcome Caravan" and "Stars of Bethlehem." Among their duties they listed: marriage makers and shakers, preservers of Arabic culture and party throwers, immigrant sponsors, and children-police. With thirty-two members, from ages ninety-two to forty-seven—"the baby"—the Pontificals were the touchstone to a small but irrepressible Syracuse-Arab community. Their criteria for admission were mysterious and implacable, and Fatima had been told repeatedly she might have to wait for someone to die before she could be considered. After all, Mrs. D. Hind Abdulaboud pointed out, they were ambassadors to the United States of America, with personal connections to the Lithuanian League, the Catholic Youth Organization, the Greek Mothers, the Malaysian Socials, the B'nai B'rith, and most important of all: the Daughters of the American Revolution.

As an aspiring member, it was all Fatima Mawadi could do to try to live down the ongoing faux pas perpetuated by her brother and his two girls—both still, she thought, thank God, virgins—or at least the local grapevine hadn't turned up anything new on that score. She knew it was a risk to ask her brother to play for the Archbishop, but she also knew this could be the favor with enough pizzazz to entrench her once and for all in the Ladies' good graces.

"If only that daughter of that brother of mine would wear a little bit Maybelline," she scolded her husband, hovering over him in four-inch heels as he sat on a metal

chair in the still-deserted auditorium. "It would kill Jemorah? A little foundation? Maybe some eyeliner?
Maybe, God forbid, brush her hair? Are you trying to
tell me that would kill her?"

"Fatima," he said. "Is only just me, Zaeed, your husband. Don't get exercised. I never said nothing about
no makeup."

"I know that, you Jordanian moron!" she snapped and
walked away, scolding to herself. Spotting her nieces
outside, she marched to the front and yanked the glass
door open. "Jemorah, Melvina, my babies have arrived
at last!" she cried, kissing their faces at right angles, then
vigorously pinching each. Melvie swatted her hand
away. "Pale, pale, so what's new?" Fatima said. "You
think you live under rocks. A little tanning booth is all
it needs, my babies."

"Suntanning produces photoaging, sun poisoning,
and melanomas," Melvie said, still in her coat.

Fatima cocked one eyebrow at her. "Such wise, wise
words! By the prophet's holy name that such a girl exist
who is so wise to talk back to auntie!" She turned to
Jem. "Show me your fingernails. No, no! This are terrible! This will never do. What man will come near such
fingernails? All right, let's get these over with"—she
began shucking the coats off them—"I knew it! I knew
it! Still looking like rats! Starving rats. Your father
doesn't feed you a thing. Don't you eat the *meglube* and
mjeddra I brung?"

In the twenty years since their mother's death, Fatima
had been coming to their doorstep once a week with
pots of food and bags of cast-off clothing that Melvina
wouldn't even let Jem unfold for fear of mold spores.

Jem usually spotted sequins or fire-engine red among the piles of clothes before Melvie packed them all off to the Salvation Army. Matussem fed the smoky cauliflower and lentils to Peachy Otts's tomcat.

While neither of the two sisters was malnourished, neither of them had the dramatic figure that Fatima arranged herself into with corsets, belts, and plunging necklines.

"The heartbreak of it is you're not even trying," Fatima said. She brandished her cleavage like an opera singer, hoisting her shoulders and holding her hands out, palms up. "Look at that. You don't think I'd lost these rose-blush of a teenager."

"Those are mammary glands," Melvie said. "Not hood ornaments."

"What did you say?"

"I *said* those are mammaries. They're glands, sacs that produce hormones and lactate throughout pregnancy."

Fatima dropped her hands. "How dare you speak to your flesh and blood auntie like that? *Ya'Al-LAH!* I, who sacrificed having my own family just to nurse this orphans!" She appealed to the ceiling. "I'm not raising a daughter, I'm raising a snake! Listen to that! Do you hear?" She turned to Jem, asking furiously, "Do you hear that belligerence? You who let your fingers go like a boy's! Just to spit on me!"

OTHER FAMILIES BEGAN to arrive. It wasn't until Zaeed saw Amy air-kissing Fatima at the entrance that he knew he could relax. Now Fatima would stop worrying about ministering to him and would tend to her other obsessions.

Amy was his mistress in name only. Zaeed found women too exhausting to be involved with more than one at a time, and the one he had was more than enough. He'd let Fatima select Amy for him in the same way she matched up other friends and relatives. Zaeed was sixteen and Fatima was fifteen when they were first married, and she would ask him about other women. "But don't you ever think about it? Aren't you even curious about other women?" This he misunderstood as teasing. Gradually she became more insistent until, some years after they'd immigrated, she began speaking only in English and saying things like: "What wrong with you? Are you man or blob? All the husband of Ladies' Pontifical Committee are having affair. Am I to put up with your big husband demands all by myself? I am a wife or a maid, I want to know!"

Zaeed allowed Fatima to steer him in Amy's direction. She was of good Lebanese stock (with a streak of Irish), American-raised, with nice light skin, good teeth, and a secretarial school education. It was a perfect arrangement for Amy: an Arab "involvement" to distract her parents from her Jewish boyfriend. They were ever hopeful that Zaeed would take advantage of the Law of Mohammed and take her on as an additional wife. Every other Wednesday afternoon Zaeed and Amy met in a downtown parking lot, drove to a Motel 8, drew the shades, and silently played pinochle. Rumors flourished like grapes on the vine; friends were grateful for the gossip.

Amy was kindly and compliant. When they met at social events such as this, she brought Zaeed scotch and sodas from the bar.

"Look at this poor Fatima," Zaeed said to Amy, nodding at his wife who was greeting people in the lobby, moving among them with manic energy, her head at a fixed tilt. "She so discontent. She attach to fancies, then she disappointed because they don't make her then so happy. Crazy type lady, but cute."

Amy handed Zaeed his glass. Her parents were also there that night, watching them with pleasure. She curled up on the chair beside him, and her smile delighted people; they took it for the glow of illicit love.

SOMEONE HAD TURNED on the church's PA system and little girls in party dresses were standing on the linoleum tables, play belly dancing to World War II–era Arabic tapes. Matussem was beginning to set up equipment on stage. He was adorned in silver rings, chains, and bronco belt buckle. All that plus his hair, which appeared to have been dipped in car oil, made him look like a cross between Elvis and Dracula. Another man helped Matussem cart out amplifiers and cables. From across the room, Zaeed watched with pleasure as Larry Fasco moved around the stage; he reminded Zaeed of a tropical fish that Fatima had owned for a week or two before it went belly up in the tank. It had an almost completely transparent body; you could see the gem of one eye and the tiniest spiral of innards. You could also see your fingerprint if you scooped it out of the water, as Zaeed had liked to do, to examine it on the tip of an index finger.

This man floated back and forth with the same bright fish eyes. Zaeed could almost see gills working on the transparent neck. Though, he thought, that might just be his third scotch and soda.

Matussem couldn't get the sound check right; nearly every time he touched the mike it sent piercing feedback through the hall. Diners would drop their forks, clutch their ears, and send forth Arabic curses involving drought, blight, and leprosy. "May God strike you with lightning!"

"Jesus H. Christ, Mat," Fergyl Otts said. "I mean, Jesus H. Christ."

The Ramoudettes were getting nervous, unaccustomed to being surrounded by so many—in Owen's words—"non-Americans." What they were accustomed to was the Key West Bar community. Matussem, on drums, was the only musician among them, which left them thin on melody. Owen on bass guitar and Jesse on maracas took their lead from Matussem. Luckily, Fergyl rounded out the band with a Hammond organ complete with electronic saxophone, trumpet, accordion, violins, and harp, which helped fill out the bald spots. What they lacked in finesse they made up for in volume.

The real reason they played so loud was that the Ramoudettes had half-deafened themselves with rock music inside the echo chamber of Lil' Lulu's Garage. After the three of them had been working there for over twenty years, practically everything sounded good to them; all music mellowed through the opaque drums of their ears, rolling in, rich and diffuse, like singing in the shower. The world was musical: cars sluicing down Route 31 through Euclid, dream racers not even seeing the tiny hamlet; voices—any voices—melodious words tripping in random notes: "Fill . . . er . . . up . . . please . . . high . . . oc . . . tane." It all had internal cadence. As long as it didn't sound like the *ding, ding* of the garage's rubber hose bell. Under the constant onslaught of kids riding bikes over it, of cars backing up in the drive, and people stomping on it, the Ramoudettes were testy and skittish as Pavlov's dogs. Fergyl had gone so far as to disconnect the chimes button from his organ, lest he inadvertently touch it and traumatize the group.

On most days, when the highway was empty and the fields were standing still, a passerby would hear the garage's radio music making its way along the weedy plot, up, faintly, to the Ramouds' kitchen window. Matussem first noticed this not long after he and his daughters had moved to Euclid. One morning several months ago, Matussem had walked over and presented himself at the gas pumps. He wasn't certain how to make introductions so he jumped up and down on the chiming hose. A ferocious man with crooked teeth ran out of the office and told Matussem to quit it.

Matussem took one look at him and thought, okey-dokey, Mr. Snagglepuss. This person didn't have a speck of music in him. Matussem walked home and returned three minutes later, rolling his car over the hose.

This time, a man in coveralls came out of the garage. The skin laid on his face like a shadow, his lips pulled in, vanishing. Matussem thought of tales he'd heard of men held captive by giants, waiting to be roasted for dinner. Matussem beckoned the little man over and said in a low voice, so as not to be overheard by his boss, the Giant, "Excuse, Sir, I just happen to notice—as your new neighbor—that you are like me, a big lover of music. I want to says, if you don't mind, that I am thinking that a man of such big feelings as you are being is all wrong in job like these."

Fergyl squinted at Matussem. He was trying to read his lips because Matussem's voice, lowered and foreign, made it impossible for Fergyl to get all of what he was saying. He did catch the words "wrong job." He said to Matussem, "Hang on. I got some guys I want to hear this."

Fergyl reappeared in triplicate. Matussem couldn't remember to whom he originally had spoken, only that out of one came three, like the Christian trinity. And when he saw them, dressed identically, emerging from their pit of music, he sat up and said, "Hey, we got a band!"

JEM DRIFTED AWAY from Melvie and Fatima, walking through the reception lobby. She stepped into the chapel and saw the stained-glass panels, triptychs of saints; her face and shoulders shone in the light. The Eastern-styled icons, heavy-lidded and owl-eyed, smiled at her in blessing.

Back in the reception hall, the long tables were filled to capacity as servers brought out vats of stuffed grape leaves, squash, tabouli, rice, roast lamb, and loaves of Arabic bread. There were bottles of *arak*, which the men

called for over and over. The smell of cooking rose in
a wet fog. The church janitors had spontaneously called
all their friends and relatives. Now a large group of them
were performing tribal dances against the back wall,
brandishing long swords.

The Archbishop sat up front at a private table. He was
a tiny man with a giant smile that seemed as permanent
as his nose. He also appeared to have few teeth left,
and after Fatima met him, she'd crept over to Jem and
Melvie's places where they sat with Uncle Zaeed and
hissed, "A country bumpkin! These one's a throwback
to camels and tents, my God. What will the Americans
think now?"

The Archbishop reminded Jem of someone, and on
closer inspection she realized that he resembled the
chapel's stained-glass saints with their full lips and dipping eyelids. He raised his finger, using their gesture of
benediction. He was seated at the place of honor beside
his hundred-year-old mother. From time to time she
would blot a piece of food out of the Archbishop's beard
with her spit and napkin, while crooning in Arabic, "My
boy, tut tut, my baby boy."

The honored guests sat with the High Secretary of the
Ladies' Pontifical Committee, Mrs. D. Hind Abdulaboud, a woman with an iron hairdo and black rhinestone
sunglasses on a pearl chain. Mrs. Abdulaboud had acted
as their mistress of ceremonies, shuttling the Archbishop
and mother from place to place and contriving to let as
few people as possible speak to them. She was hunched
over her guests at the moment, watching the Archbishop's mouth as he ate, as if she too would have liked
to blot food from his beard.

"Look at her," Fatima hissed to her friend Estrelia. "She must be wait for him to cough up the golden chicken bone."

Estrelia grunted, gnawing on a shank of lamb that she held between dagger nails like Fatima's. "She's a prune's ass. Have another drink; relax your nerves, honey."

"No time for nerves," Fatima said, surveying the room. She took a long swig on her mai tai. "Time is for arranging. Husband time."

Jem and Melvie pretended to be busy eating stuffed grape leaves, trying to ignore Fatima as she towed a man to their table. Fatima moved directly over them and plucked the grape leaf from Jem's hand. "Wake up, girls!" she said. "These here nice Mr. Farah Farah come to meet you. Fifty-eight years of age and no wife ever. Pure and clean like a baby."

"Now wait just one second." Melvie was rising out of her seat, pointing at the man. "Our father already brought this one home ten years ago!"

Mr. Farah Farah was tremendously fat. He slowly spread his hands, palms up, on either side of his great belly. There were multicolored stains all over the front of his shirt. "Still available," he said. "All for you."

"And wonderful, beautiful job, with pension!" Fatima said, clutching Jem's shoulder. "Accountant!"

Mr. Farah Farah drew himself up at the mention of his job and squinted at Jem. "You know how to cook, clean shirts, refinish floors?"

"You, sir, are morbidly obese," Melvie said, prodding his belly with her index finger. "I'm appalled that you would even think of presenting yourself as a suitor when you're already courting heart disease."

Mr. Farah Farah spread his hands even wider, as if to touch the poles of his vast desert-belly, and his eyebrows descended, meeting at the top of his nose. "These one!" he said, staring at Melvie. "*Ya'Allah,* Fatima. You tell me she is change. She is change like eyes of the Sphinx. Not once in a thousand year. These sister-in-law I cannot take!"

FATIMA RELUCTANTLY SURRENDERED Farah Farah. As the party progressed, she moved through the crowd with predatory concentration, scanning tables, her hands grazing a shoulder here, an arm there. She moved like a sheikh, with the sword of her gaze tearing away veils, appraising family trees, bank accounts, and social standing.

At one point Fatima hesitated at a group of young men with soft jaws and plummy lips. They slid their eyes like sparks in Jem's direction as Fatima pointed, but Jem could hear one protesting, "No way, no Arab girls for me! I want an American girl who'll chew my ears up." Fatima swatted the top of his head, but they all nodded agreement. She only moved away from the group when she heard they were about to start tenth grade.

FATIMA PRESENTED HER nieces to Tony Il-Kaseem, saying, "What you think? You want marry one? These only second cousins."

Melvina groaned and rolled her eyes. "Mistake," she said.

Tony ran his hand under his butter-yellow muscle shirt. "Oh, Auntie Fat-eema!" He tossed his head, laughing, and a lock of black hair fell back in ordered strands. "You know I swing whichever way the wind blows, darling. But marriage? I'm not climbing into *that* closet!" He curled one hand under Jem's chin and made a kiss-mouth at her. "Gotta go, I'm off to belly dance. *Call* me, Jemorah—you don't get out enough, sister."

Fatima watched him gyrate his way through the crowds, hands above his head, stirring the air. "All riddles and dancing!" She shook a fist at the ceiling. "By Allah, would you send us a husband!"

F A T I M A ' S   L A S T   C O N C E R T E D—and to her mind, most electric—matchmaking attempt of the evening was an old-looking young man named Salaam Alaikum. His face was so thick with sorrow it seemed to hang in the folds of his skin. His eyes appeared to be liquid, about to leak into the seams of his cheeks. His lower lip trembled slightly, and he was so still, propped in the chair Fatima had pushed him into, he seemed to be scarcely breathing.

"Hello," he whispered, lifting his hand to Jem without raising his head. Jem took it and felt a brief touch of dampness before he withdrew.

"A *university professor*," Fatima hissed. "Teaching *poetry*."

"Emerson, Thoreau, Gibran, Dickinson, Whitman, my true loves," he said, scratching his head and producing a little snowfall of dandruff. "'Press close barebosom'd night!'"

Jem felt a wave of cold wash over her, and she looked up to see a woman dressed and veiled entirely in black who had moved between her and Salaam. There was no hint of her face except for a pair of aviator glasses propped over the veil. "I am the mother," the woman said in Arabic, then began rummaging through Jem's hair.

"Cease and desist this instant!" Melvie said, jumping up and swatting the woman's hands.

"I am the mother," the woman commanded. "I want to look over this daughter-in-law." She circled around Jem and grabbed her jaw. "Open."

Jem jerked back as Melvie grabbed the woman's wrist. "Unhand her!" Melvie cried.

"Naughty, naughty girls!" the mother said, while Fatima sighed heavily as if to say, I know, I know. "How can I know my daughter-in-law before I know her teeth? You told me she was a good, obedient girl, sweet as a chicken."

"Back off, lady!" Melvie raised a fist. "I'm warning you."

"Allah the merciful and munificent! A demon-*ifrit*."

Melvie and the mother began bickering, waving their hands at each other. Jem turned from them to see Salaam staring at her, his eyes wide and pale as ghosts, so steady that Jem felt, for a moment, undressed, and put her hand to her throat.

"You want to be alone, too, don't you?" he said. "You're like me. You want to live the rest of your life blissfully alone."

"No," Jem said, too faintly for the women to hear. "No. I don't."

◂ ◂ ◂

FATIMA HAD GIVEN up on her groom search
for the evening and was now on her fifth sloe-gin fizz.
"She did it at least one halfs from spite," she was saying
to her friend Estrelia. "No, I take back, she did it one
hundred percents from spite. I'm tell you, she died to
make us looking bad."

Estrelia, who was five ten and had about seven inches
and forty pounds on Fatima, was tipsy. She stared at
her smaller friend and wondered if Fatima was going to
pass out any time soon. Estrelia had been a flight attendant for thirty-five years and called herself a "vet." She
claimed to have lived through two nose dives and one
midair collision, and had navigated countless angry,
sweaty travelers, businessmen with martinis, first-class
tickets, wives, and roaming fingers. She'd survived
boozing it up with stewardesses and pilots in airport
lounges, then staggering in a crowd onto the wrong
planes. She'd seen the cities of Bangkok, Tai Pei, and
Geneva blur together. She could drink till her lips got
heavy, her mouth fell slantwise; till she was paging
phony names ("Mrs. Hazel Nuts") on airport intercoms
and couldn't recognize her own voice anymore.

When she heard her friend Fatima saying her brother's
wife had died to make her look bad, Estrelia knew they'd
entered the danger zone. She tried to hush Fatima. The
band had been playing for some time and there was a
huge crowd up front trying to dance to Matussem's jazz.
The Archbishop and his mother were clapping their
hands, absorbed in the entertainment. No one noticed
Fatima at the last table, bitterly chewing over the facts
of life: ungrateful husbands, unappreciative Ladies'

Pontifical Committees, impossible nieces, and dead, interfering sisters-in-law.

"C'mon, Fatty," Estrelia tried to joke, using a name Fatima allowed no one to use. "How do you contract typhus out of spite?"

Fatima only nodded more vigorously, throwing spray-starched hair around her shoulders. "She doesn't get the vaccine, these is how! Who get typhus anymore? And die in one night, boom? Nobody but for silly-silly tourists who don't get their shots and come to Jordan to show so superior they are!" She finished this statement in a scream and several heads turned.

Melvina jumped up from the next table and Jem rubbed her forehead. "Oh no," she said.

"Excuse me, but what were you saying just now?" Melvie asked Fatima, fists on her hips.

Estrelia tried to wave Melvie away, but the confrontation thrilled Fatima; gin was boiling through her, mingling with a hundred petty grievances and irritations. Zaeed was up on the dance floor with Amy; there was nothing to constrain Fatima; she was free. Soaring on a hot wind of anger, she shouted, "Your mother dies on purpose because she hates Arabs!"

Melvina slapped her so hard that Fatima spilled out of her chair.

Later people got the details mixed up. Some said Fatima was threatening to kill Melvie, or herself, or the whole family; others knew it had something to do with mothers; everyone knew Fatima was upset over being left her mother's ugliest dresses. Some said Fatima slapped first; others, that Melvina pulled a switchblade.

Jem saw it all, from the slap to the riot that spontaneously combusted around them. Estrelia grabbed Melvie, and suddenly a hundred men were yelling and swinging at each other, launching into a free-for-all. Everyone was shouting in Arabic, shrieking about mothers, Arabs, Americans, and patriotism in general. From what Jem could tell, the men—though all drunk—swiftly factionalized, Saudis with Saudis, Lebanese with Lebanese, and so on. There was civil war at the back of the St. Yusef Syrian Orthodox Church.

At the front of the church, the party was going strong. The women and children and the men too old or blasé to bother with brawling, as well as a few bewildered American spouses, had crowded forward into the spaces the other men had left behind. The Archbishop appeared to be oblivious to the chaos behind him. Then the custodians had the idea to herd the brawlers, like cowhands herding cattle, back into the big cloakroom behind the dance hall. Jem watched as the still-fighting crowd was custodian-rounded-up through the double doors. She peeked into the cloakroom and saw that the men were now so crammed together they could no longer swing out, but hung on each other's necks, twisting and pushing like an unruly chorus line. Some of them had already started singing.

Fatima had swooned in a cloud of gin vapor and was flat on one of the linoleum tables while several women hovered over her. Melvina had disappeared.

THE DINNER PORTION of the party was over and, as far as Jem was concerned, her sister had issued the final comment on family relations for the day. Matussem and the Ramoudettes were engrossed in their music; Jem's father had entered a Count Basie trance with occasional riffs from the soundtrack to *The Ten Commandments*. He hadn't even seen the fight. But in the moment when the fight passed from the women to the men, Jem saw the pale, eel-skinned Larry Fasco flicking among the brawlers, a fin cutting through the churning water.

The party itself ended an hour later when one of the Lady Pontificals discovered that a huge group of drunken, sweating, singing men was making it difficult to get to her wrap in the cloakroom, and that, furthermore, they were threatening to storm the stage with Arabic drinking songs. The Lady Pontificals called the police, and Jem peeked through the church door just in time to see three police cars, sirens and cherry lights flashing, pull into the parking lot. She stood quickly.

"Hey Jemmy," Matussem said when Jem walked over to him. "You're just in time for help us carry out equipment. I think party's about winding down."

The police, huge in storm-blue uniforms and squared-off shoulders, waded through the little mothers who clucked at their children and scurried out of the auditorium. The officers were holding clubs; the Lady Pontificals had described the fight to them as a full-scale Mid-East uprising, possibly an international incident. By the time the officers reached the cloakroom there was nothing there but settling dust, and Roorhoud, the hunched-over caretaker, restoring coats to hangers.

"Whad you want?" he said. "Whad? They go boom-boom, boom-boom, big fight, *kelbe*-dogs, boom-boom, Roorhoud have to fix. Whad bullshit."

Jem helped the band pick up cables as the police left,

closely followed by an indignant pack of Lady Pontificals. She looked at her father. "Where's your manager?"
she asked. "I thought *he* was in charge of this stuff."

Matussem straightened and turned toward her. His
hair oil had broken up and locks fell in spikes across his
forehead. He touched a finger to his lips as if imparting
a secret. "Who knows?" he said. "Larry Fasco is like
moon and tides, he comes, he goes, there no telling.
Guy is eighth wonder of the world."

J E M H A D A cable slung over each shoulder and a
microphone in each hand when Roorhoud ran up to her.
"Some guy is call for you, there in office. Maybe one
to marry you finally!"

Jem answered the phone, and Gil Sesame said, "Hey,
hey, guess who this is!"

"Gil Sesame!" she said. "How on earth?"

"Well darlin', after I called your house, I tried calling
every other Ramoud and Arab-sounding name in the
Mona Library's Syracuse phone book, figuring y'all
knew each other. Which turned out to be about right.
Also talked to a couple Turks and a Frenchman. They
were the ones told me about the party, since most everybody else was already there. Must been one hellfire shin-
dig—whyn't you invite me?"

"Well, why would I? Where are you, anyway?"

"Hell, you're a regular welcoming committee. Well,
gal, remember how I said I was in Salt Lake City? All
right, that was just the hind-end of a little white lie.
Actually, I'm in a little bitty town just outside of Salt
Lake, called Mona. I've been unexpectedly detained, but

I just received word—in no small part, thanks to you—that I'll soon be able to hitchhike on out of here, untarred and featherless."

Through the door, Jem watched Aunt Fatima sit up and give Roorhoud an appraising look from her table.

Jem switched the phone from her right to left hand and dried the sweat off on her dress. She hesitated. "Gil, what's going on? What's in Mona?"

"Hell, all kinds of things are here, stuffed owls, a grocery shack, a fishing tackle–religious supply store, just same as in New York. Also, there's this prison, see, well, more a kind of jail, you know, nothing that imposing, y'understand—"

"Uh-huh—"

"Well, y'see it's like this. Y'all know how I possess this special gift, so's to speak. You might even say disappearing art form, like Indian pottery—"

"You mean hustling?"

"Well sure, yes, to put it baldly, to call an eight ball an eight ball, *hustling,* yes."

Jem glanced back into the party hall. Matussem was draping a *khaffiyea* around Fergyl's head, saying, "Better than Peter O'Toole."

"Go on," she said.

"Well, Utahans are a special breed, y'see. Second cousins to Nebraskans, which means they're the sportin' kind. Hell, y'all can hardly blame them, spending half their wakin' hours gettin' churched up. You have any idea what one of them Mormon services runs to time-wise? Looks like seven, eight hours from where I'm standing. So who's to blame them if they look to a little relief, is what I'm saying—"

"Gil, is there something you want to tell me?"

"Well, that's what I'm coming to, Miss Jemorah, if y'all'd let me get around to it. Damn it all, you New Yorkers can be the pushiest kind of pushy. See, about a month back I won me a wife—"

"*Up*state New Yorker. What did you say?" Jem switched hands again.

"Now, girl, listen. This was not *my* wife. Exactly. More like there's this feller from somewhere outside of St. Anthony, the *wilds,* and he wanted to keep playing. I mean he's the kind so dumb-ass dumb, you can't help jerking him on the line a little bit longer than is absolutely necessary. And that, Miss Jem, was Gilbert Sesame's first and only mistake, if indeed mistake it was."

"Uh-huh."

"I mean to say, the guy's dumb as a stick and just as poor, too, only he wants to keep playing, even after I got him mortgaging his granny's grave and selling the fillings in his teeth. So he's bet every last tooth in his head, what's he possibly got left to give away?"

"His wife."

"Prophetess!"

"And you let him?"

"Miss Jem, when a man's betting, you gotta be accepting. It's a holy rule, eleventh commandment. You gotta know when 'tis better to receive than to give."

"Gil, what happened?"

"Well, there's an answer to that question. But to get to it, I've got to tell you, for starters, that the Dumb-Ass's wife was fifteen and five-eighths, though she looks about a full decade above and beyond. And being fifteen and five-eighths would not be such a complete difficulty in some of these parts, only the damn Mormons can be so sticky about insiders, outsiders, and whatnot. Not to mention the gal happened to be the daughter of the owner of the biggest Pinky Binky supermarket this side of the Mississippi—owner being best friends with the district court judge—who'd just as soon his gal stay with the first husband, not that the pa was so all-fired hot on the original article. Fact is, the Dumb-Ass is still serving a sentence. We each got hard time—community service—dishing out mashed food at the Mona Seniors' Recreation Center. For trading and carousing. Ha! I'd like to see them make that stick. Besides which, I never laid a finger on her. She wouldn't let me near her. In all actuality, though, I got Mona-style justice—no mashed spuds long as I could give them the name of my far-off sponsor."

"Your what?"

"You, of course, my bride-to-be! The custody is just in *theory,* of course. No actual doing attached."

"Is that legal?"

"Buttercup, it's called the Law of the West. Mona Ordinance 107: criminals under the age of 60 may be released into the custody of a sponsor if said sponsor resides at a distance of not less than 1,392 miles from downtown Mona, population 27."

"Criminals under sixty?"

"Most of the town is over seventy. I can't explain the mileage part. Ordinance 108 says no mules in the dry goods store. Makes more sense to me than the sponsor law."

"That's why you started calling me last week!"

"Now, now, Miss Jem, I know what you're think-ing—" Jem heard a scuffle in the background, the squeak of a palm over the receiver and Gil's voice, muffled, saying, "All *right,* already, you'll get your damn spuds." He came back. "Pardon the interlude, these senior citi-zen types are something else. But as I was saying, *A,* I only have eyes for you, my muse, my guiding light, and *B,* I'm gonna beat this pathetic rap without a tear or drop of bloodshed. My lawyer, Rex Biggs of Wee, Biggs, and Howe, says to lay low back East awhile—in hiding, so to speak. We'll sue their shriveled hides for defamation of character and then catch the glory train back out West together. In the meantime, little darlin', when do we rendezvous?"

"I don't know what to say, Gil. It's all so . . . strange."

"Yes, indeedy, ma'am. Doesn't everybody love a sur-prise? There are so few such pleasures in life. Like your Arab hoedowns—when's the next one? How many are you hiding from me?"

Watching Fatima steer Roorhoud in her direction, Jem blurted, "No, none! They're practically every weekend, but—"

"Fine, perfect! Bravissimo! Okay, I gotta go now. Till then, *arrivederci!* Till we meet again in Rome!"

MELVINA STILL HADN'T come home by the time Jem got into bed that night. Jem fell asleep wonder-ing where she was. Her dreams were jumbled, the color of sloe gin; she saw long hair, trees bending. Somebody was saying, "This is your husband," behind her sister, who was shaking her head no.

When she woke the dawn was gin-colored. She went to her window and could faintly see a small figure walking up the Otts's field toward their house, a black dot in a pool of rose. She pulled on her robe and went outside. The air was pink, and she wasn't certain of what she saw: it appeared to be Larry Fasco walking through the fields carrying Melvina.

They were shining like the tall grass. Larry Fasco's arms, neck, and face made a prism of the sun, a spectrum. He winked in and out of the light; at times Melvie seemed to be floating, her skin wine-dark against the brightness. She was brimming, eyes closed, skin taut as a fruit's.

The only sound was Larry's legs switching through the weeds. He brought Melvie across the street, onto the front lawn, and placed her next to Jem. As soon as she slid from his arms, Melvie returned to herself. She straightened, brushed at her dress, and shook hands with Larry Fasco, saying, "Thank you for a pleasant evening, Mr. Fasco."

Larry Fasco didn't look ready to leave, but Melvie folded her arms.

"Damn. Couldn't you at least call me Larry?" he said.

"That would be fine, Lawrence. Don't swear."

He twisted his hands in his pockets, kicked at some grass, then said, "Well, okay then," and walked back in the direction from which he'd come.

Melvie began humming and fixing her hair in a window reflection. "Melvie," Jem said and stopped. She squinted, trying to shut out the white morning shadows; Melvie was looking at her. Finally Jem said, "Melvie, was that you just now?"

"No, Jem," Melvie said gravely and shook her head. "That was not me. Not at all."

Jem decided to go back to bed; it was still early.

Chapter 8

WHEN JEM WAS nine, she liked to kneel on the couch and pull a brush through her mother's hair, so it crackled like fire. Nora's fingers around baby Melvina were long and slender as tapers. When Matussem came back from work in the winter night, he was snow-flecked, his lashes wet and silk black. Matussem stamped and the snow shook from his coat. His hair was all black then and curly, like his daughters'. After he was dry again and they had eaten dinner, he gathered Jem up and sat next to Melvie and his wife.

"Now, well, girlses," Matussem said, his English at the time unwieldy. "Tonight I tells you about moon and gazelle. There was and there was not one nights when the gazelle see these moon in water place, a lake, like ink these lake. The gazelle she ask moon in sky, 'Whad now? Who these in water?' These moon, joker, she like the laughs. She say, 'This my sister moon of the water. Don't drink her up or the fishes will swim out of the water to find her.' But these gazelle, she tries drink the moon out of the water, because then gazelle will be beautiful like the moon. She think the fishes will make parties and go dance around her. She drink and sister moon goes from water, and a hump come there, on her back, and she turns to camel! And moon—she laugh, laughing moon! So lesson for daughter, if you listen to moon you get turn to camel. So go to bed when Mama she says to."

Then Melvie, who at two was already impatient with her father's semitranslated proverbs, would run to Matussem, slap her tiny hand on his arm and shout, "Da! Fight! Fight!"

IN JEM'S DREAMS the moon became Jordan, the place where her father came from. Her father was the gazelle and he waited by the black water's edge, staring at the moon. Sometimes she woke crying from this dream, and then her mother's face would replace the moon and her fingers like candles would smooth back Jem's hair. "Hush. Hush," she said. "Those are only stories."

Nora would leave the room then, vanishing like the tail of the jinni's lamplight.

Twice a week, Aunt Fatima and Uncle Zaeed came over for dinner. Fatima and Zaeed had faces like Jem's father's, the same clear tint of earth. Fatima looked at Jem and Melvie, her eyes black as cups of Matussem's coffee, and she murmured in English, "Beautiful! Beautiful babies! Pure as water. You come back to home soon, come back to Old Country, marry the handsome Arab boys and makes for us grandsons!"

Nora's lips tightened to a streak. She stood and left the room. Melvina rushed over to her aunt, tiny fists raised, shouting, "Fa! Fa! Fight! Fight!"

Later at night, Nora bent over the girls, tucking them in. "Your home is here. Oh, you will travel, I want you to. But you always know where your home is." The ends of her straight, long hair brushed their faces, its bright red fringes swinging and making sparks. Soon they would be flying to the moon to visit their other family.

NORA HAD REFUSED to get all of the shots and vaccines the family had advised for the trip to Jordan. "Typical Arab patronizing," she'd said to Matussem. "According to your sisters, young women don't know how to take care of their own bodies." They rented an apartment for a month in the center of Amman, Nora insisting that silent Baby Melvie would surely cry all night. "*Amerkani,*" the aunts, who'd borne thirty-eight babies between the six of them, said to each other. "Too good to stay with us!"

No one knew how long she might have walked around in pain and with fever without saying anything, not knowing the danger. She had seemed fine for most of the visit, then one night about two weeks after they'd arrived, Jem had been awakened by her mother's breathing. It was ragged, vibrating through her. Jem went into her parents' room, drawn by the rattling, and she was shocked that her father could lie asleep next to this woman who lay turning into stone.

Jem had touched her mother's leg and it was hot and

stiff as rubber. She pulled back the sheet and her mother began to tremble. Jem could see her mother's eyes open, watching her. "Please cover me," she said. "I'm so cold, I'm freezing." Her lips were blistered and scorched; her hair looked tarnished.

Jem sometimes felt that the disease should have carried her off with her mother. When Jem was very young, her mother had told her that when she was first born they'd had German measles together and had lain in the same sickbed with fever for weeks. Sometimes Jem dreamed of that early time. The illness would be there; moist and warm, it clung to them like a vapor as they held each other. They breathed together, in and out, sharing breath. Her mother's arms encircled her. The fever was smoke, fire in their skin. The smoke filled them, thick in Jem's chest.

AUNTIE REIN TOOK over the family in the weeks following Nora's death. She was seventy-nine years old, straight and strong. She'd outlived her five siblings, including Matussem's mother, her younger sister Amira. Rein had married a rich cousin in Forty-seven and emigrated from Nazareth to a grand house in Beit'oon, a village on the outskirts of Amman, Jordan. After Nora had died, they brought her body into Rein's large stone bathroom. Nora's hair floated around her, red as lit tobacco against the marble column of her body. There seemed to be a haze in the room that rose from the steaming water they emptied over her. Rein's new tub had running water, but they had to pour it into buckets, cart them down the stairs, and set them on the stove to heat. Fatima, who'd flown back home from the States the day she'd heard of the death, had carried the buckets two by two. In the tub, Jem's mother turned into a cloud, her features drifting apart; when Rein lifted her body out of the tub she seemed to scoop up a current of water.

Rein was short and heavy, but she could run up and down the stairs like a girl, and she squeezed the breath out of Jem when she held her. Rein wore her white hair in a long, thin braid that fell past her waist. After washing Nora's body, Rein brought Jem into her bedroom, which was filled with carved wood and brocade curtains and vaulted ceilings. They stood together by the mirror and Rein undid her braid so her hair spread and shimmered like a silver mantle, and she drew it around so it cascaded over Jem's neck and shoulders. For a few moments inside that white tent, Jem felt comfort again.

AFTER THE DEATH, time unmoored itself and went drifting down Auntie Rein's marble halls, pooling along the stone floor. Jem felt like she was living inside the Waterbabies tale that her maternal grandmother used to read to her—fairy-children like mermaids swept along the world's currents. She swam in loss, and it seemed other children were different, at great distances from her. Only her cousin Nassir, who had recently lost an eye in an accident, seemed able to understand. He stayed at her side, and they took walks to the corner store for bubble gum and eggs. "*Atini atnosh beyda*," she would say. The shop owner placed the eggs in a paper bag and Jem, used to the protection of cartons, would then run home and present them to the kitchen staff smashed and leaking.

In Jordan the pleasures of the familiar were gone. There was little available milk; making pancakes was an exotic production that attracted attention in the neighborhood. The ice cream was thin and oddly flavored; vanilla tasted like perfume. But every day at noon Jem and Nassir went together to the main square for cones. There were also boys who walked the cobblestone streets in the early morning holding trays of warm, seeded bread rings on their heads. Each morning Jem and Nassir ran to them. *"Atini kahk,"* Jem would say and then share with her cousin.

Her mother was also somehow there, her memory residing in the steepening streets. She was a jinni, whose real activity Jem could scarcely remember, less a memory than a presence who might fly out from any crook or corner, perhaps from the tubs of corn and butter vendors carried on muleback. A week after Nora's death, Jem began to wonder if her mother had ever been real, or if she was just a sweet story that Jem had told herself.

Nassir and Jem rode through the village together on shaggy burros. The bedouin women admired Jem and petted her; when they brought Melvie along, the husbands liked to hold her hoisted up under her arms, feet dangling down. Aunts and uncles took them to visit huge, ringing churchyards, banked in tier after tier of wildly colored flowers. In one chapel, they found a shining altar where the infant Jesus was supposed to have been born.

Jem and Nassir sat together on the stiff horsehair sofas of her great-aunt's house, eating plates of the salty basket cheese and yogurt *lebneh* and Syrian bread, staring at the television static, or watching relatives who congregated around what was the only telephone in Beit'oon.

At other times after the death, Jem wandered Auntie Rein's limitless house, feeling the flesh-ache of her mother's absence, continually expecting that she might still find her mother alive and waiting for her beyond the next hallway, mistaking the backs of other women's heads, the curves of their hands, for her mother's. The house went on and on, its rooms opening to patios and great flyaway windows that she could step through; it was hard to know where the house stopped and the outdoors began. Jem stood by an open window that looked out on the flagstone walk and a night wide as the Dead Sea. She felt herself drawn as if pulled toward the open space, as if her mother had reached for her in that moment, as if her soul had just slipped through one of the big windows, out to the sky.

At night, schools of stars shone through skylights and tall, arched doorways and lit the marble floors along with constellations of lamps and hanging chandeliers. Jem saw little of her father, who was sequestered behind the study doors. Rein had shut him away to protect him from the flow of visitors and their communal grieving. There was a television in nearly every room, but the reception was poor and there was little being broadcast; the static Jem heard drifting in the halls and through the windows was only occasionally interrupted by reruns of *The Saint* and *Car 54,* dubbed in French or Arabic. There were servants who brought her plates of cheese and sweets and the hard, dried balls of yogurt that she liked to gnaw on. Jem lingered under the vaulted ceilings, amid food and noise, and tried to give herself up to forgetfulness. Melvie, who was two and some months, had taken to a wet nurse—a local mother Rein had employed—as easily as an infant, and her skin glistened, though she fussed and constantly demanded to see her sister and mother.

Rein meant for them to stay. Her own family was grown, involved in their own concerns, and she'd outlived her husband. She would hold Jem in her lap for hours, brushing the little girl's long hair back with a boar's-bristle brush till it shone with a blue steel light. But they stayed for just a few weeks, the body stored in a hospital morgue, then Matussem finally decided to bury his wife in her home earth. He had begun to look as if he'd been winnowed away, his shirts and suits all too big. Jem was frightened of the shadow that Matussem had dropped into, and she cried because she didn't want to leave. Matussem, too, seemed startled and nervous when he looked at his daughters.

An hour before they were to depart, Auntie Rein took Jem to her garden. There were sunflowers and mint, and farther back, Rein showed Jem where the baby cucumbers grew, curling on their knotty stems. She brought in a basket of the tiny things, each just big enough to fit into the palm of her hand. They rinsed them under the kitchen tap, and Rein set out a dish of coarse salt. They sat at the table and dipped the ends in salt; the skins were soft, not at all bitter, and the sweet and salty cucumber was delicious to Jem. Once they'd finished them, it was time to leave, and Rein held Jem and told her they had vegetables just like that back in Jem's own country.

▲ ▲ ▶

FATIMA CLAIMED THAT Nora's death was a "failure of modern medicine." "Shocking, too much," she said, flicking her black hair back with one long fingernail. "Jordan so modern, like suburb of New Jersey. Such thing don't happen in the Modern World," she'd say, then add, grim faced, "Your mother. I know she didn't really liked us."

Back in the States, Fatima played at mother, dressing them in ruffles and singing endless Arabic lullabies, until one day Melvie, who was then two and a half, bit her wrist and drew blood.

Their father said the relatives had snubbed Nora and gossiped about her, driving her to despair, the relatives and neighbors and their "attitude." "Sure," Matussem once said, "all those Jordanian crones, making like they never see red hair before. Like redhead Arab women haven't been crazy in love with henna bottles ever since Cleopatra. Like they never seen *I Love Lucy* reruns! Give me break."

THE DAY THEY'D returned from Jordan with a body in cargo, Nora's parents had met Matussem and the children at the airport. Matussem had seen them all the way across the terminal as the noise of the crowds faded into a silence that filled his ears and weighed down his legs. He was carrying Melvina; Jem, who was nine, held his free hand. The closer his wife's parents came, the less recognizable they were to him. Their features melted apart in despair, becoming stranger and stranger, until, as they drew near, he forgot what faces looked like.

They cried, they spoke to him and gestured, the words falling into pieces, broken, repetitive noises, until at last the sounds were hammered down into a glowing brand, a heated sign; a passage in his mind was thrown open and he heard his wife's mother saying, "You killed her. You. You killed her. You. You killed—"

His daughter's hand in his was iron hot.

His in-laws never forgave him. Although they called the girls on birthdays and holidays, they wouldn't see them in person. "It hurts too much," his mother-in-law had said to Jem, "to see so much of our daughter mixed up with the body of her murderer."

Whenever she'd called, the girls' grandmother had closed the conversation by saying, "Tell your father to tell you the *truth*."

Melvina, when she was six, answered her, "I already *know* the truth."

Jem had said good-bye, hung up, and asked: "Dad, what *is* the truth?"

Matussem looked down, shrugged, and said, "How could I ever know?" Then he put on a Coltrane record and said, "Listen, here's the gospel according to Saint John." And Jem stood in the living room, thirteen years old, listening.

A YEAR AFTER they returned, Matussem moved his family from Syracuse to Euclid, to nights of pure dark, caught in the teeth of stars, the ventriloquist crickets calling to them. He saw their country home as a place of perfect forgetting, lost in a gully of trees, boundless fields ragged with Queen Anne's lace and this-tles. It was built into a rise, to be entered on two levels, downstairs in front and upstairs in back. The bedrooms were downstairs facing over the front lawn, living and dining rooms up; everything was a little odd about the place. Jem liked its windows and clarity. She tried to forget the bleak forms of priests and beetle-browed neighbors crisscrossing the cool stone of the bedroom floor in Amman, her mother's hand turning from hot to cold in her own, the black-suited doctors clustering around the bed, the flock of relatives, faces nodding at her, hands of claws, the plumage of mourning, and out-side the wet streets, cats crying like babies at night. In their Syracuse house, when they'd first returned, the ghosts were so thick that Jem had wanted to scissor her arms through the air, to place her hand over Melvie's eyes to protect her.

Jem loved the new house. It was sprawling, almost haphazard in design, as if the earth had buckled and red timber and glass had risen from the rift, just as natural as the slate, blue spruce, and lilacs that flanked it. In the suburban subdivision where their mother had once lived with them in a house of particleboard and balsa wood, a train track ran not fifteen feet from the back door. At times the track pounded so loudly that small objects danced across the floors. It was a dark place, close with memory, the scent of absence. In the country, Jem would take to the lawn chairs on a warm evening and feel she was rising up to a shelf of trees and acres of the lightest air. She felt the change in herself, as if her mother's life had been a river paddle that, in leaving, had churned swiftly through her. The trees had a black midsection, a soft belly near the earth where the bluest needles lay down and swept the grass.

Chapter 9

*E*UCLID, NEW YORK, was virtually the same as it had been one hundred years ago when two roads intersected and that point was named. A couple of years after Matussem bought their house, there was something that the locals called a "mall scare." The farmers and welfare families were up in arms because a Syracuse architect had the idea of locating the Great Eastern Canada-Maine-York Mall in Euclid.

Nothing ever came of the plan, but for a while some of the local families dreamed about selling their land at staggering profit to dumb-ass city-mall developers, and the farmers shot off their rifles to show what would happen to any fancy planners who tried to slice into their crops to build the highway for their Great-Big-What'sitsname-Mall.

"They put up a mall here, you just set and see what happens. You'll have every bozo and his brother from here to Baldwinsville saying 'Let's visit up to Euclid today, yuk, yuk,'" Hilma Otts once said to Matussem.

Actually she was shouting it because she was standing on her property across the street. About a foot of cotton housedress hung out under her down jacket. Her legs were thick, planted against the ground, and Matussem thought he could see the outline of her biceps straining at the parka as she held her arms folded across her chest.

Hilma thought of Matussem as "that cute little brown guy." She never minded that her youngest, Peachy, liked to spend time over there with his girls, but she had to keep her own distance. She knew about Arab men, and if Jupiter Ellis, that sonofabitch who'd vanished into thin air years ago, ever got wind of Hilma hanging around with a smooth-talking, darky foreigner, well, she remembered even after a decade or two the kind of bad temper Jupiter Ellis had.

So her and Matussem's conversations were amiably conducted across wide spaces, usually across the street or over the aisles of Bumble Bee Groceries. Matussem considered this distancing another of the myriad American eccentricities he'd discovered since he arrived. He liked to tell his relatives, "I don't care how many *Bonanza* you watch, nothing get your brain ready for real America!"

Hilma Otts was not the sort he wished to get too close to anyway. Her fingers unnerved him. He'd seen the way they dug into a head of cabbage or throttled her daughter Peachy's nape when she was up to no good—Hilma had the kind of fingers that made surgeons, pianists, even jazz drummers cringe. He hadn't been with a woman since his wife's death, and Hilma convinced him he would never try again.

In the hundred years since Morgan Road bisected

Route 31, the Otts family had grown like a dynasty, spreading and mingling with Brooms, Ellises, and many sundry others, all immigrants from more ancient upstate hamlets, like Cicero and Phoenix along the old highways.

Without the mall, Euclid remained an amoeba of a town, thirty miles straight out Route 31 north of Syracuse. It took in dirt farmers, onion farmers, and junk dealers and produced poorly clothed and poorly fed children, who'd wait for driver's licenses then leave in rotting-out Chevies, going as far as a case of Black Label would take them. Usually just far enough for them to come back for good.

"No one ever escapes this place," Peachy Otts told Jem when they were children. "You want to think twice about moving here. It's like that show—*The Twilight Zone?*"

Peachy turned up, barefoot and hair sticking out like a bushy doormat, on the Ramouds' front lawn the day they moved in. She immediately took Jem aside and began telling her stories.

"I hope you won't cut the grass in the fields, 'cause it'll piss Dolores off." Dolores was one of her older sisters. "I used to sneak up here and watch Dolores and Darren Brummett doing sex in the weeds."

At nine, Peachy had buttery skin and rolling blue eyes. "We're white trash," Peachy told Jem, leaning against the post that marked off the Ramouds' lawn from the open fields. "You're moving into a white-trash town. Crazy nuts, goof-heads. Like once when Glady wouldn't make sex with Darren Brummett, he went to the fruit stand and stole their ax and chased Glady right around that house you're moving into."

"Geez." Jem looked back around the house, as if she might have seen them running through the fields. All she saw, though, was three-year-old Melvina in the kitchen window, watching her sternly. Peachy flipped back her knotted hair, and in that moment, Jem thought she looked like a mermaid, with her pale skin and sea-broken eyes. Mermaids were supposed to become sea spume when they died, Jem remembered, unless they found a mortal to love them, to give them a soul.

HER FIRST YEAR riding the school bus, Jem saw how the countryside could brim with pain. At the Wisters' she saw the oldest man in the world, a face like a white raisin, leashed to a post in the front yard. He moved around on his elbows and stomach and moaned at the school bus. His hands moved constantly, scratching out dirt patches. This was the first stop after Jem and Peachy's. Hanky Wister would always get on, force down the window and shout, "Shut up, Granddad!"

The first time they picked up the Brooms, Jem thought there was a mistake, that the driver was lost. He drove off the road, across a field, and stopped next to an old city bus propped on blocks in the middle of a lot, about a mile out from the main gravel road. A band of seven children, ranging from around ten to eighteen, emerged from the defunct bus, crossed the lot, and climbed onto the school bus. Jem noticed a clothesline loaded down with diapers. The Broom kids looked savage. Their faces were sharp and blank, branded with grime. Jem felt heat rising from their hands, their mouths, the way they ran, banging down to sit in the last rows in the bus.

If Peachy wasn't sitting with Jem, she was swaggering up and down the aisle, sizing up the others. She liked to jump into a seat then turn and leer into the faces of the children behind her. Her hair was matted and there was something dreadful in her eyes; often the children would flinch. When this happened, Peachy leaned forward and spit in their faces. Her body was compact, dense with fire. She was alive with limbs, loose energy, somehow stunted, a permanent child-god of destruction. She smelled; she hummed; she stuck herself in the leg with safety pins and watched the points of red appear under her skirt. Other days, though, Peachy was subdued; she'd tell Jem about how her older brother pushed her down in the bedroom, stopped her mouth with a hand that smelled like axle grease, and sweated and groaned his face into the pit of her neck.

Peachy was Jem's only friend on the bus. The other children taunted Jem because of her strange name, her darker skin. They were relentless, running wild, children of the worst poverty, the school bus the only place they had an inkling of power. She remembered the sensation of their hands on her body as they teased her, a rippling hatred running over her arms, legs, through her hair. They asked her obscene questions, searched for her weakness, the chink that would let them into her strangeness. She never let them. She learned how to close her mind, how to disappear in her seat, how to blur the sound of searing voices chanting her name. One day someone tore out a handful of her hair; on another someone pushed her down as she stood to leave; on another someone raked scratches across her face and neck as she stood, her eyes full, the sound of her name ringing in rounds of incantation. Waiting to leave, she could see her name on the mailbox from a half mile away, four inches high in bright red against the black box: RAMOUD. Matussem had been so eager to proclaim their arrival. There was no hiding or disguising it. She would run off the bus, straight to her room, but the voices would follow and circle her bed at night.

None of the other children had ever helped her, not even Peachy Otts, who would watch blandly, without surprise. By the time Melvie started school, the bus route had changed to accommodate new subdivisions, the tentacles of suburbia reaching from Syracuse toward Euclid. New children rode the bus, mild middle-class children with combed hair, cookies and raisins in their lunch. "Faceless," Melvie complained in seventh grade. The bus no longer took the long, gravel road south to the shacks and trailers, as if the school had forgotten those children were even there.

As Jem moved toward graduation and college, her tormentors scattered. The kids on the bus dropped out or got pregnant, went to juvenile homes, foster homes, penitentiaries, turned up poverty-stricken, welfare-broken, sick, crazy, or drunk. After a while, no one was left to remember the bus. A kind of relief and loss: no one to bear witness, and Jem did not let herself remember. There was no room left in her to think about any of it; she knew those children had been right. She didn't fit in even with them, those children that nobody wanted.

THE LAST TIME Jem had talked to Peachy or seen most of those tough kids together was twelve years ago, when Jem was a high-school senior and Peachy a repeating ninth-grader. They were riding home from school when a police car came up behind them. The red light fluttered behind the bus; they pulled over and the kids started shouting, swallowing stashes of drugs, even cigarettes, jamming knives and pipes between the bus cushions and under the seats. Someone hurled a tiny pistol from the window and Jem watched it wing past the railroad tracks into the ragweed and Queen Anne's lace.

Two police officers boarded, and the bus fell into silence. The officers went directly to Jem and Peachy's seat, and Peachy—who'd been eerily quiet in the moments before—began protesting in a high, altered voice, "I didn't do it! You got the wrong kid, I swear! You got the wrong kid!"

As soon as they laid hands on Peachy, that thin voice turned into a terrible wail. She fought with her hands and feet, the way Jem had seen cats scrabble on their backs, claws flying, teeth bared in her dirty face. The police wrestled with a fury of thrashing limbs; Peachy's face was squeezed past recognition in rage and fear as they carried her out.

Jem never did find out why they'd taken Peachy. After that, Jem rarely saw her. She never returned to school.

Sometimes Jem saw her working at Onondaga Orchards, the big produce stand up the road. There, Peachy seemed serene, even at home among the vegetables, though in many ways she never seemed to Jem to have grown up; her skin remained milky beneath the dirt, too clear, her eyes nearly vacant, sweet and dull as molasses. Though only in their late twenties, Glady and Dolores, Peachy's older sisters, looked haggard as old warriors, harrowed by poverty and pregnancy. Jem had once heard Peachy's mother, Hilma, say of her youngest, "This one could go either way, could almost grow up to be pretty. More likely though, she'll stay what she is, a goofy devil-child, too slow to get ugly much or tired. She'd need some more smarts or to have a kid like herself to get older."

Chapter 10

THEIR FATHER USED to tell them, "Za'enti da'ar the beauty of the house. She sit upstair in her bedroom window and look down on everyone. 'I so gaddamn beautiful!' she think. 'They all look like ants from here!' she think. Well, one day the house of Za'enti da'ar gets on fire. I know what you thinking, like maybe the folks gets tired of her saying they are like ants and there a reason for fire. But no. That is just how these old-time stories are: there no reason. It just all of a sudden on fire, okay? So anyway, here come her father, carrying out furniture, running and holler and who know what, he crazy, right? It is bad news. Next come Mama with the clothes and pots and pans. Next the sisters and brothers and babies and all that, crawling and crying and punching everybody. Oh no. Next come grandma, grandpa, auntie, uncle, the whole gaddamn tribe come out and stand in the street and they look up and there Za'enti da'ar, still in the window, her hair just right above the fires. All they yell to her, they yell, 'Za'enti

da'ar! Za'enti da'ar! Come down here, you crazy ass.'
And stuff like that. Only she don't listen. No way, unh-
un. And you know why—"

"Because she was Za'enti da'ar," Melvie and Jem
would say.

"That right. She is Beauty-of-the-House. And she
says to them, 'No way, you must be crazy. I am beauty
of these house. I don't care if it is on fire, you don't get
me out in the street.' And so, because she Za'enti da'ar,
she burned up completely. They could hear her screaming out in the streets, *aieeehhhaaa!*" The girls would already have their hands over their ears. "There nothing
left of her after that but a gaddamn golden doorknob."

Melvie hated that story, even back when she was eight
and Jem was fifteen. Even though she'd sit patiently
through it and provide the requisite answer at the proper
time, Jem suspected she was waiting for the ending to
change.

"But that's so stupid!" Melvie would burst out when
the story was done. "She must have been emotionally
disturbed! What does being in the house have to do with
anything? And why didn't they just drag her out? And
how in the WORLD could anyone turn into a golden
doorknob? She'd just be bones and ashes, that's—that's
so—incredible!"

Their father had hundreds of instructional stories,
many of them paranoid, vaguely morbid, a rogue's gal-
lery of characters. Matussem was on a first-name basis
with all his characters and was forever running across
them in the world at large. The unsuspecting butcher at
the Bumble Bee he called "Raof el-Ghazis," who
was the-man-who-tried-to-train-his-camel-to-eat-air

because Matussem suspected him of resting a finger on the meat scales. Whenever one of the girls was too slow or reluctant about joining him on one of his out-ings—usually to drive out to hardware stores to look at lawn ornaments—he would clap his hands and say, "Come, Za'enti da'ar! Don't take so long!"

He populated America with figures from his child-hood's stories; Jem thought it sharpened his focus on the world. Motives and actions would fall into place if he called a woman "Yasmine Al-Hassan" (the-woman-who-screamed-a-lot) or a boy "Semia Abouq" (the-boy-who-ate-hot-*mensif*-and-then-didn't-warn-his-father: Father: why are you crying, my son? Boy who has just burned himself on *mensif:* because I'm thinking of my dead brother in heaven. Father who proceeds to burn himself on *mensif:* I wish you were up there in heaven with your brother!). These were childhood friends; if Matussem recognized them everywhere, this country couldn't be such a foreign place after all.

Jem wondered what language he thought in; his dis-placement was a feature of his personality. He wouldn't have been the same father, she knew, if he had stayed in Jordan and raised them there. His removal was part of that soft grieving light behind his eyes and part of the recklessness in his laugh. His eyes were so steady at times Jem thought they were taking in the whole of the world and all its expanse of loneliness. The few times Jem had asked Matussem about her mother and he had tried to tell her, the words swelled in his throat. He would stop and smile as if in pain and trace a pattern on the kitchen table with his finger.

Who was her father, Jem wondered, in this country

without shadows? Matussem flickered thin in the family mind, every step always the first, poised over his drums, raveling beats through the air, telling story after story through them, like Shahrazad, giving life. When he wasn't telling fables, the girls heard their father's stories about his childhood, about the way the enchantment of America had eventually drawn him across an ocean. "Every week the same movie! Flash Groodan! Flash Groodan! American spaces ship!" he said. "All the kids wanted to hear about. America."

His bosses at work, Mr. Magal, Mr. Boink, and Mr. Gastowe, all told Matussem that he had to shape up, quit wasting so much time on music, or he'd never be promoted out of the basement. Melvie once overheard Mr. Boink refer to their father as "the dirty sand nigger."

Their aunts and uncles, who were forever calling from overseas, liked to remind Jem and Melvie that they were Arabs, brushing out their mother's Irish-American ancestry in lectures and bedtime stories. Aunt Nejla would say, "Never mind about silly Fatima living over there; she's married. America is no place for young girls like you." Every summer one or more relatives arrived from the Old Country to tell the girls that America was a flight of fancy, their lives there a whim of their father's overactive imagination. The mirage would someday melt and they would be back in the family home where they belonged. On the other hand, male relatives like Uncle Fouad and his sons were expected to be footloose and even, as Fatima said, "crazy in the head." A man was different; he could let himself fly into the world like an arrow and, the aunts told them, no matter where he flew, he would still be an arrow.

Chapter 11

B Y   D A Y,   T H E windows of the Ramoud house
reflected the open spaces of upstate New York:
Euclid, Boonville, Canton, Minetto, Utica, Fulton
("City with a Future"), Hannibal; lost tribes of toys on
front lawns; children on bikes pedaling down the streets;
chickens in the road, always getting hit by cars or captured and thrown out attic windows by little boys. The
silence was an afterglow of abandonment, a cry through
the port towns: places left with just the skin on their
bones, their eyes black windows, their hearts doused
lamps.

The Ramouds wouldn't have said that their neighbors—what neighbors there were—were particularly
cordial; most of them were better described as invisible,
tucked away in ancient farmhouses with backyards
awash in toys, tools, auto parts, and cars on blocks.

About half a mile up the road from the Ramouds'
house, a small girl stood in the weeds, face smeared
with crumbs and dirt, and bottle leaking gray soda

pop. Next to her, a boy and girl were slapping each other.

"Shut up, you!" their mother screamed through the window. "Shut up, shut up!"

Dolores Otts fell back on the bed and stared at the TV screen, its faint image lost in Friday's mid-afternoon glare. She was thinking, and she knew she just had to quit doing that. Whenever she started thinking she seemed to get closer to things than she really needed to be, the kind of things that made her crazy.

She remembered a lot: this was her great misfortune in life. Her ma said Dolores had a flypaper brain, sticky all over. She would read something or hear it on TV and get every word in her head; she never knew when some of it would fly right out of her mouth. She knew from some TV show that baby turds held polio. And whenever she happened to think about it, she saw how the field around their place was piled up with diapers, plastic disposables, each with a nest of baby shit. It was, of course, the same place where those babies liked to play.

She was thinking: "When does life start?" It wasn't her question originally—she'd heard it on one of the talk shows. It was, she knew, a crazy question; the kind that could get her in trouble.

At what point—

Because she *knew* that she'd been born nearly thirty years ago, but she wanted to know when her life would begin: she hadn't seen any signs of it yet.

Maybe, she thought, that was why she'd turned herself over so many times to that damn man, *that damn man* being many men, forty, maybe fifty, or even a hundred.

Who was counting? It didn't matter, they were all the same, parading around with their dicks like trophies, and nearly every one put a baby in her. She'd thought there'd be at least one infertile Joe in all Clay County, but if there was it didn't look like she'd ever be introduced.

It seemed it was like Reverend Murabito said: things didn't get better until you died. But Dolores had seen corpses—grandparents; her aunt Joe; Patrick and Brian, her fourth and fifth kids—and none of them looked like they were having a party.

She took a hanger out of the closet and started to unbend it. Just a week before she had noticed a bumper sticker with a picture of a hanger with a red slash through it and the words Never Again underneath. This was in the parking lot of Bumble Bee Groceries. She'd pointed the sticker out to her mother, and the two of them had stood there trying to unpuzzle it until the car's owner walked up with her groceries.

"That's to say that abortions should be kept free and legal in this country," the young woman said.

When they kept staring at her she said, "Because before abortion was legal, women sometimes would use coat hangers to try to make themselves miscarry."

"Really?" Dolores said, "Does that work?"

The young woman laughed and shook her head as she unlocked her car. "Well, if you want to die, it works."

Now what did that mean? Dolores wondered. It sounded like some kind of smart college answer with more than one meaning. She hadn't liked the way the young woman's hair flew into her face and the way she wore so many buttons with things written on them. She looked like a hippie freak. And there, she had a nice running car and could buy all the abortions she wanted. As Dolores and her mother walked to the store entrance, Hilma started in on her: "Dolores Otts, you do not mean to say that you went out and got knocked up again."

Dolores rolled her eyes. "No, Ma, I do not mean to say that or anything else on this earth."

It was a soft spring day, but Hilma was wearing the down jacket and nightgown she always wore. She stared at her daughter, and Dolores noticed that Hilma had pulled her hair so tightly into curlers that it smoothed wrinkles out of her forehead and lifted her eyebrows.

"I swear to God, Dolores Otts, you pull some damn, stupid-ass coat hanger stunt, knocked up or not, you'll send me right to the crazy nut house. I swear I'll go live with Ellie Broom down in the shit shack, how 'bout that?"

"I guess you think I'm a complete retard?"

"I think it's exactly the kind of stunt you love to pull."

AT WHAT POINT?

Either end of the wire looked sharp. She hadn't gotten out all the kinks and coils, but it looked straight enough to do a fair amount of damage. She wondered if it could be much worse to put this between her legs than anything else.

Maybe it would kill her. It seemed like she was looking at that in either direction. One way she'd be in charge, the other way would be in the hands of a red, bawling baby, a critter, as Peachy called them.

It was like living in a barnyard. Except it wasn't like those kiddie songs, "and on this farm there was a cow. . . ." Here it was animals with bottomless eyes and slots of mouths, just eating and shitting, and when a new one came along, it sucked the life right out of Dolores's body.

Tin walls, the kids slept on old sofa cushions and bus seats, they cooked on a Sterno camp stove. Sometimes she put her hands on her hips and said, "Is this my life?"

The kids were all outside somewhere; she was alone for once.

So she was thinking about it, thinking and thinking and thinking, as she guided the wire gently, even tenderly, between her legs, and up into herself. She stopped a moment before it went too far and reached over to change the channel on the TV. The screen blinked, and through its snow she could make out one of those TV talking people, a man with a thick, white cap of hair. Now that was funny. She couldn't think of the name of this man, as familiar to her as a member of her family; she couldn't name him for anything.

She lay back down and brought the wire back into her; she was thinking.

"C'mon!" the man was saying. His face was a mask of shock, eyebrows disappearing up under the bolt of hair. "C'mon, you don't *really* believe that!" he shouted at a woman in his audience.

"I got news for you, bright boy," Dolores said, moving that wire slow and certain, thinking her way to the very point. "She really *does* believe it."

DOLORES DREAMED OF a red ribbon that sat bright-bowed in the hair of the baby who was supposed to be dead. She dreamed death covered Euclid. It stood in the sewers where the children ran along the concrete troughs. It walked the marsh around the trees. It echoed in the singing from the makeshift church in the water-control building. It was in the tightfisted faces of the men in the Euclid Inn, where the one-armed old-timer balanced the stick against the table, made six in the side pocket, and took a swig on a bottle.

All over Euclid, people were sleeping, floating with Dolores in a community of dreams. There were people in Euclid who never stopped sleeping or who woke at night and worked like moles in basements and garages, brewing beer, working on cars, or creating private inventions—machines that would tow their inventors up, up into the eye of the country.

Chapter 12

"THERE'S ONLY SO much you can do to
become an American!"

Early Saturday, a week after the Archbishop's party,
Jem could hear Melvie shouting at their father in the
front yard. It might have been that Matussem had gone
for a walk in his boxer shorts—as he liked to do in the
fleeting warm weather. Or Melvina might have caught
him calling another toll-free TV number for Christian
broadcast transcripts, self-sharpening knives, and Voodoo Aids. Matussem was also susceptible to charity and
foster-child programs, and many times Jem had come
home from work to find her father pondering blood
plasma donations or psoriasis research. He had donor
cards in his wallet for virtually every bodily organ.

Jem was on the phone, trying to concentrate on what
Fatima was saying but distracted by the wrath in Melvie's voice. "There is such a thing as one flamingo too
many. I drew the line at the seven dwarves and now
you come home with another bird!"

"Is that your evil sister?" Fatima said. "*Ya'Allah*, I can hear her all the way here. Bring me my brother."

"Hold on a sec, Aunt Fatima," Jem said, putting the receiver down. She walked to the window, opening it a crack, to watch her sister and father tugging at opposite ends of a large, plastic flamingo.

"What American about this? I don't ask to see passport," Matussem said. "Besides, see right there: Made in Taiwan! This ethnic bird. She beautiful."

"That's not what I'm saying. You're deliberately trying to *provoke* me," Melvie said. She let go of her end and Matussem sat flat on the lawn with the flamingo in his lap.

Every May since their move to the country, their father went through fits of exuberance, driving to the local hardware store and bringing home lawn decorations of deer, flamingos, and Disney characters the way some people bring home stray animals. The front lawn was littered with cartoon figures and exotic birds. Matussem didn't arrange them with any particular design, but sprinkled them at random, even propped them up out in the fields and weeds, much to the delight of Peachy across the street. Then, a few years ago, in a fit of irritation, Melvie had taken it upon herself to cart a couple of the figures away to unadorned lawns deep in the suburbs, thieving them away in the dark. This became her springtime ritual. Matussem either didn't notice or pretended not to, merely adding to the menagerie when the notion hit him; in this way the lawn population remained stable.

"Dad, it's Aunt Fatima on the phone," Jem said.

Matussem looked up from where he was still sitting on the grass. "*Ach du liebe, Augustin,*" he said.

Fatima was soaking in Oil of Paris Midnight Bath Balm. "Baby brother?" she said. "I've decided to put curse on these dirty-hair neighbor boy who I see always peeking, peeking at Jemorah, so that they will have a stroke tonight and maybe drop dead. Okeydokey?"

"Okeydokey? What okeydokey? What?" Matussem cried. "Fatima, why me? Why now? What neighbor boy? You can't leave it alone? No voodoo, no curses, no evil eye, I begging, just give me one breaks."

Fatima kicked her feet in the bath. "Fine, fine! You want your daughters all around with serpents, criminals, and gruesomes, that's fine! And here Fouad coming to-morrow from fifty thousand miles away. You want Uncle Fouad think we just crawled out of the gutter, that's wonderful! Maybe you hoping I'll drop the phone receiver and electrocute myself to death. Wait a second, I'll call Zaeed and have him bring the radio in, too! Zaeed!" she shrieked through the wall. "Bring the Sony in here!"

"Fatima, please," Matussem was saying. "Would you talk like a human being?"

"He thinks he's the only human being in the world!" Fatima shouted at the phone. "Fine! Good-bye, King Human Being! Now let me talk to your daughter."

Zaeed stuck his head in the door. "My mistress calls?"

"Bring the radio here and drop it in. I want to fry."

"Ah," Zaeed said and shut the door.

As soon as Jem picked up, Fatima told her about the very attractive boy with the Lebanese eyes who was holding up a construction sign out on Route 690. "Such a smile! For the gods! *Just* your age. The way he wave to me—"

"He wanted you to slow down."

"I can see the babies now. Come, come, I drive you there these minute after my bath. I remember exactly where he is working, have it wrote down."

"Aunt Fatima, no."

"'No,' she says, all the time 'no, no!' Thanks God your mother not alive to see these. Now instead she have to be seeing it in heaven. *Ya'Allah,* I can hear her beating on her holy chest! Enough aggravations already, let me go finish my beauty bath."

In her thrashing around most of the Oil of Paris Midnight bubbles had gone flat and sat like an oil slick on top of the water. Fatima thought about herself sitting there until she rotted away in her own miserable bathwater. Probably Zaeed wouldn't even miss her. Probably she would have to wait until busybody Auntie Nyla got bored and came poking around.

"They see how spotless Fatima Ramoud Mawadi keep her bathroom," Fatima said out loud in her orator's voice. "See there? Three bottle Mr. Clean! Not these cheap generic crap the Abdulabouds buy."

"Let's face it, you're a first-rate person in a second-rate world," she heard Zaeed shout from downstairs.

Fatima nodded, but it wasn't much consolation. She yanked the plug from the drain and watched the water curl into a tiny whirlpool.

"These water like my life," she said, watching it. "Whoosh, there it goes." She walked naked to the bedroom, defying the full-length mirror, and picked up a pad by the side of her bed, her book of lists. She considered the first one:

What I can stand about my life
1. Want be in Lady Pontifical Committee (Good deeds etc., etc.)
2. Good bust (not much sags)

She added 3. and wrote: "Husband who understands a couple things and is not too much of a big pain in the A all the time. Cooperates."

Under that was a second list:

What I CAN'T STAND about my life
1. My America nieces (Jemorah and Melvina) who are going to send me to the mental hospital with so much worries about who are they ever going to marry.
2. Melvina's Queen of World attitude—why does she have to dress like that every minute and why won't Jemorah file her fingernails and use cuticle stick?

Then some words in Arabic that Fatima crossed out in a fury.

Chapter 13

*L*ATER THAT MORNING, Jem—driving
with a wary eye out for Lebanese construction
workers—was on her way back from the grocery store.
She stopped for gas at Lil' Lulu's Garage down the street
from their house. Lil' Lulu's owner, Fred Beevle, didn't
believe in self-service gas. He used to say about it:
"Everyone gets cheated, you, me, everyone." So his
attendants, the same three for over twenty years, Jesse,
Owen, and Fergyl, jumped up for every car. Their skin
had turned gray from oil, and they perpetually had some
car hoisted on their pneumatic lift. Sometimes when Jem
drove up, she could see Fred himself, fat as a buddha,
enthroned behind the glass walls of the office, leaning
back against the cigarette machine and winding dollar
bills around his fingers.

Fred was not anywhere in sight that day, and the rock
music rushed from the garage. When Jem looked up,
she saw that the hand on the pump was not the hand of
Jesse, Owen, or Fergyl. It was a new hand, long fingered

and well shaped. Her eyes climbed that limb, arm and shoulder, collar and hair. The attendant's head was lowered to the task, but the posture was familiar; she'd *seen* that stoop somewhere before.

Then the curtain of hair—black, dirt-straight—lifted, parted with a shake and there were those eyes again, looking at her. After more than ten years, it was Ricky Ellis, one-time disturber of her dreams, hoisting a gas-pump hose. She could see the oil in the seams of his hands as he handed her the credit-card slip, and her own hands were just slightly trembling. Then she could have sworn she heard him say, "Jemorah." His gaze was still and she looked back at him through what seemed like a dark mantle of years. He drew her into his gaze, and in that instant she was asking, "Do you remember me?"

Ricky left the garage door open, the pump on, the rock music blasting into the underbelly of a Ford, went around to the car door and got in next to Jem. He left the bells chiming unanswered, and when Fred called to check up on things, the pay phone went on ringing.

JEM PULLED OUT onto Route 31 and they drove past fields, still silver-blue in places, and velveteen cows. In winter, the snow had etched lines of frost into the trees, the creeks stood white and still, the long grass sparkled with ice. Now everything seemed to be dissolving and in movement. She stared straight out the window, balancing her breath high in her lungs, trying not to think about the strange man in her car. They passed shacks with folding, rain-broken walls, tar-paper roofs, old trailers with sides the color of rain. Dolores Otts's trailer was set back from the road in a clump of weeds, trash, and toys, dropped there like a lost key. Rags of curtains billowed out the small windows and the trailer looked still and ghostly.

Ricky was quiet. He seemed uncomfortable in the passenger's seat and spent a lot of time twisting the radio dial until he settled on a country-western station. A man was singing like the words were coming straight from a vise around his heart, a pure, Western tenor.

"Guess he's got his jeans on too tight," Ricky said, sliding down in his seat.

"Guess I owe you one," he added, a moment later. "Or your dad, I guess."

"Why, what do you mean?" she asked, her voice oddly high.

He shrugged. "Way lard-ass Fred tells it, Fergyl, Jesse, and Owen have got this 'damn fool idea' into their heads to be musicians, and it all has to do with this 'damn, fool, foreign A-rab' that lives next door. These days they're calling in sick a lot, playing around with the damn, fool, foreign A-rabs, so old Butt-Face has to break down and hire local scum like me to do the job ten times better than his regulars at one-tenth the pay. So tell your dad thanks."

Jem didn't know quite how to answer that. She just stared ahead and said, "Okay." Some moments passed, then she said, "I haven't seen you for a while."

"Yeah, well . . ." he shook his hair back. "Spent a couple years in juvenile detention. Not exactly sure why. That was fun. Got this tattoo. Tried working out on the rail yards. Got kicked out. Seems like people just don't ever like my looks."

She glanced at Ricky once, quickly. There was a tattoo on the back of his wrist; she caught a greenish blur of it, heard the soft hum of his breath in the silence between them. *What kind of man is he?* she wondered, her breath slowing. Those are the clothes he wears. She had a flash of jeans, a flannel shirt, on a floor somewhere, soft and stale from him. Frightened, not thinking, she lifted one hand and touched his hair.

Ricky turned away. "This wasn't the greatest idea; I ought to get back," he said. "I left the whole shop open. Fred will shit."

Jem went hot with embarrassment, made a U-turn in the center of a wide, empty highway and started back. She decided to let Aunt Fatima pick out the men from now on. The sad singer stayed on the radio, singing about desolation and longing, his voice hammered to steel. Ricky put all his concentration into tuning the station. The countryside rushed at them, acres of overgrown fields beaded with moisture. Then Ricky flipped off the radio, sat up, and said, "What did they tell you about my father?"

Jem turned to look at him. She eased her foot off the gas, and they coasted in neutral. It was the first time she had dared to look at him straight on. With the windows open, his hair flew back and revealed his features, the straight nose, the blue disks of his irises. Outside, the long-stemmed wildflowers were blowing. Then a man on a shaking piece of farm machinery appeared before them, whirring and crawling and taking up the whole lane so they were forced to slow behind him.

"They told me that he blew himself up working on a car, I guess," Jem said at last.

Ricky looked at her sharply, then he nodded. "Well, that's wrong," he said and looked back out the window.

Jem tightened her grip on the wheel, listening.

Ricky kept silent, chewing on a fingernail. Then he grinned and said, "Well, maybe I never had a father."

"What do you mean?"

His eyes were polished river rocks behind the locks of hair. He looked at her and said, "Just what I said. I might never, ever have had no father to begin with. I might've got born all by myself, just the same way I'm gonna die. I just wanted to make sure you got your story straight."

Chapter 14

$\mathscr{F}$ATIMA LAY ON her bed, gazing at a magazine. Did anyone understand her? No, probably not. She pulled out her book of lists, reread item three of the *What I can stand* list, and crossed out "Husband who understands a couple things."

What she wanted was so simple, honest, and pure: *she wanted everyone to be happy!* Yet she was thwarted at each step. She had a speech that she often made to her nieces:

"It's terrible to be a woman in this world. This is first thing to know when the doctor looks at baby's thing and says 'it's a girl.' But I am telling you, there are ways of getting around it. It helps to have a good bust, but don't worry. At least you didn't get that Irish Catholic skin of your mother's, may she rest in peace. Everyone knows the Irish are pretty-pretty when they're young, but let them hit thirty and that skin? Gone! Horrible! Okay, so let's say it, you're built like starving rats and not so pretty now, but you girls wait, when you're forty, forty-five, everyone will say how *handsome* you

116

are, I guarantee it. But what good will handsome do if you don't already snagged some man to see it? There are things you don't know yet that I know perfect, and first and last is that you must have husband to survive on the planet of earth."

All right, so it was probably a lost cause with Melvina, since she was born an old maid, fresh from the womb with a face on her like Auntie Miriam's, but at least that was respectable. Jemorah, with that look of a child lost in the woods, anyone might take her home. Hadn't Fatima herself struggled to guide the child, even to drag her through life? But the stubborn girl refused.

You have to *make* children see, Fatima thought, even if it meant scooping out their eyes and pointing them with your own hands. Jemorah and her innocent face were locked like a clam against her aunt's good efforts. She simply would not use hair spray or padded bras, no matter how Fatima wept and railed. She listened nicely, then turned and did the opposite. Fatima knew terrible things waited for her niece in the world. Many times she had told Jemorah, "A woman's reputation is her soul. It's her heart and gizzard. You let them rape and murder you before you let them do anything to your reputation." The child never listened.

And for that matter, what did her brother know about anything? He was an innocent. Nine months, twenty-three days younger than her and he might have been born last Tuesday on another planet. Fatima stared hard at the beautiful heads and bodies in her glossy magazine. Was there really a place in the world like this? Young, lovely women, laughing, sitting on rocks, tawny as cats, while young, lovely men fanned them with palm leaves. Ha!

SHE LOOKED AT the pretty-faced models and thought of her sisters' softer, browner faces when they were children.

There had been seven girls: Rima, Nejla, Yasmin, Suha, Nabila, Lutfea, then Fatima. When Matussem was finally born, Rima had told her much later, there was at last ease in her parents.

But something happened. An accident? There was another baby after Matussem, a daughter. Fatima herself couldn't have been more than four or five. The infant was small and weightless as a rag doll in Fatima's arms, scarcely moving. She didn't cry so much as whimper.

They were going outside the village, to a branch of the river she remembered moving thick and dark as blood, the body of a headless creature sliding through the earth. It was a strange day, as were the rest that followed. On this occasion, when Fatima was four or five, there were clouds in the desert sky, amazing in a place usually swept clean. This sky was dense and vaporous, the clouds full.

They went to an isolated spot, far from where they drew water or where women washed their clothes. Her mother was digging a hole in the earth with her hands. Her father hadn't come.

Fatima placed the baby girl in the hole. As she was told to do. As she must have been told to do. The hole was like a cradle. The infant stirred, and for a moment

Fatima thought it might cry, but it merely bleated, a small, weightless sound that rose through the years, always floating near the surface of Fatima's consciousness. Sometimes still she heard it in the sound of bathwater or beneath the noise of a crowd. Sometimes when she awoke, very early, in the stillest part of her mind where her dream opened into the dawn, came the tiny bleat—scarcely an echo, but enough to push Fatima from her bed to wander the house and yard, vaguely listening.

Fatima remembered the infant eyes closing against the first handfuls of dirt. The baby stopped moving almost immediately, as if the sheerest blanket of earth was too heavy. They covered her then in this tender, sandy clay, adding the heart, breath, and substance of the creature like a new pulse to the earth.

Fatima recalled assisting in two, possibly three other furtive burials. None came back to her with the immediacy of that first—if indeed it had been the first. The memories moved in and out of her; she returned to them, moving aside this object and that in order to gaze through the half-light at the event itself. She did recall, on what might have been the final occasion, her father stopping her and her mother at the door, his white robes winding around him as he rose in her imagination, tall as a specter, saying to her mother, "She's getting too old now; she will begin to remember."

Her mother looked at Fatima with a gaze touched with rare gentleness, or perhaps it was only the softening of fatigue and heat. Her mother then turned and said, "Yes? And what of me? What do you think I will remember?"

▲ ▲ ▶

FATIMA LAY AWAKE on her bed, trying to get rest, to push memory out of her mind. She had a picture in her head of a door opening on a door opening on a door. She stepped from room to room, from the tiny rooms she and her mother dug in the earth, to the constant invasions of relatives, sixteen sharing five rooms, to a room on the border of two countries. It was unclear what countries these were or where precisely the dividing line was drawn. She was sixteen in this picture, and the notion of America sparked in her like a lit fuse. She and Zaeed planned to emigrate. But at some point in 1956—perhaps she was crossing the street to the marketplace, perhaps merely standing at the edge of the road—the border twitched again and she was seized without warning for crossing that line.

The merchants and villagers had fled before the foreign truck. No one had spoken to her; if they did she did not hear them. They gathered their possessions and ran. And Fatima, who was alone at the time, who was visiting relatives in the village, merely stood, watching. She held a paper bag containing a dozen loose eggs. The men wore army jackets; they did not speak Arabic. They put her into a truck so crowded that she couldn't turn around. Her bag of eggs was smashed and liquid pressed through the paper.

The men threw hoods over the prisoners. When the hoods were removed, Fatima saw a room the color of which she would never forget, though there was no word for it in Arabic or English. Later, if she saw this color—in a stranger's eyes or flitting through the pattern of a woman's dress—she would have to sit and put her head between her knees.

Fatima lived for two, three, four days without a visitor, without food, just a bucket of water in the room. She tried to scoop up what was left of the eggs, now just shell and a spot of liquid at the bottom of the bag, long fibers of egg she sucked from her fingers. She tried to eat the shells, which cut her mouth; finally, she sucked on the bag itself. She curled into herself, into the clear curve of an egg against both light and hunger. What happened? Nothing. She was released. A mistake, the man turning the key said. He spoke English. Nothing happened. She was not beaten. She was released into a blue doorway of light, empty, the desert road. Some merchants found her there and drove her back to town. Her family rejoiced when she returned. They rejoiced without asking where she had been. Not her husband. Not her mother. And she found that she could tell no one. Years later, she and her husband emigrated to America. She and her husband.

Sometimes she would tell herself a story about that time, the day in the village. She would think: *I was left in a room somewhere, and I waited. Such waiting is worse than a beating. Worse than death.* Then she would feel ashamed for thinking so. All the same, it was true. She was released into a blue doorway of light, empty, the desert road. They believe they let me out of there, she thought; they never let me out. She would close her eyes and mentally close a door, the door on a tiny brown room of earth. *I've been waiting to go out, she thought, room in room in room. I am waiting.*

Chapter 15

*E*VERYONE CALLED UNCLE Fouad "Uncle Fouad," even Matussem and Fatima, his brother-in-law and sister-in-law. He was related to them through his marriage to the eldest Ramoud sister, Rima, and was a distant cousin to Fatima's husband, Zaeed. Rima had not returned to the United States since the World's Fair in New York, at which time she'd been goaded into taking a ride on a thing called the Whipper-Snapper and had vomited cotton candy and hot dog across the faces of several bystanders.

Every year when Fouad urged his wife to renew her passport, she would respond, "That may be what you call fun, Fouad, but I'd rather fall down a well."

Fouad heard this with glee, since it meant another summer vacation of flirting with skinny American women and playing Sugar-Daddy from Amman. Now, as he pried himself out of the black Trans Am rental, he tried to decide if his brother-in-law's house was getting smaller or if he was getting larger. His hands explored the vistas of his belly, then pushed the hair back from his scalp. He wore it long, combed back into stiff, greased curls around his collar. He always kept a comb marinading in a jar of hair tonic with him, as well as a big bottle of lemon-scented cologne, and found that with these implements it was possible to dispense with bathing for days, sometimes weeks, at a time. Two of his teeth were gold, one was silver, and one had a little diamond embedded in it. He wore thick chains of twenty-four-karat gold around his neck and wrist, and designer shirts that he ordered from Niagara Falls. He hung beads around the rearview mirrors of his Lincoln Town-car and his Cadillac Seville to keep away the evil eye.

The family's attitude toward Uncle Fouad was that since he made more money than all the Ramouds and Mawadis put together, he was boss.

Melvina came into Jem's room and peered out at Fouad through the bedroom curtains. "Look at him!" she hissed to Jem. "*Preening* like the emperor in his taste-less new clothes. He won't even knock on the door. He's waiting for us to come out and abase ourselves at his feet."

He did seem to Jem to be doing just that as he posi-tioned himself—as usual, two and a half hours early—in the center of the front lawn and ran his hands over the stomach that pushed between his designer buttons. He was wearing long sleeves, and the expensive fabric of his shirt was already stained with deep V's of sweat in front and back. Jem knew from past experience that in-side of fifteen minutes he would have the shirt tied in a turban around his head and he would be lounging around in gray Fruit of the Loom boxers.

Matussem crept up beside his daughters. It was eight-thirty in the morning. "Go on there, somebody, and see what he want so early," he whispered. "I'm not done watering."

Melvina turned around in indignation. "What do you *think* he wants! He came all the way from Jordan for our *family picnic!* He wants *family fun!*"

Matussem sighed. "That's what I am afraid of. He scares me," he said. "He is weird dude. Always trouble with him and the dancing girls."

The three of them knelt together for a while on Jem's bed, watching Uncle Fouad as he stretched and patted himself and modeled various profiles. Then a black Lincoln Continental turned in, roaring up the driveway.

"Fatima," Melvina said.

"THIS FOOD TERRIBLE," Uncle Fouad said, gnawing on a chicken bone. "Miserable, I say. Nothing like home."

"Oh, I know, I know," Fatima said, shielding her eyes from the sun under a screen of polished nails. "Is all what I have to work with, the quality, the materials—"

"I would feed this maybe to my cat," he said, reaching for a drumstick. "To kill him with. And I want my coffee; why aren't you bringing me my *ahweh?* You are wanting to shrivel me up like a black fig?"

They were sitting on blankets in the backyard. Fatima had begun unloading baskets of food the moment she'd arrived while Fouad moaned over how they wanted to "starve him alive" by making him wait to eat until ten-thirty. Matussem had called Larry Fasco at ten, pleading with him to come over with some beer. Now Zaeed and Larry were playing a limp game of badminton over on the other side of the lawn, and every once in a while Fatima would stop cooing over Fouad to turn and scream at them, "Stop it, stop it, stop it! You giving me a FIT with your BALL GAME!"

"Actually, Uncle Fouad," Melvie was saying, "coffee is a stimulant and a diuretic, it—"

"Yes, yes!" Fouad shouted. "Melvina, my favorite! Come here, yes come to me, give me kisses, here and here. Come, come, you little bamboozler, you flabbergaster. What a heartpicker, *look* at this face. Your father hides you in the closet so the boys won't catch you. And Jemorah, what are you doing there hiding from Mr. Wonderful Uncle Fouad? Here, put me kisses! My favorite! Somebody bring me cheeseburger and baklawa, too."

Jem kept her nose to the right of Uncle Fouad's ear as she kissed him, which seemed to help mute the smell of lemon cologne. Behind her, Melvina was refusing to fetch Fouad a cheeseburger and holding forth on diet and health services. "In the words of La Bruyère, 'There are certain things,' Uncle Fouad, 'in which mediocrity is intolerable: poetry, music, painting, public eloquence.' End quote. To this I would add nutrition and nursing. Actually, I would place those first." Then Melvie broke off, and Jem heard her say, "You! It's *you*. I never forget a criminal face."

Jem looked up. It was Gilbert. Gilbert Sesame, in person, back from the grave, in clothes like winding-sheets, torn and spinning into the air around him. Yet he was basically the same, slightly bruised, perhaps, shrunken somewhat with age, but still Gil Sesame.

"Ah yes, the once-in-a-lifetime Melvina," Gil said, raising his arms without moving toward her.

Then Gil turned to Jem. There was still the shyster smile; the diamonds flickered on his fingers as he reached toward her. "Jemorah, queen of my Nile."

"Who is this blob?" Uncle Fouad asked. "What now?" He turned to Matussem and said in Arabic, "Every day in this country more bullshit!" To which Matussem shrugged and said, "*Yimkin naam, yimki-naah.*" Maybe yes, maybe no.

Jem embraced Gil gingerly. "Gil. Well well well," she said.

"Excuse me, Mr. Sesame," Melvina said, marching toward the back door. "I'm afraid I'll have to alert the FBI to your prison break now. Do not move off the perimeters of this property."

"Excuse me, Ms. Ramoud," Gil said, producing a piece of paper from his back pocket and waving it. "Completion of community service. I got time and a half off for behavior above and beyond the call of duty. I turned my talents to preaching to the senior citizens. Saved the souls of at least three men and brought several more at least halfway closer to their Lord. Mormons will *not* argue with a good savin', I find. I may have something of a calling." He twisted one of his rings, eyes modestly cast down, then looked up. "Course I had to part ways with the Lord to catch the last red-eye freight out of Mona by way of Salt Lake. He can fend for Hisself just fine back there. Anyway, I come at long-awaited last to make my pilgrimage to you, Jemorah, and worship at the altar of your feet. I'm here to save *you* now, darling, with effervescent wit and extraordinary presence. We'll make babies and live in your father's attic!"

Fatima perked up. "You are want to *marry* her?"

"This house doesn't have an attic," Jem said, her throat dry. "Didn't you want to stay out West?"

Gil pulled a crumpled bandanna from his pocket and wiped the back of his neck. "Well, honeychild, I thought I explained. The truth of the matter is there's a little . . . *delicacy* there. Between me and Idaho. And Utah. And a few others. We finally worked out a kind of agreement. Just temporary, of course. Just for the immediate future or so. We've agreed that I would go away—a mere two thousand mile radius—just for a spell, just to show there's no hard feelings. See, that's the problem with being a hustler, you can get a little too familiar. Then I started thinking about all the beauty and excitement that New York State has to offer. Why, Syracuse is a world-class city."

The back screen door slammed shut behind Melvina.

"Well Jem, honey dumpling, listen, you didn't want to move out West! Shit, Utah ain't nothing so much like a bunch of people so prayed-out and pregnant that they're all like balloons with the air let out."

"But—what about—Mecca, artists, land—" Jem said, almost disappointed. "You said the whole point was to move *out*—find a new place."

Fatima, Fouad, Zaeed, Larry Fasco, and her father all leaned forward.

"So help me, Jem," Gilbert placed one hand upon his

heart, the other in the air, "I swear to you, I *swear* as a man of honor and the highest, most pure and innocent of intentions, Mecca is right *here* where you already are." He seized her hands with both of his. Jem looked down into his milky eyes, his loose cheeks, hands soft as hankies. "Moving out doesn't make life better. Marry me and I'll prove it. Like the poet says, every town is the same town. Just say to yourself, 'There's no place like home. . . .'"

Chapter 16

THE SENSATION HAD been one of traveling: out the trailer window, past Moyers Corners—Euclid's farthest signpost, past Bumble Bee Groceries, Three Rivers Inn—and the Clay County line, beyond the antique buildings of Syracuse, then above Route 81 where it gashed the mountain valleys, past teardrop ponds, men in waders among boulder-broken rivers and pines carpeting the earth.

Then Dolores opened her eyes to see a girl with the bearing of an angel, neck flowing into the fine cast of the head, eyes concentrating, the mouth making her think of the story princess whose mouth spilled rubies.

The girl looked up and said, "I am Nurse Melvina Ramoud, head nurse. Now that you've come out of it I'll inform your doctor, but before I do, it's incumbent upon me to make clear how near death you were and what an incredibly stupid stunt that was—"

"You've been talking to my ma, haven't you," Dolores said.

Melvina clicked her pen against the clipboard she held. "This is your *life* we're talking about, young lady," she said. "Every last synapse and enzyme of it, and I'll thank you not to forget it."

Dolores lifted her head an inch or so from the pillow and peered at Melvie. "Hey, I know you! Didn't you ride the bus with my Wally? You did!"

Melvie's eyes flicked to the name on the chart: Jane Doe #1675. She'd been admitted through emergency after the paramedics had been summoned on an anonymous call—a child's. There was a note from one of the drivers that a group of children had run into the woods when they saw the ambulance. Melvie imagined them fleetingly, dirty children scattering like doves. "That's unlikely—I'm twenty-two, you must be around thirty-six."

"Twenty-nine. I had little Wally when I was twelve, hey, it wasn't my idea—what do you think! You would've been in sixth when Wally was in first. Little Wally got held back in school, like forever, until they got sick of him and booted him out completely. So he rode the bus with a whole lot of different people. Sad to say, that kid is half-moron and half-psycho. He's my oldest."

"That would have been my assumption."

When Dolores lifted her head off the pillow a roaring started in her ears like she had seashells clapped over them. She liked the sensation, but when she tried to do it again, Melvina reached over with a hand cool as steel and pinned her flat by the forehead.

"Hold still, you're overexerting," Melvie said. She scrutinized her patient, reading the lines that touched her skin and the yellow of her eyes. "Perhaps you enjoy suffering," she said.

"Honey," Dolores said, suddenly tired with this woman's hand on her head, her eyes inside Dolores, taking her over, making her let go. "Maybe I just plain don't know the difference between that and anything else." She closed her eyes. "Tell me one thing."

"If possible."

"Am I still preg?"

"No." Melvina turned and walked out. There was no point in telling her that she hadn't been to begin with.

Chapter 17

JEM PARKED AND walked past the hospital grounds crew and gardeners on her way to work; as always, she wanted to toss her files and get on her hands and knees with them, to dig into the soil and feel the spring sunrise blooming on her back. She envied these workers their simple intimacy with the summer—a rare and precious season in Syracuse. Every year, summer emerged from the dark corners of the woods, delicate in its skin of light. The gardeners' fingers knotted into the soil; apprentices to the season, they lived with it like lovers, their minds still as the air. For Jem, there were few moments more difficult than walking through the hospital door and leaving the summer morning behind. Even though it was only June first, she already anticipated the winter rolling over the countryside with its iron and ice, the long tongue of cold.

She felt disturbed and disoriented by Gil's sudden appearance the day before, as if a prehistoric creature—a thing of memory and distant fancy—had suddenly lifted its thorny head from Onondaga Lake. For along with his unsettling presence, Jem had lost her brief dream of the West, white Salt Lake City, a place like its name, town and lake bound in great crystals of salt, like an ice palace, alone on the salt-swept prairies. A place that she probably never would have seen, but loved to think about, nonetheless.

Without her white dream, something protective and constricting had been stripped from her, and she knew she would have to do something herself to change her life. She was going to quit her job.

Seven years after graduating college, she found that she was jealous of people who liked their jobs: the man throwing pizza dough in the store window, the meter reader quick and easy on her scooter, the lucky college students, laughing, taking up the morning like it was all theirs. Even Melvina liked her job, *loved* it, in Melvie's way. She was up at four for a six-to-three shift. Sometimes Jem saw her darting through the corridors, sailing in whites like a nun, her face pious. Melvie had begun playing nurse when she was three, bandaging her older sister in dish towels. She had taken an accelerated course in nursing just after high school, two years of studying nine to nine, year round and on Sundays, to become an R.N. as fast as humanly possible. Every morning Jem saw her younger sister, dressed in a uniform the starkest white, adjusting her cap like a sergeant, always on duty, on guard against the invisible and the insidious.

Jem waved whenever Melvie passed her corridor. Melvie would tip her head briskly in reply.

Melvina had turned down a medical school scholarship while still in nurse's training. "No time for that nonsense," she said. "Doctors are so namby-pamby. I don't have time to wait for them. There's a world out there that needs saving and I've got to get to it."

THE DEPARTMENT MANAGER, Portia Porschman, had over the years taken to hanging around Jem's desk. Portia was about five foot two and weighed in the neighborhood of 250 pounds, but she managed, somehow, to keep it all to herself, dense and pressed against her bones, packed into navy dresses with bits of lace at the wrists and neck. She was one of the toughest women Jem had ever seen, possibly rivaling Melvina. They called her the Iron Maiden when she wasn't around. She was manager of the business wing and her life's goal was to be promoted to chief, an office currently held by Mrs. Pinoire, an older woman with frillier blouses than Portia's, held in check by an undertaker's suit.

The business office never knew when Portia would go on the hunt, looking for mistakes, someone to suck into her office. Sometimes it might happen twice in a week, sometimes not for months; she was sneaky. She could move in perfect silence, blending 250 pounds, frills and all, into the landscape of computers, printers, and gray carpets as completely as a chameleon. She moved like the air, stepping on feline feet, flattening between machines. Sometimes the only clue that she would be "checking up," as she liked to put it, was the silence itself; the staff would glance toward the glass doors of Portia's office across the hall, darkened like the eye of an angry Hawaiian god. A moment of alertness would ripple through the office, the silence before an earthquake when birds flush from the woods together. Glances would pass among the women, blood-seeing, spreading doom across the office. There was nowhere for them to run. Like an evil jinni, Portia hovered and watched. Whenever Portia spoke to her, Jem's shoulders inched up around her ears and she saw light glance off Portia's teeth. She could never remember what Portia said or anything of what she wanted. She retained only a body-deep terror of the woman that proved to Jem that her unhappiness went beyond the job itself; she had the sense that Portia could do worse things to her than fire her.

She'd say things like: "Jemorah Ramoud. It seems like you just got here." She tended to speak in the abbreviated style of a Zen master:

"Nice weather. Today."

"How do you feel. Today."

Or sometimes just "Jemorah Ramoud."

The hospital business wing was called "the land that time forgot." The rumor was that once an employee got in, she never got out again, not voluntarily. She either died in office or was sucked into the murky waters of Portia's office, never to be heard from again. Jem's supervisor Nancy liked to point to Portia's door from time to time and say, "Abandon hope, all ye who enter."

The office was filled with women aged eighteen to eighty-eight. Jem had the impression the office didn't allow its staff to retire; they preferred that employees keel over on their keyboards. One woman, Virge, the eighty-eight year old, told Jem she'd started work at the hospital adding machine as a blushing bride of twenty-one. She swore to Jem on her grandmother's grave that Portia—who couldn't have been more than forty-five as they spoke—had handpicked Virge to come work for her. "If I'd known then what I know now . . . ," she said, lifting her gray eyebrows ominously.

So not only was Portia all-powerful, but immortal as well. Jem had begun to think of herself as a Jonah, trying to slip out from between the mighty jaws of her boss. The more Portia floated around her desk, the more uneasy Jem became.

That Monday, after Portia had wafted by for the third time, now saying, "No rain. Yet," Jem began to have second thoughts about quitting. Nothing was worth facing Portia; better to stay on at the business office, until she was as bent over from punching keys as Virge.

If she did, this would be the seventh birthday she would see pass in that office. Since starting her job, Jem experienced a nostalgia for her years in college so piercing it could make her catch her breath. She wished for the elegant, self-determined passage of her days again, the pleasures of the mind, of sculpting a theory or looking into the mechanisms of a psyche. As an undergraduate, she'd been enchanted by the term "professional student." Every class had suggested new classes, every subject expanded; attending courses was like throwing a handful of gravel into a pool and watching the ripples. The only thing her aunts wanted her to graduate with was a husband. "You're still pretty, aren't you?" her Aunt Rima had said to her long-distance from Jordan, her Arabic flashing in and out of what sounded like the Atlantic Ocean. "So what do you need brains for?

You're twenty-one, still pretty, so what's wrong with you?"

She took geology, anthropology, political science, hand weaving, calculus, astronomy, poetics, physics, studio art, journalism, zoology, Restoration drama, chemistry, and abnormal, adolescent, and Freudian psychologies, among others, enjoying all.

Her statistics teacher told her there was a vital, physical beauty to a well-wrought equation, like that of a painting or a poem. "Numbers are my first language," he said. Jem felt that way about people; she was a natural listener. If she could have, she would have stayed on in college, reading about emotion and motivation. Yet she chose a major in psychology almost by default, by adding up the number of credits she'd accumulated in each area. She somehow assumed that her career would fall naturally into place.

When classes came to an end, Jem graduated without a plan or a husband, so Melvie insisted that their father arrange a job for her sister in the same hospital where he worked and she was candystriping. "Temporary, till you go back to school and get a useful degree." Virtually every year after that, Melvie insisted that Jem fill out graduate school applications. Jem would get through the whole process of transcripts, tests, and essays, then become discouraged at the last moment and throw out the application.

"You like me, bambino," Matussem said from his La-Z-Boy whenever Jem fretted over her lack of planning. "Your mind all wide open, you hears too much, you hungry for whole big, crazy world."

"But it's ridiculous," Jem answered. "All that time in

college and I never actually thought about what I'd do with it after I left. And I stay in a terrible job in the meantime. How did I get this way? Why aren't I more like Melvina?'"

"Bambino," Matussem said, "the world need of only one Melvina. And one you."

AFTER CHANGING HER mind for the fifth time that day, Jem slipped her notice onto Portia's desk while she was on lunch break, then returned to her own desk and stared at the piles of filing left to do. She tried to imagine what would happen to her after she had left the office for good, but all she could come up with was Gilbert's old broken dream, the West, white deserts, cactus, temples made of salt. The place, he had said, of escape.

She remembered going to Palmyra, to the annual Hill Cumorah Pageant, an event her mother had enjoyed. Hill Cumorah, sixty miles from Syracuse, was a sacred place, where the Angel Moroni presented Joseph Smith with tablets containing the Book of Mormon. The Mormons reenacted this event in a brilliant pageant. Every summer, Jem's family would pack blankets and a picnic lunch and drive to Palmyra along with Aunt Fatima and Uncle Zaeed. But the events of the day were so plain and regular, even in celebration, that they mingled in her mind, echoing each other. It was all one day, one pageant, when they would pull into the dusty town with its sparse taverns and shops, desolate as Euclid. Jem marveled at all the license plates from Utah; she'd been acquainted with only the occasional Pennsylvania, New

Jersey, or Ontario plates speeding through upstate. She remembered pointing them out to Melvina who, though just a baby in her mother's arms, still looked at the plates with her stern and disapproving baby stare, as if condemning the impracticality of people making such a long drive.

They'd spread blankets and lawn chairs among hundreds of other picnickers all along the incline of the hill. The afternoon would be taken up with eating and sunning, while pageant organizers and church officials fanned out across the hill, handing out pamphlets, information, and copies of the Book of Mormon. Her father always made sure to get a new copy—each of which he'd store on a special shelf in the basement. At the pageant, he would read aloud from his book, words that Jem remembered as arcane prophesy.

He and his brother-in-law Zaeed would comment on American theology, arguing over fine points and appreciating what they found good.

"You've got to admire a religion whose guru is named 'Joe Smith,'" she remembered Zaeed saying. "It's like calling your god 'Joe Blow' or 'John Q. Public' or 'Omar the tent-maker.'"

Fatima painted Jem's stubby nails the same color as her own long, lustrous ones. Dragon Lady Red. Jem showed the shining red tips to her mother and sister. Her mother was nursing Melvina and as Melvie eyed Jem's nails over the slope of the breast it seemed to Jem that if she'd stopped sucking she would have said, "Too garish. Take that stuff off."

Jem roamed around the hillside by herself, picking her way among burr, hollyhocks, and thistle. Her mother had taught her the names of trees and flowers. She'd told Jem, "You should learn about the place where you live. It's like knowing the color of your friends' eyes."

Though quiet, she was curious about other children. She would canvass the hill, sometimes coming upon caches of luminous towheaded children or sunset redheads who all talked a language that sounded half-melted to her, as if they held the words inside their mouths a long time and parted with them grudgingly, conversing with little more than a slow "Howdy," or an "Is that right?"

One time some children pointed out slips of white fabric at their parents' wrists and ankles. These, they told Jem, were called "garments" to be worn under clothes at all times; they were full-body casings to keep the flesh sealed away and pure. Their baths had to be performed in stages to keep as much of themselves covered as possible. The garment wearers' children, however, were quite eager to expose themselves, boys named Jeremiah, Joshua, and Job, and their sisters, Rebekah and Ruth.

While the adults were reciting scripture, the children would run to the trees at the base of the hill where they would partly unlace and undo, and display their private parts. Jem was always more impressed by the names these children gave their privates than the parts themselves: she still remembered "my wangle-do," "tin whistle," and "Sailor John," for the boys, and "sweetie-pie," "wah-wah," and "Aunt Betty," for the girls.

Jem remembered little of the pageant itself, beyond nestling into her mother's lap as the dusk faltered and the colored spotlights began to dash the mountaintop. Melvina was perched on their father's lap, following the lights with a close, shrewd eye, skeptical as a theater critic. Jem could not remember ever hearing her sister cry and she could scarcely recall her sleeping either. But she remembered quite a bit of those black baby eyes being sharply watchful over a world that, to Melvie, required attention and governance. She was a guardian angel, Jem thought, mysterious and potent as the Mormons themselves.

Jem remembered the palm of her mother's hand soothing her forehead; footlights; men moving in colored gowns; a thumping hide-covered drum; turning, seeing the pasteled spectacle in Melvie's eyes. They shared only a few years of this, until everything slipped away in Amman, their mother's bed sheets reflected on the bitter drops of her sister's eyes.

ALL AFTERNOON THE back of Jem's neck was prickling. She took extra care with her filing: ten minutes work she stretched to an hour. The electric stapler bit her carbons at exact right angles, papers were bedded perfectly in folders. She restrained herself from consoling patients over the phone with false promises of understanding and forbearance. She knew her co-workers clamped down on late payers, trapping them in debt, threatening ruined credit, dispossession, and general devastation. Jem felt guilty every time she told a weeping patient not to worry, that everything would be "just fine." Their desperation was suffocating; she grasped at lies, the abatement of despair, fairy dust.

"A rock and a hard place," she'd say to herself. "It's you or them, Jemorah, sink or swim."

The shadow of Portia was upon Jem. She dared not stray one inch from the Way of Johnson-Crowes Hospital, which was to reveal nothing at all times, without favor or mercy. "I can't help you, but if you give me your name and number, I'll give a message to your patient rep," she said to each hysterical caller.

She knew Portia would be coming for her. The anxiety was contagious: people seemed to move in slow motion, speaking over great distances from each other. All afternoon Jem was on best behavior, but as the hours passed she felt increasingly like a traveler in the snow. She thought of saying to the women, "I can't make it. Go on without me." But she saw in their eyes that they were already miles away. By three, a thing like freezing had overtaken her and she lolled in her chair in a stupor. The filing was all done, and the only thing left was to answer the phone and look busy, but even that was beyond her. The phone, for once, had stopped ringing, and even though she knew it would enrage Portia, Jem slipped off her shoes, stared out the window, and a wide, blank wasteland filled her mind. Across this surface, she saw faint buttes and canyons; she saw butter-lipped children; she felt the gentling of a hand across her forehead; then quickly the hand melted into a shadow. Jem turned and looked up at Portia Porschman.

Portia's lips began to move in almost imperceptible degrees and it would be an eternity—Jem knew—before any sound came out at all. Jem tried to decide what her defense should be in case Portia flung her notice back in her face. She rehearsed the words, "You can't stop me, I—quit" a few times, then considered singing out, "'Take this job and shove it,'" then went back to "I quit." She hoped that Portia wouldn't say anything so devastating that Jem would be too frightened to leave. But then when the sound finally caught up with the movement of Portia's lips, Jem heard her saying, "Jemorah Ramoud, isn't it? You remind me of your mother. How long have you been with Johnson-Crowes?"

She had no idea what the answer to this question was. Neither did she have any idea what, if anything, Portia had accepted as an answer. All Jem knew was that in the next moment she was presented with the round of Portia's back, like the dark side of the moon, receding from her into the orbits of the outer offices.

THE NURSES WERE laughing. They slung their arms around the backs of their chairs in the Won Ton à Go-Go, threw their heads back, hair slipping free, and laughed.

Even Melvie was laughing. She had gotten rid of Snow White that morning, a lawn ornament that had been giving her particular difficulty, yet the one that had perched, black bobbed hair and all, on their front lawn the longest. "I think there was some kind of Freudian mother-substitute syndrome thing going on with me and Snow," she had told Jem, who'd spotted the bare section of lawn on her way to work. "I felt guilty about taking her, yet she was in the poorest taste of all. I'm afraid I might have been slipping, possibly even forming an attachment. Her removal was a test of character. It's a mistake to let such nuisances take hold. You'll always regret it. It's a character flaw that'll spread wide open like leprosy, once you let it get started. You've got to *cut it out at the root!*" She slashed her hand through the air and Jem could see Snow White beheaded, the black bob tumbling across the lawn.

Melvie continued using this gesture as they all sat around the table and she began grimly describing a recent patient-episode. "I kept saying 'Stop it! Stop that unholy din this minute!'" Melvie sliced at the air as if she could carve the noise out of it. "And she just *stood* there, *right* in the middle of gerontology, hanging on her broom and bawling like a cow—"

"That's Missy, I'm telling you," the young nurse, Hazel, said. "She's like that sometimes."

Missy was a hospital custodian. Her real name was Corinne, but she called herself Missy. Jem often watched the custodians, trying to decide if they had a better job than she did. She felt at times she was an unhappy impostor at her desk, meant to be out swabbing the floors with the others. Her father had begun work at the hospital by scrubbing commodes and washing laundry, and Jem felt that this was her legacy. She didn't fit in; she was too restless and curious, all wrong for a carpeted office. Jem saw a version of herself in Missy's eyes, alone and roving through places where she didn't belong. The custodians wore white like the nurses, only their uniforms were grayer, stained, and wilted. They were almost always African American or Cuban, or had bodies in various states of extremity, intensely thin, or, like Missy, loosely rolling with fat. Missy was also mentally retarded.

Jem liked Missy because she could sustain a steady, chirping stream of conversation, whether anyone was listening or not. She called everyone she met "Honey bunny."

"Honey bunnies! Honey bunnies!" she'd call out when she entered the business office to empty trash at day's end. Mostly the women ignored her, but Jem was helpless before Missy's advances, and, understanding this, Missy would rush to Jem's desk first.

"How is Honey bunny? Missy's fine, she's working today," she would say, always referring to herself in the third person. "Did Honey bunny work hard? She looks pretty today."

Missy never bothered with yesterday or tomorrow or anything outside of today. She seemed to approach the job as her life's appointed round, a natural circle. She would clean all evening and return the next day to the same disarray, an eternal task. She carried out her chores with efficiency and an eye to detail. Matussem told Jem that sometimes the custodians' supervisors would put pennies in the corners to test the painstakingness of their employees and that Missy's pennies were always gathered.

Then, Melvina said, late yesterday afternoon, Missy suddenly buckled over her broom and began lowing like a cow.

"When I finally got her to quiet and talk, she told me she had to go to the bathroom—" Melvina said.

"Oh no—" Hazel said. "Not . . ."

Melvie nodded. "We helped her into a stall, fool that I was for not seeing it right away—she was just making such a racket and who would've thought *Missy*—anyway, we sat her down and sure enough she started having it in the toilet—"

"Having *what?*" Jem asked.

"A baby!" the nurses shouted in unison, then laughed; Melvie folded her arms and frowned.

"We got her onto a table and she finished delivering right there."

"Popped right out," Harriet added. "Slick as a weasel. Poor thing was already half-drowned hanging upside down in the toilet. But it came back with a good loud scream."

"She'd had no idea what happened," Melvie said. "She didn't know she was carrying, she didn't know the father, she didn't know how she got pregnant. When we gave her the baby she said, 'Look, a puppy.'"

Jem was silent. She distantly heard the nurses speculating on the tones of the baby's skin and on potential fathers, ranging from Elroy in linens to Jésus in security. She thought then that this was not the universe her little sister would have organized. God had to be someone like Gilbert Sesame, King of the Wiseacres, ruler of the gaming board, who kept them all placing bets, thinking they could still come out ahead, while he laughed up his almighty sleeve.

Chapter 18

O N   T H E   N O R T H E A S T   corner of the inter-section, Ricky Ellis worked, hidden in the back of Lil' Lulu's Garage. Draped with oil, he would some-times slide out from under a car, eyes moving from the dark of repair work to that of the garage. He would get up and start walking around the pumps and up into the fields behind the station. He would step on thick berry briars and branches and deer droppings and push aside the maple limbs. He would come almost to the edge of the field and stop, cloaked by bushes and night. He would stand silently, watching Jemorah Ramoud folded into her lawn chair, eyes closed, or taking down laundry with the grace of a jinni.

"O K A Y ,   N O W   I T   the creation, the destruction, and the meaning of world as in big eyes of Mat Ramoud, big, *big* Daddy Ramoud!" Matussem shouted into the microphone, swirling a snare brush around on the surface of the drum. It shivered, alive, and Matussem hunched forward as if about to play upon the backs of jungle beasts.

Fergyl was working out a saxophone riff on his Hammond organ, which Owen and Jesse refined and outlined on bass and maracas. This was the band's specialty: rhythm, supercharged rhythm springing from the tips of Matussem's sticks, rhythm that conjured up trees and swinging vines, waves and palpitating wings.

"Calls me Big Daddy," Matussem chanted on. "I am Père, Abu, Fader, Señor, Senior. Call me Pappy, Pappa, Padre, PawPaw, Sir! I big Arab coming at you, guy, flying in towel, fifty thousand mile a second. Come down from big daddies of time, of Cozy Cole, Coltrane, and Charlie *Bird* Parker. I honk, I roar, I do shimmy shimmy on kitchen floor! A million big daddies from all time and more right here, starts here in juicy jazz and America the beautiful, the fat, the big eater, peripatetic, so on, so on. You got the picture."

It was just rehearsal, down in the Ramouds' rec room. Matussem would never have said all that in public, even in a public as laid back as that of the Key West Bar. But he knew his patter tickled Jesse, Owen, and Fergyl, who, he figured, didn't get all that much fun out of life working at the garage with the Cyclops-boss.

Fergyl tried a little aberration on the actual organ keys before retreating to the safety of pushing the sax button. It was the kind of attempt that would move the patrons at the Key West to stamp their feet and let go two-fingered whistles. Inspired, Matussem bellowed: "Call me Big Daddy! I've got a car and two daughters, I'm free! Is my life's work, is the work of the world, is nice work if you can get. My greatest work, a father! Now for fathers out there in fatherland, a little song we're making up as we go, I call 'Big Daddy'!"

Uncle Fouad groaned loudly. He'd already extended his ten-day visit and now seemed to have no plans to leave. He lolled in a chair in the shadows, emitting terrible groans from time to time.

"This goes out to my two beyootiful daughters, *ach du liebe, Augustin,* they are cute! And to the favorite movie star of Big Daddy Ramoud, who is Myrna Loy!"

"I'm bored," Fouad rumbled from the dark. "*Ya'Allah!* So boring!"

Jesse, Owen, and Fergyl snuck glances toward the corner. Fouad was almost completely cloaked by shadow, making him more menacing. He shifted his weight in tidal movements and threw his hands out, projecting like H. G. Wells. "I say, this *is* boring!"

Matussem laid into the drums and said, "Let there be air!" and tried to bring about gusts and winds, gales and rolling monsoons of drumming. To appease Fouad, he shouted, "And these also go out to some fabulous type guy, my wild, out-of-control brother-in-law, Wildman Uncle Fouad. Lets the rains come, lets heaven open the basement door and sees what we cookin', let's soak it up you ding dong, yabba dabba doobies!"

From Fouad's corner came a moan, thin and dry as from the crypt. "I'm too bored to be true," he said. "You guys are suck. We have back home twenty, *thirty* times good as this. In the Old Country sound like music, not like here, like gas pipes."

Owen stopped playing and stared at the ground. Matussem knew he wanted to ask why Fouad didn't just go back—what all the Ramoudettes had been grumbling for the past week whenever Fouad's back was turned. Instead, though, Owen looked teary eyed. The rest of them stopped playing, too.

"Now look, Uncle Fouad," Fergyl began, then looked toward Matussem.

Matussem pretended to be studying a ceiling fixture. Fouad's mere presence was as oppressive to him as the jinni-heavy lamp had become to Aladdin. Fouad's personal hobby was cultivating guilt and penance. Ever since Nora's death, Fouad had made sidelong comments, used furtive, needling questions: How was her typhus caused? How might it have been prevented? Nora must have had a sickly constitution after all. The message that Matussem tried to ignore was that he'd been wrong to marry an American, that it was time to marry again, an Arab this time. Still, the mystery and waste of Nora's early death took root in his heart. From seeds of doubt sprouted a garden of shame and regret, leading Matussem to question almost everything: his choice of a job, a home, a school for the girls, and, finally, a place to raise them. Uncle Fouad, hoe in hand, dug at Matussem, nurturing fear wherever the ground looked fertile. Every year he began anew. He had as many stories as Shahrazad, regaling his audience with the charms of the Old Country, while pointing out the vulgarity and all-around inferiority of the New.

"You see!" Fouad would announce at the sight of a car accident, a woman in a skimpy bathing suit, and/or a gunfight on TV. "You see the place you raises this daughters? Drugs, pimps, pushers, every kind of slime coming up through the sewers at night and taking over.

In Old Country there nothing like that, just the beautiful grandchildren, dancing around your knees. Here, I don't look out these window after sunset, jinnis and white eyes everywhere. But what do I know? I am only the uncle. And then you says you want to raise your daughters *here* where this winter rips the skin off your face and tears your heart out. Okay, fine, that's a big *o*-kay by me!"

Now Fouad was moaning in the shadows. He curled his fingers around one arm of his chair, as if to rise, but merely groaned, "Somebody get me a Michelbo."

"Uncle Foua-ud, Uncle Foua-ud!" Gilbert Sesame called. He clumped down the stairs, a grocery bag in each arm. "Y'all can stop torturing your family and friends now. Lookee here, look what there is—Heinekens and Doritos!" He placed each sack at Fouad's feet like an offering, then snapped off a bottle cap and handed the bottle to him. The night after Fouad's arrival, Gil had taken a job as Uncle Fouad's valet and party consultant. Fouad rented Gil a room in the High Chaparral Motel and bought him a black Trans Am to chauffeur his boss around in.

"This man knows quality," Gil said to Matussem, smoothing down his designer shirt newly donated by Fouad, only slightly worn at the elbows. "Right now he's just cranky, see. Time for his nap."

Since his arrival, Fouad had sought relief from chronic boredom by staying out all night and sleeping most of the day, guided by Gil, who added "Hell-Raiser Extraordinaire" to his job description. They favored a nameless strip-joint/after-hours club halfway between the Ramouds' house in Euclid and downtown Syracuse, one of the dozen or so structures that orbited Euclid, including Grange Hall, a firehouse, dilapidated farmhouses, and a Pap's A.M. The club—a Quonset hut with a neon light in the window—was just the kind of place where Fouad loved to smoke cigars and wrap his shirt around his head.

"Uncle Fouad and me, we're like this." Gil held up two entwined fingers to Matussem.

"You don't says, my friend, Allah be praise." Matussem and the Ramoudettes packed up and carried the beer empties upstairs.

JEM WAS SITTING at the kitchen table. "What the hells I am going to do?" Matussem said to her. "Fouad is putting out hairy tentacles and vines and roots. He's all over the place, like invasions of the body snatcher. He's mashing the buns-shape in my La-Z-Boy all wrong. What if he never leaves again? What if is us and Uncle Fouad and that Gilbo Sesamoon forever and forever? *Ach du liebe, Augustin,* my brains falling out. Let's go to Key West Bar for escape." He and the Ramoudettes left through the back door.

The basement door slammed and Uncle Fouad walked in and sat down. "That guy with beer. Your boyfriend Gilbo. He's okay driver, but I don't like him. He is a blob. A blob, I'm tell you."

Jem nodded. "I know, believe me," she said.

"He is like this tree-stuff you have in this country, stick everywhere he touches. And I tell him to wash my car and he doesn't do it. He say he draw a line. What line? A blob. He leave oily lips on back of my hand."

"It wasn't my idea," Jem said. "He started it. I was going along for fun."

"Yes, fun. In these country all the time this big thing. Fun." Fouad sighed and tucked himself back on the chair. He ran one hand up and down his belly. "I'll tell you what, Jemorah, my favorite niece, you want two thousand dollars easy?"

"That will depend on what you have in mind." Melvina was standing in the door, arms folded across her chest. "Do tell."

Fouad's smile expanded, revealing a spectrum of teeth. He said, "Perfect! Melvina, I make deal, five grands for two of you."

Melvina sat between Jemorah and Fouad and folded her hands. "State your terms, Uncle."

Fouad nodded. Jem watched him change from uncle to businessman. He tucked in his belly and thrust out his lower jaw. "Easiest money you ever makes. As favor to my two favorite nieces. I says, be nice to your poor old Uncle Fouad and drop this blobby American boys you got here, there, everywhere . . ."

"And?" Melvina pressed.

"And, as you are knowing, I have many sons. All unmarried, two in especial—the oldest, Saiid and Kier, who may yet turn to be human beings. There's no telling. We must take a wait and see attitudes. I want to get them married up good."

"Put clearly, you want us to marry them for all of five thousand dollars," Melvina said.

Fouad frowned, waving his hand delicately. "Tut, tut, a meeting, a little bit dinner, my dear ones, all we requires. All the rest is not here, not there. Back in home we know the scores, like Jem is in marriage emergency. Thirty years of age in months and then what. So okay, we start with trip to restaurant, maybe a little drinks, maybe you see where is Saiid and Kier on evolution scale, the rest takes care of itself."

"Why are you bringing this sort of matter to *us*," Melvie asked, leaning back, her voice cagey, "instead of speaking to our father?"

Fouad lifted his head and hooded his eyes. "Melvina, you think poor, old, miserable Uncle Fouad just falls off the banana boats? This is all New World. We know how things get done with who." From his wallet he fanned out five thousand-dollar bills upon the table and in the same beat Melvina put her hand on them.

"All right, then. The deal's done," she said. "One date—five G's. But I'm warning you, no body contact, no funny stuff, no marriage contracts. We don't even have to talk to them. This is free enterprise."

"Of course so, O heartpicker," said Uncle Fouad.

AFTER FOUAD AND Gilbert drove off in a spray of gravel to the Shake Your Booty, Jem went to hang the wash. The early summer evening was still warm and Jem moved among sheets fragrant with moisture. As she worked, her memory opened like the white sheets sliding between her fingers: rooms full of parties, Arab men in their living room in Syracuse, women in the kitchen, the air gathering the rich smoke, the black coffee, men talking, voices intensifying, and finally shouting. Fighting percolated in the air. The television was always on. The newscasters brought daily body counts, TV screen leaping through leaves, the camera sinking and leaping through whispering bushes, vines, recording the shattering sound of bullets, white explosions. Her mother was always slipping out, always in another room.

Jem remembered once when Uncle Fouad had run into the kitchen hysterical and attempted to telephone Walter Cronkite.

"Hullo? Yes? Hullo," she remembered him shouting. "Yes, is this Walter Cronkite? No, I want Walter! Walter, Walter, is that you? Hullo, yes, Walter! I called to say that you and the entire American newspeoples are bullshit! What's that? Yes, I say, bullshit!"

"Fouad," her father had called from the next room. "Come back. That *can't* be Walter, Walter is on TV right now, talking."

"Yes, and everything he's says is bullshit!" Fouad shrieked. His face was shining. "Yes, do you hear, old boy?" he shouted back in the phone. "Complete, all the way, bullshit!"

JEM SAT ON the lawn, watching sheets billow and blouses lift their arms in the breeze. The air was still warm, scented with goldenrod and ragweed and lilacs that wagged purple heads in the wind against the sides of the house. The fields were dissolving into pink twilight.

She wasn't surprised then when Ricky Ellis appeared out of the trees, wind, and tall weeds, his eyes clear and wide. He walked up through the fields, sat down, and laid his head in Jem's lap. He did it without speaking, and Jem let him. She didn't let herself think about what Melvie or Fatima would say if they could see them sitting together like that. She just held very still.

"I missed you," he said. "I had a lot of fun driving with you that time."

Her fingers touched his forehead. She thought that she could look at him a long time and not know a thing about him. Distant sounds of children reached her, lapsing in and out on the back of the wind. The voices, so thinned out, sounded sweet and discordant. Then Ricky closed his eyes and began singing, his head still cradled in her lap.

The sound was eerie, elegiac, climbing the bones of her legs back to her spine, the song bound to the rhythm of weeping. It sounded vaguely familiar to her, a lament for a dead soldier. What was most remarkable about this singing was the purity of his voice, going true to every note and giving it flight. The sound of a faun, Jem thought, or panpipes. She'd never heard anything like it before. While he was singing, she was afraid he would finish, and when he finished, she wasn't sure if she wanted him to start again.

He sat up then and said, "So, what do you think?"

She opened her mouth. Before she could speak, he said, "Do I sound like Elvis?"

"Elvis?"

He nodded, grinning and looking down at his crossed legs and bare feet. "Stupid, I know. He's kind of a god to me, even if he is dead and all." He squinted up at Jem, plucking a blade of grass and leaning forward to put it between her lips. "Sometimes I like to think that Elvis was my real dad, you know?"

WHEN FIREFLIES BEGAN to show against the dark, Ricky took Jem's hand and kissed the inside of her wrist and the tip of each finger. He dusted off his jeans and walked back down the road, toward the haze of the gas station. Jem stayed out a while longer, listening to crickets, bullfrogs, and the deeper silence that welled up; it filled the shadows and permeated the night air. There was a lingering smell of cut grass and if she walked a bit farther, toward the creek at the edge of the trees, she knew there would be a faint odor of human waste. In the summers, she and Melvie and other Euclid kids used to wander the concrete-bottomed creek in the Otts's fields, through stagnant water full of tadpoles and surface-skimming insects. It ran through a tunnel that cut into the earth's slope and children would walk in as far as the light reached.

She had sat with her mother, holding her hand through a night like this, like a span of water. Her mother's last words were flecks of light on the surface of that water. What were they? A request for a blanket? The names of her children? Her husband? Jem held her mother's hand, as the fever turned body and words to ashes, then cold. Jem sat through the night, stiffening, as if in step with the process of death. She was afraid that if she made a sound and broke the spell that held her mother's silence, her father's sleep, and her baby sister's stare through the bars of the crib, that she would shatter something holding them together.

When light touched the room and their father opened his eyes, the first thing he saw was Jem holding her mother's hand. He said, "Jemmy? *Yabah,* couldn't you sleep?"

That smell of dormant water and waste was in that room. Melvina, who was two, was sitting up.

Chapter 19

A man shriveled around his own skeleton, his face raw and red as a bone joint, came into the hospital early the next morning. He was more carried than walked in by a tall woman with big, horsey bones, all muscle and skin that was burned and peeled and burned again. She was wearing a bullwhip for a belt, her hair hung in shafts of tangerine yellow, chopped above her forehead as if by a tomahawk; the name *Marvella* was stenciled across her prominent sternum.

The security guards watched on their monitors as she steered her companion out of the Emergency Room and walked him across the hospital to the Critical Care nurses' station. Melvina saw them straggle past the glass wall of her office and sprang up.

"You there! Halt!" Melvie said, marching toward them. Nurses and orderlies were standing around, watching the pair, but no one seemed inclined to interfere with the whip-woman. "Stop right where you are."

The woman stopped, hoisted the man a little higher on her shoulder as if adjusting a dress sleeve, and turned around. She squinted at Melvie and walked a few steps closer. "I don't believe it. Hank, does that look like a human-earth-being to you? Now don't get your hopes up, but I think it might just—"

Hank was having trouble focusing. He nodded in Melvie's general direction and croaked, "Hey, bay-bee."

"What can I do for you?" Melvie said. She hooked her clipboard against her hip like a six-shooter.

"First tell me," the woman said, dragging Hank back down the hall toward Melvie. "Are you a human being or a robot? 'Cause we don't talk to robots. My friend here's sick and I'm looking for somebody to heal him, not finish him off like the robots downstairs were trying to do."

Melvie stared at them. She loathed rule bending, but she never tiptoed past the truth when she heard it. She also liked the way that whip looked looped through the woman's jeans.

"I'm a human being," she said to the woman. "We're all human beings here."

WHEN ASKED TO describe his symptoms, Hank said, "Heat and fuzz."

"Heat and fuzz—" Melvina's pencil wavered over the chart; she stared up at him. "Elaborate, please."

The man nodded. "I got this fuzzy *heat* right here." He pointed to his solar plexus. "Heat. And fuzz. Somebody gave me something to drink; it had bubbles. I think there was something bad in it, gave me this heat, it spreads up and down and moves around—"

Melvie noticed his fly was torn open, exposing a dark thatch of hair. He smelled of something more lethal than whiskey. "When did you drink this substance?"

"Last week, or maybe it was a month ago."

Harriet, Melvie's staff assistant, leaned forward and asked, "Honey, did you want to see someone in psych?"

Hank stopped his drifting head for a moment and looked at her. "I'm not crazy," he said.

"Honey," the whip-woman said to Harriet, "you think this is crazy, you don't even know what crazy *is*."

"Home address," Melvie said.

"Just passing through."

"Employment."

"This and that, bay-bee, this and that."

Melvie stared at him, tapping the pencil point.

"Well hey, hey, that's kind of a personal question now, ain't it?" he said. He had begun to shrink during their interview, his mouth retracting in his head as if recoiling from the effects of sobriety.

"Next of kin." Melvina's eyes glittered with irritation.

Hank's head did a slow orbit. He looked back at the whip-woman, lounging in Melvie's office door. "What was your name again, bay-bee?"

THE MORNING OPENED onto a white, salt desert. Jem hovered around her desk and stared at the carpet. On the other side of Hill Cumorah, beyond the

Mormons, beyond even Utah and Gilbert Sesame's wild promises, Jem was left with Ricky Ellis, a thought like an echo. An hour after arriving, she left her desk, aiming in the direction of the rest room, and while Portia looked away, she kept right on going, out into the hospital. She was looking down corridors opening on corridors, winding entrances without exits.

She wondered if she was in love. She marched down to the main lobby and passed the information desk. *Love.* The word buzzed around her head, a mosquito with a secret vessel of blood. The air around her hummed. She passed teaching classrooms, festooned with anatomy charts and mounted skeletons. The empty desks were golden in the late afternoon. Nothing was left in her mind but a single thought.

Had she sought *him* out, him in particular?

She passed medical records, housekeeping, security, where she could see the back of two officers' heads surrounded by the glow of their video screens.

They had talked little, knew almost nothing of each other. She'd never seen his home. His father, he said, had never existed. He was dark as mahogany from dragging rags over windshields, flipping open gas lids; there was car oil and grime worked into his skin that wouldn't come off under scalding showers and Ajax cleanser; the musky perfume of gasoline was in his hair.

He had one year of junior high and spotty high school vocational BOCES repair classes to her four years of college. Jem had many relatives; he said he had none. He claimed to have been born in the automobile graveyard that moldered off the back traces of Route 31, brought about by spontaneous combustion, like the spark's crack in a piston chamber, there in the piles of wheels, upholstery, and iron parts shedding their paint in New York air and acid rain.

Fred Beevle hired Ricky on part-time for his expert repair work, but he wouldn't buy Ricky a pair of coveralls for fear of letting customers know he actually worked there. Jesse, Owen, and Fergyl had beards and wild eyes and looked like they'd tumbled down from a mountain cave, but Fred was afraid that Ricky's history of loitering would frighten customers away, make them think that Lil' Lulu's employed criminals.

Jem looked out one of the corridor windows and saw the sprinklers dashing water across the hospital lawn. Inside, the hospital was a vacuum; the walls curved toward the floors, all dull edges. The faces of the people she passed, too, were dulled, marked by their proximity to illness and sterile procedures and the attempt to contain pain.

He hadn't given her anything, not a flower, bonbon, nor promise, only his company, his greasy jeans and torn-up sneakers beside her in the car. Then on the lawn. She thought of his skin, his coarse shave, and his eyes that seemed to want everything, ask nothing. Over the years he had sometimes appeared in her thoughts at night, without warning, in the way she'd sometimes seen kestrels suddenly soar from the tree line, splitting the twilight along their wings, claiming the sky. Her heart did a loop at the sight of him. They were almost too shy to speak; they barely knew each other, and she was afraid of strange men.

An elderly male patient in pink flannel pajamas stopped her outside the psych ward, taking her hand and saying, "When I see people like you, I think to myself, 'O brave new world, that has such people in't!' Do you know what that's from?"

She stopped, then said, "Well, there's that book—"

"Aha!" the man said happily. "Aha! You think you know, but you don't know." He started to stroll away, back down the corridor. "It's *The Tempest,* my dear! *The Tempest.*"

She watched the patient wander away, laughing to himself.

When Ricky had turned away from her that evening, she wondered, did he forget? Perhaps Ricky would only take in so much of her, the sight of her knees, or the measure of her movement, and then forget, their visits spilling down the sides of his memory, like water from an overfilled glass. She knew little about Ricky's life outside the ring of the station and the round bulbs of the gas pumps. If she were to go looking into his private life, lived in a world of weeds and swamps, in Euclid's sad houses, what would she find?

She punched out early and headed for the bar.

WHEN MELVINA ENTERED Hank Bovine's file in the computer bank it brought his name up with a string of others trailing after like tails on a kite:

Hank Bovine, also see: Perry Pensch, also see: Mandingo Fred, also see—and this stopped her and stuck in her head and went on to bother her for the rest of the day—Jupiter Ellis.

Her mind, Melvie liked to say, was a steel trap; no important fact or figure worked around the teeth of it.

Somewhere inside its jaws, the name Jupiter Ellis went pinging off the sides. Later, at the Won Ton à Go-Go, she stared at her sister across the table, until Jem turned to Melvina and said, "What *is* it?"

Melvie looked away, pulling the bar window's curtain back with one finger. The Syracuse sky was full of milk-weed seeds, blurring in the heat. "I don't know exactly." A bird, black-winged, tail tipped white, wheeled and dove. No one was in the streets; the heat had put everyone to sleep. "I have a patient I think might interest you."

THE NAME ON the bedchart said Hank Bovine, but written in, in pencil, was Jupiter Ellis.

Jem had heard the name from the Broom kids, from Peachy Otts, and from Larry Fasco. It was the name of the man the kids on the bus said had blown himself up, the man Hilma Otts was "saving" herself for, and the man Ricky swore had never really existed.

He slept in a fetal curl under the sheets; his body looked soft, his shut eyes and lips downy. He sighed as he breathed, a weathered, battered sleep, as if tumbling through his dreams. The two sisters watched him. Beyond the bedside window the clouds were radiant. Jem looked away from the bed. She remembered that, on more than one occasion, this man had bagged groceries for her at the Bumble Bee.

"Ricky's father," she said. "I don't believe it."

The man opened his eyes at the sound of her voice. The eyes were mild; they were Ricky's eyes, ocean-pale.

"Hey, hey, hello there," he said, lips moving numbly

over each other, his voice lifting from sleep. It was
motor deep and a wreck, but could, possibly, have once
sounded like Ricky's. "Nurse," he said to Melvina. "I'm
parched, darlin'—could you fix me—could you—"

"There's a water squeeze-mug on your bedstand, Mr.
Bovine," Melvie said, towing Jem from the room. They
walked to the end of the hall where they stopped.

"What's wrong with him?" Jem asked.

"He's been poisoning himself," Melvie said. "He
drinks rubbing alcohol when he can't afford whiskey,
and the toxicologists tell me last week he sampled a little
hydrogen peroxide. That stuff wipes out brain, liver,
and stomach, to name just a few of the big ones, which
is apparently the way some people like it."

Jem felt dizzy; she put a hand against the wall. Melvie
made her sit in a lounge chair and lower her head between her knees. When she came back up for air, Melvina said, "Jupiter Ellis is listed with the police as a
missing person. The entire population of Euclid talks
about him as if he'd vaporized. I personally cannot tolerate that kind of mass delusion."

Melvina's words rushed around Jem. She knew that
Melvie was saying, we can't afford to spare a single life.

RICKY ELLIS LIVED in hibernation, under the
lights of the gas pumps and in the blue lair of the garage,
wrapped in the mist of gasoline. He shook back his long
hair to look up the road at the house where Jem lived.
He waited for her to come to the station again. He tried
not to think about her. There was something about Jem,
perhaps the light of her skin, her secretive expression,

that made him know he did not belong with her. Still, the thought of her could come to him at anytime at all, little bubbles of air in his blood, desire so strong it would ache in his shoulders and arms as he bent to pump gas: the need to rise out of his life, walk up the street to where she lived, and touch her hand.

Ricky could not understand himself. He'd had too many stepmothers; he was numbed by his father's absence, by years of aimlessness and television. He was drawn to cement stoops, porches, garages, to any protected place where he could sit. He didn't know quite what he looked like; he saw fragments of himself in the steel gas pumps and the chipped mirror in the men's room. His eyes weren't really his. They opened like screens. When he looked in the mirror, he didn't know how to feel; something would move in his chest and he'd look away. He kept his head lowered and let his hair fall back over his eyes. Flat on his back under a car chassis looking into metal mazes, he could lose himself between the floor and the engine.

Someday, he believed, she would wake from the house inside the trees, that house banked in bushes, weeds, and dark windows. He was afraid to call her.

If he breathed very quietly, though, touched her with the lightest fingers, if he sang to her, he thought, she might sink deeper into her sleep, the sleep of Euclid. Perhaps she would stay with him, though he felt, deeper inside, that she would someday leave.

Ricky felt these things without ever saying them. The words had gone with his father and mother, absorbed into his stepmother's lost stare and into the TV sets. Instead he sang, he howled, he bayed and wailed.

Sometimes he dialed Jem's phone number and when she answered, he sang old songs, words that came to him from out of nowhere, as if he were making them up as he went along: "'And I'll be there in sunshine or in sorrow . . .'" Ricky could hear Jem breathing while he was singing, her pulse behind his voice. Then she would say, "Hello, Ricky. Do you want to come over?"

The ugliness, the memory of his own face, would shift inside him, dark, round, a serpent's egg that split into inky songs while he sang, then sealed again when he stopped. He always hung up.

Chapter 20

DOLORES WAS HAVING a great time. Her roommate Lana liked all the same shows as Dolores, and they kept the TV on from *Sunrise Sermon* until the national anthem. They watched as many game shows and soap operas as they could squeeze in between nurses, switching with their remote buttons as soon as a commercial came on.

Lana had a three-foot stack of true-confessions magazines, featuring incest, rape, and Martians, at the side of her bed, and these she shared with Dolores, saying Dolores needed an education in what was "out there." Whenever Lana's husband or kids came to visit, they brought her a couple more. She'd been in the hospital for a month and promised to show Dolores the ropes.

"You got to haggle with these people," she told Dolores. "It's the only language they understand. Nurse wants to stick you? Doc wants to look up your nose? You say, *hey,* you want me to cooperate, what's in it for me?"

Lana would have been the perfect roommate, except that she had a coffee-grinder voice and a cough like a hacksaw. She'd just had a total hysterectomy, described in blow-by-blow detail to Dolores her first day there. Sometimes Lana would lay back, close her eyes, and moan from a deep and constant pain, especially around three or four in the morning, in the space between her last pain injection and the anticipated morning hypo.

At times the entire floor resounded with sounds of anguish. Dolores heard sobs, wails, and sometimes screams rattling up and down the hall. But for all that, it was still a step above Dolores's house: a place where all she could hear or see or smell was babies, on and on, forever. Her mother called now and then and the background of each talk was overlaid with the sound of Dolores's children screaming and fighting, and her mother's voice, like a solitary cry from the wilderness, asking when are you coming home? After each talk, phone tucked into its cradle, Dolores felt those children's voices wash away from her, leaving her rinsed and light as air.

A couple days after Dolores arrived she was watching TV, and in the middle of *Wheel of Fortune*, Lana propped herself up and said, "You know, I'm gonna die soon."

Dolores slowly turned from the set and looked her over, trying to tell if she was bluffing. "What is this. What're you talkin' about? The doctor tell you that?"

Lana blew a stream of smoke through her nostrils. She had three cases of filterless cigarettes stashed under her bed. "Naw, these people don't know about nothing. They scraped out my below-boards to which I say good riddance to bad rubbish. But the real problem is I got tar paper for lungs. My days are most certainly numbered, hon." She took a long drag and held it for a moment before blowing the smoke out in a luxurious column. "And I wanta go the way I wanta go, so says Lana."

DOLORES THOUGHT IT would be perfect to die to *The Right Price* or *The Six Million Dollar Word*, or, for that matter, to any of the other afternoon shows, the soap operas and talk shows. The programs gave a cadence to her life, a sense of momentum, like waves on the ocean—just as soon as one story spilled out, another was gathering force. It was so different from her life in Euclid, where everything detracted from the pure pleasure of watching one show after another, straight through the days, where the problem was the day itself, the late welfare checks, the broken TVs, the babies. Nothing changed; her home was a house of mirrors, repeating itself at every turn. In the midst of all those children, she had turned toward the curving trailer walls, felt a silence stirring dangerously, in isolation, in her center: a flame, like the one at the end of her Bic lighter, touched to a curtain, an upholstery ruffle. Every day she saw Lil' Lulu's Garage, Jesse, Owen, and Fergyl working on the same cars that wouldn't stay fixed; she saw the same pickups parked in the lot of the Key West Bar; she saw Harvey, the one-armed pool player, watching nothing happen from the window of the Euclid Inn.

At the hospital they told Dolores she was in recovery, but as long as Lana was fading, Dolores thought she'd go along for the ride. Dying hadn't frightened her for a long time. It was like the people on that show *Back from the Grave* last night said. All those heart-attack people saw the same thing: a tunnel with light at the end. Like her hospital room, a tunnel of sheets and magazines, blank walls like her mind, no men, no chores, just a light at the far reach of awareness, the television, drawing her farther and farther from herself.

That is, until that nurse came back.

Head Nurse Melvina Ramoud was the first person Dolores had ever met who meant business. It figured, Dolores thought, that she would have to return when Dolores was involved in dying. Dolores was on a floor far from her office in Critical Care, and hadn't seen Melvina since her admission days earlier. She liked the angry light in Melvina's eyes, the way she held her neck and shoulders like a warrior, like Dolores would have if she'd had the strength. Dolores had always been attracted to trouble. Melvina sat on the edge of her bed. She was carrying a clipboard and drummed a pencil against it.

"So, Dolores Otts," Melvina said, ticking her pencil over and over. "Dolores, Dolores. Did you know your name is Latin for 'sorrow'?"

"Well, does that surprise me one bit?" Dolores said, trying to laugh. "No. That's just the name for how my life goes. Not much else to add to it. I was named after Grampy Otts's ferret who used to nip people."

Melvina nodded, then she said, "Maybe I'm thick. I simply don't get it. *Explain* to me, please, why a person would ever want to die. I mean, *want to*. To put themselves in the *way* of death. I try and try because there really isn't that much that I don't grasp—but this one particular . . . phenomenon. Don't they care about the people they leave behind? What about them?"

From the other side of the room, through the curtain that nurses pulled for privacy, Dolores heard Lana start hacking, a telegraph they'd worked out: *Don't let the bastards trick you!*

Dolores knew she had nothing to fear. At that moment she felt as if she'd never feared anything in her life. Her body was slight, emptied of care, and she floated, suspended in lovely weightlessness between Lana's warnings and the nurse's questions. The nurse, she knew, was looking, trying to bring her back, but it was too late. Nothing really mattered anymore. She folded her arms and looked Melvie in the eye, amazed at the power dying gave her.

Melvina stared back, then said, "Wait a second." She left the room. Then she returned with a hairbrush. "Our mother liked this, I think, I remember. . . ."

The brush passed through Dolores's hair, soft bristles taking Dolores down into herself, separating her into fibers, each worry and memory and name falling down the gentle slope of the brush through her hair, and that woman's hand upon it. Dolores sat up a little. She could almost feel it. It was almost like peace.

THAT NIGHT, DOLORES was transfixed by the TV and her roommate's perpetual groaning and muttering. Though Dolores stared at the screen, there was something different in her head. When they shut off the lights at night she saw it more clearly on the ceiling. It was her son, Wally, on a bicycle. He had never owned a bicycle, but in this picture there he was, flying along, arms extended. And she was standing there hearing him scream, *Mommy, Mommy, Mommy!* as she'd heard so many times before. And she was hating him, wanting to knock him down and break that word in two. Dolores closed her eyes against the picture, but the screaming went on and on like the sound of game shows.

Two days later Dolores refused to stop ringing her summons bell until the head nurse was brought to her.

"That's right," Lana coached from across the room. "Demand your G.D. rights. They're gonna kill us anyways, they got to do it on our F-ing terms."

When Melvina was finally located, Dolores could hear her steps clicking all the way across the ward. Dolores's hand fell from the summons bell, and for a moment all she could think was, where were you before I got here, when I really needed you?

Melvina appeared in the doorway and said, "Ms. Otts! You are creating havoc and total disruption on this floor. This behavior is counterproductive and will not be tolerated! There are two nurses and, if necessary, an entire station already designated to attend to your needs."

"Okay, okay," Dolores said, letting her head fall back among the pillows.

Melvie moved closer then, staring. "Look at you, what's wrong with you?" she cried. "Look at the color of your eyes. And your skin!" Melvie looked Dolores over deftly, checking breath and pulse. Then she went to the chart on the opposite wall. Her eyes ticked over the information and Dolores watched as Melvina seemed to read the whole story there.

Their regular day nurse came in and Lana cried, "Here she is, The Terminator."

Melvina scowled at Lana, then towed The Terminator out to a whispering consultation in the hallway, just close enough for Dolores to make out crackling phrases:

"Why didn't you—"

"—need that bed—"

"What, is this a war movie?"

"She's a faker—"

"—jaundice!"

"—no insurance, a self-pay—"

"—call yourself a nurse!"

The words danced, little sparks. If Dolores squinted, she could see her death out there, in the fields, waiting. They would send her out to meet it, out behind the trailer, among the nests of baby shit and cans of spaghetti sauce; she could see it, a shard of glass on an empty hillside. *Live by garbage, die by garbage,* she thought, then wondered if she'd heard that on TV.

Melvina reentered the room, staring at something that didn't quite seem to be Dolores's face. She said in a tired voice, "Dolores Otts."

Dolores closed her eyes and said, "Okay, I just want one thing."

Lana hacked loudly: *Go for it.*

"I'll have to hear it first, Ms. Otts."

"I want you to get Peachy into college."

Lana coughed again, but a quick, short one, an accident, as if she didn't know whether to be disgusted or proud.

Dolores had surprised herself, too. But the more she thought about it, the better she liked the idea. She was very taken with it. "I mean, what if she has a brain in her head? We should see about it," she said.

Melvina seated herself at Dolores's side, "Well," she said, "certainly there are all sorts of vocational programs—training schools—or community col—"

"No!" Dolores said. Lana was nodding her head, holding back the curtain and watching. "I want her to go to the university. To Syracuse. I want her to join one of them things? A fraternity? And wear pink and date boys and have one of those hairy coats and wave one of those flags like I saw that guy—what's his name with the sweater in the movie yesterday?" she asked Lana.

"Yeah, Jimmy Stewart."

"Yeah, like he was doing. All of that!" she cried, the idea glowing in her now. She loved it; it was beautiful. She looked at the TV and saw Peachy at her graduation in gown and mortarboard, holding a scroll covered with writing. Peachy, savior of the Otts family, the sparrow that would rise on a warm current and float past them all, up so far above Euclid that the scrap heaps and car graveyards and sewers would vanish. She would forget it all, forget pissing in buckets and throwing it out the back door, forget the things that Dolores guessed their brother Joe had done to her when she used to get home first from school. "I want her to go to tea parties and wear white socks and to—I don't know—get her head full of all kinds of stuff, about math and reading. Maybe she could even teach me then."

Chapter 21

*I*T WAS THE second Monday in June, two weeks after Uncle Fouad arrived, and Melvie had run into Jem's room at five-thirty in the morning, on her way to work, clapped her hands together in four smart cracks, and barked, "Up! Up! Up! Up!" She'd noticed Jem was starting to get a hangdog look and knew it was up to her to snap her out of it.

Melvie liked to compare herself to Atlas, whose huge wrought-iron likeness in front of the European Health Spa she'd admired for years. Without people like her or Atlas, the earth would cease to turn as efficiently and consistently as it had done. She saw to it that hearts ran on time: a heart in every chest and a stomach in every belly. She was there, also, to see that people thought the right thoughts, felt the right feelings, and that Jemorah didn't go off track. No one understood Melvie, this she knew; it was a given. She was like a deer in the woods; her true nature fluttered from behind dark shapes and obstacles in flashes, the white beam of a tail lifting as the deer flees. Even in her own mind this was true: she fled from herself.

She expected that when she died she would trade in her job with Atlas for a position with St. Peter, in charge of moral accounting. She was as well versed in the responsibilities of death as in those of life; she had met with death personally. When she was two and a half she'd sat up in her crib in her parents' bedroom in Jordan and watched it come in through the window.

It had cascaded through the air in a veil, like the ones that flew around belly dancers, a veil like Salome's. It turned over and over, tumbling in folds over their heads as Melvina kept watch. Though this was long before she became a nurse, even then she knew instinctively, inarticulately, that death came to people in personal guises: one would see a fly where another saw a fish or a star. This veil, she understood, would be the way death revealed itself to her. She had kept the memory of that night intact, complete in its detail.

The veil fell lightly toward her mother, and behind the bars of her crib Melvie was helpless to move her out of the way as she would push someone out of the path of a truck. She watched it settle in the shiver that crept over her mother and glazed her sleeping skin; she watched the veil work its texture into the skin and through the body as if flesh were made of air. And it was as if some part of that veil had fallen over Melvina, too, covering her with the memory, a network of sensations that she could never tear away.

She claimed that from that night on she knew she was called to pursue the greatest of professions, the most physically, emotionally, and intellectually demanding of any field, the most misunderstood and martyred, the closest to divinity: nurse.

People flourished under her care. Patients thought to be inoperable were restored, the suicidal regained hope, the lingering ill were healed. Not so many that anyone called Melvina a miracle worker, but enough that the staff in her hospital and the hospital community at large knew and respected her and honored her commands. Doctors consulted her as a matter of course. Patients and their families sent her flowers, chocolates, even jewelry—which she promptly returned, not wishing to appear compromised. She could look into a patient's face, read the irises, lips, the confluence of thought and shadow, and recognize an illness.

There were also those who had evaded her.

Melvina referred to death as her Achilles' heel. It caught her off guard. Jem, on occasion, pointed out that Melvie's feelings might be a natural response to death, but Melvina always said, "I'm a nurse, not just some *person.*" She believed that the pang she felt over it was the one flaw that prevented her from being the Total Nurse. "In hospital personnel, regret is a form of secondary complication, like infection," she'd said. "It must be flushed out.

"Nurses must strive for complete inner harmony," Melvie said. "Their minds and hearts as clear as light, water, and fire. They have to be truthful and spontaneous, so the clean blade of knowledge and action can flash from them to patient without interruption."

Daily, death pressed on her from newspapers, radio, television.

She remembered an article she had read four years

earlier about a boy who'd gone walking on the ice of Lake Ontario. Ice-walking was the bane of the small college that was perched on the lip of the lake. Out of cabin fever perhaps, or natural curiosity, many students were enticed out on the frozen borders. The boy Melvie read about had worked as a photographer for the student paper and, even though being caught on the ice meant automatic expulsion, he decided to chance it and went with a friend to take pictures.

They went out too far—someone always did—out to where they could see the belly of Ontario still uncovered by the ice, deep and wild enough to resist freezing. It was as if the lake itself had dared them—its waves lifting a hypnotic voice—to go on and on, to discover its secret life under the frozen dead sheets. Once the boys were out far enough to spot the waves, they heard a loud crack under their feet. One boy was able to run to more solid ice, but the photographer began to drift away on a small floe. His friend hurried to shore for help.

Campus security backed an emergency boat off the end of a pier where lake water ran channels between frozen currents and they motored toward the boy, chopping their way through the loose ice with axes and the hull of the boat. The boy was difficult to spot through the wind and snow. One moment, they saw him crouched on the slippery floe, the next, he was in the gray waves. His boots and winter clothes were instantly waterlogged, dragging him down, but he kept his head above water, and, as the boat came in, he was still able to lift his hands for the rope and life preserver they threw him.

Though they cut the engines, the boat stirred up water, and as the boy laid his hands on the preserver, the hull smashed through two great sheets of ice. Massive shards broke free, rushed at him, and the light went out of his eyes as he was crushed in half at the waist, pinned between ice panes. They dragged in his head, arms, and torso with the skin of his palms frozen to the preserver; his hips and legs went down. The place where he had stood was already mending, ice knitting back to ice.

Every year students were lost to the lake, just as in other places, people fell down gorges or were caught in undertows. In the graying, crystallizing darkness, when Onondaga Lake went still and the bowl of land seemed to swim with its ghosts, Melvina thought of the boy she'd read about. She thought about the future he might have lived and imagined the possibilities trailing after him, and she marveled at what little power to protect others anyone had.

MELVINA DREW BACK and snapped the stone, then watched it skip once, twice, three times over the lake. "This is salt water," she told Jem. "Syracuse used to be called 'Salina'—*salt*. At one time it was the world's biggest salt producer."

Jem looked at the water. "Now it's not worth much, huh."

Melvina looked at Jem sharply. "Don't say that, Jemorah." She looked over the water. "That's a defeatist attitude. Move toward your *light* energy. This is practically saline solution, almost blood."

"*Hemo the Magnificent*," Jem said, remembering the health movie they showed at Clay Elementary on every assembly day. That and *Treasure Island.*

Melvina reached down to her big, white patent-leather pocketbook propped between some rocks and pulled out an envelope. She handed it to Jem. It said Syracuse University Office of Undergraduate Admissions. "I just walked over to the admissions office after work and picked this up. Do me a favor," Melvie said. "Fill that out and sign Peachy Otts's name to it."

Jem sat on one of the flat rocks that flanked the lake. She'd never heard her sister say or do anything dishonest; Melvina was as righteous and unyielding as Moses. Jem shaded her eyes and gazed at Melvie. The sun reflected brilliantly against her uniform. Jem thought perhaps that the mosaic of lights, the blowing trees, had confused what she heard.

Melvina skipped another stone hard, six hops, and Jem knew she'd heard right. "I'm amazed . . . I mean . . . you . . . not to mention we'd never get away with it," Jem said. "Melvie? What is it?"

"It's just—I don't know how to do this, and if I don't do this, I think she's going to die. It's going to happen again." She skipped another stone, turned her face into the wind.

"Who? Peachy's going to die?"

"Dolores Otts."

Jem thought a moment, trying to remember. She recalled a pale blonde girl, swollen with pregnancy, standing at the windows of the Otts's house, waving to the bus she should have been riding. "I didn't know she was one of your patients."

Melvina sat opposite Jem and pressed her knees against her sister's. "She just can't die. She's got her whole life ahead of her yet. I won't let her, not this one."

Chapter 22

THE CALL CAME to Jem's phone. "Hello, this is the Atlantic City Police calling for Ma-TOO-sim Ramoud."

She rerouted it and minutes later, Matussem was in her office. He saluted Portia, whose back was turned, then hurried to Jem's corner. "Fifty thousand mainte-nance men all working on change one light bulb. So okay, I try to get half to work on another bulb. That my job. 'Manage,' they tells me, I'm suppose to manage. *¡Ay caramba!*" Matussem ran his fingers through his hair till it was ragged. "Your family," he said, "let me tell you—first they warm them up in hell, then they come here on vacation. How you like that?"

Jem was separating all inpatient bills into piles accord-ing to insurance carrier, a job she'd once heard her super-visor describe as digging a big hole and then filling it up again. Tomorrow, when she'd finished with stapling, they'd ask her to divide the patients according to type of coverage. The next day they'd ask for it to be changed

184

back to carrier. And so on. No one would ever look at the filing. She put down the two piles she was holding and said, "Well. Do you want to tell me more?"

Matussem checked for Portia, then sat on a typing table "Saiid and Kier—do these name mean anythings to you?"

"Besides that we're supposed to go out with them next Saturday? Oh no, what? Say it quick, please."

Matussem nodded. "Okay, no pussy-footy, in a few little words: your cousins are in the slammer up the creek."

"Use a few more words."

"Like this. Okay, your cousins are wild men, what can they say? They want to come to America to get a little bananas. Your Uncle Fouad, as you figured out, gets a little fruitcakes, too, sometimes and he mails them money to come. Only he mails enough so they go buy a Lincoln Continental, too. Your Uncle Fouad thinks because dollars don't look like dinars they're not as serious. Okay, here they are already last week, in America, in a black Lincoln Continental, and in Atlantic City—"

"Wait—" Jem started to say, then changed her mind. "Keep going."

"Right. So they are, you can say, living in their Lincoln Continental."

"Really?"

"Well, yes. They're eating and sleeping there. And doing a lot of hanging around. Also, they have a pet—"

"A *pet?*"

"A baby dog who lives in back and messes, but they're a little crazy so they don't notice."

"Ugh."

"So what happen is they bet everything in casinos; they lose everything without question. They bets the money; boom, boom, boom, they lose the money; they bets the car; boom, boom, boom, they lose the car. Who know what happens to poor dog. Next thing Saiid and Kier are half-naked on the boardwalk, talking crazy, drugs, who knows what, and the police goes get them, then goes looking in the phone books, saying, let's see, who the biggest horse's ass in world, oh yes, it must be Matussem Ramoud. Now because Fouad is God-know-where what place, I have to go get them and bring them back alive, dead, whatever. How you likes that?"

"Aw, Dad, don't do it."

"It's family troubles, no choice. Fifty thousand nephews in the world and I have to got Heckle and Jeckle. What for? I'm ask you." Matussem eyed Portia as she slowly began to turn, her face like a prow. "I got to go. Don't tell Melvina."

ROUTE 81 WAS dark as a coal chute cutting through the upstate river valleys. The landscape reminded Matussem of a picture he'd seen in a magazine: mountains at the tip of the horizon, dyed blue with distance. Before them, foothills, desert brown, matted like buffalo hide with scrub and thick sage; rose-and-purple banded hills; wheat, gold and ragged—America.

Matussem was wondering if Fouad was right, if it really was just stubbornness, remaining in Euclid. Was he turning away from his origins, away from knowing? He had once overheard his eldest sister, Rima, say that their mother had borne fourteen children. Why, then, did he know only eight? If he looked too closely at it, fear would stretch open inside him like a black hole, a space where all the unaccounted-for children went. He was afraid of being swallowed up too, like his relatives, back into that history. Everything depended upon the new country, on looking ahead at every moment. Going forward meant that he was still alive; he pushed against jazz; drumming was living.

Still, Fouad's voice would slip through his mind: Was it right? Was it natural for his daughters to go on living with him, unmarried? When both his parents and in-laws had died over a decade ago, it had been a release, he thought. But their ghosts returned to accuse him, bedeviling him with fears for the girls and their happiness. He would never throw them away into unwanted marriage. But what was right for them? How could he ever know?

As a boy growing up in a house full of sisters and their friends, aunts, and female cousins, Matussem had never known there were any other sorts of women in the world. He knew, watching and overhearing his sisters at night, that it was a bitter thing to be a woman. His mother had cradled his head between her breasts, even when he became gangly, arms and legs spilling from her lap. She had stroked his head, called him *my eyes*, even as she had lifted her voice, a shard of anger at his sisters, saying, "Move faster! Awkward, donkey, beanstalk! Lower your face, rude girl!"

When Matussem looked into his mother's eyes, he felt that he was tumbling down a well. He saw murky waters turning and clouding, and he did not understand. He didn't think then that he would be able to bear looking into a woman's eyes again.

Then he met Nora. She taught him how to speak a new language, how to handle his new country. His American lover. Through the year of their courtship she took his hands and fed him words like bread from her lips. Together, they sleepwalked into the region of love. Testing language in their bed, they roamed a new earth, black as pitch. She drew him away like Eurydice, into the world inside herself, into the world under the old one. She took him into a new creation, the corners of the map, her fingers on his skin.

As MATUSSEM DROVE, he thought about the first time he had met his wife. He had been only twenty at the time, at his first job in America, pushing a straw broom in a place called The Moral Pharmacy— Where Drugs Are Not for Fun! was painted on the sign out front. He knew how to say "homburger," "coke cola," and "not now, Moorvain" (his boss's name was Marvin). Thirty years later, Matussem wondered if Marvin had engineered the meeting. His mother and sisters had been the only females he'd ever spoken to directly, and he was so timid around women that if they asked him for the time he would flee the room. Luckily, his wife-to-be had entered the store in one of what Matussem called her "disguises." These were moods or gestures that might, briefly, shadow her loveliness. To him, she was a lightning rod to beauty, attracting it so the sun shone more brightly on her face, the wind filled her

hair more deeply. She could lower her face, douse her
expression, and the beauty would dim—like that! Two
fingers pinched to a flame. *Disguise,* Matussem thought.

He saw her seated by the door, alone in a booth, and
after her order was taken he asked the waiter, a Greek
friend, if he would let Matussem bring the meal to her
table.

Matussem brought her a tray with hamburger, milk-
shake, and fries, and when she saw him—or so he
said—she lifted her face and it was there, like striking a
match, the flaring of beauty. "Thank you," she said.

Matussem, in true Ramoud fashion, fell to his knees
on the checkered drugstore floor and asked through his
tears, "You me marry?"

THERE WAS A gray clearing in Matussem's
thoughts where the memory of his wife's death suddenly
changed colors, moving from accident to suicide. There
were times when he saw her fleeing his family and
friends at their parties; she would serve them without
speaking, vanishing into the kitchen or bathroom or
bedroom, curling into herself like a jinni disappears into
air, telling him when he came for her, it was too much,
the food and the music and the language rushing into
the walls of her head. She would unroll from the bed
into his arms, her face in tears. Or, lithe and dancing
when they were alone, Nora laughed like a bell; she
would pull the hair back from her face with a single
finger, like a child.

After her death, the mornings opened in Matussem's
bed like gray blossoms, like sharp-winged birds slicing

dawn in two. Something always reminded him of his loss: seeing the back of his wife's head in a crowd, the flicker of her pale eyes in Jem's dark ones, or Melvina catching her finger to the nape of her neck like her mother.

MELVIE TURNED TO Jem and Jem sat back. Melvie had come straight from work, wanting a drink. Jem could still smell the floor on her—patients' rooms, disinfectant, and Betadine; there was also the air of exertion, a kind of sadness and fatigue that Jem rarely saw in her sister. She hadn't said much all evening; she seemed angry, stabbing at her drink. Jem saw something starting in the top of her sister's eyes and felt a twist of premonition. Zombies made Melvie dangerous, and this was her second. Melvie leaned across the table. "I just want to know one thing, Jemorah," she said. "I just want to know if she did it deliberately like Fatima says. I need to know if she wanted to die."

Jem knew the question well; it had moved, in various guises, between the two sisters for most of their lives; anything at all could set it off. There was no answer, only a way of pushing it back into the current between them to submerge and surface among the years. But this time Melvina's eyes were fixed on her.

"I don't even have to know *why*, okay? One step at a time. I just want to know if she *did*. On purpose."

"Melvie—" Jem stopped. She was walking into the current; there was nowhere to stand. The Won Ton à Go-Go had gone still. "I . . . can't. I just don't know the answer to that. I wish I did, but I can't—"

"You can't, you can't, you can't!" Melvina shouted at her. Harriet said, "Uh oh," and Merv was smiling and nodding from across the room. "I'd like you to tell me what you *can!* You never tell me about her, you never talk about her. It's as if you're trying to punish me for something—"

"God, no, *Melvina*—"

"Don't you think I feel responsible, when I was right there in the room, *watching?*"

"For heaven's sakes. You were two!"

"It's as if she were your personal secret. Like you want to keep her all to yourself. Well, what about me, Jemorah, I'd like to know what about *me!*" Melvie banged both fists down hard.

J EM   T R I E D   T O think of a way to begin. She turned the tall glass in her hand then looked up at the bar, glimpses of eyes, hands, colored liquids, flecks of light moving with the randomness of memory. Melvie wanted reasons, a mending of this open question of the past; Jem had only fragments. She had never meant to withhold their mother, but she knew that she had lacked some courage.

"I remember a time," she began, "when there used to be a lot of pictures of starving children on TV."

"Date, please," Melvie said. "Location."

"I just don't—Biafra maybe? They had big, swollen bellies. I remember flies crawling over them, in their mouths and eyes."

"Bilharzia, cholera, yellow fever," Melvie commented.

"I asked Mom why the children looked so sad. Since they used to say in Catholic school that when you died you went to heaven. And these children were going to heaven soon."

"So what did you say?"

Jem shook her head. She couldn't have been more than six or seven at the time. Melvie was not yet born. It was a memory of a memory. She couldn't have known, as a child, how rare and essential those memories would become. Jem could scarcely recall anything of her mother's reaction, the pinprick of the story: her mother looking at her with a clear, gray-eyed gaze, as if the question was too hard to answer. Nothing more.

Jem shrugged, staring at her glass. "If she answered me, I honestly don't remember it. I don't want to make anything up about it—I don't want to do that," Jem said. "She just looked at me that way." *What is a look?* Jem thought. Didn't a mother look at her child thousands, millions of times during their life together? Could the looks be separated? Or was it one single gaze, one that suffered interruptions, but which stayed more or less the same, from the child's birth on into memory?

THEY WENT BACK to Melvie's office where, propped between *Medical Surgical Nursing* and *The Drug, the Nurse, the Patient*, she kept a family photo album. It was one she'd claimed for herself years ago, the one that dated from before their trip to Jordan. It was heavy, bound by a red, tasseled string, and the white-bordered photos were held by black glued-in corners. Now the glue was drying out and the corners were coming loose.

To Jem, it was a collection of half-thoughts, gestures, and messages from her mother's life. Her mother was smiling in every shot. There were wedding and baby pictures, school pictures, and shot after shot of festivals—their mother's favorite pastime—Moyers Corners Fourth of July, Erie Canal Days, New York State Fair, Hill Cumorah.

Jem didn't turn to the beginning—which contained mostly unnamed, ghostly babies, she and Melvina floating among them—but put her thumbs together and split the album open at its center.

At the top of the page there was a photograph of Matussem, Jem, and her mother, grandly pregnant, visiting the Onondaga Reservation Spring Festival.

"How young she is!" Melvie murmured. "A child. Now she reminds me of someone there. Who does she look like?"

"She looks like us," Jem said.

The images were amorphous, eerily indistinct. There was the small, dark round of Jem's face, wearing a toy headband with a feather; their mother lighter skinned, her precise features caught on the brink of a laugh; the high wall of her stomach vying for attention, assertive enough for Jem to know that only Melvie could be in there. Matussem's hair was plastered down with something like shoe wax, and he stood with one arm slung around the neck of a man who looked like a chief, his headdress full as sumac trees, their noses bent alike and skin matching.

"It's odd. People are always saying how much we look like our father," Melvie said. "Not like our mother."

"People see color first," Jem said.

Under the photograph were the words: Onondaga Indian Reservation, 4/68.

Jem remembered the Spring Festival: clay beads, ceremonial feathers, drums, dances, and tourists. Dancing men, women, and children, circling, stamping, arms and hair flying level; drums; chants; high sustained vowels; and the belly-deep summons to spring. The movement was the coil upon which the seasons and orbits rested. The dance brought back summering birds and the gentling of the northern winter. The dance offered hope to the frostbitten, soaked, and gloomy of upstate. Jem was drawn to the spiraling Iroquois dances and knew they were turning the earth around each year. The dried land where the Indians danced was an oasis, and the junked cars, the beer bottles, the pieces of trash moved out to the periphery of things; there was nothing but the plain, bare ground where they danced.

Jem could remember Matussem, with his arm around the man's shoulders, saying "This dude read me like a book." She also had some recollection that the man's name was Chief Dean Martin. But after several Spring Festivals, Autumn Harvests, and the sharing of Matussem's jazz tapes, Dean Martin changed his name to Chief Stormy Weather.

Melvina was staring at the handwriting in the album, so like her own—clean, broad strokes, open-mouthed vowels. There were dates, names, and places. Until the trip overseas. Then she shut the album. "Enough. I can't do any more right now."

"But what about—"

"I can't!" Melvina's voice rose. "The pictures are too

solid, they get in the way, they crowd out . . . what I have left of her. It's all I have left, all that's just mine. These tell me nothing about her or any of us."

AFTER THEY LEFT Melvie's office, Jem continued to think about the last photograph in the album: nearly all white, just the bare, gray outlines of a smiling bundled-up child in a pretty woman's arms. Snowflakes drift around them thick as maple leaves, flocking on the child's arms, veiling the woman's hair, both faces turned, inexplicably, up to the brilliant sky.

Chapter 23

I SAY! IT'S BEEN a long time since I've met two such complete and utter bullshit booby-heads!" Uncle Fouad shouted at his sons. Saiid and Kier sat propped against each other, looking too sick or miserable to sit up on their own. Saiid had no shirt and wore what looked like a pair of mutilated pajama bottoms; Kier was wearing only boxer shorts that said Sunny Buns across the back. The television was on and they stared at MTV. Fouad snorted at them, tossing his head and popping a designer shirt button. Then he tore the shirt off completely so all three Mawadi men were in various states of undress. Matussem, watching the spectacle with a mixture of repulsion and appreciation, backed into the couch across the room from them.

"But Pop, be cool, man," Kier said. "They, like, *took* our clothes!"

"Oh, God! Oh, my God!" Fouad shouted at the ceiling. "Can these be the real sons? Give them back, I say, I want the real sons back, not these blobs!"

Fatima prowled through the living room, peeking through the curtains at every window. She was certain that at any moment one of the Ladies' Pontifical Committee would take it into her head to drive the twenty miles out to Euclid, sneak into the Ramouds' bushes, and press her ear against the wall. Fatima went around whispering in a high, strained voice, "I dying! The humiliation! I dying of this!"

The more distressed Fatima became, the higher Fouad's voice climbed. He beat his chest and called upon God several times, mingling Arabic and English. Then he switched to Matussem. "Matussem, forgive, please, I beg! I beg!" Fouad shouted at his brother-in-law who was trying to disappear into a corner of the couch, wishing they would all leave so he could watch the TV. "I throw myself under you," Fouad cried, getting down on his knees. "That I has such infidels as this boobies in your house!"

Fatima ran over and began plucking at Fouad's sleeve. "Don't do this to me. They'll see! They'll all see!" she whisper-screamed. "I'm going mad. I'm going for certain to the crazy house."

"Hey, Pop, we're not infidels, man," Kier said. "You're blocking the TV."

"How would you like if I knocks your heads together?" Fouad said to his sons, trying to stand up. "Maybe that would put you some brains."

"Oh, yuh, I really think so," Saiid said.

W H E N   J E M   A N D   Melvina drove home that day, Fatima was standing at the door, wringing her hands.

Her eyes looked shriveled, as if she'd spent the day staring down Morgan Road—all the way through the dwindling reaches of Euclid into the village of Liverpool and on into Syracuse. Fatima's black hair was piled up in an obelisk over her head, and she had on the red embroidered caftan that she never wore unless she thought it would impress some American. It furled around her in a red plume.

"My babies!" she cried in a tiny grandmother's voice. "My babies are getting married!"

"Dream on," Melvina snapped, trying to push past her, but Fatima stood her ground, glaring at her niece. Melvie sighed. "All right. What's your problem, Aunt Fatima?"

Fatima took one of Jem's hands and one of Melvina's—which Melvina snatched back—and gazed at them. Her olive face flickered like a pale flame and those long-suffering eyes were ghostly. "My babies, I'm here to tell you the happy day has arrived! Your husbands, they have come for you early. They were so full with all these love and yearnings they could not wait until next week!"

Jem pulled her hand out of Fatima's. "Oh no," she said. "Big news."

Melvina put her knuckles on her hips and stood with her feet braced apart. "What husbands? What? What is this? I'm busy, Aunt Fatima; some of us live in the real world."

Fatima stamped her foot and a sound went up behind her. For a moment the sky behind the house darkened with birds, their wings knocking against the quiet, their calls scrambling as they rose. Fatima was startled, and

Melvina took advantage of the distraction, rushing the door like a halfback, Jem close behind her.

"No!" Fatima cried, clutching at them. "They're not ready. Not before your wedding!"

Saiid and Kier had been spying on them from the front hall and Melvie nearly ran into them.

"Whoa-ho!" Saiid said. "I must be in heaven, man. You are our cousins, man? This is completely, like, my mind is psyching out. I take this one, dude." He pointed at Jem.

"Kowabunga!" Kier started dancing around, hopping on one then the other foot in a kind of victory dance. Then he came eye to eye with Melvina and stopped. "Wait a sec, man," Kier said.

Fouad and Fatima converged on them, each closing in from different angles, and Jem saw that she was trapped. She tried to back up and looked at her sister. Fatima was crying at them, "Not yet! Not yet!" Fouad was saying, "So what do you think of the miserable, suffering sons of bitches?"

Saiid, the one who'd claimed Jem, was eyeing her up and down. She took in nervous glimpses of him: torn pajama bottoms, a stomach that drooped sideways over the waistband, hair that stood out from his head like black plaster of Paris—there seemed to be leaves, feathers, even small twigs stuck in it.

"I'd say," Melvie said, "that we got *rooked*. Shamelessly! Your own nieces, Uncle Fouad! This was supposed to be a *date*, not Robinson Crusoe night."

"Robin what, man? What's that?" Kier asked anxiously.

Jem saw Fouad drop his eyes, and suddenly she

realized that the bribe amount was ringing higher. Melvie was bargaining like Monty Hall.

"Ah, Melvina, you little heartpicker, you bamboozler, you should be the prime minister of England," Fouad said, meditatively sliding hands over stomach. He looked at Jem. "So Melvie says to me over my oatmeals that you can be the savior of this crying-out-loud family? You want go to these graduate school?"

"Now you're talking. Let's do business," Melvina said.

Chapter 24

THAT MID-JUNE NIGHT the house was
quiet. Gilbert and Uncle Fouad were at the horse
races. Cousins Saiid and Kier had been banished by their
father to the High Chaparral Motel, ten miles outside
of Euclid. Matussem was playing drums at the Key West
Bar. Melvina was at work. Solitude softened the air
around Jem, the warm night moved, and she felt something in her chest opening. Jem went across the yard
and cut through the field where the trees had Posted No
Trespassing signs, toward the light of Lil' Lulu's
Garage.

She recognized his legs, stretched out in jeans and old
sneakers under a car. And she felt her pulse slow as she
approached and put her fingers on the cool skin of his
ankle.

Ricky sledded out from under the engine. He sat up,
turning metallic-blue eyes on her, and reached up with
one hand.

She moved back. "Why'd you lie to me?"

"What'd you say?"

"I met someone—" She stopped, her spine turning sharp as a fishbone, fingers curling. She said, "*Someone*, right! Your *father* is who it was. Why'd you let me believe he was dead, like the kids said, that he got blown up? He's lying over there in Johnson-Crowes Hospital, right in plain sight. Jupiter Ellis!"

Ricky stood and moved into the rings of light around the pumps. He looked emptied, eyes and lips stone yellow. "I thought maybe he'd done it by now," he murmured, then stamped on the bell so it squawked. "He *had* to have! After all this time. I thought—well, I don't know what I thought. I haven't seen him for years. I certainly didn't want *you* to know about it."

Jem stared at Ricky's face and remembered the man at the Bumble Bee, bagging groceries, carrying them to the car, skin like parchment, gray, sodden, the smell of old clothes and something like rotting fruit. She remembered him sliding the groceries into her car, twisting a smile at her, mouth collapsed like wet tissue, a pair of dentures peeking out of his shirt pocket, a blurry, green tattoo on his bicep.

"And Hilma Otts has been looking for him for all this time," Jem said. "I used to see him working right over at the Bumble Bee."

Ricky nodded as she leaned against the pump next to his, regular leaded. "Yeah, she's seen him all right," he said. "She just doesn't recognize him. Or she don't want to. The explosion didn't kill him, only burned off his shirt and hair, some big burns on his face and neck. They healed. None of that stuff, whatever Peachy and the rest of those kids said, was true. They just wanted to believe it, and I just wanted him to die. He used to drink till he stank and his body shook like he was crazy. He'd try whatever he could get his hands on after his money was gone. That day he'd been drinking Lysol and rubbing alcohol. Sometimes he tried to beat me to death, smash the face off my head. He used to hit me with a broken pipe wrench, see here?" Ricky pulled his shirt down and showed her a fat, white scar that snaked over his shoulder and around the base of his neck. "Damn near smashed my whole head off for me one time."

Jem's fingers uncurled inside her pocket as she stared at that white seam. "God, I was wrong," she said. "I'm stupid. I'm so stupid."

"Nah, nah, you weren't. No more than I am about things. I mean, what do you know about this stuff? I mean—well, I guess that's how I love you, not knowing, just the way you were up there riding that school bus, looking at this stuff but never falling into it like the rest of us. I mean, you were the first person who saw me. I mean . . . I mean when you looked at me, I could *feel* it." He moved close to her and put his fingers on the nape of her neck under her hair, and she shivered. They shut their eyes together. "Tell me you still see me," he said, his voice descending to a whisper.

He was slick with grease, his hands black; he held them out and gathered Jem into himself, her chin going over his shoulder, his arms pulling tight. "Okay," she heard him saying under his breath, "okay, okay, okay." His knotted body cut into her arms and ribs, and his voice, his single word was like a war cry and a sob.

"Okay, okay, okay."

Jem opened her mouth, not wanting to say or see

anything, nothing in their future, in the unanswerable questions, nothing in their past. Then there was only the pressure of his mouth against hers, starting her on a short, dark journey of forgetting.

She went with him to the bushy grass behind the garage where it was dark and hidden. She was dizzy, wanting Ricky, want flooding her. They took off their clothes and the grass cut them. Everything was sharp, Ricky's tongue and fingers, their kisses piercing, fine as powdered glass. Jem sagged under the weight of a kiss, falling with him, then pulling back.

"Wait, wait," she said. "We have to use something."

He reached into one of his jeans pockets on the ground and pulled out a small wallet. The money compartment was empty except for some crumpled petals and a single condom. He tore it open with one corner between his teeth and rolled it on himself clumsily, hands shaking. He lifted her and she pushed down onto him. He turned his eyes to her so she saw the way the blue fled inward, into the black woods of himself. Behind the garage, she heard a faint backdrop of *ding ding, ding ding*, the roll of car tires, coming and going.

The movement of their bodies together was a chant, a sacrifice of the distance between them. The feeling was honed and Jem pressed against him, to feel it all the more. "More," she said.

J E M S A T U P and felt the night cooling, the moon on her back. She stood and helped Ricky up. They dressed, Jem feeling the wet heat through her clothes, their bodies speckled with dirt and leaves. A breeze came, riffling grass and pushing Jem's hair into her eyes. Ricky stood beside her and, holding her, put his face into her neck.

They walked the fields, now amber with moonlight. The ground seemed to shift under their feet. Jem was quiet, her body finely charged. She also felt a stab of conscience. Melvina would not approve of Ricky, his mechanic's hands, the beer on his breath. Jem saw just ahead a flash of wing, blue-gray against the dark, ascending. "It doesn't matter," she said aloud, then laughed and sang, "I don't care, I don't care, I don't care."

They marched through the sparse woods; above the treetops Jem could see a raft of clouds blown back, a crescent of clear night and moon. Ricky seemed to Jem to blend with the trees at times, his eyes dark as fireflies. They both saw the movement at the same time, something rustling up the hill and across the Ramouds' lawn. Both Jem and Ricky stopped and stood looking through the trees; Jem felt her breath diminishing as she stood hand in hand with this silent man, staring into her own front yard.

There was the same movement again, swifter and broader than at first, a spot of white and then a voice singing. The singing emboldened them, and Jem and Ricky walked closer. From the edge of the trees, Jem could see across the yard; it looked blank and velvety, mysteriously empty. Then suddenly she realized Melvina was in the center, moving, floating, her toes grazing the ground, and pinned to her back were two hands, white and pointed as starfish. Then Melvie turned, and

Jem saw Larry Fasco was twirling her and singing, somewhat off-key, "Waltzing, Melvina, waltzing, Melvina, will you come a-waltzing, Melvina, with me?"

Melvina's white dress flashed and floated over the lawn, and when the clouds hid the moon, the dress turned dark as fir trees, their blue-green shadows eaves of pinecones.

Melvie was laughing and saying, "Stop! Stop, Lawrence, or I'll call the police!"

"Call them, call them all if you like!" Larry shouted. "I won't dance with any but you!"

Melvina sank her head upon her partner's shoulder, and Jem sensed the evening being shored up and moved back by degrees.

Chapter 25

LARRY FASCO WAS entertaining Peachy Otts in the Ramouds' rec room the next morning.

"It was at this bar in Havana, see," he said. "Me and a few sidekicks and ol' Ernie Hemingway. You know ol' Ernie?"

"He bags groceries down at the Bumble Bee."

"Pathetic! What do they teach in reform school these days?" he said. "Anyway, I says to him, I says, 'Ernie, how can I become a great writer like yourself?' I ask him this after I buy him a few beers. He liked Genny Cream."

"Oh, really."

"From the mouth of God, I'm telling you, every word is true," Larry said, pointing at the ceiling. "So I lube him up with a few Gennies, ask my question, and you know what he does? Do you?"

"Hunh-uh."

"He says, 'Get lost, you lowly vermin.'"

"No way!" Peachy chuckled.

"He says, 'Take a long walk off a short cliff, you lowly vermin, scum of the sea, armpit of the earth.' That's how he talked. That's what he thought of me. That's how writers show they like you."

"Cool. Even if I don't believe you."

"Then me and my bud Jupe Ellis, we decided to go visit my ol' bud Willy Shakespeare who was writing stuff and hanging around, trying to get my opinion. You know Willy the Spear-man?"

"Hunh-uh."

"Lawrence Fasco, what are you doing in my basement?" Melvina said. She was standing in the doorway.

"Aha, here's my buttercup," Larry said. Peachy stared at him and said, "Melvina?"

"That's right." Larry stood and did a little shimmy in Melvie's direction. "She's the devil-woman and I'm a devil-worshiper, yee haw!"

"You better not say that," Peachy said, chuckling. "She'll get you, man. She does that—I've seen her in action."

Melvina stood her ground before Larry's shimmy and crossed her arms over her chest. She eyed Peachy then turned back to Larry. "And where, pray tell, is Mr. Ramoud, the supposed owner of this house?" she said.

Larry dropped his outspread arms and walked back to the card table where he'd been sitting. "Well, hell, he's in the bathroom, as usual."

Melvina snapped her fingers at Peachy, and Peachy jumped up and followed her out.

Jem was upstairs in the living room, the school application form fanned out before her. It depressed her, having to look at the layers of such applications again: test scores, essays, grade reports. They covered the table. Melvie had Peachy sit between herself and Jem. Melvie folded her hands and said, "Now, Peachy Otts. How would *you* like to go to college?"

"No way," she said.

"Oh," Jem said. "I don't know about this."

"Why should I?" Peachy said. "College is where the brains go, like Jem. That's where all the suburbs kids go."

"Right," Melvie said. "That could be you, too."

Peachy was shaking her head again. "No way, you guys. What? Look, I'm stupid and teachers hate me. Dolores is the brain, send her. Ma always said me and Glady had can openers for brains. All I ever learned in school was stuff like how to make fart noises on my arm. Perry Hardcaster showed me when I was flunking out of fifth." She started to lift the crook of her arm halfway to her mouth, but Melvie lowered it with the tip of her finger. "I never made it out of high school, and I never want to!" Peachy said.

"Peachy, look," Jem said, and picked up a page of the application. She pointed to a question that asked about Peachy's educational objectives. "Just hypothetically. Could you think up *something* to say for a question like this?"

Peachy stared at a point somewhere between the page and Jem's finger. Her eyes were motionless, and her face tightened. Finally she looked up at the two women and chanted, "Mary had a little lamb, its fleece was white as snow—"

"Peachy . . ." Melvina sighed.

Peachy grabbed the page, crumpled it up, and threw it down on the table. It bounced off onto the floor.

"Young lady!" Melvina went after the paper, but Jem was looking at Peachy. She turned to the first page of the application and pointed to the blank that read: Name, last, first, middle initial. "Can you read this?" she asked.

This time Peachy didn't look at the page at all, but stared Jem in the face. She didn't blink. Jem looked away. She thought about middle school, Peachy in sixth and Jem in eighth, on the bus where Peachy would stare off while she pricked herself with safety pins and let little points of blood come to the tops of her thighs. Staring and humming. She had a smell, at times almost unbearably sour, like dill pickles. Once Peachy told Jem she was pricking the letters of a girl's name at school into her leg, so the blood would spell out Janet. Only when she was done she hadn't spelled out the girl's name at all. Instead, little *x*'s and *o*'s and snaking lines of blood twisted over the surface of the leg, a collection of hieroglyphics.

Jem heard Melvina murmuring: "That says *name*. Peachy, can you write your name?"

With great deliberation, Peachy put her fingers to the page and drew a line of crosses and spirals across the application.

"Peachy Otts," she said, then grinned and stood, moving toward the back door. "You're lucky," she said. "I don't write that for just anybody." Then she ran out the door.

Melvina lifted her eyebrows at Jem. "Well."

"It's a start," Jem said.

▴ ▪ ▴

T H AT E V E N I N G , W H E N Jem and Melvina went
outside, the trees were yellow in the lowering sun; the
tall grass, bright splinters; the woods, deep and fragrant.
The fields were littered with white and purple clover.

"Jemorah, I'll explain the world to you someday,"
Melvie said, opening the car door. "It's all starting to
come to me. The trick is you can't rush it."

Jem leaned against the house, inhaling deeply, seeing
the spans of telephone wire threading pole to pole, past
wildflowers and hills, moving back past half-burned
silos and the wreckage of barns, the sky awash in evening colors.

"And you're not getting away that easily, Ms. P.
Otts," Melvina said to the highway.

Chapter 26

*A*T 4:45, J U L Y fourth, Saturday morning, the phone beside Jem's bed rang and she caught it in trembling fingers, startled awake. A woman was screaming something on the other end, as if Jem had picked up the extension on someone's fight. It was Arabic screaming, and Jem recognized the hydraulic hiss of the overseas cable.

"What have they done with my husband?" the woman screamed. "Where *is* he? Why won't he come home? He's dead, he's dead, oh, God, I know he's dead!"

There was a squeak, and another voice, internationally cool, modulated as a flight attendant's, came on speaking in English, "Hello darlings. To whom am I speaking?"

"Uh, Jemorah Ramoud," Jem said.

"Jemmy! How sweet! This is your Auntie Salandria." Jem had a flash of recognition. She hadn't seen this aunt since she was nine years old. "Remember Auntie Sally?"

Fatima had recounted Sally's story—one of her favorite fairy tales—over and over to Jem and Melvina
when they were younger. Born in Howkville, New
York, Sally met Jem's cousin Raife forty years ago at
a roadside stand where she hosed dirt off pumpkins
and turned them bruised-side down. Raife had picked
his way through the mud and fertilizer in Italian loafers
just to talk to lemon-haired Sally. He lifted one
of the squashes from the stand and found it gritty
and satisfying. She showed him how children would
carve faces into it, and there, holding a pumpkin that
looked to Raife like a setting sun, he asked her to
marry him.

It was this way with the Ramoud men—proposing
quickly, repenting at leisure. It didn't matter to Sally
that she was the fourteenth girl Raife had proposed to
during his two-week vacation in America. She agreed
to fly away with him, on a magic carpet if he liked.
Then she called her mother on the county phone, ten
feet up the telephone pole, and gave her the happy news,
as well as the information that sister Em was allowed
to wear Sally's clothes until further notice. Sally's
mother had what the family referred to as a "heart-attack
scare," while Raife and her daughter drove to Bill Hole,
the closest town with a justice of the peace.

In forty years Sally had returned to America only
twice, both times for fashion shows. Sally of Howkville
dwindled and faded, while Salandria of Amman
emerged, painted in Mediterranean Technicolor, eyes
ringed with makeup, limbs heavy with jewelry, voice
heavy with hauteur, a cosmopolitan twinge, although
she hadn't quite finished tenth grade that fateful year of

flight. She re-created herself in a place where she had no high-school history, where Howkville was a mystery, a place in *New York*. She went on to self-publish a book of her own poetry, dipping into Raife's big pile of money to produce *Woman Entire, Moi*.

"Jemorah, *habeebi*," she said, lilting. "How old are you now, darling? Why, you must practically be in junior high. Are you going out for junior varsity cheerleaders?"

"Well—actually, I graduated from college seven years ago."

In the background the other woman was still screaming in Arabic, "What have they done to him? Fouad! Name of God the merciful! Fouad! I know it's another woman, they've got him with some prostitute!"

"Really. Out of college? But that's silly, no, no, that's impossible, dear," cooed Aunt Sally. "Don't be giddy, darling. I'm barely out of college myself. Perhaps you are older than I thought, I'm becoming so—oh, how do they say? Oh yes, *absent*, yes, that's it, *absentminded*. Dear me, I'm even losing my *Engleesee*. I'm afraid I've turned quite *Arabee*, you know."

Sally's voice broke off and there was a sound like a wrestling match and for a second the other woman's voice screaming *"Murderers!"*

Then Sally was back, voice still modulated. "Jemorah, darling, not to trouble, but does your dear uncle Fouad happen to be any place convenient?"

"Uh—Uncle Fouad—uh . . ."

Fouad had been going out with Gilbert Sesame later and later every night. During the past week or so he

hadn't reappeared till dawn, sometimes not even till
lunchtime. Jem was about to offer to go check on Fouad
or to make some other meaningless suggestion when
Melvie walked in. Even though she had weekends off,
Melvie liked to go in to the hospital every day for at
least an hour or two, just to check up on things. She
had been in the midst of putting on her uniform, a ritual
she performed in early darkness with the ceremony of
a nun. On rare night-mornings when Jem was awake,
she would watch Melvina fitting her cap, her hands and
clothing bluish in the lamplight, her face intent. Melvina
did not like to be interrupted. She entered Jem's room
clutching her cap in one hand, the uniform half-zipped
up her back.

"What is this ruckus?" she said. "This mumbling is
quite distracting."

Jem shrugged and handed the receiver over, then laid
back among her blankets and listened.

"Yes. Yes. No. No. Uncle Fouad, I'm sorry to say,
is undoubtedly out at this moment, engaging in who-
knows-what sorts of immoral, unsavory, and unclean
practices. He has taken to consorting with local criminals
and shady characters, and there's really no telling what
he'll do from one moment to the next. It's my professional opinion as an R.N. and head nurse—what?
No—I'm twenty-two. No, I'm younger than Jem. No,
by seven years, two and one-third months. What is that
noise? That's a dishwasher? To continue, it's my professional opinion that Uncle Fouad may be suffering from
a form of mild schizophrenia and possibly one or more
forms of venereal disease. I'd recommend immediate

professional attention—in the more beneficent air of his own country."

Somewhere between "shady characters" and "professional attention" Jem slid into sleep, into dreams colored by medical terms that grew round and bright as balloons and carried her away.

Chapter 27

ATIMA CAME OVER that morning at nine with a towering bag of used dresses in her car. Going to her bedroom window, Jem watched Fatima hurrying toward the front door. Then Jem saw Melvie run out from the other side of the house and try to stuff Fatima and the dresses all back into the car. Fatima began wailing, "Jemorah! Jemorah! Oh, God, help! Help me, help me!" Uncle Fouad staggered to the top of the basement steps, covering himself with a single facecloth like a pot-bellied goblin. He said, "*Ya'Allah,* what the fuck is that?"

Jem walked outside where Melvie and Fatima were wrestling over the bag of dresses. When Fatima spotted Jem, she began screaming, "Jem! Come, hurry! She make you dress like her. You be going on your date like a white nun and they won't talk to you and you'll miss your last chances to get a man, forever—ever!" The last word of this speech broke into a loud, sustained wail, and the bag tore, dumping its dresses, a gauzy pile of spangles and satins, red as lipstick.

Melvina bent down and lifted a dress between two fingers as if it were a specimen. The dress quivered, covered in sequins, almost alive. "We are going on a *date,* Aunt Fatima," she said. "Not trying out for a Vegas chorus line."

"You see? You see?" Fatima whirled upon Jem bitterly. "This her plan. To keeps you old-maid-nun-nurse like herself. All white, fat ankles, fat shoes—"

"Leave them alone, *ya* Fatima." All three women turned to see Fouad standing on the patio, genitals cupped in a facecloth.

"Clothes, Fouad, clothes!" Fatima cried.

"Clothes? Yes, clothes I have, O sister of wife"— Fouad indicated the facecloth—"I hold in front when coming, in back when going." He demonstrated, achieving a modicum of coverage for the retreating half-moons. He turned back. "But you, why you are always buzzing and buzzing, Fatima? You put me thinking of mosquito up my arse. You bug me with this problems of yours."

"Oh, God the merciful, God to me on earth!" Fatima moaned, rolling her eyes. "What are the neighbors saying? They saying, 'The Ramoud speak with naked mens in street!'"

"*Ya'an deeneck,* you drives me to drinks, Fatima," Fouad said. He walked over to them, picked up a red cocktail dress from the broken bag and draped it across his loins and backside, knotting it at the hip. "There. Nice, fine. I have, truthfully, back home, twenty, thirty nice as these."

"*Aie!*" Fatima clutched at her chest. "The party dress is wreck!" She dashed back into her car.

"Bye-bye! Bye-bye!" Fouad waved at the car as the girls turned back to the house. "That woman," he said. "She an attack of runs."

T H E   P L A N   W A S that while the girls and their cousins went out, Uncle Fouad would take Matussem to Moyers Corners Fourth of July Firemen's Field Days.

"Your dad, he is too much of a party-poop. All the time with his drums. Always creeping like mole. I fix him up, just wait. We're going to get crazy-insane, him and me," Fouad promised.

Melvina looked at her uncle narrowly as she plucked hot curlers from Jem's head. "Ow, ow!" Jem said. Melvina was oblivious. "Uncle Fouad, I will not tolerate any violence or mayhem," she said. "Frankly, I think you and my father might have a more constructive evening if you were to stay home and have an encounter session or a game of chess."

"Melvina, you gas, trust me! Or, wait a sec—why don't you forgets my miserable sons and marry your wonderful Uncle Fouad?"

"I have no time for levity, Uncle Fouad," Melvie said, combing and yanking on a lock of Jem's hair as her older sister writhed. "My sister is a complete ruin and a bundle of nerves. Look at her! Not to mention—and I hope this doesn't bear repeating—our contract stipulates four years of graduate school for Jem in exchange for a *date* with Saiid and Kier. Certainly not marriage to you, otherwise known as polygamy."

Fouad raised one finger and said, "Ah, but in the Law of Mohammed—"

Melvie tore at a snarl in Jem's hair so Jem squeaked. "Too bad," Melvie said. "This is the Law of Melvina."

Just how terrible, Jem thought, grabbing her hair, *would this marriage business get?*

THE LAW OF Melvina also stated: Be dressed, ready, and waiting outside the front door on the lawn at least fifteen minutes before the date. Even better, arrange to meet *at* the restaurant, so that you can take separate cars. Which is what happened when Saiid and Kier phoned a half hour late from the High Chaparral Motel to say they were having trouble picking out what to wear.

"Okay, let's go," Melvie said. She walked out of the house, jingling the car keys, over to where Jem unhappily sat on the lawn in sausage curls and Melvie's white pinafore. "Jemorah! Grass stains!"

Sulking, Jem got into the car on the passenger's side and Melvie said, "Can't you *pretend* to be more animated than that? You're semicomatose."

As they were pulling out, there was a slight movement in one of the bushes. "Now what?" Melvie said. "I don't believe it, there's a Peeping Tom in the hedge." She stopped and jumped out of the car. Jem felt some presentiment and hurried after her sister, her heart quickening. "Melvie! Melvie, wait!"

Melvie was marching toward the bushes like Patton. She'd handled people who were crazed with drugs, had even managed to disarm people who came bearing knives and guns into the Emergency Room. Her shoulders were squared; she was afraid of nothing. "You there!" she shouted. "Drop your weapons and come out with your hands up!"

The bushes moved again, then parted. The intruder stood as the wind lifted the long ends of his hair up and off his face, and Jem said, "Oh, Ricky."

Melvie dropped her shoulders, hands on her hips. "Ricky?" she said. "*Ricky Ellis?*"

He stepped out of the bushes, brushing dirt from his jeans. "I was coming to visit," he told Jem, apologetic. "I saw you out on the lawn, but then when I saw your sister walking out of the house—I don't know—something came over me. My first thought was to hide."

"Oh, it's all right," Jem said smiling, making a near-curtsy in the white dress. "Lots of people feel that way."

"I take it you two know each other," Melvie said, narrowing her eyes and looking back and forth from Jem to Ricky. "That is, if you really *are* who you seem to be."

"Melvie, don't you *remember?*" Jem said. "Ricky went to our school. He lives down the street. He works at Lil' Lulu's."

"It's possible," Melvie said, focusing on him, her stare like a scalpel; he shifted. "Of course, anything's possible around here—no one tells *me* anything. As a matter of fact, I thought I heard you were in jail, Mr. So-called-Ellis," she said.

"Oh no, that's my cousin Rusty. Or maybe my big brothers Teeny and Scott? Although Teeny's only my half-brother." He looked past her at Jem. "Hey, you look nice," he said. "Your hair"—he raised one hand toward his own hair.

"Oh." She touched one starched curl, laughed and blushed. "It's terrible."

"Are you going somewhere?"

"Oh," she said and looked at Melvie.

"Well, as a matter of fact, if it's any of your business, *yes,*" Melvie said and started marching back to the car. "In *theory,* yes. If we can ever get this show on the road. Since it's ostensibly not necessary to call the police, then I suppose I'll just go wait in the car by myself."

Jem was watching him, trying to read the way his hands slid into his pockets, the way his eyes turned away from her, along the ground. *What do I mean to you,* she wondered. What if he answered her? What if, like Uncle Raife, he were to take her hand and say: Marry me now, once and for all. Who was he to her? Bad teeth, dirty hair, penniless. Still, somehow, as he stared at her hands she knew she wanted him.

"I'm going on, um, a kind of—date," she said.

"Oh," he said.

"It's not real. The date. I mean, well. See, we're doing it for money."

"Oh," he said, his expression flattening.

"No, *wait!*" she said. "I'm not getting this right. I mean this doesn't actually mean anything. It's just dinner, me and Melvie, with our cousins. They're new in this country—it's like a favor to my uncle."

"Right," he said.

As soon as they left the driveway, Melvina heaved a heartrending sigh.

Jem turned to her. "What?"

Melvina shook her head. She said, "Going from Saiid Mawadi to Ricky Ellis—I'd say that was jumping from frying pan to fire, all right."

Jem thought about that for a moment. "Well, I'd rather burn than fry, I guess," she said, then laughed.

Melvie cocked an eyebrow at Jem. "Ah, liberal arts talk. I believe that's a metaphor. You're talking about death, or maybe sex; standard human functions decorated with words. I have nothing against sex. Even if it is a waste of valuable time and energy. I'm not quite so unsophisticated as you think, Ms. Bachelor's Degree." Melvie called Jem Ms. Bachelor's Degree whenever she was piqued. To Melvie, it was one of the most withering things a holder of an R.N. could say to an N.N. ("non-nurse").

"As a matter of fact," Melvie went on, "I am well aware of the excellent secondary and tertiary by-products of sexuality. But the act itself is problematic, to say the least, rationalized by all sorts of nonsense and neurotic behavior. Well, I've tried out sex in its purely recreational format and I find I don't have much use for it. Perhaps I'll try it again someday, preferably not for at least another ten years or so. I've got too many other concerns to attend to right now."

Jem slid a glance at Melvina—she wasn't sure if she was more surprised by Melvie's swearing off sex or by her having had any at all. Then the thought of her own secret lover pulsed once through her. After years of her cool, flat childhood bed, she felt entangled in the memory of gravel and weeds in a single warm twilight, the musk of gasoline, the lip of a kiss as he pushed into her, after so many years of not having a lover, like a bite, bright almost-pain. Jem tried to think of Melvie letting go, reduced to taste and touch. Perhaps it had been with a patient, a semiprivate room, a blue seam of light under the door, after visiting hours, Melvina climbing into the already warmed sheets.

JEM AND MELVIE took a table up front when they got to the restaurant. Jem ordered a coral okoboji and Melvie ordered club soda. "I have to be on the alert," she said.

The two sisters passed about half an hour twirling the straws in their drinks, discussing work, avoiding any suggestion of marriage or boyfriends. After about twenty minutes had passed, Melvie said, "You see? Now this isn't so bad, is it? And you were so worried."

For a moment Jem thought, *she's right,* then she remembered that Kier and Saiid hadn't actually arrived yet.

Melvie decided they might as well go ahead and order. Fouad had given them three hundred dollars "spending money," in case Saiid and Kier forgot to bring—or had somehow whittled down—the money he'd also given them for the date. They were feeling expansive and ordered lobster thermidor. Some friends from the hospital stopped by and chatted for a while. They had baked Alaska for dessert. Then after-dinner liqueurs with more friends.

Melvie clinked her glass with Jem's and said, "Here's to blind dates."

"I guess so, huh?" Jem said enthusiastically.

Then Kier and Saiid appeared, each of them escorting

a young woman. "Hey, cousin-babes, we made it! Did you think we dried up and blew away, man?" Saiid asked.

"I'm not interested," Melvina said. "You're two hours and twenty-eight minutes late."

"Well, hey, what are you expecting?" Saiid said. "We look in the closet, none of our clothes is cool tonight for having wild times, and then we went to buy more."

The women with Kier and Saiid wore tall, lacquered hairdos, combed out from their heads and painted with gold stripes. Jem noted their matching lipstick and nail polish and spidery coats of mascara: they could have passed as Fatima's nieces, the ones she was meant to have.

Kier said, "This guys are Jen and Heather from the mall. They was selling us our new clothes for tonight, man, and we just said, like, hey, why don't you guys come out with us, too!"

Melvina was giving Kier a look as clear and pure as ice. "You brought these women on our date? This will cost Fouad extra."

"It's cool, cousin-babies," Saiid said. "This is even more fun—four babes, two guys, see? Let's go dancing."

JEM WAS THINKING about the women in the other car, with their nails and lips flecked red as blood, their glittering hair. They seemed secure in some animal knowledge of how the world turned, how they were supposed to look and behave. Jem didn't want any part of this dancing business; she wouldn't know the steps, or where to put her hands or feet. But Melvie was driving to Cloud Ten anyway, her hands in a death grip on the steering wheel. "It's part of the deal, it's a *date,* we've got to have *fun* on the date."

In the parking lot, Jem watched the two salesgirls float from the car, dresses soft around their legs, hair crystalline under the lights. They giggled at everything.

At the door, Saiid asked Melvina to pay the cover charge. "I pay you on Tuesday," he said.

"Credit card companies charge twenty-one percent interest," Melvie said, cracking her purse open. "I'll charge you twenty. Compounded daily."

Jem watched the salesgirls string their fingers along the boys' arms, humming their voices in the boys' ears like steam. As soon as they got inside, Saiid led Jem and Melvina away from the others into a quieter section and took out a checkbook.

"Okay," he said, writing. "Here we goes."

Melvie put her hand up. "Wait a second," she said. "That's not necessary. The agreement is for Tuesday payment."

"Hey, hey!" he laughed. "Is not for that, is for *fun!* On our *date!*" He tore the check out of the book and handed it to her. It was made out for two thousand dollars.

Jem and Melvie looked at the check, then at Saiid.

"It's good, these check," he said. "They knows me here, these bartender dude, he cash for you easy. So you go have fun, me and Kier go have fun, is a good, fun-time date, okay? Okay."

Jem watched Saiid fade slowly, walking backward, his smiling face receding like an eclipse of the moon, until he was lost in the lighting and crowds. Melvie's face was set, eyes and mouth drawn into fierce lines. "We'll see about this."

She presented the check to the bartender, who took one look at it and burst out laughing. "This is from the Rubber Chicken Boys," he said. "Everything they touch bounces! I'll give you two bucks for it—I'd love to frame this over my cash register as an original piece of art."

Melvie reclaimed it, saying she'd need it for evidence. "Passing fraudulent checks," she said, slipping it into her purse. "The FBI will get my full cooperation."

Jem was ready to call it a night, but Melvie stood firm. They had to stay until midnight, she said, so that it would technically be considered a full evening. "We've come this far," she said, pointing to the neon clock above the bar, which read a little after ten. "It would be like walking halfway across the desert then walking back again."

"So what's so big on the other side of the desert?" Jem grumbled, but she let Melvie buy her a drink. The only open table overlooked the dance floor; from there they watched Kier and Saiid drinking and working through an endless variety of women. They started with the salesgirls, went on to two others, then two others, and so on. The dance floor pumped with music, people rising and drifting on tides of it, hair and clothes becoming kaleidoscopic, and Kier and Saiid turning at the center of it all.

The boys found their cousins again after an hour or so, during a break in the music. "Hey, dudes!" Kier shouted; Saiid appeared to be holding him up. They fell into seats simultaneously. "When did get you here? Where I knows you from?" Kier said.

Saiid breathed whiskey into Jem's face. "So is this a fun-o date or what about it?"

"Well, if it isn't the Rubber Chicken Boys," Melvina said, swirling her drink.

"How is this?" Kier said. "You—you look like someone," he said to Melvie, leaning back so far in his chair Jem doubted he could see her. "Holy baloney! Just like Mama!"

Saiid looked at Melvie. "No way. No no no no no way, man."

"Will you marry me?" Kier asked Melvie.

"Hey, I tells you what!" Saiid said. "He's so true. We needs wives, man, for this side; we already have for the Old Country."

"Have what?" Jem said.

"Wives, man! We got wives, babies, a black Trans Am, *everything* there is in Jordan!"

The sisters looked at each other. Melvie's eyes were sharp. "Does your father know about this?" Melvie asked.

"Oh, mans!" Saiid shouted and then for some minutes the two boys were laughing and saying "Oh, mans!" over and over again. When he finally regained control, Saiid told them, "He knows more about it than we do. He say, wives, wives, the more wives, the more like normal dudes we gets. We got to get ones for America. The ones in Jordan are all wore out, man. It's sad, they're dragging."

Melvie hoisted her purse up from the back of her chair and produced pen and paper. "All rightie," she said and directed herself to Kier whose mouth had gone slack and who seemed to have entered a trance while the music and lights boiled around him.

"You want to marry me?" she asked. Jem looked at Melvie, a dart of worry.

Kier nodded, his mouth an open slot, eyes hanging upon her face.

Melvie pushed the pen and paper at him. "There, write it *there!*" she said. "And sign it, bub."

Kier took up the pen, and Saiid, in slow motion, tried to intercept him. "No, wait, man," he said. "Wait, it's a trick—I never see it like this before, on *napkins,* man—"

Melvie only shrugged, eyes lowered, and Kier was not to be put off. With drunken single-mindedness, he brought pen to paper.

"Oh, mans," Saiid moaned. "Now you do it, now you put us in the bed you made."

Chapter 28

*T*HE BALL WAS suspended in air by two oppos-
ing arches of water. The Moyers Corners firemen
were playing Baldwinsville, each side trying to maneu-
ver a ball over the opposite side of the wire with their
hoses.

"This, my friend," Fouad said, indicating the game,
"is so sad and boring."

Matussem was transfixed, watching the ball upon its
ruffle of water, dancing on shafts that turned white
in the early evening sun. It was almost magic how the
ball seemed animated and free floating, and time and
again he wished the ball would float endlessly, that
neither arc would prevail. But again the ball faltered,
tripped over one side of the wire and plummeted,
streaming ribbons of water. Then Matussem turned
away to face his brother-in-law and felt, suddenly,
very tired. "What is it, Uncle Fouad? In the Old
Country you have bigger hoses than these, better balls,
what?"

"Old Country, schmold-country," Fouad said and clapped his hands together. "What kind feast is these? Where the drinks? Where the dancing girls are?"

Matussem was annoyed; they were just a few feet from the fairway, from snapping whirl-a-gigs, the dive of the roller coaster, the cascade of the Ferris wheel, all the joints and mechanized parts of delight, and just a few doors down, a booth for the Bearded Lady. "*This* is the fun, Uncle Fouad, *here,* can't you even tell? *Ya'Allah,* this is Moyers Corners on the *Fourth of July.* It practically a holy day here, every guru and saint in America is out today!"

Fouad watched a tremendously fat man in overalls eating french fries walk by. "Okeydokey, which one is Mister Tubby there?" he said. "Saint or Imam?"

Now Matussem was angry. "Mr. Tubby!" he said. "*Mr. Tubby* know secrets *of universe.*"

Matussem's vexation didn't last; it was chased away in the thunder of metal rides, the small children rampaging everywhere, the clicks of the Wheel of Fortune. Even Fouad couldn't help surrendering to the charms of the mob and the greasy air. For the better part of an hour, Fouad fixated on trying to drop a clothespin into a milk bottle. After about eighty dollars worth of chances he won a small, blue toy poodle. Matussem watched him evaluating the prize, turning it over and over, holding it up to the light and sniffing it.

"Will you give that to Rima?" Matussem asked.

"My wife? Good heavens, no. Why I am wanting to do that? This my dog. Let her win her own gaddamn dog."

Several containers of steamed clams and innumerable

beers later, Fouad said to Matussem, "You know what your problem is, O younger brother of my wife?"

Matussem watched Fouad douse another clam in hot butter. Matussem had stopped several clams back, but Fouad seemed to have limitless capacity, his designer shirt streaked and printed with thick fingers of butter. Matussem was fooling around with his plastic forks, drumming on the table. He remembered that Melvie always referred to the Moyers Corners Firemen's Field Days as a "bloodbath and a bacchanalia of germs and acting up." In the carnival music, grinding calliope and loud rock, he heard the call of jazz again, its banner, over the too-loud, wild-eyed fest.

"Your *problem,*" Fouad continued, "is fun, yes, children, no. I am meaning, what is it now, Matussem, why you should be holding on these daughters when they should learning to be good girls back in Jordan? Maybe you think they are too grown-up for learning, but never for girls, especially when not married. These no place for them. I tell you what, I stay here, give one my return ticket and I buy another for other girl. They keep my wife company, give her someone new to scream at. Ha ha! I even tell you what—I give *you* a ticket to go, too. Time for your sisters to find you new wife. Now Goobert Abdel Sesame is even there to help. I send him last week to watch business and so my wife doesn't blow a gasket. It's time for you, Matussem, time to put family back where it belong." He pointed openly at a woman in a flannel shirt and a headful of pink curlers. "Degenerates! You are wanting your daughters to be around degenerates, I guess? These daughters without the saint-arms of a mother?"

Matussem scuffed at the gravel beneath his feet; above their heads the tent canvas billowed with wind. He ran one hand back through his hair so it stood up like exclamation points, then looked at Fouad's shrewd face, unreadable as a pork belly. It was almost impossible for Matussem to think fondly of his old home through the smudge of years, the sense of poverty, so many lonely sisters, the social restrictions that kept them home. The loneliness had welled up in his mother's stunned eyes. Did Fouad know something Matussem didn't know? He looked now, full of clams and Budweiser and sun, as if he'd been born at the beginning of time. He looked like a caveman, from his hunch over the salt potatoes to the territorial way his hairy hands curved around the clams, threading them with salt and butter and eating a containerful at a time.

Fouad was opening his mouth again either to make a big pronouncement or swallow a contingent of clams, the black hole sliding wide, teeth stumped as horse molars, when a woman sidled up to their table and picked up Fouad's poodle.

"A stuffed poodle—cute, cute," she said, turning it over.

Fouad snatched the poodle and clutched it to his chest, snapping, "Get back!"

The woman looked immobile as a mountain. Her breasts swelled at the edges of her tube top, gleaming like dolphin flesh. Her jeans were too small, left half-zipped at the fly. A leather jacket was slung over one shoulder, and a studded dog collar glinted at her neck. She ignored Fouad and leaned against the table, facing Matussem. "Ooh, honey-child, you're like chocolate

Cream o' Wheat, you're a gleam in my eye, I could suck you right up."

Matussem smiled down at his hands, staring at the way his fingers held the plastic fork. His face warmed with pleasure and confusion.

"I say! I say, Miss Big-Fats!" Fouad cried out behind the crescent of her wide shoulders and rippling waistline. "Go away! We are not a charity organization."

The mountain-woman creaked her head a quarter inch in Fouad's direction. "Shut your hole, you ol' gas-bag." She turned back toward Matussem, put her hands on her great hips, and said, "Are you related to Nurse Melvina Ramoud?"

Matussem sat up in alarm. He looked carefully at the woman before him: she looked strong enough to hoist the picnic table over her head. Her jeans were forced open by muscle and bone as wide as the Brooklyn Bridge; the muscles radiated out, suspended from her sternum. The hair that floated from her head changed colors, burnt and opalescent in the late light, and something resembling a bullwhip snaked through the loops of her jeans.

"What has she done?" he said in a failing voice.

"Now wait one bloody second—" Fouad said. He attempted to stand, but she put the flat of her palm on the top of his head and held him, for a moment, in mid-crouch. Then he slowly sank back to the bench.

"Well, shit, she ain't *done* nothing," she said to Matussem, and cracked a smile with a diamond like Fouad's embedded in her incisor. "Nothing but save the life of one of my best friends and biggest fans—a half-crazed, no-good, lecher rowdy, but well-meaning overall. Well hey!" She slapped Matussem a blow on his back that resounded through his body. Her smile, in that leathery face, was sweet and light as cream. She jammed herself onto the bench and muttered, "Scooch over, Slugbutt," to Fouad, who grunted, glaring down at his clams.

"I searched heaven and earth to find you, big boy," she said to Matussem. "Or, I should say, *your daughter.* I was thinking of telling her if she ever got sick of nursing she should come on my rig with me and see the country. I could use a partner like her—they just don't make 'em like that any more—"

"Rig? Rig?" Fouad grumbled. "What is rig?"

"Why, it's that little beauty right over there." She sat up and pointed. "Y'see that eighteen-wheeler on the front lawn of the Presbyterian church? That baby's mine and the First National Bank's. We see the world together, hauling whatnot from point A to point B. You want to go for a ride?" she asked Matussem.

"No way, José," Fouad said. "We busy mens, all the time getting busier. We got things to do like you don't wanta know about."

Matussem was looking at the truck. He liked the way it tucked itself so neatly onto that patch of lawn, half-turned like a creature with a crooked neck. The cab was painted with swirls of red that appeared to flame from the windows, a fiery jungle. The side of the cargo box bore the legend Prime Movers.

"Maybe yes, maybe no," Matussem said. He looked at her. "How did you find me?"

She shrugged and dipped her fingers into Fouad's container of clams. Fouad was turned away from them completely, drinking a can of beer in a sulk. "Hells bells, all

Euclid knows you, all twenty-two of 'em. They says, you go looking for Nurse Melvina Ramoud, you better report to Big Daddy Ramoud first."

"No way. Really?" Matussem said. "Probably they mean the other way around."

Fouad snorted.

"Oh no, no," she said. She held another butter-shiny clam above her lips and tilted back her head as if anointing herself, then caught it in her mouth. "Anyway, everybody says, go to the Field Days. Hell, it's the only show around. This thing has drained the population off six, seven upstate counties. Shit, the only person left in town is some little greaser-ghoul at the gas station. He sent me here and the guy at the clams booth showed me your table—"

"You see? This is done because of me," Fouad said. "They says, 'Who eats the most clams? Who has the nicest, cutest belly? That is Uncle Fouad!'"

Matussem stared at this woman, awed. There was something that he recognized in that feather of a smile.

MATUSSEM AND FOUAD drove home as the evening lowered. Matussem had forgone the chance to ride in the truck, but the memory of the woman stayed with him, slithering through his thoughts: her feather-smile and tough face. The house was dark as they pulled up the driveway. Then he remembered—his daughters were both out, swept away by their cousins; Matussem imagined the places Saiid and Kier were opening to them, halls of seductive music, glimmering veils floating in the air. Perhaps he would never see them again after such a night. He remembered the way his parents had married several of his sisters to men they had never seen before in their lives. As a child, Fatima used to sneak out and take secret looks at the suitors who came to visit, to describe to her sisters. He remembered his sister Lutfea tearing all her dresses to pieces because from Fatima's perspective in the bushes outside the suitor's window one of his eyes appeared to be larger than the other. "The evil eye," Fatima had pronounced at age nine, pulling back one eyelid with her finger. But Lutfea married, despite the deformity that, to Matussem, was invisible. All his sisters married, even Fatima the Terrible. He had never questioned it before: marriage as regular and perfect as clockwork.

They went back inside together, Fouad belching and swaying from too many clams. Matussem watched Fouad lumber down into the rec room, stomach preceding him. After Fouad disappeared down the stairs, Matussem stood in the doorway. This was not, he thought, a night to stay home alone. He heard the purr of the VCR through the floorboards. Fouad would be watching *Oklahoma! Fiddler on the Roof,* or *Zorba the Greek,* movies he'd brought with him from Jordan and continued to watch on a nightly basis. Soon he'd send his usual cable to his wife in Amman saying, "Can't leave yet. Still needed desperately. Love, Fouad." Then, as the last strains of "Oklahoma, O.K." were fading, he'd be off to the strip club.

Matussem left the house quietly, like a teenager breaking curfew. Without turning on the engine or lights, he slid the car down the driveway into the cicada-filled evening.

He thought, as he drove, how it had felt at one time like there was pure joy in his life. If he had been asked, when had he really been alive—when had life been most vital?—he would have said, without pause, in the arms of his wife. The moon was washed with darkness, a portent of things to come. But then it seemed to him that he had spent the last twenty years seeing the world cloaked, day and night as drapery, where the appearance of life was not life at all, only gestures toward it; *life* was whatever lay behind the curtain. The world, to Matussem, was lying in wait, a place that he would go to someday and resume living. He was fifty-one already. How had that happened without his noticing?

He pulled into the drive of the Key West Bar. Larry Fasco kept a set of drums ready for Matussem anytime, day or night. Matussem even had a key to the bar—not that it was ever closed; Larry got strange from time to time and locked himself out. What Matussem had grown accustomed to over the years of playing there, what he scarcely even noticed anymore, was the way his pulse leaped whenever he entered that parking lot, the way his blood sped like quicksilver. It was at his drums that he returned to life, raw and green, like a wind-whipped branch.

THE KEY WEST was dead, as usual. There was quite a crowd, but few of the patrons spoke, laughed, or danced. They reminded Matussem of turtles; they had the same hide-skinned eyes, made the same event out of blinking. There were dairy farmers, junk dealers, and mechanics. Matussem picked out half-figures in overalls and seed caps, bent over their drinks, waiting like lost souls. At the center, sending out streams of light, was Larry Fasco, his bloodless skin shining.

"Matussem Ramoud!" Larry called out over the quiet. "My old friend, my swarthy friend. Come here and buy a small businessman a drink."

The figures at the bar shifted and Matussem stepped up. Larry poured a whiskey for himself and a shot of peppermint schnapps for Matussem. Matussem touched the shimmering green glass and was swept by a desire to weep. "Larry—my girls—they're not babies any-more," he said.

It was a hot night and the heat of the air tilted up like a wall. Larry watched him with his ice blue eye. He took a swig of his whiskey and said, "My friend, it's the great American tragedy, that's all. Don't let it get to you."

Matussem nodded and began to feel his way along the bar, among the patrons, the schnapps cool as a tile in his hand. He wanted his drums. The patrons scarcely noticed as Matussem began to tighten his instruments, testing the drumheads. He knew some musicians believed there was no point to drumming without an overlay of melody, that drums had to follow guitar or saxophone, as a body follows its spirit. Matussem knew different. Even the first time he'd held drumsticks—still a young man, already a widower, looking for something to help the pulse of grief in his throat, in his hands—even before the drumsticks, he'd known about drumming in his body.

There had been a drummer in his family village, a vagrant, who pounded at hide-covered drums with his hands at sunup and sundown. He had gone to weddings, funerals and births; the other men would sit with him, overturn pots and kettles and drum with three fingers and the heel of their palms, singing, the women ululating their high voices into the desert. The memory of singing mingled with his memories of the Muslim muezzin, caught like a princess in the tower of the mosque. Five times a day, his call to the faithful went out. In the still of morning, the settling of dusk, the domes of the mosques glowing, the song went out, passing through the elements, falling like dust, the voice twining, a serpent of prayer on its path toward God.

He'd known it when Chief Stormy Weather and other men of the Onondaga Nation spoke of sun dancing and ghost dancing, of their movement together to the weaving of voices and drum, to the sound of their own bodies, tattooing the earth with the drumming of heart, blood, lungs, and spirit.

That was what he knew, that it was all one and the same, the divinity of the body, the holiness of the voice, of the drums, that *they* were the spirit as well as any trumpet or harp, that they fled together into the rising up and dancing of life.

"This go out to my wife, this go out for myself," he sang softly, sticks rippling across the snare.

The patrons watched him.

"This go out to everyone who is tearing their hairs out over their children—"

A broken cheer went up.

He played for a long time; people came and went. Larry left his place behind the bar from time to time to accompany Matussem on harmonica. Customers would step up and take a stab at singing a cappella. For the

most part, Matussem played alone, until, somewhere in
the far stretches of night, a brawny woman, with fast
eyes and hair like quicksilver, stepped up.

"You're good, Matussem Ramoud," she said, looking
straight into his eyes. She laid the back of her hand
against his and compared them. Strips of light fell over
her hair and face as she bent toward him. He lowered
his sticks.

"Don't you think you want to buy me a drink?" she
said.

"Right now?"

She backed up, curling one finger at him. He followed
her like a sleepwalker, mesmerized, into the recesses of
the bar. There were a few people left; a cathedral glow
clung to the bar. Drinks were already waiting at their
table. "Here's to you," she toasted him. "Father of great
nurses."

"One. Nurse, I mean. The other daughter is . . . not
a nurse."

She nodded. "Father of great all-around women,
then."

Matussem sipped at his peppermint schnapps, and she
grinned at him, something glittering in her teeth. "I like
a man who can drink green syrup," she said. "Not many
can." She knocked back her shot and sighed. "Bourbon.
Cleans your tonsils. Watch out, I'm breathing fire
now—the fifth one always does that to me!"

There were no clocks, no time, no movement. It was
the magical night, Matussem thought, the Fourth of
July. The evening did not move, but churned at its
edges. Matussem finished his schnapps and she was leading him again; she had his hand and he was navigating

the air. She was towing him like a kite, and he saw things from a great distance. Larry Fasco and Hilma Otts waved from the bar and he waved back. He felt exhilarated and melancholy; he was a kite, a balloon, perfect stillness at his center.

They left the bar and outside the truck was gleaming with the moon and stars as well as the pink neon sign of the Key West that struck the sides of the rig in iridescent bursts. In this light, at close range, the truck was breathtaking; it looked like a living thing.

"*Mama mia,*" Matussem said. "*Ach du liebe, Augustin.*"

She turned to him and gestured toward the cab. "Want to come up and see my etchings?"

"Oh. Well. But the fireworks!" he said, his throat suddenly tight. "It's the Fourth of July, I gotta meet somebody—I can't miss—"

She was already waving one of her conjurer's hands in the air. "You missed that, buddy boy, it's over by *hours.* I watched them on the way over here. How long you say you been in this country?" she asked, climbing up and popping open the door to the cab.

H E H A D N O good answer to her question, not in this country of hers, where time flew away on pointed wings and left no trace. The cab was as tall as a tower. He sat behind her oversize wheel and peered outside. "You drive all the way up here?" he asked.

"That's not all I do, junior," she said. Sliding aside a panel behind the seats, she said, "Get a load of this."

Her bunk was deep and high, dominated by a king-

size bed in its center. There was a remote-control TV
built into one wall and a stereo system in the other.

"Here, try it out," she said, patting the bed.

When he sat on it, the thing moved and he leaped
up. She laughed. "What's the matter? Don't you know
about water beds?"

"Beds of water? Yes, of course," he said, frowning
and eyeing the thing.

"And look up," she said, pointing.

He turned and saw the source of the soft light in the
truck; it was moonlight filling a glass ceiling. He could
see the night clouds doubled, turning their bodies. Inside
the bunk, the light moved, nuzzling her hair, touching
her eyes as she leaned against the other wall, watching
him.

Then he saw what would happen: he saw himself
pouring into the center of that bed. As he was doing it,
the images came to him, each a moment before. He
knew the weakness that would stun his limbs, filling his
head like sleep, too heavy to move. He had been in this
country before; he recognized its signposts and was
pulled down its path. Her waist, shoulders, and legs
moved into his hands as she joined him at the center of
the bed of water, clothes peeling open, her mouth peeled
to its softest flesh, to water, the shambles of their bodies
as they joined, turned to cinders.

His mind was not with him, his languages left him
as he poured into her. They rolled together, into the
current of the bed, the room, the stunning night above
them. They turned and turned and turned again. Over
her shoulder, Matussem saw the moon set and was lost

in that face that the night sky could show him when he looked up too long from the layers of heat and gravity of his own home. He stared until he was lost somewhere alone in those tangled stars and looking down into the damp sheets and then up again, her hair in his mouth, her fingers at his neck, at the inner crease of his knee, and he was seeing the colors before dawn, a flicker of an unfamiliar star.

HE WOKE WITH his wife's name in his head and turned to see the sheets were mussed and shaped in the way they used to be when she had just left them. But she wasn't there anymore. His wife was too young for him now, laughing and lovely, twenty-nine, and here he was fifty-one; how had he left her behind? She had been nineteen, he twenty, when they'd joined hands, promised to follow each other into the world.

The light now was coming hard through the glass dome of the bunk and when he sat up in the shifting bed he had the taste of peppermint and lipstick in his mouth and a feeling of having done something momentous, rash, and astounding. He found a small curtain just over the head of the bed and drew it to one side. At first his eyes were muddy and the light hurt them. Then, as Matussem began to focus, he recognized the door of his own house: they were parked on the front lawn.

"Well, good morning, Cowboy Bob," the woman said, pulling back the panel and sticking her head in.

"Good morning," Matussem said and drew the bed sheets up to his neck; he was blushing. "You know, I thinking maybe I don't know your name."

She laughed and tossed her head so her hair floated back in a bright floss. A seam of gold glittered in her smile. "Well, hot-buns, everybody just calls me Train."

J E M W O K E L A T E the next morning to the familiar sound of Melvina calling the police. She was saying something about a kidnapping, a truck, and a "disfigured" lawn.

For a moment the air in the room was still and sweet. Jem closed her eyes and tried to float, to let her mind clear like a pond. Piece by piece, the previous night came back to her. There was that business of marriage, all that writing down of offers on slips of napkins, pushed back and forth across the table between Melvie and Kier, as if they were haggling over the price of a car. Kier's writing bled into Arabic and tended to say things like: I Give Everything. Melvie's said things like: #1. I will be allowed publicly to claim to be married to you, with caveat A: that we are not officially married, and caveat B: that I am allowed to renegotiate this contract at any time.

They borrowed more money from Melvie, then bought her and Jem a row of fuzzy navels and coral okobojis. When the disc jockey switched to slow music, Jem found herself and Melvie out on the dance floor. Jem was too tired to hold herself up; she leaned into Saiid's arms, her shoulders leaning against his, eyes dipping. The evening was sliding down around her shoulders. Points from a revolving mirrored ball shifted around the room, inside her eyes. It was lovely to let go, to be held. At one point she saw her sister's face, calm as sleep, tucked into Kier's neck; Jem did the same,

closing her eyes, putting down her head, and she wondered, was this what it was like to be married?

Hours later, she was still feeling that fatigue in her
arms and legs and even the top of her head. Now, alone
in bed, she was pinned by her own body, so she could
move only her eyes to follow when Melvie marched into
her room and went directly to a window, yanking open
the curtains and admitting a pillar of sun.

"Well, you'll be happy to know that there is some
sort of truck monstrosity in the process of obliterating
our front lawn, and that I have good reason to believe
that our father—who was not in bed last night—is being
held captive somewhere in its confines," she said.

Jem struggled to lift her head, then gave up. "A truck,
you say?" she said feebly. "What exactly do they *put* in
coral okobojis anyway?"

Melvie wheeled from the window to look at Jem.
"Well, there goes our good name! I'm sure that evil little
man Gilbert Sesame has some long-distance hand in this.
Maybe that's his truck! Maybe it's Uncle Fouad's!
Maybe it's to transport drugs over international lines.
Oh why, oh why have I procrastinated so long in buying
a handgun!" she wailed and marched back out of the
room. "A baseball bat will suffice for now," she said
from the hall.

Melvina rummaged in the hall closet as Jem worked
to get out of bed. She gradually sat up, pulled a sheet
around her shoulders, and moved toward the window.
It looked as if all outdoors floated in a watery color that
had descended overnight, bathing everything it touched.

On the front lawn, gleaming like an idol, wedged
perfectly between two flamingos and a Doc, was the

truck. It was painted in primary colors, the cab lashed by painted flames, trumpets of red, borders of blue, white and yellow edging the cargo box and the words exploding in a sunburst at the center: Prime Movers. To Jem, it looked more like some divine agent than a truck, the sort of thing God might ride.

"Wowie," Jem said. Then she heard the front door slam and saw Melvie, baseball bat in hand, start up the lawn. Jem ran out after her.

Matussem was having something like an out-of-body experience. He felt his mind skimming along the cabin ceiling, looking down, regarding his body propped on the bed, eating chocolate doughnuts and drinking milk from the O–G market. Next to him, a woman in chartreuse halter and matching hot pants sipped at a bottle of lite beer, while only a few yards away stood the house that held his daughters. He turned and pulled the curtain open for just a peek. "Uh oh," he said. "I should just known it."

"What?" Train leaned across his legs to the window and started laughing. "Will you look at—what *is* that?"

It was Melvie, gleaming like a statue in her white off-duty clothes, brandishing a baseball bat, and shouting. Jem was running after her barefoot and in a nightgown.

"That's my daughters," Matussem said, rolling back and sighing. "They crazy 'bout me."

"Oh yeah," Train said. She moved back, looking as if she'd rather not deal with it. "What's she saying?"

Matussem put his ear against the window. "She says she sees someone peeking at her, the police are on the

way, they have the license number, we should give ourselves up. She won't use deadly force unless she has to,
and she won't negotiate with terrorists."

Train nodded. "*Damn!* I could use that gal on my rig.
What say you ask her for me?"

Matussem ran a hand over his face and then peeked
at her between his fingers. Train looked damaged by the
morning. The hair that was fine spun by evening's light
was now thinning and bleached. Her face was canvased
by a network of lines and infinitesimally small cracks,
like an aged hide. There were wells of shadow under
her eyes, and her lips, without paint, rolled in and disappeared. All the same, Matussem felt that instant the panic
of her leaving, and anxiety rushed over him. He felt a
crushing press of time, a need to hurry.

"Don't leave me," he said, grabbing her hands. "No,
I don't want you to go."

She laughed and fluttered her eyelashes, then extracted
her hands. "Well, aren't you a sweet pair of sticky
buns?" she cooed.

"Or, maybe I could come with you," Matussem said.
"Please, Miss Trains—"

"Just *Train*, dear heart."

"Train, I'm serious. I could be keeping you company,
reading maps, I wash the truck, change the radio station,
what you say, okay, I do it." He was almost out of
breath. He was imagining his daughters, Fouad and Fatima, the guys in the band, Zaeed, and Larry Fasco; they
would be standing on his front lawn waving good-bye
as he sat next to his tower of a woman, a pair of tom-
toms in his lap. He and Train would head for the gray
swath of highway as he played the drums.

Train was looking at him blandly. "Matty, honey," she said. "I think you must've hit your head last night or something. I hate to have to tell you, but it takes a certain kind of *something* to be a truck driver. It's not your run-of-the-mill personality, not for these big babies." She stroked the wall of the bunk. "I have to tell you, Sugar Nose, I think generally speaking, there's usually only but one trucker born per family, if any, and in this crew, it ain't you."

Matussem nodded, slightly relieved. He knew there was no way Melvina would ever stand still on the front lawn waving while he rode off with a lady trucker.

"Look, Big Daddy," Train said, setting herself against him so the bed swooned; she laid a ham-heavy hand on his shoulders. "Everybody puts it in reverse once in a while. I mean, if you're the kind that lives on and on in one place, then you're always dreaming about going away. And if you're like me, always going, then you dream about staying put. It's the human curse, I'm telling you. Here I'm thinking what a sweet deal you've got going here, sugar-plum fairies and apple pies and all. Living with your daughters and your fat-slob brother or whoever that creep is—"

"Fouad."

"Yeah, and this house, and these flamingos on the lawn, and God knows what, neighbors I guess, a corner store—look, you're *lucky,* you've got a place you can stay in. It may be boring, but look at me, running so long I lost track of my legs. When I die I'm gonna have to be cremated and have them dump me in a river so my ashes can go on and see the world. I don't like it, but I can't stop. It makes my bones ache when I stick around too long, and I've got more bones than average. Stay where your heart is, Big Daddy—not to sound like a Valentine's card—but then you'll get the best deal. Look, you just live in your house and I'll come to visit you."

"You really meaning you will?"

"Spit on my grave and hope to die."

A crashing sound like a metal gong rang through the length of the truck, the floor shivering under their feet.

"What the fuck," Train said, looking out.

Melvina was poised, bat in both hands. She'd just struck the truck and was preparing to launch another blow while Jem struggled to restrain her. They could hear the girls' voices raised in disagreement, muffled through the truck window. Then Melvina, fixed on her intended target, shouted, "If you value your lives give yourselves up! The police are here and you are surrounded!"

Matussem looked over and saw the Clay County sheriff's car parked in the driveway, the sheriff lighting a cigar.

"That girl has initiative," Train said.

Jem thought even Melvina seemed a bit taken aback by the sort of noise she could produce by bouncing a baseball bat off the side of a truck. Melvina shouted a few more things, and then they stood there in the bowl of reverberation that the bat had hollowed out of the air. Sheriff Giaconda sat in the driveway; he'd been summoned by Melvina several times over the years for various "disturbances." Generally he didn't bother to get out of the car anymore. He'd pull up, someone would lean out the living-room window to wave him on, and he'd drive away.

When the truck door opened, Melvie hoisted her bat again, pointing it at the door. The first thing Jem heard was Matussem's voice. "Melvie? Is Daddy-o! You can put down your cannon, we are coming." Matussem climbed out, waving at Sheriff Giaconda, who started his engine. The sheriff stuck his head out the window and shouted, "Hey, you want to come over for the Orangemen next weekend?"

Matussem shouted back, "Yeah, I call you, dude-man."

They all watched as the sheriff backed out, waving the tip of his cigar at them.

Then she was there. Coming through the door of the cab right behind Matussem, more and more and more of her, big as the Statue of Liberty once she was all out. Jem stared and said, "Oh, boy." Melvina pointed and shouted, "You! It's you!"

The woman looked like she was trying to shrink so they couldn't see her behind Matussem. But there was too much hair, halter, torrential thighs. She grinned and said, "Howdy, gals. Things got a little carried away, I guess. I was just giving your daddy a lift home."

Melvina squared off with Matussem. "Well, well, Mr. Ramoud," she said, looking from him to the woman, back to him again. This was not what Melvie had expected. She mentally arranged and rearranged the two plaques on her desk at work, the ones that said Right and Wrong. She said, "Need I remind you, Mr. Ramoud, of the sacred memory of our dear, sainted mother, may she rest in peace."

"Holy shitskis, I had no idea. A dead mother," the woman said.

Matussem shrugged. "We didn't have whole lots of talk time."

"And you." Melvina swiveled toward the woman. "I singlehandedly saved the life of your reprobate, if not to say criminal, man friend. And this is how you pay me back, hijacking and corrupting my father. What more do you want from me, maybe a bone-marrow transplant? Heart, lungs, liver, or kidneys perhaps?"

The woman tucked in her chin and averted her eyes. "All right, let's cut the morals." She reached for her back pocket. Melvie braced herself, hoisting the bat, but the woman only produced a gray square of paper. "My card," she said, handing it to Melvie. "Anytime you and your baseball bat want to come aboard, I got a place waiting, kiddo. You can tell them robots down to the hospital to take their job and shove it."

Melvie read the card and placed it in her jacket pocket. "Evidence," she said curtly. "Now if you're quite through, Madame, I'm warning you, move that truck or I shall make a citizen's arrest."

Train shrugged, climbed back up, and waved to everyone. She leaned out the window toward Matussem and said, "Matty, baby, my philosophy is don't torture your kids. It never works out." The truck rolled off the lawn, churning up two tracks of earth, grass ground into the tire treads.

Jem made a sound, lifted her hand to her temples.

"Jemorah," Melvie said, taking her sister's arm. "What? The lawn? Talk to me, tell me what's wrong."

"I—I don't—there's nothing really wrong."

"Is it that trucker woman? Did she upset you? Should I go after her?"

The truck was already moving through Euclid's flashing red light, gears shifting and a puff of smoke like the Wizard of Oz's. Jem shook her head. "Mom." Her voice was quiet. "She—that woman—she didn't look anything like her. I don't know why, but something about her reminded me of our mother. I couldn't stop thinking it."

Matussem turned, his eyes lifting. "It was mouth," he said, drawing his fingers across his lips. "Her smile. The same. Like a feather is."

"I don't believe you," Melvie said. "I would have remembered. I have perfect recall." But her eyes softened almost to shadow and followed the diesel smoke as it faded on the road.

FOUAD WAS CRANING to watch everything from the window in the living room. "Look at that. Did you see that? What going on out there? What car I see in the backyard? They having the party time of their life, I want go see."

"Forget it, O greasy Fouad," his wife, Rima, said in Arabic. She was sitting against him on the couch with one hand clamped on his wrist. "Lucky for you, my *sons* at least will still talk to me. Them and that Girbert Abu-Sesame. That's *their* car, the latest that you bought for them. They're the ones who gave me directions here. A nice quiet car, so quiet I can sneak in the back and they don't notice. You are going nowhere now, Mr. Slippery."

Matussem and his daughters walked into the house and found them sitting there, Rima ramrod straight and Fouad so slumped down his head was practically on the seat of the couch.

"Sister!" Matussem said and hurried to her. He touched her and kissed both cheeks over and over. *"Ah'lan wa sah'lan, keef ha'lick!* Long time no see. This is a really a day and a half!"

She sat in queen bee fashion, eldest of the Ramoud women, counting up everything life owed her. She turned wooden eyes to Jem and Melvina and held out both hands. The girls kissed their aunt's hands and felt her fingers tighten around theirs as she dragged them closer and peered into their faces. "Still not married, written all over them, ha!" she said in English and released them.

"Oldest sister of mine, how many year has been?" Matussem said. "I don't believe these is you in my own house."

"Enough of bullshit, Matussem," Rima said. "I come get husband back before you murders finish him. Putting him some—some *prostitutes* and all the time booze, bad foods, poisons, so now look see!" she struck Fouad's chest with the back of her hand. "He looking like a hanger, hangnail, what you call that—all crumple? I have to come get before you are kills him all."

Rima and Fouad stood up, Rima in a full-length caftan

glittering with gold thread. Fouad patted his stomach
and nodded at everyone. "America life, my friends, is
like eat clams, can't digest, and so too much."

Rima muttered to Matussem in Arabic, "If God wills
it, we will meet again, the day you finally come back.
Where you belong. In the meantime, send your daughters to me. I'll fix them up with some half-decent
matches. Never mind my hopeless sons. If you come
back home, we can find *you* a new wife, too. *Au revoir,*
baby brother."

Once their car had driven away Matussem said,
"Fouad remind me by the jazz guy who say, 'The large
print giveth and the small print taketh away.'"

THAT NIGHT FOUAD was asleep on a jet, dreaming of a dancing girl in Syracuse under whose veils and
spangles he had drunk. America faded behind him, the
parties, the nights out, as well as the charges—several
thousand or so for furniture, clothes, ceramic animals—he'd rung up at Montgomery Ward, Sears, and
elsewhere, giving Matussem's address. He was dreaming of the soft crush of the dancer's thighs and the way
he and all the other men watched and drank and waited
until it all evaporated in the daylight like a mist.

Matussem, asleep in his house, dreamed he was looking into a mirror; his face, thin and ghostly, slipped
across its surface. He was dreaming of what his wife had
seen when she looked at him, the dark of his skin, deep
enough to fall into.

In Jem's dream she heard her mother's voice telling

her, as she had used to, "Be bold, be bold. You should learn about yourself by learning the world. See how things come apart and go back together again."

JEM WOKE FROM her dream in the middle of the night thinking of middle school Earth Science. In May of their second year in Euclid, toward the end of seventh grade, Jem went strolling in search of a science fair project and found the fields glittering with perfect, translucent bones, partial skeletons, beaks and claws. The neighboring farm was too close to the road and its chickens were always getting hit by cars. The carcasses would putrefy in the sun until the bones were stripped clean by field animals. Jem carried some home and washed them in the bathtub.

This was three years after their mother's death. In the quiet around their house in the country, Jem's project became a matter of going to the secret insides of life. Melvina would sit in a big chair cradling an anatomy book filled with bones, muscles, crosscutting ligaments, and the staring eyeball of a skinless chicken, supervising as Jem worked with toothpicks and Elmer's Glue-All. Melvie would not let Jem substitute even a vertebra that seemed a little "off." The fieldcombing went on for weeks, Melvie dragging the anatomy book in her red wagon, searching for the precise tibia, the perfect left claw. Each bone was a particle of understanding, Jem's mind growing deft as she began to know what she was building.

In the end they had to support one faulty wing tip with a toothpick. Melvie woke Jem with a flashlight at midnight before the fair to request one last bone hunt. But the model was entered as it stood. After it received awards for creativity, accuracy, and a blue ribbon, Melvina announced to everyone that her sister was going to become a scientist. But Jem thought about the mirror her work had shown to her, turning her inside herself, and she knew that she wanted to study the mind.

ATUSSEM DIDN'T *WANT* to go back. Not even when, three weeks after leaving, Uncle Fouad had gone ahead and mailed him a plane ticket. Not even, as Melvie put it, in restitution for emotional anguish and physical hardship in having to deal with Fouad.

"What do you mean, you don't want to go?" Melvina barked at her father over the dinner table. "I can't believe this. Your ticket is for *tomorrow*."

Matussem shrugged, sitting on his hands and eyeing his salad. He wouldn't meet Melvie's eye. "Don't want to go, they don't know how to have fun there."

"Fun!" Melvina's voice. "Who's talking about fun? What do you care about *fun?* I thought you were such a big American—don't you want to learn how to be a tourist like everybody else? Look at me, *I* don't care about fun. Jem doesn't care about fun! Hilma Otts across the street with six more kids, do you think she cares about fun? No! Besides, being a tourist *is* fun, don't you know that? You see new things, you have an educational experience—"

"Already seen it," Matussem said, mashing his mashed potatoes with his fork. "*You* go, how 'bout?"

Melvina looked at him piously, her voice dropped to a devout level. "This is your *homeland*, your *people*, this is a journey to your *past*, to all of our pasts."

"Boring. No fun."

Melvie turned to Jem, who simply shrugged. It was possible that Melvie might have surrendered then and there, but a dangerous furrow came into her brow. Melvie crossed her arms and said, "'Well now, something here reminds me of Za'enti da'ar, and people who don't even realize when they're looking out the window of a burning house.'"

A wave passed over Matussem's face; he glanced up from his potatoes. "So well, well, what *that* suppose to mean, Melvina, you heartpicker."

Melvina turned blasé. She lifted her palms in the air and said, "It's your story, you tell it."

Matussem put down his fork and knife, recognition opening in his face.

M a t u s s e m w a s s t a n d i n g at the kitchen window that evening, staring out, seeing wild mustangs, box canyons, buffalo jumps, and desert basins. He could see all the way from the swamps of Euclid to the Wild West. He imagined wandering there, shedding his skin in the seams of the earth.

He remembered that as a child he'd listened to sailors and soldiers. They played the music of the world to him, sang in his village's marketplace, danced with each other on holiday. One of them played a tape machine in the village center and Matussem heard Dizzy Gillespie walk over the ocean, part the veil of dust, and speak. It was his first intimation of home.

Euclid, lost to the rest of the world, was Matussem's private land, like the country his parents tried to leave as they made lives in Jordan, as they let go of their children's memories and let them grow up as Jordanians. Matussem was only two when the family left Nazareth. Still he knew there had been a Palestine for his parents; its sky formed a ceiling in his sleep. He dreamed of the country that had been, that he was always returning to in his mind.

After they'd moved to Euclid, he found there were ways to lose himself in a place. Euclid, my misplaced past, he thought when he walked the gravel roads, past shacks and barking dogs. When he first saw Euclid he remembered it, every silver leaf and broken-backed creek. Nora had been his history once; now only the land was left.

HE WOKE THE next morning an hour before his alarm would go off and lay back into the unexpected interval. It was his most vulnerable time, the moment of waking, when things rushed into his mind. He would be leaving for Jordan today. He watched sunrise touching his windowshades and in that moment he recalled his dream: a terrible golden snake. He stared at the shades, remembering the day he fell into the well.

He had been a young boy living in Beit'oon, his father's village where almost everyone was related in some way. The well was off in a corner where no one ever went, only half finished and abandoned, yet quite deep to a young boy, a child of seven. He and his cousin Faisal liked to balance on the squat stone wall that encircled it. A dangerous game, he had known even at the time, that had proved irresistible.

At first it was easy, like balancing on any rock. But more and more Matussem felt compelled to look down into the hole; there was no helping it. One day he looked into that pushing, pulling center of gravity. In one tilting moment his arms flew out; he fought for balance, then the speck of light at the bottom, like the gleam in an eye, flew up at him.

His hands and feet swept the webby stone sides, then he crashed into two feet of mud and water at the bottom. He had gone rubbery with fear and shock and somehow landed with just a few scratches. When he attempted to stand, the mud seemed to rock and suck him in. He craned back and watched the opening above him perform a feat he later saw repeated in Hollywood thrillers: the opening telescoped back. So that while it was only fifteen feet distant, it looked nearly as faint to Matussem as a star.

Falling, he'd heard Faisal shout, a private peal of terror. When Faisal's face failed to appear over the edge, Matussem knew he was going to die. The air at the base of the well was foul; it smelled like old dung, and he tried not to remember if this was one of the places he and his friends would stop to piss while playing outdoors.

The walls were almost close enough for him to touch his fingertips to both sides at once. He felt the slime of the wall, brittle crud covered by slickness. His feet disappeared into gray mud; he shivered; he heard a sound like a squeak. Then he felt something slithering between his legs, twining around one ankle.

Till that point, he'd been resigned to a clammy death by suffocation. Now suddenly he found his lungs filling up, his throat producing a piercing, magnified cry up the stone sides like a voice in a megaphone. When the men came running with ropes and he emerged, coughing, soggy, caked in mud and lime, Faisal was sitting all the way across the courtyard on the ground. He looked over at Matussem blankly, as if to say, Where did you come from?

For years after that, Matussem had dreams that he was being pursued by snakes, fat ones, little ones, that raced behind him, tongues flickering. He became afraid of water. Sometimes he woke in the morning and felt they were still chasing him.

MATUSSEM WALKED UPSTAIRS to the living room. He sat by one of the long-paned windows and watched the dawn. Small birds went by, flat as Ontario snowflakes, off into the sky. Clouds were etched into gradients of blue, from the crown of the sky to the nape of the hills. He moved again, and from the kitchen he could see the gas-station lights by the edge of the creek; the firs along the hill still black with night.

When he was sixteen and finished with his schooling at the small country house in Beit'oon, seventy-one relatives came from all around Jordan, the West Bank, and Beirut to the party his father threw for him. The men arranged their seats in a huge circle, shoulder to shoulder, and Matussem and his father sat in the center, as his father held forth on the subject of "life." Matussem remembered more clearly than anything in the world the tent walls flapping, the edges of the wind, and his father's voice, the sound of his Arabic, intelligent and complicated: "Trust only your enemies. Women are the possessors of magic. The devil resides in a bored man." Though the family had struggled with poverty, their father was generous to visitors with food and shelter, respected by all the village for his insight and sense of justice. His powerful voice evoked his blood ties to royalty, mathematicians, and ancient poets. It was the voice that Matussem would later draw from his drums; in their undercurrents, he heard his father speaking again. He had known—even as he had listened to his father speak of history, of continuity—that he would be leaving someday, to a place where he could create himself. Two years later, his father was dead and Matussem left for the New World. His drums were now the only way back to his father's voice.

He would make himself return, to please his daughters, his relatives, but most of all to get to that pinpoint of anxiety and longing inside his brain, the skip in his dreams, the whisper that it was all a mistake, that he was in the wrong place, that he never would be at home here.

He would leave his green-sided hills and dairy valleys, his country of surprise and transformations. He'd seen a picture of the South Dakota badlands once, a place where the earth crumpled around snaking depressions, peaks and ridges flash-tipped white, clawed-out scoops.

Everywhere was veined white, the mountains shining. This was hidden treasure to him, a place that he had wanted to see. Yet now he would leave it and who knew if he would ever return?

AMERICA WAS THE place where his world began, away from the webs of family. In the new, wild western country, family flew into particles, relatives moved, changed courses, sifted around each other like the snow, the amazing interwoven flakes sweeping off the belly of Ontario that meteorologists called "lake-effect." It was the lake-effect family that swept together and meshed in the icy blasts. It was all they could do to lock hands against the whirling air. It shocked him awake; it was so dangerous to create a new kind of family, to be so vulnerable to the elements. This was the kind of living he had come to want for himself, the choice to live together, to love.

THAT AFTERNOON, THEY drove to the airport. Matussem appeared to be wearing every piece of clothing he owned—a three-piece suit, an ascot, an overcoat, a scarf, overshoes, gloves, and a gray felt fedora he'd bought on his honeymoon in Atlantic City in 1960. Melvie kept shooting angry glances at him in the rearview mirror she'd pointed directly at him. Matussem positioned himself at the center of the backseat, hands on his knees, chin pointed up. "Are you trying to convince all the relatives that you're in the Mafia?" Melvie asked, halfway there. Jem resisted turning around to look at him.

Matussem cleared his throat and adjusted his hat.

"It's August first!" Melvie said. "It's eighty-four degrees out. You're going to the *desert*. So now you've decided to give yourself heat stroke, just to provoke me."

Matussem coughed a dry little noise and pulled the edges of his coat lapels more closely together. "These my threads, can't go no places without threads."

Melvie was having second thoughts about the whole trip. The day before she'd given her father diet cards with long lists of foods he was not, under any circumstances, to touch. She'd also given him a paramedic's first-aid kit, full of things like surgical thread and booster shots for malaria, hepatitis, and typhus—especially typhus. Earlier today Jem had found the kit stashed beneath her own bed.

When Jem had asked Matussem about taking his drums he'd said, "It's okay, they are wait for me. I have try to go these ones alone."

Later, when they were leaving, the creamy surfaces of the drums, like lotuses floating on the water, were the last things she saw when she turned out the basement light.

AT THE GATE, Melvina went over a specially prepared list of flying essentials prepared by the Flight Attendant Guild of America: mystery novel, flashy magazine, gum and candy to clear the Eustachian tubes, a toothbrush for after gum and candy, celery sticks, de-congestants in case of increased cabin pressure, motion sickness pills, a pillow, extra blankets, Melvina's phone number at work and at the Won Ton à Go-Go, camera, film. . .

They all took pictures of each other waving at the door to the ramp, and Melvie said, "See, Dad? It isn't hard at all. You just walk down that little hallway and get in the plane and look for the seat number on your ticket and get in it and go to sleep. Your feet don't have to touch the pavement."

Matussem gazed at Melvie as she spoke, but he didn't appear to be taking it in. He walked stiffly to a waiting area seat. Jem thought, with alarm, that he didn't look quite real—as if he had mentally slipped out another door. His eyes moved, but they were an odd bluish gray, not black; his hair stood up in sweaty spikes.

"Dad?" Jem said. She looked at Melvie. "I don't think the flight part is the problem here. He's nervous about going back there. I certainly would be. All that pressure."

"Thanks a lot," Melvie said. "Thanks for the pep talk."

"Mmm?" Matussem made a buzzing sound, turning his eyes mechanically. One leg was crossed over the other and his suspended foot was tapping out a vivid tattoo against the air. There was a whooshing electric sound and a voice announced boarding. Jem watched the blood in her father's face fading. His fingers curled, white-marbled around the armrests of his chair, and he whispered, "Girls, girls, I can't move, something happening here, I am . . . par-zalyzed. . . ."

Melvina looked at the door then at her father; she folded her arms. "You're not going to do this to me right this very second, Mr. Ramoud, because they're beginning boarding now."

Matussem continued staring ahead through the window. Off in the gray wash of the Syracuse morning the planes wheeled, some about to rise, others descending, heavy and cloud-bound in the distance. "Par-za-lyzed," he whispered. "Can't hardly move my lips. Can't go to Jordan, neither." Both his feet were planted on the floor, hands locked to the armrests.

The attendant counted off the first set of rows to board.

"You're not paralyzed, Mr. Ramoud," Melvina said. "I *work* with paralyzed people all the time. *You* work in an administrative office where you don't have anything to do with paralyzed people. Frankly, you're just afraid to stick your head outside your little office tower to learn anything about the world. Believe me, you don't have the first idea what paralysis is!"

Matussem kept vigil on the window; he wasn't taking the bait. "Par-za-lyzed," he said. "Legs are crumble."

They called off the next set of rows to board.

Melvie smiled and said, "You know, this amuses me. Really. It does. You forget I'm a nurse. I've lifted three hundred pounds and more of paralyzed patients. That's three hundred pounds of *dead weight*. You want to play games with me, Mr. Ramoud? Think your answer over very carefully. Because *if* you do, you see, I am prepared to carry you *on my back* and strap you into your seat. And everybody on the plane, including the pilot and the attendants, will laugh at you."

Matussem's eyes moved just an inch or two in Jem's direction. "She could does that?"

Jem thought that might violate some federal aviation regulation, but then she looked at her sister's face and said, "You better keep in mind who we're dealing with here. Hey, maybe you'll have a really great time."

Melvie was down on her knees, prying Matussem's right hand off the armrest. "That's it!" she said. "I've had it."

"No, no!" Matussem's left hand flew over to the right side, and he clutched the same armrest with two hands. He was now half sitting, half crouching. "I won't do it, I won't go!"

"Oh no? Oh no? *What* won't you do?" She'd already pried two fingers free. "*What* won't you do? Huh?" Her hands were indomitable. Jem grabbed Melvie's arm. "Don't break his fingers!" She looked around for airport security, but no one was paying attention, as if this sort of thing happened there all the time.

They announced final boarding.

Melvie squeezed her fingers under Matussem's remaining grip and grabbed his hands before he had the chance to reattach himself. "Ha! Child's play!" Melvie announced. "Try again? Double or nothing!"

For a moment the two of them wrestled together, eyeball to eyeball. "So what's it gonna be, Mr. Ramoud?" Melvie's hands were locked onto his, her eyes wild, her skin gleaming with the intensity of sheer pleasure; she was smiling, her teeth brilliant. "What's your game?"

Matussem's shoulders fell and Melvie let him straighten as she felt the fight go out of him. He shook his fingers then picked up the fedora that had fallen free during their altercation and put it back on his head. "What you mean?" he said with his eyes wide. "Melvina, you little heartpicker, I was just pulling on your legs. Little joke. I going, sure, I going all along. Can't *wait* to see family."

When he kissed Jem good-bye he whispered in her ear, "Don't let her kill you. Such crazy fingers."

Chapter 30

*I*T WAS DOLORES'S time, the hour of death.
Illness had invaded her, creeping into her lungs
and coloring the air, closing her mouth like a mask; she
was a mummy. She was Lazarus, brought back to life
just to prove someone else's point, just long enough to
see her death coming.

They were releasing her from the hospital before the
sun was even up. There was no sign of Melvina. The
nurses had trundled Dolores into the wheelchair; they
said she was well enough to eat, sleep, and move, all on
her own. Behind her, back in the room, Lana was saying, "Hey, where you going with her? Hey, she's *sick*,"
and trying to flash some kind of SOS on the venetian
blinds by her bed. Dolores heard the television playing
early morning music in the background.

She knew she would be leaving her sister Peachy behind, the only one of them all she could spare a thought
for. Dolores saw herself climbing to the top of their
windblown field; it came to her through the walls and

mirrors of the hospital as they wheeled her along. She could see it in the eyes of the nurses and orderlies: the broken trailer, the strewn bottles, her muddy feet. She would climb to the top of that field, no matter how they cried and clung to her skirts. She would stand where she could look at the trailer and at Euclid and lay it all down. So she could step out of that body of hers at last, the heavy flesh, the teeth, the hair, lay it aside and go free.

Chapter 31

*H*E RAN HALF bent, hands before him, eyes half lidded, through the brush, the tall shrub, the belly-high fields of tall grass and weeds, cattails and pussy willows. He moved along the back fields, around marshy areas where the land folded into water. He didn't know why he ran, only that his hands lifted of their own accord, that he sank toward the wind, that the wind pulled on long seams inside him, from his neck to his feet, and he seemed to fly, as he did in his wonderful dreams, night after night, waking with his arms full of air.

He came to the edge of the field, to a guardrail where the highway started, and walked through the gravel cinders and bristling plants. He crossed at the flashing red light, trying to avoid his boss at the gas station across the street. He was supposed to be at work.

Ricky Ellis, the homeless boy, the orphan boy. He smiled because he'd made it all up. His father had survived, ridiculously, several bouts of drinking toxic chemicals. His natural mother was long gone. She'd been a fifteen-year-old runaway off the Onondagan reservation in Nedrow when she met his father. Ricky would check himself from time to time for signs of her, the edge of bronze his skin took on in the light, the way his clear eyes would seem to change suddenly and blacken, and something else—there was always something else—shifting inside him, the slant of the bones and muscles in his face, the river-quickness of his limbs, his body running with the currents that forked through upstate.

He remembered when she had cooked for them, Ricky and however many children were there at the time, his brothers and sisters, his father's kids from past marriages, overlapping marriages, future marriages. They sat in a crowd around the table, some against the wall, eating canned beans, macaroni and cheese from the box, while their father ate meat loaf—there was only enough for him. There was also the old woman who lived with them. His mother's mother? She never left the living-room couch. He remembered his father saying the old lady would be a bum if they didn't keep her off the streets. She saved apple cores, crusts of bread, kept them under her pillow. Sometimes, while the old lady slept, one of the dogs would sneak away from her couch with a steak bone in its mouth.

He didn't have a clear memory of that time; he didn't think it had lasted long. He didn't know what happened to the old lady. She used to lie flat on her back, turning beads in her hand and saying words that sounded like prayers. They weren't English words; his father called them crazy-ass words. She never did speak any English, but Ricky liked the sound of her talk. He'd fade to sleep sometimes on the floor by the couch, letting the syllables lull him, as if the words were part of him and his body understood what his mind couldn't.

Ricky's mother was like him, fleet, with a runner's spirit, yet capable of sitting and playing endless games of solitaire in the kitchen, the bulb over the table rattling with flies. She taught him how to play a game called Napoleon's Tomb. She kept track of her score on a scrap of paper, and every now and then she would slap her forehead and say, "Oh, ding it, Mary Lu!" That was her name. Mary Lu. The other name, like a whisper, Hínuga. He remembered. She had never talked much.

He remembered that she used to watch him while they all ate. She herself never seemed to eat; she was tall, thin, and leathery as a piece of beef jerky. She'd hold that black-bottomed frying pan to her chest like a shield and it matched her eyes exactly, black as something burned. He wondered why she stared like that, like she was plotting to swipe him one night, like the old-time Indians used to do, and steal him back to the reservation with her. He thought he might have liked that better than where he did live. Even though the words *Indian reservation* called to mind a big, fenced-in place, like a fairgrounds, with campfires, tipis, and guards at the entrance. He didn't care; he wished for a place just for himself and his mother and the old woman.

In the end, she did run, but without him, and the old lady on the couch was gone soon after. There was no note for him, no souvenir of any kind. No one cooked for them anymore; dishes spilled out of the sink and grew crusts. Their father would cash his workman's comp checks the moment they came and there'd be a day of good eating—hot dogs and beer and canned sauerkraut and Twinkies—then, nothing but whatever scraps the neighbors could spare. Their father would disappear again.

After his mother left, the kids ran wild. Nothing could hold them, not foster homes, not detention centers. Some of his half sisters were grown-up by that time, and they took the younger ones in. Ricky lived for a while with his stepmother, Hilma Otts, and her kids. He used to sit on the edge of the back doorstep and look at the garbage that had seemed magically to rise up out of the fields. He was only a kid, maybe eight or nine, but he noticed that some kinds of garbage would break apart and disappear, and some kinds, like beer cans, would roll around and around like tumbleweeds, set adrift across the fields. Years later, when his half sister Dolores Otts set fire to her trailer, he was not surprised. He remembered her eyes when he kicked in the door, craning toward the sky, as if she were drowning, her stacks of magazines, beauty hints, marital advice, and recipe cards, those collected towers of garbage, dried and bound, going up like matchsticks. Those piles had gone to the ceiling. If Ricky hadn't found the garden hose in time she might have killed herself and all her kids.

When Ricky was nine his father blew up a car in their backyard with a blast that rocked Euclid, knocking glass out of the windows of Lil' Lulu's Garage. Ricky had come running out and saw that the whole rear wall of the house was scorched, bits of ashes and sparks rising from it. The car, a Camaro, which had been up on blocks, was blasted into great shards as if by a giant's burning hand, pieces rocking and smoking, strewn up and down the street and over the hill. His father was across the yard, sitting, his legs straight out, his eyes white holes in a blanket of soot. The volunteer fire department came and took him away. The next day, kids on the bus said that Jupiter Ellis had been blown to smithereens.

Ricky didn't say anything to discourage the story. In fact, he started crying because the idea was so sad and appealing all at once. His father should have died, Ricky thought. He certainly deserved to die, and, once dead, Ricky could relax and begin to like him a little, even to miss him. He had sniffed and wept and worked his way up to a full-scale, fevered wail, which made all the other kids shut up and stare at him in pity. The bus driver, Mrs. Lagarty, with her heavy red arms, had pulled the bus over and yelled, "All right, what the hell's going on back there now?"

Ricky yelled back, "Nothing, I'm having a heart attack!" And he was so surprised by the way one of his father's very own expressions had popped from his mouth, in what seemed like such a clever way, that his father stayed dead from then on. Ricky dropped out of school a couple of months later.

THE OTHER THINGS weren't true. The things they said about Ricky. He wasn't bad. Hilma Otts said he was like a kid raised by a pack of wolves. So what was wrong with that? he thought. None of the human beings he knew did such a great job.

He cut across another lot, this one thick with trees, and into a spray of weeds that he drew back like a curtain with one arm. Through the dried, late-August stalks and pods, he could see her house, the redwood that Max Blemer had built, charging everything to the limit and beyond on his twenty-five new credit cards. Somehow Max had gotten his name on a kind of pre-approved list, even though he had only been the town garbageman and unofficial dogcatcher. He had filled out every single application form he got and received the cards every day in the mail over the course of three glorious months of spending. No one was too surprised afterward when one day the Blemers suddenly weren't living there anymore, leaving behind the big newly built house, wide-hipped and resplendent in its woods.

Jemorah and her family lived there now. The day they moved in, Ricky pedaled his half sister Kathy Broom's bicycle up and down the wide country road that bordered the house, fascinated with the new girl who was nine or ten at the time. Her hair was darker than any he'd seen, except perhaps for the crown of black he remembered edging his mother's part, beneath a wash of red dye. He circled the house slowly, taking care not to touch the lawn, hiding among the trees, deep in the places where the men came and stuck them for their sap. His mother used to say they were bleeding the trees.

Meeting with Jem was a thing he couldn't bring himself to hope for or feel that he deserved. The sight of her was enough to slow his heart to a near stop. He had watched her, settling himself among the leaves and mossy earth by the house, more often than she would ever guess. The single time that they had made love was already unreal, eluding him like a half-forgotten dream. Once again Ricky was alone in the fields, watching.

There was a strange scent in the air—tart, almost spicy—and it took him a moment to recognize it as smoke. He turned suddenly, facing the highway, and saw a black streak rising, billowing out in charcoal plumes, from the direction of Dolores's trailer. *Probably just burning garbage,* he told himself, but a terrible, familiar sensation started in his gut, and he was walking, then running toward the trailer. Probably nothing at all.

BRIGHT MONDAY MORNING, at the first gesture of her shadow in the glass doors at the hospital, Melvina knew Dolores was gone. She did not waste time checking the patient log or calling admissions. She went directly to the room: there was a teenager with a broken hip where Dolores had been. They'd released Dolores an hour and a half before Melvina's shift, the attending physician overriding Melvina's own order to keep her in-house.

Anger wicked up her spine and her hands burned on the patient logbook. She dropped the heavy book with a crash and everyone in the corridor looked up. For a moment, Melvina seemed to hold anger palpably in her arms. She did some deep-breathing exercises then picked up the logbook, dusted it off, and went to her office. She sat at her vast mahogany desk and looked at the two plaques she'd bought for herself on her ninth birthday, Right and Wrong. She picked each of them up, weighing them.

Her phone was ringing then, the crisis line for the

fire/police department, and for a moment she couldn't bear to answer, to hear the death confirmed. If Melvina had learned one valuable lesson in nursing, it was that a thing was less powerful if she looked at it directly, but this time she said to herself, "Later." Without picking up, she routed the call to Emergency.

ON HER OFF-HOURS, when she needed to be alone to think, Melvina sometimes went to the old wing of the hospital, to the beds where they had once treated typhus patients. She sat on the mattresses and she could feel the ancient fever still there in the beds, its heat rising through her.

"Prolonged hectic fever, malaise, skin rash," she recited, stroking the mattresses. "Bradycardia, delirium, leukopenia. Intestinal hemorrhages and frank perforation, late complications."

Evenings in the abandoned ward, when she could hear nothing but the call of the crickets, she felt there was nowhere at all for her to go. She would stand at the window and feel the warmth of some maternal spirit in the air, the mother in the moon with her bare shoulders and grieving face. Then Melvie would chide herself and tear the cap from her hair, knowing that she had failed before she had ever begun, that her first memory was of powerlessness before death, that she had betrayed her mother even in her failure to remember her. She watched the moon become a cold rock, watched her reflection in the window say that people were deluded, betrayed into loving life. She would call herself a "marked nurse," and know that she was offering penance with each patient's care. Dolores was merely the most recent in a long line—the ones she had failed to save.

At these times she would touch the windowpane, raise her face to the moon, and say, "How can I forgive you for leaving me?"

IT WAS AROUND five o'clock the next afternoon, a Tuesday rich with August sunlight. Nurses off first shift left the hospital and stood outside, blinking, uniforms shining like glass, the heat rising in bands over the blacktop. They crossed the street through the glare until they were over by the cafés and bars, cubbyholes dank as autumn. There they could press their palms against beer glasses and wait for thought to return.

Today Jocelyn was on the warpath, the silver tag of her uniform zipper swinging between her breasts, her big white shoes mashing a layer of peanut shells and popcorn on the floor. Some of the nurses at their table—even nurses throughout the bar—caught the feeling; it rippled through and made them anxious. For others, it was early and hot enough outside that they still felt stunned by the air, not yet ready to give up their drugged silence.

"I'm gonna tell you right now," Jocelyn said, squeezing a half-full can of beer so Jem saw it dent in her hand. "We're suckers, all of us! I don't know a single nurse who doesn't want to be something else. They drop dead. Nurses do! We slave like jungle natives all our lives, then *bam!* Stone cold *dead,* push the body under a rock and con somebody else to take the next shift."

The problem was a recently admitted patient. In his

mid-forties, he was an advertising executive, scheduled for an appendectomy. He refused the hospital food and had his secretary run in sushi, chocolate truffles, wedges of Camembert, ruby grapes, and Italian wines from the import stores downtown. When Jocelyn had attempted to confiscate the wine, he'd deliberately leaned over and drooled on her arm.

"A long string of slobber!" she held out her hands to demonstrate. "Like the cows used to do on my grand-daddy's farm. And then he smiles at me. He *smiles* through the slobber. In his yellow L. L. Bean p.j.'s or whatever they were. And he says, 'Now clean it up.'"

Some of the nurses stared through sun-blinded eyes, a bored look saying, get used to it, that's the job. But Harriet said, "What total bullshit," and another said, "How's his b.p. medication these days?" Some of the women glanced at Melvina—Sheriff. It was the law of the Old Nursing West: if they wanted, they could have punished or killed; it was called creative medication.

Melvina sighed, crossed her arms, and ruefully considered that there was a time not so long ago when she might have gone another way. It would have involved becoming a renegade of some sort, like the Vietnam vets she sometimes treated, the ones who refused to go near the V. A. hospital. They drove each other up to the emergency room on Harley Davidsons, roaring like Zeus, in black leather, chains, and a web of tattoos.

Melvina, despite her appreciation of law and order, couldn't help a sneaking admiration of bikers. She had a sense that with a twitch of fate, it might have been her on a Harley, perhaps glued to the back of some disposable man as she'd seen many of the women; hair fluttering under their helmets, molding their bodies to the momentum, closer than a marriage vow. What was more interesting to her, though, was the thought of mounting her own engine, tearing a hole through the layers that weighed on her, house, community, family, the need to make *well* and *whole*. She'd have punched through it all and left the tattered edges behind, rising white-uniformed on the highway.

She reflected on killing the advertising executive, just one small human sacrifice, nothing spectacular, no stakes, bonfires, or necktie hangings. Just something discreet, a gradual, invisible, *accidental* misapplication of medicine, and the sliding into some choice coma, irreversible brain damage. Nothing to it. And he'd earned it, hadn't he? He'd *spat* on a *nurse!* That hardest working, hardest suffering, most unthanked, unseen, unknown of the race of visionaries and saints. He'd earned it.

"The sooner we get our patient well," Melvina said finally, looking, in turn, each and every one of her compatriots in the eye, "the sooner he will leave us."

MELVINA HAD TAKEN psychology courses as a part of her nurse's training; she knew all about what she called the "myths" of id, ego, and superego. Personally, she was much more attracted to Shintoism, whose faithful collected little god statues, spirits all around them, who kept everything in line. That seemed to her to be the way things worked. Inside the Arab-Syracuse world she was surrounded by relatives and other interested parties, the dead and the living, each with his or her own opinion and influence.

"I'm fed up with egos, ids, whatever," she liked to say. "If they want to speak to me, let them come and speak. Otherwise, I don't have time for it."

She'd duke it out with any id that'd care to put up a fight. She believed that in her own case these so-called hidden desires and violences all rode up in the front seat, everyone carrying on at the same time, like a carload of Arabs. Then there were the occasions when she would surprise herself and do something she hadn't known she was going to do. So it happened that around seven, after the Won Ton à Go-Go, she found herself turning left instead of right at the Euclid blinking red light, away from home and toward the Key West Bar.

As usual, the place was silent and lit up like a cathedral, windowless walls glowing as if holding racks of red candles and tapestries. Melvie had come to see the owner, a man with skin like marble, hair like plaster, eyes of stained glass. The saintly light in his hair and skin made him look as if the star of Bethlehem was at his brow, cherubim at his fingers. She walked up to the bar and felt an eerie impulse to kneel.

Larry's hand was fluttering over his cash register, ringing up a drink. It stopped in midflight when he saw Melvie's reflection in the mirror behind the bar. He smiled and pushed the drawer closed.

Though she'd been stopping there almost daily, since mid-May, she was still surprised each time she did. She had little use for men as a general rule. There were a few male nurses on the floor, especially good for lifting and turning patients, but often the first to start feeling wounded dignity. Their identities were often a source of confusion; it was not uncommon for a patient to assume that a male nurse was a doctor, a female doctor "just" a nurse. Male nurses were always the first to return to the outside, what Melvie called the "unreal world," where they were men again, privileged to spit and wear suits, swagger, and whistle at women.

She'd never forgotten what their mother's mother had said to her in phone conversations that had followed the death, when Melvie was still a child: "Never trust a man. Don't let them touch you, I mean *really* touch you. They'll only hurt you." Her grandmother needed a scapegoat, someone to anchor her despair. Melvie knew those feelings got tied up in the threads of a person's blood, the lattice of muscle and heart. Still, though Melvie had dismissed her grandmother as paranoid and a hypochondriac, she found some sense in her attitude to men in general.

She looked at Larry, who was now polishing the same spot of bar over and over, eyes mostly lowered. He went on with one little movement of the rag in his hand, as if his brain were caught in a tic. He was all patience, waiting for Melvina to speak.

The only other customer in the bar, Tenny Beevle, laid aside his paper and said around his cigarette, "Hear about the big blaze . . ." Then his voice faded, his eyes narrowing, as if trying to recall his thought.

No, Melvie knew, men were something beyond hurt: perpetrators, trespassers, their presence as troublesome as poltergeists, their desires far less certain. Larry lifted his eyes, stopped rubbing the bar, and Melvie said, "Take a break."

◂ ● ◂

MELVINA STEPPED INTO it, like a traveler on frostbitten plains, walking into a place where the earth mingled with ice; she lowered her head, averted her face, and pushed.

She had no interest in *why;* that was self-evident. To her it was only, always *how.* How to get the drug, to tap so many cc's into the hypodermic chamber, to test it for air bubbles, letting drops spritz free; how to tourniquet his arm for him, or his leg, to find the vein, the one standing strong and blue, the one with straight, unbroken walls, carrying its load to map out the body in blood seams, turning it into a country of snow.

Larry ducked his head. He couldn't stand to watch when she injected him. He was upset by his habit—introduced by way of muscle relaxants after an injury in 'Nam—and believed that it was another body, another Larry, that this young woman injected, graceful and deft upon the needle as another woman's fingers might be upon piano keys. Melvina brought him the drug to keep him alive, in the same way she would feed a patient who couldn't lift a spoon. She had suspected his addiction from the first moment that she'd seen his paper lips, his transparent skin. On the night of the church dance, after Melvie had slapped her aunt, Larry had come up, shuffling her through a side exit into the blue-and-gray twilight and into his car. He had pulled into an abandoned drive-in lot, weeds shagging against the car. He reached for her and Melvie pushed back his sleeves to see the track marks. He was ill, and for Melvie the decision to help him had been made long before she'd ever met him.

He received his fix in the storage room under the Key West. It was the only place in the whole building with windows, thin casements near the ceiling that sparkled with dirt and sunlight. They sat on liquor boxes. When she withdrew the needle, Melvina would sit back to watch the transformation. She brought him methadone; she called it the middle rung down the escape ladder.

Larry became an angel, eyes burned to filament. He put out his hands to her, held himself to earth, and his veils would lift, one after another, like the layers of deaths she had seen in her life. The tiny deaths rose and he emerged, his face shining from the force of it. His words became powder and he sprinkled them over her. His eyes became stars and he saw the spirit inside Melvina, that glowed with something like his own burned-away beauty, "Melvina . . . my life . . . my joy . . . my beauty." And then, "Welcome to the Room of the Absolute Present Tense."

She held her patient-lover's hand as he rose and drifted, skin limpid in the creamy sun. The windows floated away. Though Melvina never touched any drugs herself, she dutifully took his hand and accompanied him. Whitening air filled the room, their small space; in the long hours they spent together, Melvie watched figures from her memory, from Euclid and Syracuse, wander in and out like figures in a fog. She saw her father and her sister, and though she might have reached toward them, they left her. No matter how she called after them and strained her eyes, they lost themselves in the turning current of the air, just like Dolores Otts and her mother and every other person she might have saved and had lost.

When the sunset in the windows ripened and turned apricot, Larry recovered enough to look in on the bar. Sometimes that was when they parted ways, but on that night, the first week of August, Larry turned the bar over to Hilma Otts. He and Melvie drove up to the fish stands on Lake Ontario. They walked past the picnic tables and took fried, dripping sandwiches to the lakeside. The shore was broken into flat rocks where they could sit and watch the progress of the sunset. The lake was a baptismal font where the sun broke along steepening bands to a single, intense line that spread crimson against the water. The air was dotted with clouds of gnats. Larry leaned back against Melvina and said, "You know, babes, when I see days like this, I feel like, okay, now I can die."

Melvie stiffened. She wanted to dig her fingers into Larry's shoulder, to say to him, never. She put her arms around Larry: she would keep him alive as long as she could.

"Psychohealer," Larry said, still staring out. "You and my ex-wife are a perfect balance. She was the Psychokiller and you are the Psychohealer."

"I beg to differ, Mr. Fasco," Melvie said, annoyed. She straightened as if behind her big desk at work. "There is nothing psychotic in the pursuit of holistic health."

Larry chuckled faintly.

"And why, pray tell," Melvie said, "do you insist on calling your ex-wife by that horrendous name?"

"Her meat loaf," he said, with a faraway look. "Her meat loaf, and every now and then she chases Peachy Otts around with an ax. Of course, that's a Euclid kind of thing to do anyway."

Melvie carefully wrapped their scraps in a page of newspaper. Folding it up, she noticed a small item smeared with grease, *Dolores Mabel Otts, 29, Dead in Fire.*

Chapter 32

WEDNESDAY MORNING PRESSED down on Jem. She felt the eternal recurrence of work that was continually undoing itself; she could hardly bear another day, losing her life hour by hour. The team leader had talked her into staying on until they could find her replacement. Two weeks notice turned into a summer, and perhaps longer: they hadn't even advertised the opening yet. She went to work thinking, This is absolutely my last week.

She walked down the corridor to the business wing, looking at her desk, the wall before the desk, all flat and faceless. When the first phone call came, before she had her hand on the receiver, preparing the words, "Good morning, inpatient billing," she was thinking, *I'm dying*.

She thought about the passage of her life, about the fact that she would be thirty in a month, after years of summers, visiting aunts and uncles, listening to their warnings: A good girl does not leave her home. Does not go out in public, speak to a man, show her ankles, talk back to her parents, go to school, live alone.

On her walk in from the parking lot that morning, everything had felt heavy, the thick raindrops, the sight of the gardeners settled between wicking branches. Her breath wavered with the thought of Ricky's mouth. She looked into the cement-colored sky and knew she was getting older. She was determined to leave.

Portia came to Jem's desk that morning and asked her to stay on another week.

"Just until we can get your replacement trained." Portia was wearing a dress of tiny flowers that seemed to flow and ebb around her bulk, independent of the flesh beneath. Jem tried not to look at it; the flowers, white on a black field, would wink open then disappear. Jem's eyes kept falling from the woman's face to her dress. She felt herself tilting, falling into the universe of the flowered dress.

Sweat was pinching out of her skin, at her temples and underarms. Portia was smiling at her, already pleased by Jem's answer, by the way she knew things would go. Jem imagined a giant weaving in Portia's office, in which she arranged the future, a fabric Portia could wear on her back like her dress of star-flowers. The smile on her face was inexorable. How could Jem presume to alter the course of Portia's destiny?

She mustered barely enough courage to say something, and couldn't hear her own voice, but apparently Portia did, for there was the slightest rumbling. The smile quivered for a moment and Portia said, "Time? How *much* time do you need to decide? I have to know *now*, Ms. Ramoud."

Then the dress began to turn, the universe of flowers eclipsed itself, and Portia gestured to Jem with one finger. Jem was drawn from the desk, through the pathways of printers, filing cabinets, other desks, towed by her own fear toward the open door. Portia, a Milky Way of light, proceeded through it, then disappeared. It was impossible for Jem to see in, but impossible to remain standing alone outside. She turned briefly and saw the faces of her co-workers behind her as distant stars, a galaxy of passive faces, witnessing her passing. *For heaven's sakes*, she thought, a quick dart of irritation. Then, abandoning hope, she entered.

The light in the office was aquatic, like in outer-space movies; everything was hushed, the floor blanketed with darkness. Somewhere at the center of the room where a desk might have been was a shape of extinguished color, afterglow of auburn, white, and black. It was Portia herself, swathed in a kind of Oriental wrapper and reclining on cushions on the floor. "Here," she said, tapping the floor beside her. "Come sit. Let's get to know each other."

Jem sat on the floor and tucked her legs crossways before her. The floor was covered with a coarse carpet that she saw, as her eyes adjusted, was Persian. There was one large picture window, but that was tightly shuttered with blinds and admitted threads of light that stitched the room without illuminating it. She could make out shelves covered with irregular shapes, knick-knacks. Nowhere were the papers, folders, furniture, or even the telephone she expected. It seemed suddenly that such artifacts were all merely props for a play, and Portia, with her streamlined body, had no need of props.

She was the thing itself. A planet, floating close enough to touch, allowing Jem a look at the marvel of her surface.

Then Portia said, "Did I ever tell you I knew your mother in college?"

Jem held her breath; her thoughts scattered. Portia had drawn an arm through the space between them and caught up Jem's hopes in one hand. For a moment she thought Portia might be able to tell her the purpose behind her mother's death, answer the mystery of its suddenness. Perhaps, Jem thought, she had been mistaken about Portia's intentions. She'd read her all wrong, they all had; Portia might be an angel, a buddha, adrift between worlds, seeing the invisible.

But then Portia shifted, rolling herself back against the cushions, facing her ceiling. She sighed dramatically, ridiculously. Jem felt a clammy cold under her collar and in her palms; her mouth turned to tissue.

The only college photographs Jem had seen of her mother were in her school yearbook, the girls' basketball team. The girls were lanky, lined up front to back, grinning lopsided, and under each was a word in quotation marks, "Divebomb," "Blitzkrieg," "Warrior." Under Jem's mother it said, "The Natural." Jem had assumed her mother had known only women like these, laughing and athletic. Matussem called Portia *Therabit Eyn,* Evil Eye. It was all wrong, their ages were off; her mother would have predated Portia by a good ten years, Jem guessed.

"She used to be a good Catholic girl, did you know that?" Portia was saying, facing the ceiling, her face a white spot. "Used to be in our church group when she was a freshman. We all went to Mass together every Sunday and holy days of obligation. I met your grandparents once when they came down to visit. Good Christian people. They didn't see their daughter that often. It was a long drive. I suppose even then she was running from them, starting to rebel." Jem watched the white spot crane up a few inches off the floor, turning toward her. "I bet you thought I was a Jew. With a name like mine." She snorted. "Hardly. I'm grade-A all American, missy. Now *you're* the one with problems."

If it hadn't been so suffocating, the air sinking onto Jem's shoulders, if she could have remembered where the door was, through the darkness cloaking the room, she might have run out at that moment and saved herself. Instead, she pulled up her knees, drawing into herself, her heart condensing to lead, and within that an iron ember of rage beginning. Portia wouldn't stop talking, directing herself toward the ceiling, her voice going on and on, "Your mother used to be such a good, good girl. She was so beautifully white, pale as a flower. And then, I don't know. What happened? The silly girl wanted attention. She met your father in her second year and she just wanted attention. We just weren't enough for her. I'll tell you, we couldn't believe it. This *man*, he couldn't speak a word of our language, didn't have a real job. And Nora was so—like a flower, a real flower, I'm telling you. It seemed like three days after she met that man they were getting married. A split second later she was pregnant. I know for a fact her poor mother—your grandmother—had to ask for a picture of the man for her parish priest to show around to prove he wasn't a Negro. Though he might as well have been, really, who could tell the difference, the one lives about the same as the other. . . ."

There was a long pause. Jem's forehead was pressing against her knees, the anger was moving, lining her veins, dull, filling her eyes and mouth. She began to shake.

"She never did finish college after that, never got to be the woman she could've been. A husband and baby at twenty. Look at what *I've* done with my life. You know, it's not too late for you. Oh, sure, you're tainted, your skin that color. A damn shame. But I've noticed that in certain lights it's worse than in others. Your mother could have made such beautiful children—they could have been so lovely, like she was, like a white rose. Still, it could definitely have been worse for you, what with *his* skin. Now, if you were to change your name, make it Italian maybe, or even Greek, that might help some. I'm telling you this for love of your mother. I'll feel forever I might have saved her when that Arab man took her and you kids back to that horrible country of his over there. It's a wonder any of you survived that place, so evil, primitive, filled with disease! I should've spoken up twenty years ago, but I didn't. I thought, the Lord will provide, blah, blah. She could always have the marriage annulled. I thought I should butt out, let Nora make her own mistakes. Well, not anymore, now I'm telling you, Jemorah Ramoud, your father and all his kind aren't any better than Negroes, that's why he hasn't got any ambition and why he'll be stuck in that same job in the basement for the rest of his life. They'd never promote him any higher. He only got where he is now on my say-so, because I feel for you kids. And now you can go that way, too, or you can come under my wing and let *me* educate you, really get you somewhere. We'll try putting some pink lipstick on you, maybe lightening your hair, make you *American*."

"My father's mother *was* black." The statement came from the back of Jem's throat, so sudden she hadn't known she was going to say it, the words like iron. Jem leaned back on her elbows, locking them against her shaking. "Yeah, a former slave. She married her master who had twenty-six other wives. They were black, brown, and yellow, and some didn't even *have* skin."

The pale spot once again craned upward, looked at her a moment. Portia's eyes reflected splinters of light; she blinked slowly, like a cat. Then she said, "I love back talk; it tells me so much about a person. It explains why you're in heat over garbage like that Ellis kid. White trash worse than lazy darkskins. Multiplying your mother's mistake. That's what it leads to, breeding worse and worse trash. Here I am offering you a real chance and your mind's too trash-low even to see it."

Jem lifted herself off her elbows. For Ricky she unfolded; she felt delight, relief, and anger. She stood as Portia was saying, "This is my whole point, I want to save whatever of your mother's clean blood is left. For your own good, Jemorah, I *can't* let you quit. Don't you see? You stay here, we'll work together, I'll scrub all the scum right off you, make you as pure and whole as I can—" She was twisted toward Jem, propped on one elbow.

Jem stood, stepped back. "You know what?" she said. "You're pathetic. If I didn't think you were so repulsive, I might even feel a little sorry for you. You don't know me and you don't know a thing about my mother. She would have hated you, your tiny, hateful little mind. You're a bully, a liar, and a bigot. You can take your crappy job and shove it!"

Jem hurried toward the door, but in the thick darkness she couldn't find a knob, or even a frame. She swung her arms out, her hands scrabbling among the walls and shelves. The knickknacks scattered, some smashing, toppling; books fell out of place. "Let me out of here!" she shouted.

Portia was sitting up. Jem could just see the edge of her shoulder in the thin light like a crescent moon. "I'm not letting you out," she said. "Not till you say sorry."

Jem became frantic, stumbling around the room, until, tripping over Portia's legs, she fell against the window blinds. They clattered down with a huge crash, and Jem realized how much the office staff must have feared Portia not to have run in at that point. The light broke through like waking; suddenly she could see outside the hospital. She saw Crowes Street and the Physicians' Office Building, people strolling by with shopping bags and purses.

Portia's office looked makeshift and dreary in the light. The desk and files and telephone were set up in a corner; among the broken shards were several ceramic dolls and trolls, glass animals. It reminded Jem of the bedroom of a twelve-year-old. For a moment she did feel pity. Across the room, standing near the door, Portia looked shrunken and water-wrinkled, washed-out in the daylight. She lifted her palms to Jem with pleading

fingertips, her eyes swollen, and said, "I don't hate you,
I love you, I don't hate you!"

Jem began walking straight toward her, the anger
winding around her, legs and arms and face all shining.
She felt as if she was growing as she moved, tunneling
air out of the room. She had never felt so clearheaded
before. Her feet pounded the floor and she came at Portia
as if to run her over, and Portia threw back her hands,
her face drained of expression, and shrieked, "No!" Jem
charged straight past her, shoulder striking shoulder,
grabbed the door, and walked out.

S H E W A L K E D T H R O U G H the vacuum of the
outer office, past the desks of workers in suspended ani-
mation—or perhaps it was she who was suspended,
moving in silence and invisibility. Not a face turned in
her direction, every head was bent to its task, and Jem
knew then why people who entered that office were
rumored never to return: no one ever looked toward
Portia's door if they could help it.

She left the hospital and walked into a new city, a
place that had intensified over the course of her morning,
become color-saturated, where the faces of strangers
turned around her like knives. The sky was sharpened
to a crystal point, the diamond edge of coming winter.
It was hard to breathe; the air was thin and felt wreathed
in ice; it snagged in Jem's throat. She felt the points
of strangers' eyes and fingers turning toward her. And
though she waited to be stopped—feeling she had com-
mitted an unnamable crime—she walked freely to her

car. Two of the gardeners she usually passed on her way in to work were out trimming the Johnson-Crowes hedges. One briefly touched his cap to her; she couldn't manage anything in return.

It struck her after she reached the car and locked herself in, that the thin breath in her lungs and the tightening sensation in her stomach were fear. Not merely the fear of being caught, but of everything around her—of the way the strange faces turned and rushed forward, of gestures and glances, of the world of these people, who didn't know her or want to know her. Who might even have wanted to hurt her. Somehow the world had shifted; she'd entered a place that no longer felt benign.

She drove through the lot, past the security booth and beyond the parking gate to the street. Looking left and right, she felt she was seeing with Aunt Fatima's eyes; she heard her aunt's voice saying, "This is not our place, not our people." Jem didn't want to drive home; she was afraid to see her house in this way, yet she was still heading there. When the on-ramp for the highway came up, she passed it and took the smaller city streets, meandering into the neighborhoods. She drove through the Northside, with its two-story houses ringed with soot and the smells of frying onions, garlic and sausages, past porches and brick stoops, past Columbus Bread where two squat men stood in the window dressed head to toe in flour, past the Thanatoulos Bakery which had a sign on the door: Closed—LeVar's First Communion.

She imagined what the old buildings looked like inside, in their hunch against the night. She had a yearning to sit in the front parlor of one of those houses, on a horsehair couch, the TV flickering with late-afternoon reruns, while dusk came to the neighborhood, seeping in the front window, settling in pools around the set and curtains, welling in the kitchen.

She thought she'd contracted homesickness from her father, that it was passed on like a gene to the child of an immigrant. Any place might look like home: suburban neighborhoods, apartment buildings, far-flung country houses; the desire quick in her veins. She envisioned walking the flagstone path, up the wooden steps, through the door and settling in. Now she drove past blocks of barbecue grills, groceries, baby carriages, the business of the world. She was lost.

The car moved from the neighborhoods to the old shopping plazas, past the radio and TV aerial towers, down Electronics Parkway to that spot where the highway cut through open grass and fields, a stretch that Jem had seen from her school-bus window. The tall weeds shook; she felt their shiver in the pit of her stomach. They held currents of her childhood unhappiness, the fear and anxiety of the bus ride. The feelings budded open, disturbing enough that she tried not to remember.

She couldn't find a life here with Ricky Ellis, his job at a gas station, her work in a business office. She couldn't hide in Euclid and disappear. Her hands tightened around the steering wheel and the force of understanding churned in her stomach. She steeled against it, shaking her head clear. She wanted *more;* after so many years of holding back, losing herself in dreams. Her mother had left before she could show Jem where her place might be. Jem averted her eyes as if her sadness clung to the windshield. She would *not* let herself vanish. She would live.

▲ ▲ ▶

ONCE HOME, SHE checked the mail. When Jem saw the envelopes she took a deep breath. One was from Uncle Fouad, the other from Stanford University, Department of Psychology. She remembered in that moment: Melvie had fished her application out of the garbage and sent it in. Jem knew that in any case she'd completed the application so hopelessly and late in the year that her only chance for fall admission would have come if an earlier applicant turned down an offer. She tore Stanford's letter open, let the envelope fall in two pieces and in her hands was a yes.

"Ah, good," Melvie said, when she returned that evening. "There it is. Very satisfactory. I could've told you—hard work, industry, and brilliance will always triumph in the end. Of course, I would have preferred you applied in astrophysics, but I've learned the importance of compromise. Peachy, for example, may not go to college, but she'll learn to read. Now I'll take this." She snatched the letter from Jem.

"What for?"

"To make copies, of course!" Melvie glared at her. "The first is going up in the nurses' station on sixth. I'll call Dad and the rest of the family. You call Aunt Fatima."

Jem groaned. Why not engraved announcements? she thought. Melvie marched out of the room. She remembered Fouad's letter then and tore it open. There was a check inside, made out to Jem for twenty-five thousand dollars. The note on the bottom read "Year one, gradual school."

Chapter 33

*I*T SEEMED TO Jem that when the calls started, they came all at once like a burst of daggers. Begin ning in early August, a month after Fouad's departure.   "May I speak to Mr. Fouad Mawadi."

"But—he doesn't live here—" Jem would say.

"This is given as his home phone."

"He lives in Jordan."

"Jordan, near Elbridge?"

"Jordan, the country."

Usually there'd be some sidestepping, a few leading questions, a couple of sidelong accusations. Then Mrs. Baymore or Ms. Harrison or Mr. Minway would get down to business, the message always the same: we have charges here for a purple Naugahyde couch . . . a statue of a giraffe . . . thirty-five Hawaiian shirts . . . a Bar-master blender . . .

Always overdue. Not a penny paid.

Fouad had apparently begun opening store accounts and charging the moment he'd first stepped off the plane in America, two months ago. This was only the first wave of creditors just starting to tense up over missed payments; there was no telling how much he'd charged in more recent weeks. When Jem had some time between calls she would pause to wonder about what might have been going on in Uncle Fouad's mind during those apparently intoxicating moments of transaction. Was the plastic card some sort of miraculous passkey to him? Funny-money to be used over and over, like something out of a kid's dream? More likely, as the shrewdest, most successful businessman in the family, Fouad knew exactly what a credit line was. Not that Jem felt he had no scruples, exactly, only that he was able to push inconvenient matters of conscience to the back of his brain. A place where the idea of family was not real, but a kind of needlepoint that Fouad could hang over the mantel while he boarded a plane, leaving behind over a hundred unpaid bills.

In the Old World, Jem thought, family must be as abundant and invisible as air—just as precious—just as easy to exploit. In America, maintaining a family at all sometimes seemed like a miracle.

The collection calls went on day after day for a week. Nothing stopped them, not begging, reasoning, or sighing. Nothing until Melvina answered the phone at eight o'clock on a Saturday morning. Jem sat up in bed eavesdropping through the wall to Melvina's bedroom.

"Yes," Melvie said. "No, no—one moment. I'll have to ask you to state your name and business clearly before I can give out any information. . . ."

"I see . . . I see. . . ." Jem could hear her saying, *I see*, over and over as Jem imagined the expanding list of

Fouad's purchases: twenty-eight pairs of cowboy boots, two *Golf Tips from Harry Subotnik*, an emerald pinkie ring from Montgomery Ward, Kmart, J. C. Penney. In the middle of all those dry *I see*s, Jem knew Melvina was caught between her loyalty to order and her sense of personal dignity. She would be outraged that Fouad had reneged on his bills (Melvie herself didn't believe in credit), and she would be infuriated that the collectors were dunning her family in order to reach the guilty party.

It didn't take her long, though, to sort through the ethical dilemma, and after a few of these calls, Melvie began asking for the name of the caller's superior.

"Because I intend to report this phone call to the proper law enforcement agencies, Ms. Katerina Dutley of accounts payable at Daisy World. I will investigate what grounds I may have for a harassment suit. Although, if your company was foolish enough to bestow a Daisy World charge account on Fouad Mawadi, then your company has an even deeper problem than greed, intolerance, and aggression."

The calls began to trickle off as Melvina answered them. Then she began to call the collectors herself, initiating a reverse harassment campaign at billing offices and collection agencies across the country. She called herself the Joan of Arc of collection. Melvie also telephoned Uncle Fouad at his home in Amman. She talked to Auntie Rima, since once Uncle Fouad returned home he reverted back to King Fouad, who wouldn't touch telephones, microwaves, television sets, or clock radios for fear of radiation. He would sit in his private chair, a new La-Z-Boy recliner from Montgomery Ward, and eye his wife as she spoke on the phone, asking every five seconds, "Who is it? What do they want from me now? Get rid of them," as Rima ignored him.

Melvie could hear Fouad in the background, bellowing in Arabic, "What now? For God's sakes, God the merciful, the compassionate, who is it?" as soon as the phone was lifted.

Melvie thought of Arabic as the tongue of the hearth, of irrational, un-American passions, of pinching and kisses covering both cheeks. Tongues could climb Arabic syllable over syllable like fingers ascending piano keys, enabling great crescendos of screaming. Arabic represented to Melvie the purest state of emotional energy.

She began speaking to her aunt in Arabic, "May the grace of Allah and his prophet be upon you."

She heard Rima saying to Fouad in English, "A salesman."

As a result of her phone call to Aunt Rima, Melvie secured the promise of a certified check to cover all Fouad's debts as well as pre-payment for three more years of Jem's graduate school tuition and living expenses. "*Ya'an deenak,*" Melvie heard Rima screaming through the overseas cable scramble at her husband. "Imbecile! You've been screwing over my baby brother! Do you think that everything disappears when you get on a plane and turn your fat ass in the other direction?"

Melvie's father, Rima added, was out disco dancing.

A FEW NIGHTS later the phone rang at three in the morning. Jem grabbed it off her bedstand; at the

same time she heard an extension click and Melvie saying, "Well, it took you long enough. Don't they know
about phones over there?"

"Girls, girls, it's me!" Matussem shouted so Jem
flinched from the receiver. "Guess where I am calling!
What time it all there?"

"Three A.M.," Jem said, lying back in bed.

"Lower your voice, Mr. Ramoud. We aren't conversing over Dixie cups," Melvie said.

"I'm at Uncle Fouad's house, crazy or what? You
sound like you right at the next door! Fouad is waving,
everybody waving, hi, hi, everybody says hi. Fouad
give me big check he says for some kind of bill."

"Hang on to it," Melvie said. "Dad, I looked into
your return flight. You can move the return date up
without a big penalty, so if you're really making yourself
miserable—"

"Return? What return? I maybe stay extra longer.
Why come back? This place is A-okay great, not like
olden days. They got VCR, every night big parties,
food, dance. Heck with it all, Euclid is great place to
leave, let's face these. Look, Rein just put for me plate
of *megluba*, roast lamb, *koosa mashie*, why don't you girls
ever put for me plate of *koosa mashie?*"

"Well gee—" Jem started, just as Melvie shouted,
"*Koosa mashie?* You don't even *like koosa mashie!* What
is this? I don't *believe* this!"

There was the sound of a woman's voice in the background on Matussem's end and he came back and said,
"Girls, girls, your Aunt Rein want speak to you. You
remember your nice old Umptie Rein? Hang on."

The girls' aunt came on and began speaking in an ancient Arabic that Jem strained to make out, her comprehension better than Melvie's.

"I want Jemorah to marry my youngest grandson, little Nassir," Rein said. "He's a very good boy, thirty-five years of age, and he's coming to America for a little more schooling, and he needs a wife right away to watch him. I want Jemorah for him because he's an educated boy, he needs someone with brains to make him happy, God save us all. This is very important to the family and I know I don't even need to ask, because this is the only thing now that would make me happy, and if she wouldn't do it, God forbid, I would have to go and die like a dog in the street, God willing. Then there would be a family war, who knows what, may God forgive. Luckily my sister's good boy, Matussem, has already promised Jemorah to him. All done. Fine. Good-bye, good-bye."

There was a long pause; Jem could hear the pounding of her pulse mixed in with the grain of international static. Melvina's breath had grown louder and louder during Rein's announcement, until, when Matussem came back on, he said, "Melvina, you sounding like you have tornado in your nose."

"Mr. Ramoud, what was *that*? Something about marriage and Jem and war."

"Oh," Matussem chuckled. "Oh, that? Slipped by my mind. You know, with so much parties and fun. I guess I make a little marriage contract for Jem. They so serious here. But just wait, I bet you they forget all about—"

"I'll do it," Jem said, her heart shaking, feeling released and terrified, a dive off a high cliff.

"What?" Matussem and Melvie said at once. Then there was a thud over the phone and Melvie came running into Jem's room. "What are you saying? What is this?"

"I'll marry Nassir and come back with him to live in Jordan with you and the rest of the family if you want," Jem said into the phone, staring at Melvie. "I've made up my mind. I'm ready to do it."

"Wow, you don't say," Matussem said. "This a crazy world or what? Here I thinking you going to maybe be little mad, something nuts like this."

Melvie folded her arms. "I want to talk to you, Miss," she said.

Jem clung to the receiver and pulled her bedclothes higher. "Dad? I think I better get off the phone."

"Oh no!" Matussem laughed. "This Fouad's phone bill, no problemo!"

Melvie made a sound a little like a growl. "No, I really better be going now! Bye, Dad!" Jem hung up.

Melvie leaned her head back against the wall and held the sides of her forehead with her fingertips. "Explain to me—" she said, tilting her head toward Jem. "I'm a simple person, easily confused. I must need help on this one. You're going to Jordan to live with the rest of the Ramoud family? Is that right? Did I hear you correctly?"

Jem shifted sideways in her bed and propped herself up on one elbow. "I'm tired of fighting."

"'Fighting'! Do you understand that Auntie Rein is ninety-nine? Do you really plan to worry about her committing suicide?"

"You don't understand. I'm tired of fighting it out here. I don't have much idea of what it is to be Arab, but that's what the family is always saying we are. I want to know what part of me is Arab. I haven't figured out what part is our mother, either. It's like she abandoned us, left us alone to work it all out."

It looked in the night dark of the room as if a shade had lowered over Melvina's eyes.

"They're always saying that Americans don't understand or appreciate what family or community is, as if we need to be trained, like animals. Maybe they're right," Jem said. "Remember Uncle Eli? How he wouldn't even let any Americans into his house the whole time he lived in this country?"

"Wait a sec," Melvie said. "Wait a sec, wait a sec. Let me tell you something about our mother. I watched her die. I remember everything. That night is the only real memory I have of her. My consolation is that I believe she lets me know what she wanted."

"You were two years old."

"I hear her voice. Then and now. We have conversations from time to time. Talks, check-ins—I look at the moon and she answers."

"Melvie."

"Not everything can be written up for the *New England Journal of Medicine*, Ms. Ramoud. There are phenomena that evade the microscope and the rational mind every day. My own experience—call it intuition, gut feeling, what have you—is really quite modest in the larger scheme of the paranormal. What it boils down to is the sense that she didn't want us to be tied down to anything. She would say 'I want my girls to be free.'"

Jem stared at her sister, through the wet black of early morning, trying to see Melvina clearly. "You never told me this before." Jem felt something twining between them in the air, set into motion. She looked at the black beads of her sister's eyes, intent on her. She took a breath and said, "All right then, but what about now? Where does that leave us? I've spent so much of my life not daring to look up, look around at what there might be for me. I've spent so much time trying to please her, to guess what she wanted. And listening to Aunt Fatima telling me how to be good, to please my mother, to be a good girl, which means, as far as I can tell, to shrink down into not-thinking, not-doing. Well, I don't want to waste away doing jobs that make me numb. You say our mother wanted us to live freely. I don't want to keep hanging on to a place or a dream that comes from someone who is not around anymore. I'll marry and move to Jordan. And I'll be free because I'll be with people who have my name and who look like me."

"You *don't* know that," Melvie said. "You don't know anything of the sort."

Jem watched Melvie turn and leave, her downswept gaze brushing the room.

Chapter 34

*A*FTER YELLING AT her boss, fleeing
the office, and calling in sick for almost two
weeks, Jem found herself returning to work one morning, as if it were any other Tuesday. She got in the car,
snaked through the traffic, around and around the overfilled parking lots, parked, and marched up the hillside,
past the gardeners bent under trees beginning to fleck
with orange, yellow, and red. She took a gulp of air, a
look at the lowering sky, grabbed the door, and went
inside.

Jem had the sense that her plans were too drastic, too
strange really to act on. When she walked in everyone
in the office stared, like she was Lazarus, still wearing
the death rags. No one spoke to her beyond necessary
exchanges. Jem felt she was trapped in the same fear as
the rest of them, the sticky tendrils of routine, drawing
her in; she was afraid to do anything else, and she was
maddened and exhausted by that fear. The spell of Portia
Porschman and Johnson-Crowes Hospital had worked

itself into her; she was good for nothing in life but staring at blips of computer light, doomed to her phone and desk, until she keeled over on top of the filing or Portia came with leg irons.

It was a way of being that Jem had been raised with. She'd watched the ancient trailers around Euclid cave in, their siding disintegrating into rust and red tears, while families still lived inside. Dolores Otts was her age. Jem had read the small item in the *Euclid Town Crier* about Dolores's death. An "accidental fire," it said. Jem imagined Dolores wading through the newspapers, rags, the boxes of takeout food, the spools of thread her kids described in the paper, past the branches of trees forcing through her windows, taking a box of matches, and setting fire to a copy of *Good Housekeeping*. Fire leaking across the living room, rising in the doorways, racing the walls. What lightness she must have felt in setting it all aflame! What was a place like Euclid any-way, Jem thought, but a charred house, sticks and bones. A broken wish that no one could escape.

WHEN PORTIA DID emerge from her office, looking haggard and reddish around the jowls, Jem felt the air suck out of the office as if every woman there had taken in her breath at the same moment. Jem was facing her computer, fingers on the keyboard, and she could see Portia's reflection in the monitor glass, a demon wafting in from the microchips and dancing over the screen. She felt as if ice were creeping up be-tween her fingers. Suddenly she thought that Portia might not call the police at all; she might just haul Jem back into that office and mete out punishment personally.

Jem turned in her typing chair, poised to face her head on. Portia was already there. The big head nodded down at Jem, a great arm lifted, then a piece of paper, folded in the shape that kids at school used to call footballs, tumbled into Jem's lap. It took Jem a while to undo the tight, elaborate system of folding. By the time she did, and had read the note, Portia was gone. The message was written in big, black letters: "I LIKE YOU, WHY DON'T YOU LIKE ME?"

DAYS LATER, ON Friday, an hour before quitting time, Portia deposited a new note. The message was lengthy, and the gist of it was that Portia needed Jem to stay on until they found a suitable replacement, which might not be until a year or two from that date, due to hiring freezes, and that, if Jem quit, Portia would find ways to make her life "unpleasant, if not a total, living nightmare." Jem read the note over two then three times, all the while aware of Portia watching from behind her office window. Then the phone rang, and when Jem answered it, there was no response, just a sound like rain in the background, then a dial tone.

She thought she could see an eye peering from Portia's door. Jem fiddled with a few keys at her computer and tried to make it look like she was working. Even after she'd hung up, the sound of rain lingered and distracted her; it mingled with the whir of the office machinery and the murmuring of her co-workers that rose inside the office walls like water in a glass. There was no easy escape from the place. No windows, no back doors. The only way to leave was to walk past Portia. Then she thought, why not? She had quit, she had confronted Portia, she had even—though this now seemed distant and unbelievable—defied her. Leaving should have been the easy part. But she looked at that eye in the doorway, and wondered if she could do it.

The phone rang again. "Well, what are you waiting for?" It was Melvina.

"What?" Jem looked around her desk for a hidden camera. "What do you mean?"

"When, exactly, was it you first gave notice?"

"Oh, maybe three months ago, give or take a week."

"*That's* what I mean," Melvie said. "What do you think? Even our father, Mr. Chicken, finally disembarked. Granted, your escape to Jordan is a feebleminded plot, but I thought the idea might have inspired you with enough gumption just to get out and look around. Life is change, flux, movement. You move or you shrivel up. Case closed."

"It's not safe out there!" Portia's voice, on an office extension, cut in. "This *job* is life."

First Melvie's and then Portia's lines clicked dead. Though Jem could see Portia coming first, Melvie materialized at Jem's desk seconds ahead. "You're out of line, Nurse Melvina Ramoud," Portia said.

Jem could see eyes rising around her at the other desks. The mailroom girl froze in her tracks. There was a moment of great silence.

Melvina crossed her arms and said, "Don't mess with me, lady."

A murmur from the office staff swelled up, and Portia

rocked with it, her large body swaying lightly, to and fro, sizing up her adversary. Melvina's reputation had spread to all corners of the hospital, even the business wing outpost, and Portia eyed her cagily. "Hey, I'm on your side," Portia said, after a pause, in a new, offhand voice. "We're all women here, aren't we?" She lifted her hands, indicating the staff around her. Jem contemplated their faces a moment, gray and pearly-eyed like the long-drowned, the tight set of their mouths, unhappiness flowing out of them. "I hire women, you see, to help them," Portia was saying. "You know a lot of people would be saying these women should be home having babies. Not Portia Porschman."

"You're warped, Ms. Porschman," Melvina said. "Emotionally disturbed. I don't blame you for what you are, just for staying that way. You don't do them any *favors* through criminal exploitation. The business office is the last non-unionized wing of the hospital, its women the most underpaid of all staff, and they work the longest hours. Their right to employment isn't in question, but their working conditions are!"

Jem thought she heard a few voices lifted in agreement. But Portia's eyes were lit now, hands open, arms raising like Zeus's. "Don't you go using that *union* word around here. These girls are mine. They answer to me and they work for me. I trained each of them like a mother, and without me they're nothing. When I say eat, they eat; when I say breathe, they breathe. They're my flock. I love each and every one of them. When they're good, I reward them; when they're bad, I'll be the one to punish them. I made them, every one."

Melvina ran her eyes up and down Portia once, then

said, "Oh really? And who taught you to say that? Who trained the trainer, Ms. Porschman?"

Something in Portia's face withered a little. Then, feeling a shadow, Jem noticed the black undertaker suit of the mysterious Mrs. Pinoire, chief supervisor of business, briefly gliding through the back of the room.

"She's right!" A voice from another part of the room wafted up. It was Virge. Eighty-eight years old in support hose, a jumpsuit, and neck brace; she shuffled to the front of the room. "Miss Porschman's right!"

"Why, thank you very much, Virginia," Portia said, clasping one hand around Virge's entire shoulder. "What did I tell you? My women love me."

"Why yessuh, yessuh, good, white massuh," Virge said suddenly. "All us slaves is so thankful! Now Lordy, oh, Lordy, won't you let my people go?"

Portia didn't move, twitch a lip, or flick a muscle. Her face turned gray; she seemed to be turning into a wall of flesh. Then Virge extricated herself from Portia's grasp, reached over, and offered her hand, tiny and curled as a bird's claw, to Jem. Jem took it. "See?" Virge said to her. "That's the only thing my hand is any good for anymore, holding hands or adding up. The arthritis got it curled into the shape of my adding machine. It's time for you to move on, before the same happens to you, doll. You better go or I'm going to, and I'd just as soon stay, what with this hand and all."

Melvina jerked her head at the door. "That way out," she said.

Slowly and with some production, Portia shut her eyes.

Jem grabbed her pens, notebook, and address book.

One of Gilbert Sesame's telegrams slipped out, the words "My darlin'" face up. She left it on the floor. She stopped before Portia, whose eyes were still shut, then realized she had nothing to say to her. She walked, leaving a trail of silence behind. She tucked her ID into the time clock, punched out. Then she and Melvina—acting as military escort—opened the door into a slight shower washed with sun.

"You know she's not a such a bad sort once you get to talk to her," Melvie said as they walked toward the car.

"Portia? You're kidding?"

"Not at all," Melvie said. "She's got some managerial talent, I'd say, but lacks soul. Genghis Khan, you know, was an underrated manager." She opened the driver's-side door for her sister. "So now what?"

"You're not going to tell me?" Jem said, standing by the door.

Melvie tilted back her head, drizzle on her nurse's cap and on the backs of her lowered eyelids and caught in her hair. "No. Don't tempt me. I'm working on personal growth this week; reducing the need to control and colonize, for today. So I relinquish all claims on your future—graduate school, marriage, Jordan, as long as you give me two weeks notice on all decisions and an option to accompany you or veto the plan entirely if it's some unbalanced scheme."

"Well, I'm going home. Do you want to come along?" Jem asked.

Melvie shook her head. "Sorry. You go, but *I* can't just leave. Nursing to me is not an act of volition, of 'free will' if you like. It is as necessary and immediate as using my limbs."

"For you, maybe. Some nurses quit."

Melvie wagged a finger at Jem. "They're kidding themselves. Radical self-delusion. Once you become a nurse, it's branded into your flesh—like a tattoo—you can't simply rub it out—"

"In all cases?"

"Either that or they were never nurses to begin with. *False* nurses, I call them, poseurs, who never really had a calling, but were lured by the status, glamour, and other worldly enticements."

Jem got into the car. She thought for a moment, fingers on the ignition. She started the car then leaned out the window. "What about going back to school yourself? You'd make more money if you got a graduate degree and went into nursing administration."

"Hah!" Melvie propped her hands on her hips. "I'm no easy-chair pencil pusher! It's the front lines for me or nothing."

Jem waved, put the car in reverse, and the sky broke into beads over the windshield as she drove away.

ON THE HIGHWAY, Jem remembered something to tell Melvie: the time they went to the amusement park in New Hampshire, when they and their mother were visiting her relatives. Jem was nine, Melvie two; it was just a few weeks before they would leave for Jordan.

Jem had been attracted to the words "Fun House," which sounded like a charming, candy-colored place

built for children. She and her cousins, all between six
and nine, wanted to go in. She remembered distantly
that Melvie, a toddler who hated to be carried and wrestled with strollers, had reached both hands toward Jem
and kept crying over and over: "No! No! Me, me, me!"
Jem couldn't tell if Melvina wanted to be included, if
she wanted to exchange places, or if there was some
other message in this. Until their mother's death, Jem
had been called Jemmy, which Melvie had shortened
simply to "me."

When Jem entered the narrow shaft of darkness at the
door to the Fun House, she saw she'd been mistaken
about the place; Melvie's voice from outside echoed back
at her from every odd and crooked angle of the structure,
"No, no, no!" The sound didn't fade until the children
had walked to the interior recesses. Jem had little recollection of the house itself: sweeping plastic spiderwebs
and dangling tarantulas, people in warts and peaked hats
jumping out at them. What she did remember clearly
was walking, suddenly, into a room of shifting blue
lights; nothing else was in the chamber but black walls
and blue lights, soft and suspended in the room. It gave
her an enchanted feeling, like sleeping in the snow, and
if her cousins hadn't been with her, she might have forgotten about the rest of the house and hung back, captured by the lights.

She pressed forward with the rest and stepped out of
the room of blue lights into a place with no light at
all. It was separated from the other room by a heavy,
swinging door which, as they entered, flashed a blue
beacon in, briefly illuminating the other place; Jem
thought she saw faces, tongues, and staring eyes, cover-

ing the walls around her. Then the door shut behind them, snuffing out every particle of light and the flash-lit faces.

It was a darkness more thorough than she'd ever experienced before; darker than anything she could have imagined. It seemed thick, like water, a substance that would float her away. The other children put out their hands, they laughed and cried out, "Oh!" and tried to find their way to the next room. Only there were no doors out. Jem ran her hands over the smooth surfaces; there was no crack, not a breach or flaw in the walls that went on, seamless and smooth as a womb; the children moved around and around, finding that the door through which they'd entered was gone. It was as if none of it had ever existed, not the door, not the sign outside, the dancing letters laughing out the words Fun House. The outside world disappeared.

Someone began to whimper, and then it rose like a wind in their ears; one by one, automatically, they joined in, crying, climbing to full-scale wails. Jem couldn't remember how long it went on; she had lost herself in crying. Noise and darkness went on and on, full and keening with lost souls.

The next thing she remembered was hearing an even more piercing sound, a voice, "no, no, no!" cutting right through the crying. As it grew louder and closer, the children gradually quieted. Jem's mother and baby sister appeared in a rectangle of intense blue that opened from a corner. Melvie was clamoring in her mother's arms, trying to snatch the flashlight away from the fun-house employee with them, never once ceasing her alarm: "No, no, no! Me, me, me!" When she finally spotted

Jem in the ribbon of blue light she quieted down and said with two-year-old weariness, "Oh, *there* you are."

"We went looking when you didn't come out, and Melvie led us straight to you," Nora said. "This place is a maze, but she kept pointing out the way. It was really something."

"Kid's a goddamn bloodhound," the worker grumbled, holding his flashlight away from her. "Well, goddamn it." He switched the beam around the room while he propped the blue room door open. He spoke into a walkie-talkie. "Goddamn it, Hal, looks like we got a circuit out in Purgatory."

"Don't swear," Melvie said.

Moments later something flickered and the room was bathed in a red tide of light. Now Jem could make out the writhing eyes and faces on the walls; they grimaced and moaned silently, eyes bulging. Then cousin Huck said, "Hey, look here!" and pointed to the words Push Me painted squarely in the center of a yawning mouth. He did and the apparently seamless wall swung open to the next chamber. "Neat-o," he said, the traces of his tears now barely noticeable in the half-light. He walked through.

The man offered to escort Jem the rest of the way with a flashlight, but she shook her head, taking her mother's hand and allowing Melvie a fistful of her shirt. They walked back to the entrance from which she'd started.

Jem wanted suddenly to thank them for that rescue. Gratitude, love, and regret all rushed at her, like the beating of wild wings, the feeling that her mother had been there, pressing her hand for just the briefest moment. The thought came to her that she always tried to suppress: *Not fair!* To have had so little time with her, no time to show her love or remorse for whatever bad might ever have been between them. Jem missed her then so fiercely that her eyes burned and it felt like something was torn out of her.

There was no way to bridge the space. It could not be covered by travel or in the course of a love affair, not even in marriage. The space was inside her now, she could feel it, a thing to be valued, the edges of her loss. Jem looked into the sky, its canopy of rain, and thought of a pair of bright wings that might enter the gap and lift her thoughts up high, a love letter on every point of water, filling the distance. Even if it were only to come to the solitude, silence, and the gentle foundering of the body into the earth, even if it were only that. So be it. *Take my thoughts to her,* Jem thought, *let her know.*

Chapter 35

WHEN JEM GOT home that day she heard the television before she opened the front door. The house rippled with laughter and jingles. She entered quietly, trying to stay calm as she turned up the staircase, following the unearthly sounds. Melvina was still at work, and their father was in Jordan. As she entered the living room her eyes went to Matussem's recliner, which was not empty. Its back was turned toward her so she could only see the top of a head. The TV was showing a rerun of *The Donna Reed Show*, gray-and-white characters gliding about the screen.

She stopped where she was, first blank with confusion, then fear began to liquefy in her bones. She started to back up and had just about made up her mind to return to the car and drive around until whoever it was had left, when the recliner creaked, a hand held up a demitasse cup, and its owner said, "Don't you keep any decent coffee in this impossible country?"

Jem walked around the chair to see a man bearing the

322

unmistakable features of the Ramoud clan: black hair combed and oiled to drench the curl out of it, a soft, rising nose, and exquisitely lidded eyes—only in this man's case there was only one eye; in the other socket was a halfhearted copy in glass, immobile and staring.

"Nassir? Is that you?"

"*A salaamu alaikum*, my betrothed." He transferred the cup to his left hand and offered his right. "You don't mind if we don't do the kiss-kiss, do you? After all, we're in your country now. I'd like a vacation from sentiment Middle-Eastern style for a while."

Jem took the cup from him. "So Auntie Rein wasn't kidding," she said, her mind winging, wondering, *what have I done?*

Nassir was pushing the recliner levers and twisting around. "How far back does this baby go? See, that's what makes this country great—your chairs go farther back than ours. Marvelous! They do all your relaxing for you." He straightened up in the chair and looked at her. "Yes, indeed, Granny is a great kidder. That's why she lasts like she does, laughs while the rest of the family cries themselves to death. Her favorite movie is *Zorba the Greek*. She tells everyone that she and Anthony Quinn are goddamn cousins, such an incorrigible liar."

"Uh, excuse me one moment," she said. "I'll go get the coffee." She went into the kitchen and picked up the phone. "Code red," she whispered to Melvina. "Family alert."

She made the coffee and brought it out with a little dish of cardamom and saccharin pills.

"Good. Foamy on top," he said, tipping the black sludge in his demitasse. "So either the family is suffering from mass hysteria—which happens—or you, little cousin, actually took it into your head to announce your intentions to marry me, leave the world behind, and go live where the girls wear long skirts and Liz Taylor-as-Cleopatra eyeliner. Come now, my dear, tell me what the truth is."

Jem kept a wary gaze on this man as she stood before him. He was around her own age, certainly not bad looking, even with the glass eye. There was a rakish slant to his smile that interested her. She realized then she was scrutinizing him like a head of cauliflower in the grocery store and sat down, quickly, across from him. "Well, yes, I may have said such a thing, something *like* that," she said, now studying her nails. "Who knows? Maybe I even meant it, do you think?"

Nassir waved both his free hand and coffee cup at her. "Please, please, please, I implore you, Jemorah, keep your wits about you. We're both adults, both Christians of a sort; I think you need to reattach to your sense of reality. Remember, my betrothed, the family is a cult organization. In two days they'd have you shaving your head and mumbling to yourself in a bed sheet if you let them. That's what the game is all about: how *not to give in!*"

Jem looked at him; she knew he was reminding her of something important, something she had known all along and quite well. He was balancing the tiny cup on its saucer, dropping in saccharin pill after saccharin pill. His skin had a golden cast, and the black-etched droop of his eyes reminded her of a gazelle.

"There, there, dear one," he said. "You mustn't forget, I am, indeed, on your side."

◂ ◂ ◂

JEM AND NASSIR were sipping coffee, reminiscing over the few weeks of their childhood together, when Melvina and Fatima burst through the downstairs entrance together. "Nassir? *Habeebi*, Nassir?" Fatima's trill rolled up the steps before her. "Come to me, oh, my little baby, oh, my precious one!" she cried, running in, grabbing his cheeks, and kissing him over and over.

"Guess what. This is our cousin Nassir," Jem said to Melvina.

Melvie stood by scowling, arms folded over her chest. "The one Rein wants you to marry." She turned to Nassir. "How do we even know that he's who he claims to be? How do we know this isn't another one of Fatima's setups?"

"You wish for such things, bad girl!" Fatima said, clutching her nephew and drawing herself up. "This boy a prince among princes, may heavens protect him from acid rains of your tongue!" She turned back to Nassir. "This my nieces, Jemorah and Melvina. Both available, though Jemorah is more so."

"Yes, that's the general idea, isn't it?" he said, smiling at the women, eyes coal-bright, teeth shining in the handsome dusk of his skin.

FATIMA RAN INTO the kitchen to make Nassir a "safe" pot of coffee, snatching the cup Jem had prepared from his hand. They could hear her opening every cabinet door and drawer, happily singing in Arabic about the woman who washes her husband's feet. Melvie stood a foot or so away from the base of the recliner and refused to sit or uncross her arms. "What did you say your full name was?" she asked Nassir. "What is the purpose of your visit and your final destination?"

Fatima returned to the living room in time to see Melvina examining Nassir's passport. "*Ya'Allah*, my terrible, terrible niece!" Fatima said, grabbing and pocketing the passport. "She worse than Israelis, worse than evening news. She want to crush me, so help me God."

"You realize, of course," Melvie said to Nassir, "my sister is not on the marital slave block. Not yet at least. She has absolutely no intention of marrying or going anywhere with you, and if *I* have any say in this—"

Fatima began ranting in Arabic about a "family curse" and being "driven through with stakes."

Nassir looked at Jem. "What is happening here? Did I miss something?" he said.

"This is how they make conversation," Jem said. "Don't worry, you don't have anything to do with it."

Clucking, Nassir climbed out of the recliner, took Fatima's hand, and led her to the couch to sit beside him. Fatima quieted down and curled herself against Nassir like a cat. Melvie sat in the recliner and glared at them.

"There, there, anything you want, dear Auntie," Nassir said, patting her hand. "I'll do whatever you say, don't torque yourself up on my account."

"Tell me again, exactly how much education did you claim to have received?" Melvie asked Nassir. "Were you aware that Jemorah has just been accepted to a graduate program at Stanford, one of the most important universities in this country?" she said, pointing to a copy of the acceptance letter on the mantel. "She starts week after next."

"*Mabrooka*," he congratulated Jem. "That's wonderful, little cousin." To Melvie he said, "I completed my baccalaureate and graduate degrees in science and anthropology at Cambridge and Oxford respectively. I'm in this country to work on a post-doc at Harvard. I think I've got a résumé packed away somewhere, if you require one."

Fatima was smiling and stroking the side of his face. "Dear, dear boy," she said. "Fun and games. But we knows the big reason for you to visit: to continue family name, marry my darling little baby niece and take her back where she belong, make your grandmama, my honored auntie, happy."

Nassir caught Fatima's stroking hand, and as he kissed it his gaze glanced above the ridge of knuckles to the two young women seated before him. "You've got my credentials—or, at least, some of them—so what of yours?" He turned to Jem. "You still haven't answered my opener—my curiosity about whatever opened this floodgate of family feeling. What was it that turned Jem the unattainable, the American cousin, back to the Old Country? What dislodged the first stone? What trumpeted outside your Jericho?"

Melvie said, "Nothing," as Jem said, "Everything."

The two women looked at each other and Jem repeated, "Everything."

"Ha!" said Fatima merrily. "So I says."

"It's true," Jem said, speaking to Melvie. "Things are changing for me. I've started to see better, like the way

I don't fit in. I haven't put together a life. I'm still living at home, I've been working at a job I hate. I'm so tired of being a child, being good, wanting people to like me. They don't like me. They don't like Arabs."

"Americans don't like anybody! Americans don't like Americans!" Melvie said. "And what are we talking about, you *are* an American. Where do you think Americans came from, when they're not captured on reservations? They come from other places. That's what an American is!"

"No, I don't think so. I think it just doesn't work like that. It's not enough to be born here, or to live here, or speak the language. You've got to *seem* right," Jem said, lifting her palms. "Well, I don't know how to accomplish that, and I'm starting to think I won't ever learn it if I haven't by now. In fact, I don't even want to learn it anymore."

"Amen," Fatima said. "Jesus, Mary, Joseph, praise holy name of Allah the munificent—Jemorah has seen light."

"But it's incredible, do you honestly think anything is any different in the Old Country?" Nassir asked Jem, leaning forward. "Maybe you've seen *Lawrence of Arabia* lately and you think it's all the same, bedouins and sand and camels, all tied up in a time warp, like cowboys and Indians over here. Or maybe you believe, dear friend, that it has all been waiting for you since you left its doorstep in 1970, that you'll return and find the great peace of the tomb still there, that you can go back to my grandmother's home and wander without responsibility or care. Just as you've preserved it in memory. And well you might, but that world would be only your own, the isolation of a child's fantasy. If you were to step outside your enchanted circle, you'd find the same sorts of suspicions and intolerances as here. There is nothing unique or magical about the Middle East; it shares xenophobias and violences with all the rest of the world!"

"Nonsense, nonsense, nonsense!" Fatima shouted, each word an intensifying alarm. "At home, she surrounded by so much family, more family than she know what to do with! Peoples who loves her, who protects her, who cut their right arms off and give to her! Not like here in this evil of evils where she is outcast, as I have been in fifty thousand years of suffering here that I have yet to tell a person. In this country they offer with one hand and take away with the other. So she will walk away from this. As it is written, no to your honey and no to your sting! Let her go to the people who are loving her."

"And what, precisely, do you call me?" Melvie asked. "Her flesh-and-blood sister, pray tell? Let me recommend that *you* go back, if you're so maladjusted here."

"It's too late for me, naughty girl," Fatima said, tucking a loose hair into place. "Soon, soon, it become my forty-ninth birthday. Already I am standing on my deathbed."

"Forty-nine? I always thought you were older than our father," Jem said.

"Enough talk, talk, talk," Fatima said, standing. "Nassir need more cakes and coffees, he vanishing before our eyes. It is all settled. We shop for a wedding dress tomorrow. Melvina is bridesmaid. Someone is matron of honor, you choose, of course. There is no time to waste. Your father will be weeping fifty thousand tears of happiness!" she proclaimed, dashing back into the kitchen.

Melvie stood up and snorted. She was still wearing her nurse's uniform; in the evening sun, refracted through the room, the uniform glimmered, smooth as sheet metal. Her cap pointed, tiara-fashion, at the ceiling. "I will not consent to a thing until I know, exactly and honestly, what it is that both of you want. Especially you, Jem—"

"I'm not completely sure," Jem said. "I only know that I want to change my life. A new start. It would be difficult in Jordan at first, I know. I don't expect miracles. But I might fit in some ways, a general, public way, where I could walk in the streets and ride buses and go into stores and feel like it's okay. There's all our family there. I wouldn't be such an outsider," she said.

"And I'm telling you," Nassir said, "this 'home' that you seek is not there, not in the sense that you mean, not even close. People like you and Melvina, you won't have what your grandparents might have had. To be the first generation in this country, with another culture always looming over you, you are the ones who are born homeless, bedouins, not your immigrant parents. As you and your sister just said, everything and nothing. You're torn in two. You get two looks at a world. You may never have a perfect fit, but you see far more than most ever do. Why not accept it?"

"So then it shouldn't matter if I choose America or Jordan," Jem said. "It's the same either way."

"It shouldn't, but before you do, allow me to inform you there are certain things about this other potential home that may not be quite to your Westernized taste, dear friend—"

"The truth at last!" Melvie said, sinking back to the edge of the recliner and pushing up the leg rest. "Sing it out!"

Nassir leaned forward, sliding face, arms, and shoulders into a bar of light from the window. He looked tired, as if he carried the distance of his journey in the slant of his shoulders. Strands of hair fell across his brow, down to his unmatched eyes, one opaque, a mask, the other a corridor of black, spiraling into the easing and opening of the pupil. It was here that Jem saw their shared grief: the eye that remembered the other's loss.

"I remember," he was saying. "Don't think I forget about our grief, little cousin. I see her in you, and you, too," he said to Jem then Melvie. "Don't think I have lost my allegiance to our early time together. For me, that in itself is enough reason to marry you, if that is indeed what you wish. More than any of these 'fun and games' in school, as Fatima puts it. My grandmother panicked when she heard I had received a grant to study in America. She told me, don't drink the water and don't look any of the heathen women in the eye. A week before I left, she said, I want you to marry Jemorah when you get there. Believe me, a hundred grandmothers couldn't get me to do this unless it had importance for me. Say the word, open sesame, and it is my command. But first you must understand, sweet, maybe-betrothed, that your childhood is not back there waiting for you to reenter its halls. I personally do not intend to return to the Old Country until the grant has run its course, and maybe not even after that. If you were determined to move there in the near future, you would probably have to go alone, and our country does not understand or appreciate solitary women."

"And this one does?" Melvie said, forgetting for the moment which side she was on. "That's a media-induced illusion."

Nassir crossed his hands on his lap. "Perhaps so. But I first want you to imagine what our Arab countries are like, how immutable those cultures are. I attended Oxford with another cousin of ours, Rejel, who for his dissertation wrote a family history. Do you know that not once on his family tree—written, no less, for the eyes of the Western world—not once did he mention a single woman, not a mother, aunt, or sister! He whited them out of history, wrote their names in invisible ink, so to speak. Moreover, nowhere in this 'comprehensive study' does he mention Fouad and his brothers swindling their own youngest cousin, Zaeed, your husband, Fatima, out of his land and birthright, buying it from him—since he didn't know better—for the price of his plane ticket to America. Now they condescend to him like a ward out of their quasi-guilty consciences. Farewell, family love! There are so many stories of treachery and deception in our family alone, I could go on like Shahrazad, for a thousand and one nights. In the end our family chronicler was forced to purchase his degree in order to finish—but enough of all that—"

"No, tell us more, please," Melvie said, pushing the recliner farther back so her feet were parallel with her head.

"Another time. Look, I've spent enough semesters in England to learn about how the historians love to cut the world into East and West, chop, chop, to reassure themselves of their superior isolation, right-thinking, et cetera, et cetera. In the same way, the Muslims speak of themselves and the infidels, the Jews have their gentiles. What you hate in this place you will find in other places. Imagine, if you will, living immersed in endless feuds over kinship, allegiance, and possession—which is what you will find yourself doing in the Old Country. Our border is an open sore; there is nothing in many hearts and minds there now but vengeance and bloodlust. The Arabs call the Jews devils; the Jews call Arabs animals. They are as obsessed with each other as lovers. Every day on the radio, TV, in the streets, you hear the litany of the enemies' black sins: injustice is paired with injustice, tortures are compared, bombs, kidnappings, the number of women and children killed, each side warring to win the greater moral outrage, the greater injustice, till the war of rhetoric is nearly as painful as that of the flesh—"

Nassir broke off and Jem looked up to see Fatima standing in the door holding a silver tray so heaped with cookies and pastries she looked like she'd held up a bakery; in the other hand there was another pot of coffee. Jem didn't know how long Fatima had been standing, listening, in the doorway like that, but her skin had gone so white it seemed to lose its edges, and Jem thought Fatima might faint.

Their aunt slowly placed the tray—cakes and all—straight down on the floor, at her feet, as if that was precisely where it was meant to go. And then, just as precisely, she stepped over it, coming into the center of the room where Jem could see her ashy forehead, her hands and throat white with perspiration. "What are you saying, my foolish nephew?" she said to Nassir. "Am I believing my ears? What you are saying about my country, my heart and soul? You, who lost the father and brother to these horror, these enemy."

Nassir nodded. "Exactly, exactly. I lost them, and for what? I am tired of hating. I have Israeli friends who lost even more! It never stops; it's a game without end. Why shouldn't we be the ones to say stop?"

"Is not any kind of a game!" Fatima shrieked. Her neck stretched to the chords, straining. "I forbid you use such word in the house of my brother. Is no kind of game, you stupid, stupid boy. For all you lose and you learned nothing. You think you can go just cross the ocean and wipe your hands like the Roman kings? What I care for these people you think are your friends? What of my losses? What of my parents' shame, driven off the good land and sacred home the father's fathers built? When we were homeless and dying without food, what of the four starving babies I had to bury still alive, living—I, I, I?" she said, pushing her palms in their faces, as if the mark of it was there to be read. "Can I buy a bar of American soap and wash these away, as you have washed up your self? Babies I buried with my mother watching so this rest could live, so my baby brother can eat, so he can move away and never know about it. These why he came here, then," she said, turning to Jem and Melvina. "To get away from knowing. No one would tell, but still he knows there is something to fly from, praise Allah he was born so fortunate! Born a *man,* not to know the truth—"

Jem was hardly breathing. She was watching her aunt, trying to understand what she'd said. Suffering shone on her aunt's face, white as water. Fatima stood very still, standing inside the hollow place her words had cleared away, wrapped in sorrow and tears, which never left her eyes but seemed to fill the length and breadth of her body, her flesh filling with tears. Fatima stood silently, hands curled around her elbows, and when finally she spoke again, her voice was made of tears: "This the first time I say it out loud," she said. "I think, maybe if I don't say it, maybe, does it go away. But it don't. It comes, it comes, it comes! I have no kind of peace. Their spirits stay with me; there is nowhere else to go. The saints and sinner live together. When I am sixteen, and a foolish girl, standing outside alone in the dangerous street, in Jerusalem, the Israelis come for me; this is my punishment, at the hands of God. I think they will kill me, it will be starving me to death, for all the food those babies would eaten. It is on their hands now, in the camp of my enemy, bad place. I think, now an end to my bad thoughts in this room of theirs without doors. It is nothing to the room I live in, in myself!" She struck her chest with a closed fist. "*Here* there no escape. And they let me live. After four days alone with misery, I am let go of their prison, I am left even by enemies. I am returned to die again, again, again. And *this* you say," she said, turning on Nassir, "this is a laugh, a joke, a *game*, as they say in this Godforbidden country. That is what we playing at—to put a smile in your spoiled mouth!"

"Auntie," Melvina said. Fatima flinched for just a fraction of a second then Melvie opened her strong arms and took her in. "It's all right, it's all right," she said into Fatima's hair, standing and holding her, the two women moving back and forth, like a cradle. "They forgive you, they all forgive you—can't you hear them? They're here, in the air, all around us. I can hear them, they forgive you."

MELVIE STEPPED BACK from Fatima, holding her shoulders, her gaze lowered, softened. The light in the room was like butter; it slipped down their skin and gilded their hair. No one spoke; then Melvie said, "Aunt Fatima. It's all right. You can talk to me. Please. I want to know about you and our mother both."

Fatima stared at her niece who'd never before asked her a single question, never asked her for a thing. Fatima looked at that solemn face, and every accusation, bitter prejudice, and self-justification flew from her like drops of water.

"Your mother," she said slowly, "I don't know." She closed her eyes. "I really—I don't remember. . . ." But she did. She remembered the pale eyes that wouldn't close. She had flown back, though she'd sworn never to return, after the death. The eyes had stiffened open; the body seemed still faintly warm from its fever, though it was almost two days dead. The girls couldn't have remembered it. Melvina, she told herself, was just an infant at the time; Jem gazed at a point somewhere slightly over her mother's body.

Women are meant for death, she thought. These bodies bound for no good in this world, where any man might kill you. They were all guilty, the living. Wasn't the night sky with its pink-and-blue belted clouds the sky of loss? Weren't women like black orchids, in the sorrow of their bodies, meant to be used up, to wither like roses, left in rockers, over sewing and TV, left without men or children, knowing their lives had never really been their own?

"You remember," Melvina said. "Tell me. I know you remember."

Fatima carefully bent to the tray of pastries on the ground and picked it up. "She had long hair," she began. "Bangs, and she hate lipstick. She wearing size eights dress and loved many purple clothes most of all. Hair like the color when the sun goes down."

ALL EVENING JEM and Nassir listened to Melvie and Fatima's voices murmuring through the floorboards, like the spirits of the *ifrit* touching the soles of their feet tucked under the kitchen table. Jem heated up a cauldron of stuffed grape leaves and lamb that Fatima had smuggled over in her car along with the cookies and cakes.

"So Uncle Fouad was lying again," Nassir said, spearing into another grape leaf. "They *do* know how to cook in this country."

"Some more than others."

Fatima's husband, Zaeed, called. "You needing a rest? Should I come there and take her home? What stage she is at now—screaming pontifical, weeping martyr, or plain sulking?"

"I think we did something new, tonight," Jem said.

"Really! In honor of cousin? Maybe you *should* marry these guy, Jemorah. He sound influential."

Nassir was scratching at his glass eye when Jem got

off the phone. "You know I can remove this at will," he said, tapping the eye. "Want to see? It looks fabulous on a Christmas tree."

"Not right yet," Jem said, looking from one eye to the other. "Doesn't that hurt?"

Nassir sighed and finished the last bite of yogurt and lamb. "Let me tell you something, dear cousin of mine. Since tonight is the night of unburdening secrets. My secret is not so phenomenal at all." He sat back and ran his hands over his belly. "Everyone assumes that the eye's loss was wreathed in tragedy and violence, a childhood casualty of war. Maybe something that happened under the hands of expansionist Israelis or sword-wielding Muslims. Not so." He looked at her, eyes hooded.

"How then?"

"A soda-pop bottle." He shrugged and grinned. "A soda bottle and my young stupidity. The advent of carbonated water was a wonder from the mysteries of the West. As children, my friends and I loved to shake the pop bottles so the stuff would shoot spray when you opened them. We were idiots—self-mutilation was inevitable."

"Oh no."

"Oh yes, of course. Now then." He reached over and patted Jem's hand. "Don't look so troubled, it's the way of the world, O possible-bride-to-be. Fate handed unsuspecting me a bottle with a half-opened cap, and I shook it hard. When the cap shot off, it perforated my eye. Our village doctor finished the job by removing the eye and cutting it in two, like a grape, with his penknife. Why? Who knows? To see what it would look like perhaps? Then, nick-nack, he throws it in his dustbin and that's the last we ever see of my left eye. A tragedy in two acts."

"That's terrible," Jem said. "You seem so blithe about it."

Nassir leaned forward, resting his elbows on his knees and spreading his palms open. It looked as if he were tipping the balance of his thoughts forward. "You and I, Jemorah. I very well remember what that time was like for us. Don't you?"

Jem looked at him; she saw the marble walls again, the tiles checked black-and-white, receding into passages, loss.

"I'm not saying it wasn't hard, but merely senseless. I can't put a reason to it any more than I can to your mother's death. If Fatima thinks she can look to the home country and find her meaning there, then I don't begrudge her. But most of the people who come to America, the immigrants, they think that this is just another place like home, a thing they will be able to hold and understand. It's not that easy. Our family"—he paused a moment and rubbed his face in his hands, then looked up—"our family is *mejnoon*, you know? Crazy, nuts. Half Muslim, half Christian, they switch back and forth when the mood possesses them. Or they come to this country and pretend to be Presbyterians. Do you understand any of this?"

Jem looked at Nassir's hands, now lying between his knees. "I think I know," she said, "how important a place is, and the need for a particular land, a location, for anyone to live, to have that land to call home. I know that's what I want."

Nassir smiled at her, his big head tipping up. "Good, very good. A quick study, as they say. How many people know, after all, what it is to really live in a particular place, as you say. To have your past and the past of your past tied up in a patch of land, to walk on the bones of your buried dead and hear your name in every particle of dirt, to know all this, all your life, and see it washed away under the wheels of tanks and trucks as if under the force of the ocean. Who can know it who hasn't lived it? This is what our family has lived. We spring from exiles and refugees, Jemorah, you and I. We go on, to be sure, but the place of our origins is swept away. Forgive me, if I take liberties in saying this. Perhaps I say it because I sometimes feel the same as you. But I think, maybe, you believe that because she died overseas that there's still some part of your mother, perhaps her soul, remaining in Jordan, waiting for you to come back again. Perhaps the home you're thinking of is in your mother's arms."

Jem rose, walked to the kitchen door, and tipped her forehead lightly to the screen. The air through the screen was cool and black, coming, it seemed, from great distances, the flesh of night shifting, great and lovely and empty.

"Because, dear, if that's what you feel, I have to tell you, I don't think you'll find her there," he said.

"No," Jem said. "Of course not."

NASSIR HAD TO leave the next day. Since he had flown to the United States directly from Oxford he had little family news for the girls. He'd heard legends of an American man—a friend of Jem's?—named Gilbert Open-Sesame, a camel-back cowboy who wore a Stetson and bedouin robes and seemed to have power over the hearts of women, last seen headed for the Sahara driving a stretch limo with Cousin Milad, Uncle Fouad, and four waitresses from town in back. There were rumors that this Gilbert Open-Sesame would soon be elected village mayor. The same grapevine, Nassir told them, had probably also produced several children from Jem and Nassir's union.

Nassir took Melvina's hands at the door. "My dear, righteous, regulatory cousin, I remember even when you were a baby the village men would talk about kidnapping you to watch their sheep. Even then, they could all see what a good shepherd you would make."

"A profession not unlike nursing," she said.

He held Jem a moment. "Here's a proposition for you," he said releasing her. "Suppose we make it a lengthy engagement? If we string the time out long enough the family may even forget we're not married. And if you ever change your mind, dear cous, if you panic and need someone to marry you pronto, you may always call upon sweet old Nassir. I haven't forgotten our friendship, and strangers can learn to love each other. Call me anytime, day or night. Call my name into the wind as your Lois Lane summons Superman, or use the phone, if you prefer."

Jem smiled and nodded. "Where are you going now?"

"Now? Well, now, betrothed, I'm off to the hallowed halls of Cambridge, Mass. I wasn't kidding before—a juicy post-doc awaits me. After that, who knows? Archaeological digs in Tunis? Linguistic studies in Niger? I'm a professional nomad."

"A family trait," Melvie said.

"But never fear, my dears, as long as there are great-aunts in Jordan, there will be people who know how to reach me."

He said good-bye and, waving his cupped hand like the Pope, walked out to the airport taxi that had pulled up.

Chapter 36

$\mathcal{S}$ OON IT WAS going to be winter again; ice would creep up the river valleys and over the flat lands so they gleamed like sheets of marble. Soon there would be crusts of snow at curbsides, black with car exhaust. Soon, the wind-tears and the cold that froze tears to lashes, lashes to skin. The rains were starting that would strip the canopies of leaves from the trees. Soon the short days, barely enough to wake the world before it slumped back into slumber, the nights without end, upstate winter.

In California, Jem thought, there might be no difference among the seasons, or just the hint of a softening. She imagined winter there as just a nuance, an afterthought. In Jordan, the winter sky would open and the clear rains spill out. Nowhere but upstate, she thought, would the sky have that aggrieved expression, furrowing like a brow against the earth.

She remembered wandering as a child, snow-blind between the seamless white of earth and sky, as if she could walk forever without the whiteness ever coming to an end.

Once when she was very young, Jem decided to go looking for squirrels in the snow. It was a game she used to play with the older children next door; they would go on walks through the thick bramble and tangle of branches behind their house in Syracuse. On this day, though, it was so cold that no one wanted to come out. So she walked alone through tall fields of snow, through a falling powder suspended around her, melting on her lashes and mittens and hair. And it was cold—cold enough for her breath to smoke, enough to coil her fingers up in ice-crusted mittens.

In those days, she could dawdle endlessly, lose the time in a search through fields for four-leaf clovers or fossils or berries, or in lying on her back reading clouds. This was the way of her first six years, the hazy time before her mother brought Melvie through the door and, with one ferocious, sweeping baby gaze of house, father, and Jem, Melvie claimed them all. On that bitter February day, less than a year before Melvina, the black twigs in her bedroom window had called Jem outside. She remembered the trees, their dark profiles, their secret lives, tucked away in branch and bark and knot-holes. She walked deeper and deeper in, until she stopped among the glaring white banks and, growing drowsy, lay down and fell asleep in the snow.

The rest came to her in pieces, mostly told to her: their mother frantic, searching the neighborhood and friends' houses for her daughter who liked to wander down the street, neck arched back to the sky. Their father calling the police, the fire department, anyone who might help. Then her mother remembered Jem's squirrel hunts through the fields. She followed the traces of her child's footsteps disappearing as the snow fell, through a patch of trees and briar nearly impassable for an adult—unless she could bend down and creep like a child. She found Jem, sinking, already covered, barely an outline etched in blue on the sparkling surface of white, under the stuff that cleaned and muffled the world. Jem's image was fading under the surface in blue hollows like the memory of a child.

She scooped her daughter out of the snow and carried her back. Jem was so stiff with cold she seemed dead, but her life had only retreated inward to a stiller place, and it returned as she warmed. Jem had visited a pale place just before death, and while she could not remember the sleep or the rescue, she never quite lost the memory of that retreat. She had known, always, that her mother would be able to find her.

S H E L O O K E D O U T the window; the clouds and spirits of mist called her away. She was unanchored, and, she realized, vaguely lonely.

It had been weeks since she'd last seen Ricky Ellis, and on this early morning when she'd risen to see the sky turning in a scowl of rain and clouds, she'd remembered her dream of him, Ricky running through a field like a wild pony, running against a pearly sky. Even when she woke, it seemed he was still there, his movement an echo through the room.

In two weeks she would be thirty. Something had changed; it was as if the world had made a distinct quarter turn overnight. She could hear the season's first pale lash of rain across her windows. She was still alone in the bed that she'd slept in since sixth grade, still listening to the traffic out on Route 31. She wondered what would happen to the house if her father never came back again from the Old Country. She imagined the sheriff coming and putting her clothes out on the street. She might wander the junkyards and sewers of Euclid and beg for food from the neighbors. Perhaps dogs would follow her, and her hair would fill with twigs and dirt, and she would turn as wild as Peachy Otts had been, sleeping anywhere and going off with anyone. Jem already felt a kind of nostalgia for the life she would leave behind. Then she realized that Melvie would never let her do any such thing.

The phone began to ring and when Jem answered, a woman's voice said, "Hey hey hey, it's your daddy's lady friend, trucker-bunny Train! And guess what? He's back."

"He's . . . What? Who do you mean? Who's back?"

"Big Daddy Ramoud, of course, Big Daddy of the Ramoudettes—I don't think there's more than one. Yeah, he's on his way home."

Jem switched the receiver from left to right ear. "Have you seen him?" she asked.

"No, have you?"

"Well, no. As a matter of fact, the last time he called it didn't sound like he was ever coming back."

A laugh pealed from Train's end of the line. "A woman who doesn't know her own drawing power," she said. "I like that. You must drive men ape-shit. Listen, peach-fuzz, I seen some pappys in my day and yours is one stand-out, sterling character. He's devoted to you girls like A&P is devoted to selling groceries, like Mack Truck is devoted to big. And I say this from knowing him a mere day and a night."

Jem looked around the room, the furniture light-dappled, a black-and-white snapshot of her parents framed on the nightstand. "Even so, how do you know he's back?"

"Easy. Psychic c.b."

"What?"

"My c.b., my radio, peach-buns, lifeline to the world and beyond, only mine is psychic—I didn't buy it like that, it just happened, a cosmic connection between me, the truck, and waves in the air."

"Waves?"

"Sure, yeah, you know people give 'em off, everything does, trees, rocks, and then they show up over the c.b.—"

"You hear trees?"

"Whoa, sweetie, you're getting ahead of me. We can discuss that part of the theory another time. What I'm talking about now is brain waves, ghost waves, all kinds of static that comes in over the line."

"Huh. What does that sound like?"

"Hard to say. Sometimes it just seems to bypass the ears and lands straight in my mind. Like I'm just a way station for other people's thoughts and fates. Other times it's mixed into the static when I can't get no clear human voices on the other channels, and then I can pick and piece messages out of what-all I'm hearing. Other times it's like there's some ghost radar out there, picking up and broadcasting thought messages off every soul driving on the highway. That's when things get real confusing."

"Jeeze. How did you hear my father was back?"

"A little of everything told me, that's what made it so out-loud clear to me. First thing yesterday morning, snap on the citizen's band and all a sudden I hear your daddy in my head think how he hates to fly. Next, round lunchtime, I hear something 'bout Doc, Grumpy, Bambi, and pink flamingos in the static."

"Those're his lawn ornaments," Jem said. "He likes to hose them down in the fall."

"Whatever. I knew anything that weird had to be my friend Mattoo. Then, this morning, the clincher. I put on the hailing frequency, try to snag me a conversation out there, anywhere, and the c.b. ghost comes on and tells me 'breaker-breaker, he's back.'"

"'He's back'?"

"Loud and clear. So I'm headed out of Salt Lake now, and I want you to give him a smacker for me and tell him his love biscuit is on her way."

WHEN JEM CAME home that evening she opened the door to Dizzy Gillespie, the familiar music falling through her like a pulse. She ran down the stairs and found Melvie and Larry Fasco; Jesse, Owen, and Fergyl sitting on the two hideabeds; and Matussem installed in his recliner.

"Hey, Dad!"

Matussem tried to unfold himself from the recliner, then gave up and held open his arms. They hugged, kissing on both cheeks, then Jem stepped back for a better look. The seven-piece suit he had left in was gone; in its place he wore seersucker Bermuda shorts, a shirt printed with red gardenias, several gold chains and gold rings, and the largest wristwatch she'd ever seen. He was tan, steeped in lemon cologne, and his hair was waxy and far blacker than when he left. "Jemmy, what sights you are!"

"So are you," Jem said.

Matussem looked down at himself, then held up a jeweled hand. "You should see my sunglasses," he said. "They ones crazy swingers, those dudes in Old Country. Here, come back now here." He unlooped a thick gold chain from his neck and draped it over Jem; it was heavy as chain mail. "For you. I also brought for rest of this dudes. Melvie, of course, don't wear hers."

Jem looked around and saw that over their garage coveralls Jesse, Owen, and Fergyl each wore a gold chain. Larry Fasco's peeked out under a shirt that was open to an inch above the navel. Melvina, as ever, was in unadorned nurse's white. "Tasteless overconsumption," she said. "I, for one, am not seduced by such wastefulness, nor will I ever be a handmaid to filthy lucre."

"These rest," Matussem said, counting through the chains left on his neck, and rings on his fingers, "I get for Fatima, for my trucker-bunny, for gals at work, and for Wally Otts."

"The newspaper boy?" Jem asked.

"He good kid. He get gold necklace. But so then I runs out of money the first day in Jordan because these gold place is first thing we go to. So Fouad has to put for me back right away what he owes me on all his old bills so his brother-in-law doesn't make him look bad. It work perfecto! Then coming back to America, I even figured out to *wear* all the jewelry so customs won't catch me if they checked the luggage. Of course, fifty thousand necklaces, it got heavy—"

"What if they'd just looked at your neck?" Melvie said.

Matussem thought a moment. "Then they would caught me," he said at last.

"We'll discuss this later," Melvie said.

"Well, well, well, here we are, one big happy family again," Larry Fasco said, putting an arm over Melvie's shoulders.

"I beg your pardon," Melvie said. "To the best of my knowledge, my father never adopted any full-grown sons."

"Melvina, you heartpicker," Matussem said. "You girls and this guys my family. Why you think I'm coming back here in two seconds? I can't stay away; I am going crazy there."

"You always said the big happy family was in Jordan," Jem said.

"Big mistake! Big misery family," Matussem said. "All they do all day, the women go to the gold store, the men eat, drink, eat, drink, eat, drink. Gas bags. I get fifty thousand pounds fat. On top of it, they gossip, fight politics, gossip, fight politics. Okay, for while I like it, but it worn me out. How much fun you can have twenty-four hours day? Besides I am afraid you getting crazy and go marry someone like Nassir."

"You mean like you arranged for me to?" Jem said.

"*Olé*," Melvie said, folding her arms over her chest.

"Well done, Ms. Ramoud."

Matussem shrugged. "It's truth, I get enthusiastic. Is hard to help it. Everyone so enthusiastics over there. Like crazy."

"Oh, never mind," Melvina said, rising. "We sent the groom packing. And I now guess you expect us to kill the fatted calf for you, the prodigal father. Well, you can forget it. Make your own hamburgers," she said, marching from the room.

"Wait! Honeysuckle!" Larry Fasco called after her. "I was gonna propose. Hey! Wanna get married?"

"I'd rather swing from a vine," Melvie said back through the doorway and kept going.

"She likes you," Matussem said, patting his friend's knee. "Crazy about you. She's just mad because you didn't give her 'advance notice.' That's what Melvie likes, 'advance notice.' I didn't give her advance notice, either."

Larry shrugged, sinking back in his chair. Jem noticed he was looking more than usually transparent, the color of eggshell, his eyes blue wells. "Melvina hot tamale," Larry murmured.

"Train knew you were coming," Jem told Matussem. "From her c.b."

"She did? She called here? Does she miss me?" he said, sitting up. "What is c.b.?"

"She said to say your love cookie's coming back— something like that."

"*Ach du liebe, Augustin, achtung!*" Matussem said, rolling out of his chair. "Let's play music, dudes."

They were a band more in spirit than substance, but they had spirit. Jesse, Owen, and Fergyl concentrated on playing until their eyes went sharp and bright. Matussem held sway over it all like a shaman transforming, wings unfolding from his back, lifting straight into the sky, overlooking towns and counties, neighborhoods, and private lives through the roofs. He could see it all when he was playing. He was home, at last truly home.

Even Melvina couldn't resist the music, and she returned to stand near Jem and listen. She watched Larry Fasco conduct; lost in the bright music, he looked as if he might evaporate at any moment. Melvie crouched and whispered to Jem, "I won't marry him, but we may be stuck with him for quite some time. I never drop a patient."

"I like him," Jem said.

"Oh, he'll do," Melvie said.

MATUSSEM BROUGHT BACK several souvenirs from his time in Jordan, including a habit of exclaiming "hang loose!" and tipping his extended forefinger and pinkie back and forth (from some Hawaiian tourists vacationing in the Middle East); thirty-five Hawaiian-style shirts, courtesy of Fouad; a trove of thick gold jewelry; a bumper sticker that said Eat at Ishmael's Shish K.B./B.B.Q.

He also returned with a theory about drumming, that it tapped into the heart and broke the spirit free, all the colors and the flavors of the life a person had lived. There were things hidden in the core of a person, feelings and memories so deep, that with the right music the spirits of people could be liberated, new life conceived, and the dead given rest. He evolved this theory while lying awake on the Castro convertible in his sister Rima's rumpus room, surrounded in a valley of her grandchildren's toys. His body had ached for the feel of the sticks, the drumheads answering his every move. And the ache for the instrument was like the ache for his lover's body. In the light of the Old Country, place of his wife's death, he saw things clearly, fresh, for the first time in years. For so long he had felt that yearning for his wife; now he knew her memory had laid down and rested easy in him, a warmth that would never go away, at ease under his desire for his new lover. In this theory of night and day, of toys and shadows, his thoughts of drumming had become complicated, suffused with smoke. His memories had run too sweet; they needed the bitterness of earth to temper them, and the clarity of the present, of music, to bring out new life.

On the third or fourth day of his visit, his sister took him to a spot by the Jordan River, near sounds of settlement construction and American bulldozers on the neighboring bank. She pointed out a small headstone, engraved with the names of four girls, dating forty-two to forty-seven years past.

"What is this?" he'd asked Rima, his heart turning to ash, already knowing.

She told him the story of his infant sisters, buried just after birth, destroyed by their parents' poverty and despair. The older girls had all known among themselves, had pieced it together, though their parents had tried to act in secret. Matussem himself had been too young to understand; he'd been spared.

After a moment, Matussem asked, "And Fatima? Did Fatima also know?"

"As the youngest daughter," Rima explained, "Fatima was forced to assist. And she's never told anyone, not even us." Years after their father and mother had passed away, Rima said, memories began to trouble the daughters, haunting their dreams, until, a year ago, the sisters defied village and family opprobrium and put up the tombstone.

"We laid the babies to rest," she said. "You must tell Fatima. It's over. There's no one left to protect, nothing to do now but to mourn and reflect. We want her to come back, to visit and see her home and family again. To know that it's over."

Then she showed Matussem another headstone, older and slightly larger than the first, engraved with a single trumpeting angel and the name and death date of his wife.

"But her grave is in America," he said, astonished.

"I know. We had thought she might need a second bed," Rima said and smiled. "We thought her spirit might have become confused on such a long airplane ride back. So we had a second burial the week after you left. We wanted to give her soul ease."

Matussem knelt by the simple marker and touched his fingers to the chiseled hair, the windblown cheeks, the curling lips of the trumpeter. She looked like Jemorah.

Chapter 37

THAT SATURDAY MORNING Jem woke to the sound of her sister shouting. Through her bedroom window she saw Melvina pacing back and forth in front of the house. When Jem slid open the window she heard, "What country is this? No! Just answer the question! What *country* is this?"

Jem couldn't see her father, but she heard him clearly. "Melvina, you're a heartpicker, you heartpicker," he said.

"But you're not even Muslim! Your family is Syrian Orthodox," Melvie shouted. "The whole neighborhood can see you up there chanting prayers. Someday you're going to fall off that roof and *break your back*."

An hour later, when Jem walked into the kitchen, she found her father elbow-deep in a vat of shish kebab. "Dad, how many people did you make this for? There's only going to be five at the barbecue—us, Fatima, and Zaeed."

Matussem dredged his arms out of the vat. They glistened with olive oil and spices. "Only way I could figure out how to stir up this mess," he muttered. Then, "Yeah, okay, well, I thinks maybe I will be hungry. I feel a big hungry coming to get me today." The shish kebab gleamed like jewels, with bright bits of onions and peppers, ruby tones of meat and tomato.

They drove out to Fair Haven, up on Lake Ontario, an hour's drive, through Fulton, Hannibal, and Sterling, the small towns simmering in the late heat. They went down through the valley of trees at the park's entrance, then up to where they could just see the blue lip of water, its soft breakers rolling toward land.

Melvina drove while Jem sat up front beside her. Behind them, their father was staring out the window and sighing. He said, "Whenever I see a day like this, I think, okay, now I can die, now that I've seen a day like this, it's all worth it."

Melvie sniffed.

The trees bowed around them, their branches silky and streaming like the costumes of sultans, green and gold and red robes against blue water brocade. It was Labor Day weekend and the park was smudged with smoking hibachis. Children were running everywhere, as Matussem observed, "like maniacs." A Frisbee bounced off the car and Melvina braked, considered taking action, then drove on.

"America, oh, beautiful, may shed some grace on ye," Matussem sang.

"That's incorrect," Melvina said. "Those words are wrong."

"I know all the words," Matussem said. "There are

some things, as a father, I know, that you, as a daughter, will never know. I know all the words. Don't try to bamboozle me, Melvina, you heartpicker."

Matussem went through his private versions of "God Save the Queen" and "Oklahoma" while they waited for Melvina to settle on their stopping place. Then he switched to Arabic drinking songs once they'd parked and begun unloading the car. Fatima and Zaeed had been following in the car behind theirs and as soon as Zaeed heard "*Aye Ez Zain*," he joined in, clapping his hands, while Matussem beat on the top of a cooler.

"Oh, now this is delightful," Melvina said, putting down a pitcher of juice and putting her hands on her hips. "Is it already time to be making a spectacle? My sister here was accepted to one of the most prestigious universities in this entire country and my father and uncle elect to behave like extras out of *Barabbas*. It makes me tired; it makes me very, very tired."

When Jem heard the phrase, "most prestigious universities," she felt a little current of dread run through her; it was beginning to feel more and more impossible. She started walking, looking around the park, charged with a desire to run loose along the coastline. Instead, however, she swerved directly into Fatima's path. Eating utensils splayed from her aunt's hands; her black hair fell forward in a helmet; then the red-tipped fingers curled, and her darkened mouth said, "Jemorah, my darling baby orphan daughter, let us talk about your life."

Jem hesitated, then said, "How about a little later, Auntie? I just want to see what that is over there—" and began walking toward the trees.

This was a new ploy, one Jem doubted would work, but Fatima had seemed tender, even patient, since Matussem's return. Jem wandered toward the trees, waiting to hear Fatima call after her. Not until she'd nearly been swallowed in the greenery did she distantly hear Fatima shout: "Baby-darling, you *have* to get married! Time is up!"

Jem kept moving, wandering past the picnickers into the farther reaches of the park, touching the spiny backs of trees, grainy dirt moving beneath her sandals. She was walking toward the sun's glossy head, into the still trees around the lake, secret pockets of land, silence in the cup of leaves, gentle as memory. She lay back against a rise where the dirt was sun-steamed, dust sliding into air, and she was caught in her love of the earth, the green slopes and lake-torn stretches of the lap of New York, not far from the Onondagan Nation, from the time when the earth was nameless, or named something she'd never know. The land sang in its true voice, ordinary and beautiful, the rocks and grass and the sun; the voice stole her spirit away. Her father heard the voice, too, as he slipped from the office some afternoons down the fire escape, to cry back to it on his drums.

She thought of her mother and said in her heart, Please stay near.

When she returned to their table, the meat and vegetables were grilling, and Fatima was stretched out on a lawn chair, a tanning mirror under her chin. Melvie was showing Matussem and Zaeed how to start a fire with a flint, just in case.

Jem stood by the picnic table and said, "I've decided I don't want to go back to school. Why should I?"

"Yeah!" Matussem dropped his flint and stood also. "Yeah, why?"

Fatima opened her eyes. Jem saw her aunt's face twinned in the sunning mirror, the first one annoyed, but the second, the face in the mirror, looked softened and more mysterious. Melvie stood, both hands held out as if for balance. "What is this?" she said. "What am I hearing? Is this a mutiny? Tell me now, is this why we drove to the lake? So you could have me walk the plank?" Melvie looked from Matussem back to Jem. "Do you know what they do to mutineers?"

Zaeed turned one of the shishes. "Anybody hungry?"

"Hush, Zaeed!" Fatima said. "This is going to be a big fight for us."

Melvie stomped; her anger was strong, a whirlwind; she shook her fists in the air. Her arms were glowing in the translucent summer light, her black hair and eyes splendid; she was yelling at the sky, "Why? Why is my every effort trampled, cut down, denigrated?"

"This is like the Bible," Fatima murmured.

"What do you know about it!" Melvie yelled at Fatima.

It was already too late for Jem to put up a fight. She felt herself slip into sympathy for her sister. She couldn't help herself. With her golden arms and glistening hair, Melvie looked too frightening to touch, so Jem stood back a little and said, "All right, already. We'll see."

MATUSSEM HAD BROUGHT far too much food to their picnic, and they ended up offering it to anyone who walked by. "Have a shish?" he asked people, holding up a long skewer. Two young men with ponytails and beards who'd been backpacking stopped and sat with them, talking and eating, telling the Ramouds about where they'd hiked and how they'd been living on peanut butter and jelly for the past five days.

Fatima held aloof, eyeing their long hair, the dusty clothes. She'd told Jem several times that perfectly fine husbands can come out of a good scrubbing, but something else troubled her, something deeper: a sense of danger. It slid like a specter through the dark length of her eyes.

She lived among Americans, in places they had built, among their people, but despite this she wanted to keep herself, her family, and a few friends apart from the rest. She wanted what the Americans had, but at the same time she would never relax her hold on herself. It was not appropriate to mingle. Americans had the money, but Arabs, ah! They had the food, the culture, the etiquette, the ways of being and seeing and understanding how life was meant to be lived. Her wish, always, no matter what, the sharp wish that cut into her center and had lifted her eyes with hope was that her nieces should marry Arab boys, preferably in the family.

She refused to speak the whole time the boys sat at their table. At one point, Melvie rapped her knuckles on the table and said to her aunt, "Where are your manners? Make an effort!" Then, after an hour or more of eating their meat and bread, drinking their beer, of conversation, of songs from Matussem and Zaeed, fingers knocking on overturned pots, as they were leaving one boy held back and turned and took them in, one by one, from Matussem to Zaeed, to Jem, to Melvie, finally stopping with Fatima as she returned his level gaze. And he said, "So what *are* you all anyway? I-talians? Wet-backs?"

In a place like Fair Haven Park where the trees hung silky drops of leaves, where the air was sweet against the frame of water, Matussem could not believe that a deliberately wrong thing could happen. So he smiled at them openly, putting faith in the sunlight and thick grass where he chose to sit, apart from the table and the blanket, and he said, "We are Arab. From Jordan."

There was no reaction from the boy who was merely waiting for his friend. But the other, the one who'd stopped, who had kept looking at Jem throughout his meal with a hawk's glance, that boy made a strange little yelp. "*A-rabs!*" he said, his eyes now full of what looked like a twist of amusement and disgust. He turned to the other boy and said, "*Arabs,* Jesus fucking Christ. And we ate their *food.*" The other boy grabbed his friend and tugged him away. As they left, Matussem heard them laughing.

No one said much after the boys had gone. They packed up and left soon after.

JEM DROVE THEM home, losing track of time, Melvie and Matussem asleep in the backseat. The memory of the hikers fell away from her, fading into the roads, the swaying trees, the brilliance of home. She took the country roads and suddenly around her the grass sparked with rain and the wild weeds were bright as treasure. She didn't think she would ever live there again. The house looked strange as a shipwreck in a sea of country fields and telephone wires threading Euclid to the rest of the world. It could be, for Matussem, a private home, a place to create his life. But she had recognized, as the hiker turned to face her, the mystery of this hate, something she could crack only by going into it: back to school.

Jem drove past the fields where she and Melvie once hunted for chicken bones or lay on their backs and scanned the sky. A dream within a dream, the fringe of tall grass and weeds lined the road, rising to crest beyond the flashing red light, then disappearing.

The sun shower vanished. Just for a moment, everything was sliding along the air, as if the rain had left its traces in the sky like a path, a ladder to Heaven. This was worth studying, she thought, things that were hidden inside the crust of the earth and sky, the things that lay hidden in people: her father's heart in the drums, her sister's ministering fingers.

She would take home with her its finger-scratches of lakes, hills climbing into maple, pine, and mountains. Euclid gave her knowledge of the poorest of the poor, living like a secret pulse inside the country. Peachy Otts, standing in the doorway at the vegetable stand, watching how the earth carried its road up the hill and away from her, bending her head over her book, lips moving over the letters, talking to Melvie about vocational school. Maybe Jem would someday marry a person like Ricky Ellis and spend her life learning about another lifetime. Perhaps not.

There were pussy willows in the roadside ditch, their small faces brushing the air. This was a road the ghost hitchhiker was supposed to travel: the lovely, lost daughter on the way to the prom who took the sweater of whoever gave her a ride, then left it waiting, neatly folded, on her grave in the morning.

Chapter 38

𝒮UNDAY MORNING, FOUR months after the Archbishop's party, a letter from the Ladies' Pontifical Committee—on stationery thick and creamy as a slice of cheesecake—was hand-delivered by the paperboy to Fatima's door. She ran her fingers over the gold-embossed lettering, held the paper up to the light to see the watermark, then wiped at the tears that fell before she'd known they were there, brushing quickly before they dulled the sheen.

The letter read in ornate calligraphy:

The Ladies' Pontifical Committee
Mrs. D. Hind Abdulaboud Presiding
Cordially Invites
Mrs. Fatima Nyoor Hussan Ramoud Mawadi . . .

She read the letter out loud, first with a whoop and a kind of war dance, face thrown back to the heavens. Then marching back and forth through the living room, reading to Zaeed, to the cat, to whoever might be listening through the walls, holding the letter in one hand and waving the other to and fro. Once she tired of this, she ran to the kitchen to prepare a big vat of fried cauliflower and rice for her favorite brother and his wonderful, wonderful girls, but on second thought, she decided, even better, she'd buy them a real bakery cake instead.

She drove to the Thanatoulos Bakery, which had always been her favorite. Thirty years before, the Thanatoulos had provided the cake that welcomed Fatima and her husband to their new country. The bakery's neighborhood always seemed to have drizzling weather, apartments banked together on a tilting street, as if someone had built it to capture the inconvenience of old Europe without any of its charm. Wet laundry flagged the ropes between the buildings, and children with scraped knees chased balls.

Fatima could never pick out Mr. and Mrs. Thanatoulos because the bakery was always crowded with small, nut-brown women, hair knotted into kerchiefs, and equally tiny men tucked into aprons, their hair and faces and arms white with flour. Everyone spoke Greek and customers got what they wanted by pointing. Fatima was comfortable there; they lived and communicated in the same way her family in Jordan had, jostling, deliberately following each other around. They screamed at each other in a torrent of words that was their regular tone of voice. Sometimes the children—with their beautiful, nut-roasted skin and gray eyes—would run in from the back and amiably join in the screaming. The place allowed her to visit home without feeling the pain that it had held for her.

Then one day the Thanatoulos were gone. To Miami Beach, someone said. The name was still on the door, but a Hispanic family marched around behind the counter. Then a family of Asian-Indians, then one of Albanians, and then Lithuanians. Each of them, except for the Indians, was equally loud and equally possessive of the limited space behind the counter. The Indians only lasted in the bakery about eight months. Even though they were talented with cakes, breads, and all sorts of sweets, Fatima knew they had failed because of the pleasant tones in which they spoke, the sweet way that child yielded to mother who in turn worked serenely with husband. And they spoke English.

"These not American way," she told Zaeed after purchasing some of their butter cookies. "Too much smiles and knowing English. I feel they stabbing me with needle-eyes in the back." She ended up throwing the cookies out after crumbling each one in search of drugs or razors.

For the past year, Thanatoulos Bakery had been run by an African-American family. Fatima parked her car half up on the curb, just outside the bakery window, along the bricked alley, waited a moment, hand on the ignition, surveying the area, prepared for flight. Was the place any more dangerous, she wondered, with a black family in charge? Apparently not. There was an everlasting-ness about the street, eternal gloom, cobblestones smoothed pale, children shining like minnows through twilight.

Gilt letters ran across the door in a double arch, Thanatoulos Bakery/Hours: but no one—except the Indians—had ever posted hours. It was open when it was open, which meant that Fatima had gone to this place many times during the usual business day only to find it padlocked. This tradition had begun with the Greek owners who found it necessary to close for baptisms, weddings, confirmations, first communions, last rites, and other occasional sacraments. Fatima had heard they even closed up to help the children pick out prom clothes.

Sometimes, returning from a protracted church function or a late-night fight with friends and relatives, Fatima drove by and the store would be blazing with light at two A.M. In the summer, with the car windows rolled down, Fatima had caught shreds of Greek, Albanian, or Lithuanian drinking songs as she drove past. If the air was mild with predawn moisture, she would tilt back her head and listen. More often than not, she had Zaeed pull over while she ran in for a bag of butter cookies with chocolate jimmies.

THE DOOR SWUNG open under her hand and Fatima swept into the floury air. She drew herself up to her full five foot three and noted with satisfaction that despite the changing families, the women behind the counters stayed a fairly constant five foot two, though the children seemed to be getting taller with each new owner. All the women were "Mrs. Thanatoulos," in Fatima's mind, no matter the skin color or eye shape.

The present owners had introduced an innovation that had not appeared in any of the previous generations: they frosted their goods. Not just the cakes and cookies, either, but everything, the muffins, the rolls, even the breads were shiny, lacquered with a crust of sugar, as if dressed up in party clothes, tinted with cherry reds, berry blues, and sea greens. There was something irresistible about these colors, like eating the ornaments off a Christmas tree. These confections were given names like Big Chief cookies, Smokin' Joes, and Extraterrestrials. Before such innovations the goods had always been called the kind with sprinkles, the kind with raisins, the kind with nuts, and so on.

Fatima was pleased. She'd been crowned a queen that day, her scepter, the church stationery invitation, tucked in her bra. There were to be no more frivolous decisions in her life, no more pettinesses, no more mistakes of any kind. She was leaving the past behind. She went to the counter where Mrs. Thanatoulos was standing between the take-a-ticket dispenser and the spindle of striped string.

"There," Fatima said, pointing one regal finger at the case, Cleopatra herself.

Mrs. Thanatoulos brought the cake to the counter. It was three-tiered, covered in pink frosting and hairy with sprinkles. On the top layer was a yellow smiley face and the words in blue gel, Have an X-tra Nice Day!!!

"This here our King Creole Fuzzy Wah-Wah Cake," Mrs. Thanatoulos said. "Angel food and seven different kinds of marmalade fillings—it's so good, baby!"

Fatima closed her eyes, Cleopatra. She raised a hand. "Yes, these is the one just right."

Chapter 39

*T*HAT SUNDAY MORNING, Jem opened her eyes and heard singing. As if still dreaming, she remembered a wooden crib, with tiny, colorful sailboats dangling above her head, a hint of ocean air coming through the open window in the summer, and her mother walking from room to room in her dressing gown, singing "Daisy."

Jem sat up. There was no salt air, but the day was fresh and clear as a sheet. The singing filled her with purpose and she hurried from bed, pulling on her robe. When she grabbed the basement door her hand was trembling. An odd, inarticulate thought flashed in her: her mother's death was all a dream. Who really knew whose face it had been under her aunt's hand? Dreams, dreams! She ran down the stairs, through the voice that rushed up at her, notes tumbling around.

Her father, Jesse, Owen, and Fergyl were standing in a group, surrounding Ricky Ellis, and Ricky was singing in a vibrant tenor, "Tell me you love me, do."

369

Melvina joined Jem from the stairs. Melvie put her arms around Jem's waist and laid her face against her neck. Jem released her breath, a current of grief. "So sweet," Melvie said.

When the song was over, Matussem clapped loudly, then turned to his daughters and pointed to Fergyl. "These guy says there's a dude at the garage who can sing. So I go and he is there under a car, singing beautiful about hound dogs. My new discovery, Ricardo Ramoudette!"

Melvie walked to Ricky and shook his hand. "Congratulations on your rehabilitation, Ricardo," she said. She started up the stairs. At the top she turned and said, "Your voice is a gift from the universe."

Larry Fasco—in Matussem's words, mysterious as the moon and stars—linked his arm through Matussem's and they went up the stairs next, Matussem saying, "I make the coffee," the Ramoudettes trailing behind. Jem overheard Larry saying the words "love" and "marry." Matussem was laughing, his voice more distinct, surprised, saying, "Oh, my friend, oh, my poor, poor, crazy friend!" and then, more faintly, "But first tell to me, why you are calling your ex-wife the Psychokiller?" A moment later, Matussem reappeared in the doorway. "Fatima is stand here like Bride of Frankishstein and wants to know who wants cake. Okay, I'll tell her nobody."

Jem stayed in the basement with Ricky. They were silent; there was a sound like dust sifting, easing from floor to ceiling, quiet as a distant bell.

"I miss you," Ricky said, not looking at her.

"Me, too."

They were quiet.

"It's been a while," she said. "What have you been up to?"

"Working. And hiding," he said.

"From?"

He smiled and shrugged. "Just trying to figure things out, I guess. Like about us." He ran a hand back through his hair. "Me and this Arab girl who dates her cousins."

"I see."

"Hell, I don't care about that." He tilted his head slightly, eyes narrowing to clear light. "I just want you to tell me what's going on, Jem. I want to know."

Jem dropped her eyes. She noticed suddenly that his feet were bare.

"I heard you were going away to some school."

She shrugged, then nodded. "In California."

"California."

"Stanford."

"Okay." He pressed his palms together, blew out. "Okay. I know I'm a risky person. I work at a gas station. Although Larry Fasco has talked about me coming on as a partner at the Key West. Of course, *Larry* . . . well, you know him." There was a long pause, then he said, "I don't know. Maybe we could get married. I wouldn't say that I'd exactly been planning for it. Hell, it *might* be fun, marriage. We could get a big cake."

He looked at Jem. She put one hand to the well of her throat, stopped herself from saying yes.

"You don't want to get married," he said; his voice scored the air.

She took a breath. "I guess I don't. No. I really don't."

"I knew it," he said.

She stared at him, thinking of the panpipes and the faun, the impossible music, sounds that haunted the forest and enchanted animals. He turned his marine eyes to her, pale as water; she saw him on the cement steps of the O–G as she had tilted her head forward, looking through the glass. "Wait," she said.

She went upstairs and returned a minute later with Fatima's bakery box. She undid the blue and white striped cord, folded back the placket of cardboard, and revealed the King Creole Fuzzy Wah-Wah Cake. "Have some," she said, offering Fatima's special cake knife. She brought her lips to his ear. "Wedding cake," she whispered, smiling.

UPSTAIRS, FATIMA AND Melvina had already started fighting again, as if it were a conversation that never ended, like a chess game played from opposite ends of the earth, the players perpetually plotting moves in their heads.

Fatima was shouting, "What do you know about anything?"

Melvie answered, "Nothing! I obviously don't know anything about anything at all."

"Oho, Miss Smarty Pants with no respect!"

Ricky was looking at Jem. He ignored her knife, dipped into the box, and scooped out five fingers of cake. Jem covered her mouth, trying not to laugh, and said, "Fatima is going to kill, with her own two hands, I'm telling you—"

Ricky looked back at Jem with his clear gaze, the blue

teal of his irises sharp. He reached over and fed her a
bite of the spongy cake.

"Would you like me to sing for you again?" he said.
"How 'bout 'Blue Suede Shoes'?"

She pushed the rest of his handful of cake back and
shook her head. Ricky finished it and reached into the
box for more. There were sprinkles and pink frosting
on his lips; his breath was sweet as jelly.

"No, thank you," she said. "I don't want any more,
but you eat. Sing later." In a gesture that she recognized
as her mother's, she brushed the hair from his eyes.
"You look hungry, eat up."

LARRY, ZAEED, JESSE, Owen, Fergyl, and
Matussem came back down the steps into the rec room,
each holding a demitasse of black, Arabic coffee. "Jazz
time," Matussem said. "Want to hear some terrific
vibes?" he asked Jem and Ricky.

Fergyl put an Artie Shaw record on the stereo and
turned it up. The music was rich and clear, and the men
set down their cups, moving around and clapping. "Oh,
yeah!" Larry shouted. Ricky took Jem's hand and they
tried a few steps. Then Fatima screamed through the
living-room floor, "Turn that down, you are DRIVING
ME CRAZY!"

"Ho boy," Matussem said. "Let's switch." He pulled
out a battered copy of *Giant Steps* and went to his drums.
When "Naima" came on he swirled the brush around
his drumhead and gently, sweetly, began tapping. In the
swish of the drum, in the high register of the sax's voice,

she came to him again, dancing like the original mystery of her language, its jinni's tongue. Her image turned, bent to him, the world in her gesture, the mystery of her love, releasing him. "Coal-train," he said. "We're pulling out."

Melvie came downstairs. "Fatima would like you to please reduce the volume. She's also looking for her cake." She went to the table, picked up the box with one hand and scooped out some cake with the other. "Jemorah, you have sprinkles in your hair." Tucking Fatima's cake knife under her arm, she climbed the stairs and shut the door behind her.

"WHAT AM I going to do?" Ricky said, his hands on her shoulders. "I'm going to miss you so."

Jem moved closer, placing her head against his chest. They moved, ever so slightly, together, and it felt to Jem like they had begun wending their way along a path of music, finding their way. She could hear the sound of the drums through the movement of Ricky's chest, jazz and trills of Arabic music, bright as comet tails, and through this, the pulse of the world. All around her, through the thin, high basement windows, the maple trees shook; she watched them, their leaves turning desert red and gold.